Seven N

Karen Gillece was born in Dublin in 1974. She studied Law at University College Dublin and worked for several years in the telecommunications industry before turning to writing full-time. She was shortlisted for the Hennessy New Irish Writing Award in 2001 and her short stories have been widely published in literary journals and magazines. *Seven Nights in Zaragoza* is her first novel. *Longshore Drift*, her second novel, will be published in 2006.

SEVEN
NIGHTS IN
ZARAGOZA

KAREN GILLECE

HODDER
HEADLINE
IRELAND

First published in 2005 by Hodder Headline Ireland
8 Castlecourt Centre, Castleknock, Dublin 15, Ireland

First published in paperback in 2005 by
Hodder Headline Ireland

1

A CIP catalogue record for this title is available from the British Library.

ISBN 0 340 84122 2

Typeset in Plantin Light by Hodder Headline Ireland
Printed and bound in Great Britain by Clays Ltd, St Ives plc

Hodder Headline Ireland
A division of Hodder Headline
338 Euston Road
London NW1 3BH

www.hhireland.ie

For Mum, Tracey and Thomas

ELENA

1

IN ANSWER TO his question, Elena had wanted to tell him about a boy she had once been in love with. She had wanted to lean into his body and tuck her head into the crook of his neck. She had wanted to listen to her own muffled voice explaining through the wall of his chest about a love that was beautiful and destructive and real. A love that had existed in a time before he had known her. A love that had burned inside her, glowing red like the Sacred Heart in her mother's kitchen, eternally flickering. She had wanted to tell him that that was the reason.

But instead she had stood there with a hand on the banister, looking up at him and shrugging. 'Curiosity,' she had said, blinking under the hall light.

*

Somewhere between the kiss hastily plucked from her husband's lips and the taxi spilling her onto the gleaming, slippery step of the hotel, the rain started to fall. Palm trees that flank the broad entrance flex and strain in the wind and neatly clipped trees shaped like lollipops flutter and glisten at their sentry posts. Clouds move and crowd away the evening sun. And as she hurries from the taxi to the revolving door, she hears the snap of flags above her, their colours greased with rain.

She is early. There is the option of going upstairs and being among the first there. But she feels awkward, tense. Were it not for the rain, she would have got out of the taxi at the bridge and strolled the rest of the way, killing time. Or if the taxi driver had not been surly, emitting thick waves of smouldering fury, she would have asked him to circle the block a few times. It would have been worth paying the extra fare.

In the lobby she hangs back, aware of the nervousness in her movements, her fingers reaching for leaflets displayed on a gilt-edged table, leaflets she has no intention of reading. Her flickering gaze passes over empty clusters of expensive, well-upholstered furniture. Catching sight of herself suddenly in a mirrored column, she sees round, startled eyes, the colour leached from her complexion by the difficult shade of her dress. 'This is ridiculous,' she says to herself. 'Pull yourself together. Grow up.'

'The Fitzpatrick Suite'. That is what the invitation said. As she walks towards the lifts, with her head held high – a conscious effort to project a confidence she does not feel – she sees the details blinking onto a widescreen monitor: 'UCD BCL Class of '93'. Something in her chest gives a tiny kick.

Rising in the elevator, an instrumental version of 'Eleanor Rigby' seeping through the speakers, she is nudged by the sudden realisation that he could be up there now, in a darkened function room, his long fingers selecting vol-au-vents from the trays cluttering felt-covered tables. There it is again – that feeling. Creeping in around her temples, making her feel light headed, before plunging down into her stomach and fluttering insistently. She has had that feeling on and off for a few days now, growing, gathering momentum.

The Fitzpatrick Suite is on the third floor. Exiting the lift, she walks the corridor, and as she wanders past numbered doors, her mind drifts and she begins to wonder about the bedrooms here – are they painted in the same sedate palette as the lobby? This is a business hotel, after all. The lighting in the lounge is too bright to be otherwise; the pattern of the carpet too busy to be restful. She imagines wide, hard beds encrusted with crisp starched sheets, the ubiquitous pattern clinging to the bedspread, rosebuds perhaps or a paisley print, or a frenzied spread of diamonds – greens and rusts, navies and golds. Plain white walls, some benign framed prints, dark-wood furniture – utilitarian and inoffensive. Like the room she spent her wedding night in.

These surroundings are familiar to her. They have the same formal comfort and arm's-length luxury that that hotel had. It too was reminiscent of a business function. All the sheaves of flowers, the elaborate hats, the ice sculptures and piano playing and all of that champagne could not cover up the faint whiff of economics. She remembers her relief at escaping to their bedroom and how it almost made up for the disappointment at the décor, the unromantic trouser press, the abundance of leather in the desk and stationery, thick, masculine colours and the smell of Haze clinging to her nostrils. It was enough to be away from her father-in-law's backslapping, her mother-in-law's worried laugh. Free from her own parents' tense faces, her mother's hawkish eyes alert and disapproving, her father's awkward pleasantries and trembling speech.

And afterwards, she remembers lying in the darkness, starched sheets pressed against her naked body, Henry's arm lying heavily across her stomach, a slippery warmth between her legs. Light filtering through a gap in the curtains. She watched it seep into the room, finding shapes; shadows becoming a chair, a table, a suitcase and the eerie glow of whiteness from her wedding dress hanging on a wardrobe door. A woman's dirty laugh filled the corridor, throaty and raucous, before being swallowed up by a closing bedroom door. Outside, tyres crunched over gravel before swinging out of the gates. And the thought came to her – unannounced and unwanted – of a bed in a different country, orange peel on the floor, a street light flickering outside the open window and the nutty smell from her lover's skin – burnished and salty to the taste.

She shakes her head, twitchy and unsettled. She will not let it begin like this. She will not allow herself the indulgent sadness of nostalgia. *I will be strong*, she decides suddenly. *I will pretend. I will be somebody else.*

On entering the Fitzpatrick Suite, the décor confirms her suspicion that tonight is a business gathering, a benchmarking exercise to mark off who has risen and who has fallen and who has stayed pretty much as they were. The room is a very wooden affair, panelled walls and ceiling in blond woods, and much to her dismay there are no windows, which adds to the air of claustrophobia. The ceiling emits harsh light, casting the people gathered there in a pale, unflattering light. They are already forming clusters, producing language that rises and forms a cloud above them, humming and moving.

She can feel eyes on her as she enters the room, eyes that survey her hair, her dress, her shoes. Her body feels sticky under her dress and she wonders what the eyes make of its floaty chiffon layers, its daring hue. 'A tricky colour, green,' they might think, 'not everyone can carry it off.' Black would have been better. Simple, elegant, forgiving. But the realisation of this has come too late.

Craning her neck, she rifles through the faces gathered there. But his is not among them and something like disappointment touches her. To her dismay, she sees no face she recognises. Hardly surprising, she reminds herself; after eleven years people will have changed. Eleven years since sitting in the draughty hall staring up at the corrugated ceiling and listening to the deafening rattle of rain on the roof, half an hour left in the exam and nothing left to write. And at that time, she had fully expected to see those people again, at least after the summer. There was still another year before graduation. But that was before fate – and Adam – steered her in a different direction, casting her adrift for a while, her life falling forward out of control.

She moves into the room, sidling up to the felt-covered tables, approaching the trays of canapés and assorted hors d'oeuvres laid out there. A few people wander past vacantly, clutching cocktail sausages and napkins. She smiles vaguely but they move on, drifting into groups.

'A glass of wine, madam?'

Madam. She doesn't like being called that. Madam is for older women, for women who wear cashmere and carry their glasses on a chain around their necks and have hair that is dyed and coarse with age. Women like her mother.

She smiles bravely and accepts a glass of red wine from the acne-afflicted youth dressed solemnly in monochrome. Merlot, woody with a bitter kick of tannin. She remembers the stains to her teeth too late, the glass already smudged with her lipstick.

'Elena?'

Hearing her name, she turns and finds Rachel standing behind her. 'You came!'

'Yes,' she smiles as Rachel leans in to kiss the air beside her cheek.

'I wasn't sure if you would,' she continues, 'you seemed so uncertain that day I bumped into you. But look at you! You look fabulous! That dress! You know, you haven't changed a bit since college.'

'Oh, I don't know about that!' Elena laughs, feeling her face loosen into the conversation. 'And what about you?'

Rachel has changed since college. Changed remarkably. The whey-faced, anxious girl with the hurried head-down walk has been transformed into a brightly coloured creature with streaked and coiffed hair, an orange tan and quite miraculous breasts. When Elena had met Rachel by chance in the supermarket early in the summer, those breasts were hidden underneath a Ralph Lauren T-shirt. But tonight they are plumped up proudly under a black bodice. Elena wants to say something about the change, something complimentary, but nothing comes to mind and she is left gaping, aware of the expectant silence.

'I'm so glad you decided to come,' Rachel gushes, filling the silence. 'I was telling the other girls about how we bumped into each other, out of the blue, after all these years. They were amazed – couldn't believe it – that here was the Elena who seemed to have disappeared off the face of the earth, that no one had heard from in years, and all this time you've been living quietly in suburbia!'

'Yes, well…' The blood is rushing to her cheeks. Her dress is sticking to her back. She feels the need to offer some kind of explanation, but nothing is forthcoming.

'But it's so easy to lose touch, isn't it?' Rachel says quickly, mercifully.

'I suppose it is.'

'You know, we've often spoken of you. I've lost count of the number of times I've heard people saying, "Whatever happened to Elena Shaw?"'

'Really?'

'After second year, when you didn't come back from Spain to sit your Finals… when neither of you came back… some of us wondered if we would ever see you again!'

Rachel's eyes flicker under the strong lights and the searching look reminds Elena that her private life has been discussed at length. That she has formed the topic of conversation – worse than that, gossip, salacious and juicy. Girl runs off to Europe with lover. Doesn't return. Forsakes education and career for love. And by love they mean sex. And sex in a foreign climate seems so audacious, infused with the molten heat of the land, becoming something flagrantly carnal. It must have filled hours spent over coffee and cigarettes, their names tripped out at dinner parties, their affair paraded through pubs and restaurants. As a cautionary tale, Elena wonders?

'And what about your husband? Is he here?' Rachel's eyes flicker about Elena, searching him out.

'No,' she answers, drawing the eyes back to her own. 'He couldn't make it, I'm afraid. The babysitter let us down at the last minute.'

'Oh no! That's a shame!' Rachel's smile slips momentarily, before perking itself up again. 'Never mind, Elena. Let's see if we can find the girls. They'll be dying to meet you.'

*

The lie she has told incubates inside her as they drift through the growing crowd. It wasn't the babysitter. It was Henry. An icy chill passes through her like a shudder as she thinks back to the phone call earlier that day and his announcement that he would be staying at home with the children instead of accompanying her to the reunion. She listened to the purposeful insistence of his words, with the receiver crushed against her ear, while something sank inside her, plummeting down through her depths and layers, pooling in the pit of her stomach.

'What?' she asked in disbelief.

'Come on, Elena, don't be like that. You'll have a better time on your own. I've never even met any of these people.'

'I haven't seen them myself in years,' she answered frostily.

'Well, precisely! So what are you getting worked up about?'

He had launched into a hurried explanation about a deadline approaching for an important client, a hint of aggression underpinning the details – this is a nervous habit of his, as if warning her not to question him.

'Fine,' she answered in a high, tight voice, suppressing her disappointment, hiding her indignation.

And later, after he returned home, she studiously avoided looking at him standing in the doorway of the bathroom, a hand passing over his face with its fading tan, purple shadows creeping around glassy-blue eyes. Emily danced up and down, trying to get his attention. 'Daddy! Daddy! Daddy!' she called, hopping from one bare foot to the other.

But Elena refused to look up. She refused to look upon the small lines that have started springing up in the corners of his face, his hair peppered with grey, subtle changes that she has noticed lately – this new tiredness that catches in his breathing. And sensing his guilty presence there, waiting for her to absolve him, to tell him that she really didn't mind going alone, a little voice inside her was bursting to escape. She wanted to tell him that it wasn't fair, that he knew how difficult this would be for her, didn't he? She wanted to scream at him, to bully him into submission. But she fought it off, refusing to give it an airing. I will not turn into my mother, she had told herself.

But despite all this, she had been unable to resist saying to him on her way down the stairs, 'I just wish you could have told me sooner. Then I could have cancelled for both of us.'

'If it's going to be so awful, Elena, then why are you going at all?' he asked, exasperation leaking into his tone.

And that's when she said it. 'Curiosity.'

A lie, made insignificant by her casual shrug, the nonchalance with which she delivered it. But a lie nonetheless. And if she had told him the truth, would he have changed his mind? If he had known about the boy who is now a man, would he have come with her? Or would he have stopped her from going at all, with shocked indignation and breathy threats? Whispers of *No way* and *I can't believe you would…*, still other murmurs of *Over my dead body*.

*

Rachel has found Cathy and the three women stand together re-acquainting themselves.

'And you never went back to finish your degree?' Cathy asks her, eyebrows knitting with concern.

'No. I didn't… In the end I decided it wasn't for me.'

'I always thought that was so sad,' she says suddenly. 'I mean, that Adam went back and sat his Finals, but you didn't. That always struck me as being so… well, unfair.'

She says this without malice, but with a compassion that causes a sudden lump to appear in Elena's throat, her eyes hot with tears. Elena, who has always liked Cathy, feels a pressing need to move away from her. A silence falls between them, resonating with her sense of deflation. She wants to tell them that she is not usually like this. That she is normally gregarious, a busy person. She wants to tell them that her life is full, that she makes sure it is – filled by Henry, the children, her mother and father and brother, even her parents-in-law and the coterie of friends she and Henry have built up and established. She feels a need to populate her days with people and activities. It sometimes occurs to her that she might be too dependent on other people, unable to sustain a sense of solitude. This is vaguely worrying to her.

For there was a time when she was alone. There are moments stored in her memory of solitude in foreign cities, walking through streets alone and untouched, viewing buildings, monuments and museums unaccompanied. Except by sadness. She remembers the sadness. Perhaps it is because she can remember it that she needs companionship, someone by her side. She is not as self-contained as the younger Elena once was, but needs help when venturing out into the world, a buffer, a bodyguard.

'Well,' she recovers herself. 'What about you, Cathy? Did you ever qualify?'

'Yes, as a solicitor. I have a small practice – conveyancing mainly.'

Elena smiles politely and they nod at each other for a moment. The question is coming. She can feel it. 'So what are you doing with yourself now?'

She groans inwardly, suddenly feeling the weight in her legs, and wants to sit down and kick her shoes off. This question will be trotted out ad nauseam tonight. It is one that she dreads.

'Elena is one of the lucky ones,' Rachel answers for her. 'She gets to stay at home and bring up her children. There are days, believe me, when I would gladly ditch my job and become a housewife.'

Housewife. It is such a dull, deadbeat kind of word, laden with connotations of floral housecoats and rubber gloves. It is sexless. In Spanish, they say *ama de casa* – friend of the house. Such a gentle, subtle expression. At times Elena feels that English is such a brutal language, lacking the rhythms and nuances of her second tongue.

'Oh,' says Cathy, her voice lilting up and then down again through the syllable.

'I do a little translation work as well,' Elena interjects, needing to salvage something of her ego, her intellect.

'Of course – I had forgotten you spoke Spanish.'

'How do you manage it?' Rachel asks brightly. 'Bringing up children and working?'

'Well, it's only a little... sort of freelance, you see. Part-time.' Her voice ebbs away, marking the inadequacy of the words.

Cathy is asking her about the children now and she answers compliantly, somewhat vacantly. She tells of their names and their ages, their little traits and habits, and Cathy smiles and nods at appropriate moments. Why does she feel so mechanical, so cold? Unable to engage, Elena feels like she is floating above their conversation, going through the motions, her mind elsewhere. And while she listens to Rachel launching into an anecdote involving a judge, a call girl and a radio station, the floating Elena is lost, careering through time and space back to when she had choices.

How did she get here? What twist of fate, what ill-timed move or hasty decision put in motion a catalogue of events that have led to this uneasy feeling of inadequacy? She thinks of the girl she once was, with her ripped jeans and open-toed sandals, hair wraps and T-shirts emblazoned with political slogans that were not her own, and wonders what she would say to that girl now had she the chance. Would she sit her down and talk some sense into her? Persuade her to finish her degree, cajoling her with promises that love would wait for her? How would her life have turned out if she had not gone with him? Would things have been different if she had not left him, if they had not left each other?

But how could she regret any decision that has led to her children? Life without Emily and Ben is something Elena cannot consider. For the moment she set eyes upon them – first Emily, and later Ben – their purple and bruised little bodies, wisps of hair plastered to the scalp, and those florid, scrunched-up little faces and impossibly small fingers and toes – she felt something move through her, a change, an imperceptible recalibration of all her emotions and desires. She could not turn away from that. She would not want to.

Yet still, there are moments of envy. When her next-door neighbour Ian regales her with tales of his exploits at parties, all-night sessions in Lillie's, stripping Renard's bare, flirting with boybands and soap actors, she feels a little deprived. And when she hears her friend Clodagh speaking of foreign business trips to Milan and Munich,

London and Stockholm, she feels twinges, small pangs of wanting, and for a while she feels a little trapped and caged in.

Things would have been different if she had returned to finish her degree. And she could have done, if she had wanted to. He did, after all. But that would have been to admit defeat. A tacit acknowledgement that what she had done was a mistake, a folly, a setback to her education, an illogical abandonment of sense and reason. But love is not bound by such cold, sterile terms. That is what Elena thinks. And to have gone back would have been to negate everything they had shared, everything they had revelled in and all they had been to each other. She could not do that. Even if he could, she could not engage in that betrayal.

A woman who Elena does not remember ever knowing has joined them. Her hair is a shade of purple, a colour that does not exist in nature, and she holds a paper plate of canapés but makes no attempt to eat them. She has a sudden smile, a brilliant display of chalky square teeth, which she flashes at intervals, luminous responses to Rachel's endless anecdotes. Her eyes pass briefly over Elena, dropping to her legs before turning back to Rachel.

Elena looks down at the hemline skimming her bare knees. She should have worn tights. This is all wrong, this dress, this night. What is she thinking? Who is she trying to be? Her age is shouting at her. *Thirty-two*, it screeches, *not twenty-two*. It lingers like a cloud above her, sneering at her silly little dress with its Provençal pretensions, her shiny hair cut along her jawbone and oh-so-safe little earrings peeping out, diamonds lest anyone think she could not afford them.

As conversation swirls around her, Elena is suddenly weary. Assaulted by the pressing need to sit down, she waits for a natural pause in conversation, then makes her apologies and moves away. Cathy promises to catch up with her later. Rachel seems to bristle at a perceived insult and the radiant smile from the woman who has joined them fades into a thin line. But Elena is too tired, too heartsore, to care.

It was a mistake to come here. What had she hoped to achieve? Half an hour into it and she is already lost. Something urgent is building inside her, emotion boiling around her heart. The windowless room adds to the oppression, the wooden walls close in around her. To her horror, she realises that her eyes are crowding with tears.

Brimming with a forgotten sorrow, she needs to get out, to get away. Away from the reminders of failings, of wounds that she thought had healed. The room has filled with people and voices are raised, laughter rising from the crowd as it shifts and moves, like an amoeba changing shape, seeping forward, growing, pooling in corners. 'Please, excuse me, please let me get past,' she hears her voice saying, rising and urgent, her hands pressing against shoulders, her body moving against the bodies of strangers. Reaching the entrance, she swallows hard to control the rising lump in her throat. And as she pushes free from the crowd, breath catching in her throat, she sees him, standing before her as if waiting for her.

He is tall and full of angles and still as skinny as a teenager. His face too has grown angular, the shock of hair cut back to reveal a neater, older face. Skin that was once reddish-brown and freckled has eased into a subtle tan, lines sneaking into the corners. It is a shock. That boyish face has grown up.

'Hello, Elena.'

His eyes have not changed. Still sharp with irony, eyes that are greedy and unblinking, sucking in every detail of her.

'Adam.'

'You're not leaving?'

'Yes. I'm afraid so.' She feels agitated. Unprepared. She is conscious of the rocking of her own heartbeat. This is something she had not anticipated. The shock of their greeting, the awkwardness of the distance of space between them.

'I just wanted to pop in and say a quick hello.' She feels the need to explain.

'No, you didn't. You came to see if I would be here.' He says this in a flat monotone, but she senses the challenge.

'What?'

'And now that I am, you're running away?'

'I am not running. Not from you. This room, there's no air,' she explains, feeling the colour in her cheeks, the blood-flow to her face letting her down yet again. The room is clamouring amid a multiplicity of sounds. She feels them hammering at her back, propelling her forward.

'Don't run away, Elena. Stay and talk for a while. Look. See how they've already begun to notice us.'

He nods in the direction of the crowd and she watches his eyes, those wide, remembered green eyes that seem to be tipping the whole room in his direction.

'Is that why you came?' she asks suddenly, tasting the bitterness of her own words. 'To give them something to talk about?'

'I came because I knew you'd be here.'

'How could you possibly know that?' Her resentment rises, pushing lightly against the word 'possibly'.

'Because I knew you couldn't resist it. You never could tear yourself away from drama, from tragedy. I knew it in the way your eyes fixed on Carlos's body while we waited for the medics to arrive.'

She flinches at the image, the vivid stain on her memory.

'I knew it in the way that you felt compelled to go to Zaragoza to the funeral when the rest of us refused. In the same way you liked to linger after sex. In the same way you lingered after...'

'I left you.'

She surprises him with the aggression in her voice. It flares up, igniting her chocolate-brown eyes.

'I was the one who left you, Adam,' she hisses. 'Remember?'

'Yes. I remember,' he answers slowly, as though wary of her temper. 'Like it was yesterday.'

He says this softly, his hushed tone rings with sincerity. It is too much. She cannot stay. She turns from him and begins to hurry away, needing to put space between them, needing air to pour in and fill the gap between his body and hers. And as she moves, she is conscious of those green eyes, fixed on her, seeing past her and through her, as they did from the start.

2

ELENA LIKES TO think of herself as a decisive person. Someone who knows her own mind and is not afraid to act on her decisions. No dithering. No dilly-dallying, as her mother-in-law Alice might say. Alice is not someone who Elena thinks of as particularly forceful or self-possessed. 'My head is muzzy today!' she exclaims frequently, after spilling sugar or forgetting to bring in the washing or mistaking what day of the week it is. Always this declaration is accompanied by a high, shrill laugh, a semi-screech, nervous and sudden. It used to bother Elena, unnerving her and making her watchful for sudden movements. But she has become used to it, allowing it to seep and melt into Alice's persona. 'My mother-in-law is so forgetful!' she might declare, with a generous smile as if to say 'poor old thing', which she hopes is seen as affectionate and not condescending.

Cabbage-brain, nincompoop, airhead, featherbrain. These are all names Henry uses for his mother. Terms of endearment, he says. 'How are you, mushy-mind?' he might say, kissing her lightly on the cheek. Or, 'Forget to take your medication again?'

'Do you think your mum minds you speaking to her like that?' Elena sometimes asks.

'It's just a joke,' Henry shrugs in reply.

Shit-for-brains. Elena was sure she heard him say this, once, quietly, under his breath.

Elena comes from a long line of forthright, determined women. It is the Spanish blood, Henry says, earthy and molten, that makes them fiery, decisive, grounded. It is what attracted him to her, he says, that underlying air of surety. It gave her strength and a certain calmness, like a rock. It has occurred to Elena that her husband is fond of describing her in geographical terms – earthy, grounded, rock – and she is not sure what to make of this.

'You're a real ball-buster,' their next-door neighbour, Ian, said to her recently.

Standing outside their house, looking up at the TV-repair man fitting a new cable under the eaves, she watched carefully, barking – yes, barking! – instructions at him. Ian stood next to her, hands on his delicate hips, shaking his head in disbelief. 'You go, girl!' he said, grinning up into the sunlight.

Others were more inclined to think of this strength of character as a stubborn streak. Her mother, for example. 'Obstinate as a mule!' she would declare, rattling the syllables off her tongue. 'Always the same. No push. No give.'

Elena is not sure whether it is indignation or pride that her mother expresses. Is she relieved to have a daughter with a sense of herself? Is it a breath of fresh air after the years of wavering indecision she has endured from Elena's father, Vincent? A comfort compared to the fickle transience of Elena's brother, Luis?

But whether it is obstinacy or groundedness or ball-busting, it seems to have deserted her now. She dawdles in the lobby, eyeing up the weather. The rain is pulsing down, cast against the windowpanes in fleeting waves, the wind gathering and pounding against the glass. To escape into the elements would be crazy, she tells herself, she'd be soaked to the skin. That would just be theatrical. And she has already made one dramatic gesture, fleeing the scene in a flurry of tears and emotion. That is enough for one evening.

So she finds a seat at the bar, which is almost deserted now. She perches on a high stool, leaning her bare elbows on the buffed, polished surface of the dark-wood counter and orders a drink. As the vodka and tonic is put in front of her, fizz spitting from the glass, she notices her reflection in the mirror behind the bar. In among the glasses and liquor bottles is a small heart-shaped face, with sallow skin and big round eyes. The broad, slanting mouth is unsmiling, her lipstick all eaten away. Her reflection appears tiny, diminished. And this is how she feels.

'You should never go to a reunion unless you are on top of the world,' Clodagh counselled her. 'Unless you can look people in the eye and say, "This is me, this is my life and it is absolutely wonderful", then just don't bother. Stay home, eat pizza and rent a soppy movie. Pour all your angst into some piece of crap with Meg Ryan in it, but for Jesus's sake, don't spend the evening with a bunch of people who will be reciting their CVs practically verbatim!'

If only she had listened.

What is the collective noun for lawyers, she wonders? A school of solicitors? A battery of barristers? A murder of lawyers? Whatever the correct term, they fill a room upstairs and it is the immediacy of that knowledge, the sudden presence among them after all this time, that brings it home to her like a sledgehammer – she has been running. Running for eleven years. Over a decade. She is exhausted.

Behind her, there is a couple seated in two armchairs, staring around each other disinterestedly. Elena watches them through the bar mirror. She sees the girl's platinum hair, her white trouser suit – inexpensive and badly cut – her body squeezed and bulging in places. She looks bored, fed up. Her boyfriend leans forward, his hands clasped in front of him. There are gold rings on his fingers but no wedding band, and through his open shirt collar, gold chains sit among the hair that is matted there. They appear to have nothing to say to each other. Elena wonders at their presence here. Perhaps they are staying in the hotel for a weekend, a romantic break, an attempt at mending broken fences? The woman catches her eye – her gaze is hard under all that shadowy make-up – and Elena looks down, fixing her eyes on her drink. How easy it is to fall out of love, she thinks.

Without looking up, she knows that he is there. Something has happened in the room. The air around her seems to heave like a sharp intake of breath. He moves beside her and wordlessly pulls a stool over next to hers, leaning on the counter before bringing his weight down on the stool with a short puffy sigh. His movements seem enormous to her, great deliberate acts that disturb the air, unsettling the temporary peace she has found. He has followed her down here. As she knew he would.

He motions to the barman and leans towards her and whispers, 'What's that you're drinking?'

'I'm fine,' she says shortly, feeling small and tense and not wanting anything from him. Not even a drink. He ignores this and orders another of what she is having, a whiskey and red for himself.

They sit in silence until their drinks arrive. Conscious of the petty meanness of her refusal, she makes a tentative gesture to recover. 'Thanks,' she says quietly.

'You're welcome,' he replies, sipping his drink before returning his glass carefully to its coaster. She watches his long fingers from the corner of her vision, their knuckles and joints bulbous and oversized on those skinny, narrow hands.

'So. Were you waiting here for me?' he asks softly.

'No,' she lies, disturbed by his arrogance and the bluntness of his address to her. It is too familiar, too insolent after all these years.

'I think you were.'

'I came here to wait for the rain to stop, Adam,' she says coolly, struggling to suppress her rising temper. 'It's cats and dogs out there and I'm not exactly dressed for it.'

'So why not go back upstairs? Why sit in here all alone, when you can be mingling with your peers, reacquainting yourself with lost friends?'

She hears the sarcasm in his voice and senses his own bitterness towards them and all they represent. Curious, seeing as he chose to go back in the end. To become one of them.

'I won't be here long,' she says. 'Just until the rain stops.'

She is conscious of the defensiveness of her tone and repeats herself, softer this time.

'As soon as the rain stops, I'll be on my way.'

'Fair enough.'

They drink in an absent-minded fashion, staring into nothing and avoiding each other's reflection in the mirror. But Elena can sense the difference in him, the changes that have swollen in him. They send mild shockwaves through her, jolts touching her heart. His effervescence seems to have become flat over time, all the fizz has fermented into something dull and uneasy. His boundless energy seems to have realised its boundaries; it beats at the surface but is hemmed in, contained. Elena is reminded of athletes that have retired, their bodies like machines winding down, muscle turning to fat, sinew and tissue growing less taut, more flaccid. She has noticed the tired hunch of his shoulders. There is unhappiness there, she thinks.

'You came alone?' he asks suddenly.

'Yes. My husband couldn't make it.' Her voice touches lightly on the word 'husband'. It feels grainy in her mouth.

He is looking at her now in the mirror. She can tell from the change in his posture, the stillness that has entered his body.

'What's his name?'

'Henry. Henry Butler.'

'I see. And how long are you married?'

'Eight years.'

His silence is filled with something. Shock? Pain? Disappointment? *That long?* it seems to ask. *So soon after?*

She looks up and meets his gaze through the smoky mirror. It is a handsome face, but not classically so. It is crowded with angles, a mass of bones jutting through skin – high cheekbones and a sharp jawline, the mechanics visible. His forehead is smooth, laid bare by the absence of hair that once fell over it, now cut neatly, almost severely. It makes his eyes bigger. Heavy lidded and sensual, they meet hers among a gathering of glassware and she sees the pain in them. For a fleeting second, this affords her some satisfaction. Satisfaction to know that he too has felt it. But this dies away suddenly, replaced by shame at her vindictiveness, disgust at her self-pity.

'Does he know about me?'

She is shocked by his question – so bald, so direct. It is too honest, lacking the artifice and chicanery that she had expected – indeed, hoped for – from him.

'Not as such.'

'What does that mean?'

It means that he knows there was someone in the time before he knew Elena, someone vague and shadowy like a dotted outline whose colours she will not provide. Her husband suspects that this is as a result of pain caused, inflicted, suffered, but he does not – cannot – know how acute the pain was. And how, if the surface is scratched, this pain might seep up to greet the daylight, emerging from the shadows it lurks in. Besides, she was never interested in the details surrounding Henry's former love affairs and made it clear that he should afford hers the same casual disinterest. But she does not say that to Adam. Instead she shakes her head and skirts the issue, moving on, detracting from the probing nature of his remark. 'Are you in

Ireland just for this reunion, or is there something else that brings you here?'

'My mother isn't well,' he answers. 'And I felt I ought to spend some time with her before… you know.'

'I'm sorry to hear that.'

'She's old,' he says quickly, as if to shrug off any pity. 'She's had a good run at it, no one could say she hasn't had a fair run at it.'

'That's true.'

'She never did forgive me for running off on her like that, though.'

He laughs, a small tight gasp of air, and shakes his head, his chin jutting forward.

'I swear, that woman. She's been threatening her own demise ever since I left, but this time I think she means it. And do you know the funny thing?'

Elena waits.

'My mother has discussed her own death more than anyone I have ever known. There isn't a time I can remember when she wasn't saying, "One day I'll be in my grave, and then you'll be sorry", like it was a stick to beat me, something to guilt-trip me with. I even think the old bat used to get a sort of pleasure out of it, like she knew she was going to have the last laugh and there'd be no recourse for me, I'd just be saddled with the guilt that somehow I had shortened her life. And now that the big event is finally getting ready for curtain up, she's shit-scared. Really. She's absolutely petrified.'

Elena thinks of her and remembers the small birdlike woman with the transparent tissue-like skin, the same greedy eyes as her son's, although hers were always hungry for faults and failings. But most of all, she remembers that rasping voice, that ginny breath…

More drinks arrive and they are momentarily distracted.

'Is she in much pain?' she asks, and he nods his head quickly.

'It's controlled, of course, but it's still there. You can see it in her face.'

'How awful,' she says solemnly, before adding, 'please God, she'll go quickly.'

He looks sideways at her as she says this. It is the first time since sitting down next to her that he has looked directly at her and not through the reflection of a mirror.

'That's not what you used to say. I remember a time when you used to say that death should be slow, so that it could be experienced fully.'

She smiles despite herself, a sudden smile at the memory. 'So I did.'

'Death is the final experience, you used to say. And so it should be drawn out, as it was the last act of life we would have. That's what you used to say.'

'That was a long time ago, and before Carlos...'

His name escapes her lips before she can stop herself. It sits between them now, growing, swelling, it fills the room. Carlos. It sears her chest like a hot whip of air.

'Yes,' he says slowly, dragging the syllable out. 'But then Carlos's death changed so many things, didn't it?'

She turns away from those eyes, those liquid eyes, pointed and punishing. Raising the glass tumbler to her lips, she gulps, a loud, guttural swallow, and returns her drink to its coaster with a trembling hand. A storm of ghosts has been whipped up. They swirl around her, mocking and taunting.

'Do you think it will be long?' she asks quickly. 'Your mother, I mean.'

'No. She's very close now.'

'And will you go back to Spain afterwards?' she asks tentatively, awkward with the subject of death.

'I'm not in Spain any more,' he says, pursing his lips thoughtfully. 'I haven't been there in four years.'

This information races through her, unearthing a dozen spin-off questions, more coming to the surface, crowding her consciousness. If not Spain, then where? Why did he leave? Did she go with him? Did they go with him?

But she stays silent, waiting for him to provide answers to these unspoken questions.

'I left Spain because things weren't working out.' He says this with a rueful smile, but it doesn't adequately cover the hurt that's there. 'I needed to get away, to make a clean break. Half on a whim, I applied for a US green card. When I got it, I thought, "What the hell" and went for it. I've been living there ever since.'

He's there alone, she thinks. Too many Is. No mention of we.

'Whereabouts?'

'Maine. It's OK. I've gotten to know some people.'

She senses his loneliness.

'And are you practising over there?'

'No,' he says emphatically. 'I could have done the Bar exams, I suppose, but my heart wasn't in it. I guess I'd lost interest.'

Adam who was always so fickle, flitting from one thing to the next. Adam who returned to finish his degree, and for what? To what end?

'I have my own business now,' he tells her, oblivious to the disappointment on her face.

He's telling her about it as she half-listens, drifting in and out of the conversation, picking up occasional words like tax relief, staff retention, profit margins and customer base. All that syntax. Meaningless words. Economics. Why does she feel so betrayed? What right has she to be disappointed by the life choices he has made? It is eleven years, she reminds herself sharply. Water under the bridge.

'You never went back, then?'

This question snaps her out of her reverie.

'No. It wasn't for me, in the end.'

'I hope it wasn't because of me,' he says softly.

Of course it was because of you, she thinks, because of what you'd done. 'Not at all. I just don't think I was cut out for it.'

'That may be true,' he complies. 'You never were the lawyerly sort.'

This strikes her as a strange thing to say. Did he really think that? Even back then, before they left, could he already see that she was unsuited, that she didn't fit in? She thinks back to that time and tries to summon how it felt to be eighteen. Entering university and the next phase of her life, she felt nervous but not overly so. For the most part, it was excitement she experienced, a clear-eyed, hopeful sense of something coming in the future, something promised. Knowledge. Learning. Understanding. The liberation of education. The opening of her mind, and of her body too – how it longed to reach out to another. In this, she was no different from every other student seated in that lecture theatre. Or so she believed, until now.

'I suppose not,' she concedes softly.

The rattle of rain has stopped and the bar is filling up. There are faces there that she recognises, the class reunion spilling down into the bar and lounge.

'I worked for a while,' she volunteers suddenly, 'after I came home.'

'You travelled more after Spain. Belgium, I heard…'

'For a while,' she says quickly, dismissively.

She does not like to think about that period of her history, a time when loneliness consumed her, accompanying her as she beat her way through narrow streets alone, her deadened gaze passing over medieval buildings grey with rain. And sometimes not alone.

'When I came back home, I got a job. In an insurance company. Customer service in a call centre.'

He shoots her a glance of sympathy, eyebrows curling in the centre.

'It was awful. Truly awful.'

She tells him about the vacuous office, a warehouse really, filled with rows of cubicles like horse-boxes. She describes sitting in her cubicle, a headset trapping her in its vice-like grip. All those sunless days, that endless stream of invective from faceless aggrieved customers. She adds a certain comedic element to her account with facial tics and put-on voices peppered through her anecdotes. He groans in sympathy and laughs where appropriate. But what she doesn't tell him is how that job saved her. Its monotonous routine gave structure and a curious sense of purpose to her life, which had been so fraught with uncertainty and calamity up to that point. And how the camaraderie between the customer-service agents, as they were known, lifted her spirits, chivvying them out of the dark place where they had lingered all winter. And then she met Henry, and everything changed.

'Did you keep in touch with anyone? From college, I mean?'

'No.' She shakes her head.

'Why not?'

'Because I wanted to forget.'

He seems struck by her honesty, his eyes flicking over her face before looking away.

'And now? Tonight? This reunion?' He glances at the group that has gathered by the entrance, some the worse for all the free wine.

'Tonight was a mistake.'

'How come?'

'I don't know,' she confesses. 'For some reason, I felt that I had something to prove, a point to make. And, in the end, I've proved nothing at all.'

'What is there to prove?'

She feels slightly ridiculous, realising the strangeness of their conversation. He is leaning towards her in a bubble of intimacy, they are whispering conspiratorially.

'That I'm equal to them,' she finally admits. It feels strange to say it out loud, the words tripping off her tongue. 'I wanted to show them that, despite the fact that I never graduated, that I'm not a solicitor or a barrister, the life I have is just as worthy as theirs.'

'Does their approval mean that much to you?'

She is flustered by the question, regretting her honesty.

'No... but...'

'Surely what matters is what you think.'

'Well, of course...'

She pauses, feeling embarrassed and conscious of the condescension in his voice, his mannerisms. He is turning away from her, back to his drink, and she feels the pique of his dismissal.

'Your husband didn't come with you,' he remarks, the words thrown over his shoulder, but she senses the change in his tone.

'No. Something came up and he couldn't make it.'

'Does he know how you felt about coming here tonight?'

'Yes.'

This lie leaves an acrid taste on her palate. A taste of guilt. She has not admitted her true feelings about tonight to Henry, her fear of inadequacy.

'And yet he still let you come here alone.'

This is not a question, but an offhand remark, barely spoken. He shakes his head and raises his eyebrows. She senses his disappointment in her and feels herself rising to the challenge.

'It's not like that,' she says angrily.

'Are you happy, Elena?'

Again the question takes her aback. It is so sudden, so forcefully put. She cannot remember the last time anyone asked her this, and immediately she realises the answer. Tears prick at the back of her eyes. But she will not give him the answer. He has not earned it. She feels how dangerous he is to her.

'My happiness is not your concern.' She spits the words at him. 'It hasn't been for over a decade.'

A silence passes between them, swollen with unspoken bitterness. At last he raises a hand, a gesture of surrender. 'I'm sorry, Elena. And of course you are right. It's not my place to make assumptions about your life.'

She is reluctant to let go of her anger and he seems to read this in the tense posture she has adopted, her features arranged in a mask of cold contempt.

'Please, Elena. Please don't be angry,' he says in a conciliatory manner, that same quiet charm. 'Don't stay mad at me. I didn't mean it. Please?'

And then he touches her wrist lightly with those long well-remembered fingers, fingers that once knew every part of her, that have traced lines across her skin, fingers that were once hungry for her, clutching, probing, invading her, fingers that have moved her to ecstasy and calmed her with their tenderness. They rest briefly on her hand and she feels their coolness searing her bare skin, sending shockwaves through her, goosebumps rising up treacherously on her flesh. And when they move away, back to the coldness of the glass tumbler, a yearning is left behind, that forgotten desire scratching at the surface.

'Do you have children?' he asks softly.

'Yes. Two. Emily is six and Ben will be two in January.'

'You've been lucky.'

'Yes, I have.'

Another pause springs up, one that is waiting to be filled with a question that she wants to ask, but is afraid to. She has wondered for so long, and now finds herself cowed by the possible answer.

'And you?' she asks hesitantly.

'I have a son,' he replies ponderously, before adding his name, 'Carlos.'

Her breath catches. She is unprepared for it. After that brutal death and the catalogue of pain that ensued? To name his son after Carlos? It seems too much to endure. How can anyone live with such a constant reminder? His name enunciated daily? She has difficulty comprehending such a decision. What strength it must take… She knows she could not bear it. She, who ran as far as she could.

'I don't see him much now,' he says regretfully. 'He and Maria stayed in Spain.'

'I see.'

'She and I don't talk much any more. It would seem there is nothing left to say between us.'

'I'm sorry,' she says and, to her own surprise, finds that she means it.

25

'I'm hoping when he's a little older, he will be able to come out and stay with me.'

'Of course. He must be ten years old now?' she asks.

'Six,' he says slowly and drinks deeply, avoiding her eyes.

She is momentarily confused. There must be some mistake, some error in calculations. 'No. No, he couldn't be,' she says, shaking her head.

'Elena. He is six,' he replies calmly, bringing himself to return her gaze.

'But… but…'

'There was no baby,' he says, holding his voice steady, as if explaining to a child. 'It was a mistake. There was no baby. Not then. Not until much later.'

She is reeling. Something is dropping down within her, falling through her, wheeling down into the murky acid depths of her being.

'A mistake?' she whispers hoarsely.

'Elena.'

'Whose mistake?' Her voice cracks.

'Does that matter?'

'Yes!'

There is something in his face now, an expression of inscrutability. What emotions are mixed up there, she wonders? Are they anything to compare with the barrage of bewilderment, anxiety and aching regret that are clamouring around her heart? How she would like to hurt him, to spring at him and beat him around the head, to claw at those green eyes and all that they have hidden from her. A dull ache settles across her face. She is assaulted by a sudden exhaustion.

He opens his mouth to speak, but is interrupted by someone else from the reunion.

They have been spotted. A member of their class, considerably drunk, has broken away from the group and joins them, draping his arms around them, pulling them into a huddle. He laughs loudly, his cheeks are ruddy and laced with broken capillaries. His thick girth speaking of frequent drinking bouts.

'So!' he shouts at their faces, looking from one to the other. 'The lovers unite, eh? What? Back together again, yeah?'

'You're drunk,' says Adam good naturedly, a strain in his voice.

'Damn straight!' the drunk laughs. 'And what of it? Eh? What of it?'

He laughs again, a snort, his foul breath filling the air between them.

'Some things don't change!' he bellows. 'I remember the two of you, sitting at the back of the lecture theatre, mauling each other in the library, in the canteen, in the bar, always slobbering all over each other, getting stuck into one another. D'you remember? Huh? Shagging in the stairwell outside Theatre L. Do you remember?'

His comments seem to belittle what they had, to besmirch the last traces of dignity clinging to that love. It is too much for Elena. She extricates herself from his unwelcome embrace and moves away. She has stayed too long. There is no place for her here.

'Aw, c'mon!' the drunk exclaims, spittle gathering in the corners of his mouth. 'Don't be like that now!'

He rocks backwards on his heels before steadying himself, gripping the bar.

'I have to go,' she says quickly, avoiding Adam's gaze. She cannot bring herself to look at him as she turns away, hurrying through the lounge, those drunken words still clinging to her like static.

He catches up with her in the lobby as she is about to enter the revolving door and grabs her by the elbow, swinging her around.

'I'm sorry,' he says breathlessly. 'About him. About what I said.'

'I have to go,' she repeats, shamed by the sudden trembling of her lip.

'Don't,' he pleads, still holding her elbow. 'Not like this. Not again. There's still so much to say…'

She looks back at the bar dubiously. The noise and smoke and clamour of drunken conversation are overwhelming.

'We can go somewhere else, somewhere quiet?' he suggests.

'I don't know, Adam.'

'I have a room.'

The soft cadences of his voice ripple through her.

'Please, Elena. Stay.'

3

SHE HAS NEVER once been unfaithful to her husband. Through eight years of marriage, she has never once been unfaithful to him. The first Christmas they spent together, there was a party in a neighbour's house. Elena recalls a tall, gaunt-looking man with a mouth that seemed crammed too full of teeth, and how he pulled her to one side and told her in a deep, roomy voice that she had beautiful skin. 'It is sublime,' he intoned gravely, and would she mind if he stroked her face? She laughed it off, making a smart remark, something about Oil of Olay, and hovered close to Henry for the rest of the evening, conscious of the meaningful sideways glances she was receiving. For days afterwards she found herself remembering the way he had looked at her, the light of his small glittering eyes as he said those words. When she was passing her fingers over her face at night, massaging moisturiser into her skin, she imagined that those fingers were not hers but someone else's, touching the soft contours of her face for the first time.

A year ago, she shared a taxi home from the squash club with Henry's friend Andrew. As the taxi pulled up in front of her house and she rummaged in her purse for her share of the fare, he held up a raised hand to refuse her money, saying, 'Don't worry about it, Elena. Why not just come back to my place and we can fuck each other senseless for the afternoon?' She remembers the shock she experienced, not least because it was Henry's friend, but also because the proposition seemed lost in the daylight – foreign and indecipherable. Later, when the shock wore off, replaced by indignation and a real trembling anger, she recalled the language he had employed. Those words, so coarse and so brutal, spoken so casually. They seemed to bounce off the inside of her skull, worming their way around her brain. She could not get rid of them. As she was standing at the checkout in the supermarket, purse in hand, listening to the items beeping through the register, those words suddenly filtered through into her consciousness, scalding her cheeks, leaving her flushed and unsettled. Or she would be piling bundles of folded clothes into the hot press, humming to herself, and there they were again – *we can fuck each other senseless* – bubbling through the pipes and cistern. They hummed through the churn of the washing machine, they clattered above the drone of the lawnmower. She turned up the volume of the TV in an effort to stifle them, but she could not suppress the whisper of inquisitiveness they fed.

She is not familiar with this language. She has grown unused to it. Love has softened her vocabulary. There is respect in her husband's advances, an unspoken reverence that seems strangely endearing from a man with his self-effacing tendencies. His invitations are mostly wordless. Lying next to him at night, she feels his sleepily searching arms and legs reaching for her, his body moving into the centre of the bed, causing a depression that draws her own body towards him. His hands and fingers speak of his intentions, his kisses are tender to begin with, becoming more pressing, more deliberate as she responds. She is familiar with all his noises, the moans and sighs, his breath catching in his throat as her back arches, clasping him in a firm lock with her strong thighs, that faint strangled cry as he shudders and comes to rest, his body lying heavily on hers. Afterwards, as they arrange themselves side by side, sleep drawing in upon them, he whispers his words of love to her.

That is the language she is versed in. The language of love within marriage. Their expressions of desire are couched in phrases that are warm and secure, not harsh and biting. They know each other's movements, each other's sighs and noises and odours. There is comfort to be drawn from it.

But, at Adam's suggestion that they go to his room, she is suddenly cut adrift, coursing through a language she doesn't know. Is this a proposition? By accepting, would she be tacitly agreeing to something more? Despite these fears, and against her better judgement, she finds herself emerging from the lift on the seventh floor and following him along the corridor, watching his loping walk as he fiddles with his keys and reaches the bedroom door.

He turns his face to look at her, with a sudden impudent smile. 'Don't worry,' he smirks, as if reading her mind. 'You'll be quite safe. Promise.'

But there are other voices clamouring in her consciousness. She can hear her mother's harsh, reprimanding tones, syllables rattling in her Latin lilt. *Stupid girl. What are you doing? Who are you trying to fool? After everything that he has done, you still go back for more?* She can see Alice, her mother-in-law, and the perplexed look in her eyes. Alice, who frets over all of them, worrying about whether they have had enough to eat, whether they are warm enough, comfortable enough. She can hear her, the hushed voice, that quaver of fear. *Oh, Elena, I don't know about this. I'm not sure that this is such a good idea. I'm not at all sure that it is.* Alice, the counter of blessings. And alongside these voices, her own whispers to her, telling her that his promises can no longer be trusted.

He pushes the door open and walks ahead of her, turning on lights and snatching items of clothing from chairs and beds in an effort to make his room presentable. The door closes behind her and she looks about for somewhere to sit. There are two beds – a double bed occupying the central area and a single pressed against the wall. It doesn't leave much space for the collection of furniture that remains – a desk, a coffee table and two stiff formal armchairs. He stands awkwardly in between the beds and motions for her to come forward and make herself comfortable. Neither of them is sure where to sit. He opts for one of the armchairs and leans back expansively, crossing those long, skinny legs. His trouser leg rides up and she sees a few inches of pale skin covered with wiry hairs above a dun-coloured sock. As she perches on the corner of the single bed, he makes a hasty apology for his room – its size, the lack of space. She shakes her head and mumbles something about comfort and convenience.

The silence that follows is difficult. Elena does not know where to fix her eyes. Avoiding the bed and his nervous stare, she fixes her gaze on the mirror above him. The room is warm, overheated. How can anyone be expected to sleep in here, she wonders? The lighting is softer than in the lobby and lounge. A restful dimness that casts the sharp edges in shadow, erasing the hardness and the fussy pattern that surrounds the room.

'Drink?' he suggests suddenly, getting out of his chair and approaching the minibar as she gives her order.

He hands her a vodka and tonic and returns to his chair. She is conscious of the jerkiness of his movements. His long, angular body seems to crowd the room. He stoops, almost as if he feels the ceiling bearing down on top of him. His actions seem rushed, powered by an urgency she is not aware of. It makes her nervous. He was not always like this. There was a time when he had more grace, or at least more purpose to his energy. That seems to have been replaced by something fierce and erratic.

The colour rises to her cheeks. She has already had too much to drink. The little voice inside her that has been instructing her to leave has risen to screaming pitch. It is as she resolves to leave, to go downstairs and get a taxi and return home to her husband and children, to her life, that he starts to talk.

'You know, I often wondered how it would be if we met up again,' he says suddenly, the smirk dissolving into something vague, a sleepy, stalking look. 'I've tried to imagine what it would be like. What you would be like.'

She burns under the fleeting glance that passes over her. 'Is it how you imagined it?'

He shrugs. 'More or less. You're the same.'

She laughs, a short burst of breath from her mouth. It frees some of the tension lodged in her chest.

'I don't think so,' she smiles. 'I'm older now. More wrinkled.'

'Not that I can see.'

He says this in a low voice, and she thinks of the creases and lines in her body that he can't see. The lines of life that have crept over her like a road map. She is not ashamed of these scars.

'You haven't changed,' he reasserts. 'Not fundamentally. Still the same old Elena.'

'Why do you say it like that?' she asks, sensing something in his tone.

'Still needy. Still looking for approval. Always trying to prove something about yourself.'

31

She flushes an angry shade of red and a blood vessel jumps in her temple.

'It must be nice to be so self-contained,' she says quietly. 'So pleased with yourself.'

'I'm not pleased with myself,' he counters. 'Far from it. But I'm not looking for love from a crowd of people I don't even know any more.'

'I wasn't looking for love from them.'

'Respect, then. Admiration. Whatever.'

He uncrosses his legs, his eyes levelling her.

'Either way, it doesn't matter. You wouldn't get it, no matter what you had done or achieved. Truth is, they're only interested in themselves, their own little lives, their individual trophies – be they flash careers or trophy wives or fabulous wealth. The only emotion you could hope to inspire in them is envy. You'd be a fool to think otherwise.'

He finishes his sentence and looks away, drinking from his glass.

He has become bitter, she thinks suddenly. How did he get like this? Adam, who had once seemed so pure to her – almost radiant with possibility and an unspoken joy with life.

'If you loathe them so much, why did you come?' she asks.

'The same reason as you.'

'Which is?'

'To see you.'

He says this flatly with a slight movement of his shoulders, an upward tilt of his eyebrows, as if to assert that the reason is obvious.

'You think that's why I came?'

'Oh, I know it is.'

'You're wrong.'

'I'm not wrong. But you can pretend if you want.'

There is something sneering in his voice, as if to imply that he is above such dishonesty. This is an old tactic. She remembers it well. Recalling how he used to become aloof, how he would take possession of the moral high ground with ease. But there is something brittle about him now. She senses cracks in his hard surface.

'You're different,' she says suddenly, and he looks up, surprised.

'How?' His mask slips temporarily, leaving something childlike in the expectant look on his face, needing her to be kind, needing her response to be gentle.

'It's hard to put my finger on it. You seem – harder.'

'Oh.' His face falls a notch.

'What I mean is, you seem to be not as open as you once were. You used to be so pliable – so open to possibility. You used to embrace new things, almost chasing after them.'

He smiles wistfully, remembering.

'You had so much energy. There was a restlessness about you.'

'I was restless.'

'But not unhappy.'

This tumbles out unheeded. The tiredness in his body seems to wash over his face and he nods slowly.

*

'Maria used to say that I was drawn to danger. That it drew me like a magnet. It used to drive her crazy. God, when I think about it!' He laughs and passes a hand over his face, before resting his chin on his palm, elbows leaning on the armrests of the chair. 'She said that I found danger irresistible, that she couldn't understand why I was so drawn to it.'

He has slipped down in his chair, relaxing into it, his long legs stretched out in front of him.

'She may have been right.'

'It made her so frustrated. How she used to scream at me! And at those moments I always thought of you.'

She shifts uncomfortably.

'Why me? Why then?'

'Because if that was true of me, then it was true of you. I always felt we were alike in that way. Both of us like to play with fire.'

'Maybe then...' she says and stops.

'Yes. You're probably very safe now.'

He says this softly but she feels the slice of his remark.

'Perhaps I'd had my fill of danger,' she retorts.

*

Night closes in around them. The drink and the time that has passed in this room have made her comfortable, more daring.

'Do you see Maria at all now?' she asks casually.

33

'No. Not really,' he shrugs. 'As I said, we ran out of things to talk about years ago. Of course, it's impossible for us to avoid each other completely. We have a son, after all, and his needs must be discussed.'

'That must be difficult.'

'Yes,' he acknowledges quickly. 'Yes, it is. But we try to remain civilised. We have very civil conversations. Very brief, very civil.'

'I see.'

He purses his lips, thoughts clouding his eyes.

'She is so angry. I've never known anger to poison a woman like that. Twisting her, misshaping her, so that all of her beauty dies. Or maybe I just can't see it any more. I only see the bitterness.'

A shadow passes over Elena's mind, an image of a face she has tried to forget. Big, round, mournful eyes, coal-black eyebrows cut into smooth olive skin. And that blue-black hair, hanging low on each side of her shadowy face. A delicate face with gentle features and a brittle elegance. But there was a history of trouble enmeshed in her genes. It was a face full of secrets, it seemed to whisper of dark thoughts and hidden sorrows. How Elena had hated that face.

'She lives in Seville now,' he says, 'with Carlos. They live with her parents. She wasn't coping. After I left...'

The regret clings to his voice.

'She hated me for leaving her,' he says quietly, before straightening up and saying more forcefully, 'but she hated me anyway and that wouldn't have changed if I had stayed.'

His hurt and his regret are palpable. The battles he has fought with Maria, with himself, shreds of them cling to him still. And because of the boy, their son, because of Carlos, those shreds will cling to him always. For the first time she feels moved to pity him.

'Would you like to see a picture of my son?' he asks her, brightening at the suggestion.

She smiles weakly and nods.

He is on his feet now and moves to the bedside locker, rummaging among the mess of books and papers and loose change.

'Here we are,' he announces, his fingers lighting upon an envelope.

He moves quickly and sits on the bed beside her. His explanation of how he receives regular photos and letters from his son means that he doesn't see Elena's face as he sits next to her, his leg brushing against hers. He doesn't witness the flush of fear tinged with desire that colours her cheeks at the immediate proximity of his body to hers. She is at once conscious of the beds in the room.

'This is Carlos,' he says quietly, a soft-spoken pride in his voice.

It is a strange thing, seeing the child of a former lover, she thinks. What makes it strange is the possibility that this child could have been hers, or at least some variant mutation of this little person. He has Adam's bone structure, the high cheekbones, the impudent grin, that same flap of hair cast down over his forehead. But what shocks Elena more are the eyes that peer out from this small boy's face. Coal-black eyes with a strange light behind them – murky pools containing depths of history. Mournful eyes, Maria's eyes. A wealth of sorrow has seeped into his genetic make-up. She flicks through the five or six photographs and sees him captured playing, laughing, but the laughter never touches his eyes. Elena wonders if they are reflective of his own pain – the pain of desertion by a parent. As she gazes at the last of the images, she is suddenly struck by a thought – that this boy is alive because of what happened. His warm little body has life, has breath, because of those seven nights she spent in Zaragoza.

'He's lovely,' she admits softly.

'Yes, he is. He's a beautiful boy.'

He takes the photos back and looks at them for a moment longer, before putting them to one side. But he makes no attempt to move from the bed.

'Why did you name him that?' she asks.

'It was Maria's idea, not mine.' His voice is wooden and, though she cannot see his face, there is something rigid and set about his profile.

'I don't understand how she could. After everything that happened? You would think she would want to forget that name.'

'She never got over him,' he says quietly. 'Never stopped loving him.'

'But after all that time?'

'Not that long, really. Just a few short years.'

'Still. To carry that around with you, to go on loving someone like that, long after they've gone. It's incredible.'

'Not so incredible.'

He turns his face to hers as he says these words, and the intensity of his look speaks of a yearning she too has felt. Disturbed by it, she looks away.

'And how could I say no?' he continues. 'After everything she had been through, I felt I couldn't stop her from naming him that, despite the pain it caused me. I owed her that much.'

He looks down at his hands, folded in his lap, fingers knitted together.

'Sometimes I think she wishes I wasn't his father. I know it, in fact. She wanted Carlos to be the father of her child. Not me. And I proved to be a convenient – but ultimately poor – substitute.'

Elena is too shocked to answer. He has made an admission that leaves her cold.

'I've never admitted that to anyone,' he says, as if the realisation has just occurred to him.

*

The night grows and blooms. They sit alongside each other on the single bed, shoes kicked off, ankles crossed, backs pressed against the wall, hands folded in laps or idling with drinks.

'He's a good man. He's solid,' she tells him.

'Unlike me.'

She ignores this remark, aware of the self-deprecating tone, but also conscious of the question in it. She does not want to be drawn into that.

'When we met, he seemed so uncomplicated. It was difficult for me to get my head around for a while.' *After you*. But she doesn't add this. 'I kept looking for skeletons in his closet, dark secrets, hang-ups. But the truth is, Henry is a simple man. He is uncomplicated. He has no axe to grind.'

'Sounds perfect.'

He says this glibly and takes a swallow from his glass, draining the last of his drink.

'He's not perfect. Of course he's not. He can be cold and tight-lipped and secretive.' She says this quietly, feeling disloyal somehow. The shadow that has seemed to be hovering over her marriage in recent times slips into the bedroom and hangs in the air between them. But it is wrong to parade Henry's faults through this hotel room when he is not here to defend himself. She knows that.

'So he's human, then?'

'Yes, he's human.'

He pulls himself up from the bed and goes to fix another drink. Elena has lost count of how many times their glasses have been refilled. She is not even sure what time of the night it is. She doesn't protest when he takes her glass and hands it back refilled.

When he returns to the bed beside her, he seems to slide down so that his head is alongside her shoulder, his long legs bent at the knees, his socked feet disappearing over the edge. He sighs heavily and leans against her. She stiffens but does not move away.

'Do you love him?'

This question is asked quietly but firmly, without apology. He wants to know. A strange question to ask, as if he knows that maybe it is possible for her to be married to a man she does not love.

'Yes, I do.' Her voice is crystalline.

'As much as you loved me?'

He does not look at her when he asks this. She can feel the warmth from his body. It prickles her flesh, raising hairs on her arms despite the heat of the room.

'Yes.'

'Really?'

He looks up at her now, something flickering behind his liquid eyes. Doubt, fear. As if he had clung to the hope all these years that it could not be possible for her to love again in that way.

'It's different,' she explains in a small voice.

'Different?'

'It's not the same kind of love.'

'Not as passionate?'

'Not hurtful.'

This hangs between them, cutting a space between their bodies.

'Well, that's something,' he says dismissively, cooling the hot air between them and looking away.

*

And it is different. It is more honest, respectful, than what she shared with Adam. It is a grown-up kind of love. Not the heady passion of her youth, the recklessness and delirium of those early years. It is restrained, she acknowledges that. There are still times when she longs for the heat and urgency of that early passion. And at these times she thinks of Adam, and the way she was with him. He has done things to her body that no one else has dared. The memory of those acts draws blood to her cheeks. And words spoken, violent words, crude expressions of wanting, of longing, language that was urgent and compelling, language she hasn't used since, words she could not utter to another, such would be the depth of her mortification.

But with Henry it is different. She has housed his children in her body. That changes things.

*

Across the city her children are sleeping, their sweet, humming bodies oblivious to this encounter. Her husband is stretched out in their bed, arms circling the pillow under his head, the muscles in his long back pulled straight, vaguely aware of her absence, perhaps. But unaware of her betrayal.

'I thought I would feel different,' she is telling him. 'Being a mother. I should feel different. And while it has changed me, it's not in the way I expected it to. Not in the way I had hoped it would.'

He listens and says nothing.

'But lately, I've had this feeling. This nagging feeling.'

'Of what?'

'Of disappointment.'

'Why?'

'I don't know.'

Something cracks in her voice.

'I'm not even sure what it is I hoped to have achieved. I used to have ambitions...'

Tears are forming in her eyes. Pooling in the corners, preparing to fall. But she is past caring. Let them fall, she thinks. 'But this feeling won't go away. This feeling of being unfulfilled. That there must be something else, something beyond all this. There must be.'

He is holding her hand, stroking his thumb across her knuckles and the back of her hand. She cannot remember him taking it in his, and she does not draw away.

*

'It was stress. That's what she told me.'

His voice is strained with the pain of recollection.

'She was late. And she was frightened. It was an honest mistake.'

Elena thinks of Maria, her cloying need for attention, the way she used to whine and cling to Carlos. She remembers the intensity of that dark sideways stare.

'You could have left her, once you found out? Once you had realised?'

'Yes,' he answers flatly. 'I guess I could have, and no one would have blamed me. Except myself, perhaps.'

'So why didn't you?'

'She was in a state. Distraught. Irrational. I was worried for her, worried that she would do something stupid. And, besides, you had already left.'

'You could have come after me. You could have explained.'

He shakes his head, defeated.

'I wish I had done. So many times, I've wished that. But at the time, it seemed too hard. So much had been said between us. And I didn't know how I could explain to you. I didn't have the words.'

A silence passes between them, a silence that echoes, *If only...*

'And besides, I'm not sure it would have changed things. I'm not sure you would have forgiven me.'

'Probably not.'

*

The light in the room is changing. The dim grainy glow from the lamps is joined by a faint blur of light filtering through the curtains.

'I think about that time, a lot,' he says. 'Especially lately. Since I left Maria. I find myself thinking of that time in Spain before everything changed.'

They sit holding hands, his head is pressed against her shoulder now and she turns to look down at it. It is so close she can smell his hair, and if she leans forward just a little, she can touch her face to it. All the voices have deserted her now – her mother's voice, Alice, the bleating of her own conscience. All that is left now is the soft cadence of his voice floating around her in a gentle mass of words.

'God, when I think about how excited we were leaving Ireland, just the two of us. And we were just kids, although we thought we were so grown up. We thought we knew it all.'

He laughs, as if with fondness. 'I think now that that was the happiest time of my life – those months in Barcelona, with you. Before Carlos's death. Those hot, hot days. Those endless nights. I think that then I was truly in love with my life. And with you.'

She allows her head to drop against his, her ear and temple pressing against his crown.

'I don't think I'll ever know happiness like that again.' His voice aches with the weight of sadness.

'How can you be sure of that?'

'Because it was innocent. I was. We all were.'

She thinks of the four of them as they were then – all that hope, all that potential. All of it struck down, flung apart with one violent act, and the desperate and emotive acts in the days that followed. She is crying softly, tears trickling from the corners of her eyes, sloping over her cheeks, becoming rivulets, running down into his hair.

'When Carlos killed himself, he also murdered that innocence,' he says. 'And I cannot forgive him for that.'

*

Outside, there is noise in the corridor, the rattle of a trolley passing, chambermaids preparing to start cleaning the rooms. The light from the window is growing stronger, the lamps' glow weakening in the early-morning light.

'It wasn't what you think,' he says.

'What did I think?'

'That it was because I didn't love you. It was never that.'

'I know.'

'Because I did love you.'

'Yes.'

'I never stopped.'

'I know that too.'

HENRY

4

HE LEFT HER once before. The details of his leaving have become lost over time – the initial misdemeanour that caused it, who said what to whom, what words they flung at each other. He cannot even remember the source of the argument, that first grievance that set in motion a fiery chain of events tumbling forward on top of each other until he felt driven to leave the house, marching out with his head held high, as though wounded but too proud to display the injuries. What remains in his memory are the sounds and textures of that argument. Tonight, they seem tremulous and pure in their resonance, as though the event had taken place that morning, instead of several years ago, before the children. He can still feel the crunch of gravel beneath his petulant march to the car, seething rage bubbling up inside him. He can hear the sound and pitch of her voice before it was cut off by the slamming car door. He remembers the melodrama of her pleading, palms flattened against the driver's window, her round face ruddy and damp with tears. And the dismissive click as he locked the car door, before reversing back – his face a blank – away from her and her crumpling features.

He can recall the hour or two spent sitting behind the wheel, the car stationary, looking out to sea, the radio buzzing in the background, his anger slowly subsiding and reason seeping back through the corners of his consciousness. But he cannot, for the life of him, remember what it was that had driven him away. This bothers him. What stupid argument had escalated through heightened sensitivities and fragile tempers, culminating in her tears and his departure? What heedless remark or thoughtless gesture had driven him to such lengths, he wonders, had tested his commitment, threatened his marriage? And how did he return? Was there an apology, an admission of foolishness, of recklessness? And if so, by whom? These questions keep rising to the surface of his brain. He beats them down. It does not matter, he tells himself. It was a long time ago, before the children. And this is different. This is a different matter entirely.

The taxi moves slowly down the tree-lined street, carrying Elena away for the evening. He follows it with his eyes from the bedroom window. Halfway down the road, the light on the roof is extinguished. It rises over the humps in the road, accelerating between speed bumps, before finally reaching the turn and disappearing from view. Its departure leaves a stillness. The street is quiet. Leaves are changing colour, loosening on their branches, and the light is starting to fade. Children are indoors and cars are settled in driveways or parked on the kerb. He looks out at the neat row of ice-cream-coloured houses that line this street. Their restrained elegance, the stillness of the evening, the gathering clouds, all add to this feeling stirring inside him – this uneasy calm, lapping against the stone of panic wedged in his stomach. The taste of it rises to his dry mouth.

Elena is gone. And with her departure comes a relief, a sense of being able to breathe again. He exhales loudly, feels the air escaping his lungs, his diaphragm contracting, leaving him deflated. There is an attendant guilt, of course. Where would he be without the guilt, his constant companion? It settled in nicely after that pathetic exchange earlier in the day, when he told her that he couldn't go with her to the reunion. It was cowardly to tell her over the phone, he accepts that much. But the words of the earlier meeting were still ringing in his ears.

He could not tell her in person. Not after that. His face would have given him away. And so he called her with his invented deadline – a milestone that could not be missed, an important client, a key project. He would work from home, he told her, when the children were asleep. He felt her disappointment, sensed her anger in the silence that followed, only the gentle inflation of her breathing over the telephone indicating her presence. 'Fine,' she said in that high, tight voice that always accompanies her suppressed anger. There was tension in the exchange that followed – a logistical arrangement relating to cancelling babysitters and bathing the children and fixing his own dinner. After they said their goodbyes, he waited with the phone to his ear, poised to hear the loud thwack of a receiver being slammed back into the cradle of the phone, a physical display of temper, but there was only the gentle click, chased by long, slow beeps.

He turned his mobile off after that, making himself uncontactable for the afternoon. There are several messages on his machine, just from the previous day alone, that he hasn't returned, though he is fully aware who they are from – the telephone company and the RAC pressing for payments, Eagle Star with questions surrounding the halted direct debit, his EBS Visa, MasterCard, credit controllers who he now knows on a first-name basis – all of them looking for money he doesn't have. And then there was the meeting with the bank – a tight-lipped, sharp-suited executive – her words still ring in his ears. 'You've missed three months, Mr Butler.' The sweat on his back, the tightness of his collar. 'This cannot be carried forward any longer. We are going to have to insist on immediate payment.' He sat there dumbly, nodding his head, while she regarded him with cold, knowing eyes. No doubt she had seen his type before. He would not be able to pay it back and she knew it.

Afterwards, he got into his car and drove north across town, out to Skerries, parking in the lot overlooking the harbour and strolling around to Stoops. Hunched over a pint, his suit jacket slung across the back of the barstool, he mulled over how he should tell Elena. How he should lay his cards on the table, come clean. He would have to tell her everything, it would be impossible to keep things hidden now. Lately he has tried dropping hints as to his predicament – enough to give her a clue without frightening her, providing her with a glimmering of truth. He has used phrases like 'slump in the industry' and 'downturn in the IT sector'. Enough to intimate that things aren't as freewheeling as she might think. So that, later, she could not argue that she didn't know, that she hadn't an inkling – but that is a cheat in itself. It doesn't come close to touching upon the extent of his losses. He sipped his pint and thought again of when he should tell her. What would be the right moment? As the image of that inevitable confrontation played out in his mind, he was nudged by a new urge. An urge to run. It itched at his brain, rubbing against his conscience threateningly. It was achingly tempting – the only way of escaping this whole mess – to bolt, to run, to disappear. He shook his head in an effort to dislodge it, trying to ignore the seductive whisper of the idea.

Entering the house that evening, he found Elena in the bathroom with their daughter, whose face was smeared with lipstick and a lurid green eyeshadow that was snaking up into her hairline. 'Daddy! Daddy! Daddy!' Emily shouted, her face brightening as she danced about, trying to escape the facecloth wielded by her mother. His heart shrank with shame at the treacherous thoughts of abandonment he had entertained.

Elena didn't speak as he stood there. She didn't even glance up at him in acknowledgement. Instead, she stayed where she was, leaning against the lip of the bath, gripping Emily's chin with one hand as the other worked the cloth over the small greased face. Concentration was etched into her forehead. He toyed with the idea of telling her that he'd spoken with his imaginary client again that afternoon, that the client had demanded some additional requirements and that this would mean another all-nighter, thus evoking a glance of sympathy. But as he watched her angrily wiping away the make-up, he decided against it. Instead he asked, 'Where's Ben?' and she answered, not looking up at him, 'In his playpen.'

He didn't want a scene. He was too afraid of what might escape from him if he lost his temper, what admission he might make, and the fright it would give her, the reeling shock of it. Elena's irritation was apparent in the thin line of lipstick cut through her soft face, it lurked behind her eyes in hard, dark glances. Luckily, she has a habit of avoiding confrontation, shrinking from arguments. She favours a quieter, stubborn approach. She wins arguments with her silence. And this evening, as she prepared herself, brushing her sleek dark hair with quick, savage movements, he felt the ripples of her anger. She was firing short, sharp instructions at him and the children while sorting through the contents of her handbag and he had felt like he could touch the tension between them, run his fingers over the layer of discomfort that exists whenever he is alone with her. He cannot remember when this tension developed between them – what had been the precursor to it? But, lately, he has noticed that they are reluctant to talk to each other, and he worries that, despite the children and the house, they have little in common.

She kissed him goodbye – a custom that they have not yet given up on – and then she was gone. Watching the taxi disappearing from view, he rests his forehead against the cold glass. Small splutters of rain appear. Across the road, lights are beginning to come on in the tall sash windows; curtains are being drawn as the evening closes in. He turns around and surveys the shadowy room, their bedroom, which has grown dark while he has been standing there.

Emily is watching him. Round, cautious eyes in a full-moon face, Elena's face, eyes that level with him across the room, momentarily solemn, before being masked with smiles.

'What do you think, Daddy?' she asks, and his eyes pass over the garish costume jewellery that adorns her small hands and neck.

'Fabulous,' he says, trying to lift his voice, trying to pitch it at a level that is carefree, even jovial. 'Very glamorous.'

'Really?'

'Absolutely.'

His voice is hollow, it aches under the strain. But she seems satisfied and turns to admire her reflection in the mirror, scrambling to the edge of the bed.

Somewhere down the hall, he can hear the sound of his son thrashing about in his room, his voice rising above the clatter he makes with his toys. The screeching tone tells of his irritation, his growing demands for attention. It bears down heavily on Henry's mind.

He needs to think, he needs space for his thoughts to be laid out and picked over, a last-ditch effort at sorting out the wreckage of his financial affairs. But his thoughts are muddied by the rising panic and the increasingly vocal demands of his children. He tries to quell it, seeking to focus on tasks in hand – the children, their routine. Time is pressing against him.

'Right,' he says, clapping his hands together sharply and startling Emily, her body jumping inadvertently.

'Bath time,' he says sternly, before exiting the room to collect his irate son, Emily following behind.

The babysitter arrives shortly after the children are put in the bath. He forgot to ring and cancel. Henry opens the front door to a tall, gangly girl, her hair plastered to her head, standing shivering in the porch. Behind her, the rain comes down in sheets. As he explains to her that she isn't needed, that he's sorry for not calling to let her know, her face darkens, a straight line forming between her eyebrows. 'That's my evening wasted,' she tells him, deaf to his apology. Two other people asked her to sit for them, she informs him, and she had to turn them down. He suspects that this is a lie, but wearily takes out his wallet anyway, offering two crisp, clean bills. She fairly snatches them from his hand and crushes them ungraciously into her jeans pocket. Henry watches her turn back into the rain, her head bent into the wind. 'Bitch,' he says after her, under his breath. Half an hour late and she has the gall to hector him.

Upstairs, his children are splashing about. He can hear the noise of their bath-time war games – the dive-bombing ducks, the killer plastic fish, the teacup missiles and submarine bottles. He goes to the kitchen and fixes himself a drink, before passing through the hall and up the stairs again to the children. He perches on the toilet seat and sips his brandy, watching their small neat bodies, slick with water and soap, hair plastered to their scalps – so clean and new! – they look like small mammals, baby seals.

'Daddy, look at this,' Emily instructs him, and empties a bottle of bath water over Ben's head.

Henry watches as his little son gets up quickly, the shock of the sudden downpour stirring him to his feet. He stands in front of Emily, breathing deeply, his flesh dimpling under rivulets of water, and lets out a great bellow of laughter.

'Now me!' she cries. 'Now me!'

And she is duly showered from the plastic bottle, squealing with delight.

He watches them play, letting the sounds fall over him. His chest is tightening and beads of sweat are forming on his back. His children are energetic at play. Their physicality is raw and naked as they splash about. Emily's mouth is open with delight, lips drawn back to reveal the gap in her teeth and the frills of new teeth peeping out through gums. Ben's skin seems so white next to hers; he has inherited his father's pale genes – fine blond hair that appears mustard when wet, watery blue eyes and pale, pale skin. His colouring is ethereal next to Emily's rich shades of chocolate-brown hair and eyes, her skin like milky coffee. Yet there is something sturdy and strong in Ben's make-up – a tight weave of muscle and fat and bone.

He does not want to hurt his children. He is filled with dread at the thought of something happening that will damage or scar them. And yet, he is conscious that he has already injured them with his financial ruin. The meeting today has bought him some time – until next Wednesday. But already he knows that it is pointless. Within days he will lose not only the business but the house too. His mind races on to consider what will happen after that. They will have to find somewhere new to live, maybe even approach his parents, or Elena's, for assistance. A glimpse of the imminent shame he must suffer comes to him, and he closes his eyes to it. In the lidded darkness, escape whispers to him, tempting him, instructing him that he can walk away, turn his back on all of this, disappear.

Suddenly he feels as if he might vomit. He presses his mouth into the back of his hand and holds his breath. The feeling passes. It is chased by a twinge of panic – a sudden plunging down into the pit of his stomach. He is exhausted. He looks at the bathroom mat and contemplates curling up on it. But that would alarm the children. He aches to lie down, yearns for his bed. But he cannot leave the children on their own.

'A baby can drown in two inches of water,' his mother once warned him, her voice laden with gravitas, thick with doom. 'Just two inches,' she repeated, eyes bulging so he could see the blood vessels shooting into the milky sclera.

It frightened him, though. The image of his baby breathing water, the tiny lungs plumping out like balloons, the face changing to purple, then blue, the silent, unpronounceable panic gripping its small, bloating body. These images shook him, tortured him. Along with fears of falls, chipped teeth, broken bones and traffic accidents – cars, trucks, motorbikes. He was filled with dread at the thought of abduction, of shadowy figures lurking in playgrounds or supermarkets, waiting to pounce. He could not countenance what would happen then, he could not bring himself to imagine it. There were enough images to frighten him, a whole chamber of horrors wallowing in his consciousness.

He had not been prepared for it. He had envisioned the love, but not the fear. He feels the weight of it. It is always there – clinging to him, like wet clothes dragging at his limbs.

'It's only natural,' his friend Shane Smith told him. 'And it won't go away. Not ever.'

Shane is his squash partner – a corporate banker with speedy movements that defy his short, bulky frame. Often, after a match, they sit in the bar overlooking the courts and have a beer, discussing work, families, the stock market, whatever topic occurs to them. Henry enjoys these chats. He feels the casual warmth between them. Shane is easy to talk to, a man with clear ideas; there is something about his profession of thought that seems to provide clarity to Henry. Shane and his wife Kim have one child, Alex. Henry has seen photos of Alex, he has seen the small narrow face, the dark squinty eyes and expressionless mouth. He has also seen the bruises Alex has given Shane. Great vivid haemorrhages beneath the surface of pallid skin. Alex has behavioural problems. He doesn't speak, at least not coherently, only a complex series of grunts and whines, primitive expressions that only Shane and Kim can comprehend. At six years old, he has begun displaying violent characteristics.

'He's frustrated at being unable to express himself,' Shane once explained. 'He's locked inside a body that won't work the way he wants it to. It becomes unbearable for him and that's when he lashes out.'

Henry cannot imagine the strength it must take to rear this child. To pour out love and discipline and affection, and receive only pain and punishment and physical abuse in return? How is it possible? How can anyone love such a child?

'Because he's their son,' Elena said plainly when he spoke of it to her. 'You'd be exactly the same if he were yours,' she shrugged, before turning her attention back to whatever it was she had been engaged in at the time.

But Henry is not so sure that would be true. He does not share his wife's implacable black-and-white view of the world. He is haunted by vacuous grey areas – shaded and stalked by unnameable terrors. It horrifies him, the thought of deformity or incapacity in his children. He is not sure he has the strength or depth to love like that. It was different with his own babies, they were both so perfect and, still, he felt that he did not fall in love with them instantly as Elena did. It took him a little longer.

He fishes the children out of the bath, wrinkled fingers and toes and all. They take turns at being rubbed down with towels, jumping about from one foot to the other as he manoeuvres them into their pyjamas. He is not as adept at doing this as Elena. Their bodies seem so pliable when she swiftly wraps them in their nightclothes, whereas Henry feels confronted by a mass of angles – all elbows and knees – difficult joints and flailing limbs.

Eventually, they are sitting in front of the fire in the sitting room, eating yoghurts and watching TV as their hair dries from the warmth of the flames. Henry is in the kitchen, fixing his dinner. There is lasagna in the freezer and pizza too, but he doesn't have the patience to wait for them to heat. Peering into the fridge, he sees cold meats from the delicatessen, slices of Swiss cheese punctuated with holes and a salad in a blue and white bowl. But he doesn't have the energy to make a sandwich. Instead, he takes out the cold apple pie from the top shelf – a third of it already eaten away – and, finding a fork, he sits down at the table and begins to eat. He picks at the food – the nausea is still there. He is aware of his continuous lack of appetite lately. Elena commented on it earlier in the week, making reference to his weight loss, the tiredness in his face. There was concern in her voice, tenderness even, and the sudden kindness of her remarks moved him.

He does not understand it himself exactly, this creeping wariness in his relationship with his wife. He cannot remember where it sprang from. He is even less sure about the date it began. When did he start rehearsing conversations with her in his mind, having his answers worked out in advance? He is conscious of the nervy silences that have sprung up between them, invading their home. He still loves her, but the weight of his secrets and the fear that she will find him out are threatening to widen the gap between them into a chasm that cannot be bridged.

Looking at the kitchen around him, he sees marks of Elena everywhere. In the bright sunny shade of yellow that bounces off the walls. The solid chunkiness of the oversized mugs hanging from the mug tree. The bravery of the orchid that has managed to survive despite its fragility, this small piece of exotica flowering shyly in the corner of a suburban kitchen. There is order to the clutter gathered here. Elena has never liked throwing things out.

In the same way, she gathers people to herself. She is more open than he is, more enthusiastic. People are drawn to her, whereas Henry often feels awkward in the company of people he does not know so well. When they first moved into this house, he grew aware of the friendship that was struck up between his wife and their next-door neighbour, Ian. They seemed to spend hours dawdling over mugs of coffee, or chatting distractedly over the garden fence. 'He's gay!' Elena laughed when he mentioned it to her in a thin voice. But what bothered him more was the ease with which she could develop an affinity with another person. He felt a shade of envy and a degree of disquiet.

Elena is robust – strong minded and self-assured. There is something magnetic about this quiet strength that draws people to her – that drew him to her. She makes people feel safe. It seems to pervade her whole being – it is in the determined set of her mouth, in her stout command of the children, in the ordered way she controls her life and those friends and relatives that people it. Lately, he has felt like holding on to her, leeching some of her strength, her unshakeable resolve. Particularly when he wakes in the middle of the night, his pillow soaked with sweat, the same question ratcheting up in his head – where is his family going to live if he loses the house?

It is after nine when the children finally sleep. Emily struggled to stay awake, fighting the tiredness, bullish and determined. Henry fears that she senses something. She has become watchful of him lately, careful with him in a way that makes him uneasy. But eventually, her spirit caves and sleep takes her, leaving the house mercifully silent.

He passes downstairs and fixes a fresh drink in the kitchen. He is beginning to feel light headed, although his feet are leaden, sticking to the carpet. As he moves through the house like a shadow, his eyes travel silently over the rooms, taking in the things that have been gathered in this space. He views the cool elegance of the cast-iron fireplace in the sitting room, the solid usefulness of the fire irons. He absorbs the modern paraphernalia and gadgets in cool chrome and zinc and graphite. He stares at the ceiling, the creamy-whiteness of the room, the inviting plumpness of the sofa cushions. And something washes over him – a wave of nostalgia – like a sudden thirst.

'We can't afford it,' she said to him, her hands stuffed in the pockets of that old duffel coat she used to wear, the tufts of a multi-coloured scarf peeping out at her throat, her big brown eyes fixed longingly on the mid-terrace Victorian house with its shy charm and crumbling paintwork.

'There's no way we can ever afford it,' she said, the ache of regret in her voice. 'We just can't. It's ridiculous.' But she wanted it badly, and he wanted it for her. And the humiliation of going to his father, cap in hand, asking for the money – that pride-swallowing feat – was worth it, just for her reaction alone. He remembers the violence of her embrace – relief, hope, joy, passion packed tightly into her neat little body – thrust upon him, enveloping him, rolling over him in waves of happiness.

The house has been patiently restored, thick layers of paint scraped off the mouldings and banisters, the heavy, wide floorboards revealed from under sticky carpets, then stripped and varnished and returned to their former glory. He can recall the thick layers of dust, great clouds of it suspended in the air for weeks, months even, tripping down through shafts of light from the open windows, dancing dust-motes. It coated everything, the sparsely assembled bits of furniture, all cloaked in this pervading white veil, giving the whole place an eerie, ghostly feel. And in the midst of it all was Elena, a bright plume amongst the dust, in coloured shorts and T-shirt, her hair swept back in a red bandanna, on her hands and knees, sanding the wood earnestly, patiently. Miss Havisham, he used to call her when she emerged covered in dust, feeling the tightening about his heart at the beaming smile that greeted her nickname.

They made mistakes, of course, especially at the start. Young and experimental, they flirted with bright colours, sometimes lurid, creating a veritable patchwork of mismatched colours. There was the cobalt-blue wall in the kitchen – dreary and depressing. And the sunny yellow in the bathroom – dizzyingly bright at six am. It was hard work, exhausting despite their enthusiasm. He remembers Elena's work on their bedroom, painting it soft peach, her steadfast effort to create a restful environment, and how his thoughtless remark that it looked like a hospital room reduced her to tears.

They laughed about it later. Teething pains, they called it.

Henry knows he will almost certainly lose this house. He closes his eyes and passes a hand down over his features, wiping the guilt and grief away. His heart is sore, swallowed up by the scalding bitterness of his reality. He allows himself to think he is particularly plagued by bad luck. But deep down, his recklessness laps at his conscience. *I did this*, he reminds himself, feeling the stone in the pit of his stomach. *This is my doing.*

It is ten fifteen p.m. by the kitchen clock. Henry stands by the fridge, examining the noticeboard papered with receipts, flyers, take-away menus, lists in Elena's neat square handwriting. There, amongst the clutter, is the invitation, pinned to the centre between Emily's school report and a dental appointment card. It has occupied that space for weeks, but tonight it seems to be taunting him. He peers closely at it and considers the present gathering. He thinks of Elena, the stillness of her head, the quick flickering movement of her eyes as she moves among them. What excuse is she making for him, he wonders? That he is working late? That the babysitter let them down? A shiver of regret passes through him. He recalls the disappointment in her voice, the sudden anger, her half-hearted attempt to persuade him, his weary, steadfast refusal. A guilty performance – from both of them.

He thinks of her, in her green dress, its light layers brushing softly down to her knees. He imagines the tender slopes of her shoulders, the soft line of her collarbone, the pulse at her throat. He has always loved her skin, its smoothness, the way it catches the light, the rich olive colour. So different from his Irish skin with its pallor and tendency to blemish and burn. Hers is strong, resilient.

He pictures her at this reunion, her cautious smile, that faraway look taking over her features as she listens bravely to yet another boring anecdote or tedious picking over current affairs – the oil crisis, the weakness of the euro, the risé in crime. It makes him weary even thinking about it. All those nodding heads and careful suits and brittle hairdos. And Elena. Her calm demeanour, her whispery beauty. And him. Will he be there?

A vision clouds Henry's gaze, of a young man he once saw in a photograph. Tall, skinny, all elbows and knees. Greenish eyes, high cheekbones and a mop of unruly sandy hair falling over his face. Rakish. That was the word. He found the photograph once when looking for a motor tax renewal form, or something equally mundane. He was not spying, not sneaking through her things behind her back. And yet when he came across that picture, stuffed away in a notebook amid a sheaf of outdated documents, he instantly felt guilty, even though it was she who had been underhand and secretive, squirreling this fading photo away.

He remembers holding it up to the light and briefly assessing the form captured in it. There was a shiftiness in those eyes and a knowing smile – insolent and cocky – that slanted the mouth, closed over teeth. A thought darkened his mind – he should destroy it, send it on its way back into the past where it belonged. But something held him back. Loyalty, perhaps. And so he slid it back between the yellowed pages of the notebook. It could be there still. He doesn't care to know.

Leaning against the kitchen table, he drains his glass and feels a sudden flash of anger passing through him. Anger towards her and the cold manner in which she has guarded that side of her past, sending warning signals whenever he – her own husband – has tried to get close. She has set boundaries that he cannot cross, wrapping herself up in this unnameable, unmentionable grief whenever he touches upon it. It irks him, the way she holds herself aloof from him, as if he is not worthy of access to the secrets of her heart, the bitterness of her past. As if he would not understand, as if he could not know what pain felt like. It was a peculiar sort of arrogance, he thought, so at odds with her generous nature.

And she is generous. Generous and forgiving. But he knows she will not be able to forgive him for what he has done, he is certain of it. And he cannot bring himself to tell her. I should leave, he thinks. She would be better off without me. But even as he thinks this, he recognises the cowardice of this excuse, the flimsiness of his reasoning.

He catches sight of his reflection in the small mirror next to the fridge. He takes a moment to assess the face staring back at him, how it seems to have hollowed out as if the cheeks have sunk with the release of breath. Eyes that are flat and staring, his mouth slightly open, disappointment circling his face, distilling sharply to despair. A grey, pallid colour, like smoke, like paper. At this moment, he wants simply to cry.

Emotion has been building inside him all day, and now as the dam is about to burst in a sudden outpour of emotion, he hears the doorbell ringing. It sends him hurrying from the kitchen, out into the hall. Blinking back the tears, he pauses to compose himself, running his hands quickly through his hair, before moving to answer the door.

5

A LARGE FRAME fills the doorway, damp and glistening in the half light. His head is bent as if he is too tall to stand up straight under the porch, his hunched shoulders bunched into a dark anorak, made darker by the steady beat of rain sloshing around the shallow step. He leans in towards the door and the shine from the porch light is partially blocked by his head, so that the light seems to be emanating from him, like radiation.

'Miserable night,' he intones grimly, pushing gently past his son, who steps back wordlessly, allowing him into the warm house.

Straightening up, he shrugs his broad shoulders out of the wet anorak, swinging the jacket onto the banister, sending a dusting of raindrops flying – they splutter into beads on the wooden floor below. Henry is still holding the door handle between fingers and thumb; he can feel his father glancing briefly back at him, his eyes passing along Henry's narrow frame – small hooded eyes that gleam in the light.

'Well, don't go letting all the heat out,' Dan says quickly before turning into the sitting room, ducking as he passes under the doorframe.

Henry closes the front door slowly, mechanically. His blood feels hot – molten – as it pushes its way forcefully through his veins, heart catapulting in his ribcage. The tempestuous internal workings of his body are masked by a calm exterior – a still composure, cool and well practised, his features arranged into a dull, flat picture of complacency as he follows his father into the sitting room.

'Desperate night,' his father is saying, running a hand through iron-grey hair, the neat bristles damp and spiky from the rain – a military haircut.

Dan stands in the middle of the hearthrug, his arms fixed awkwardly by his sides, unsure of what to do with his hands. He looks about him, eyes blinking rapidly, a hand slipping into his trouser pocket while the other tugs at the long lobe of his ear. Henry feels the familiar irritation creeping into his voice as he urges his father to take a seat. It bothers him, this persistent habit of standing about awkwardly, this false formality, as if his father is making a conscious effort not to relax, which is probably the case. Best not let his guard down. They are both guilty of it.

'Drink?'

'Eh, well…' Dan scratches the underside of his jaw. 'What's that you're having yourself?'

'Brandy.'

He inhales noisily, peering into Henry's almost empty glass.

'Just a soft drink for me. Orange squash or something.'

In the kitchen, Henry shuffles through the collection of fruit juices and fizzy drinks before finding the orange.

'Orange squash,' he mutters to himself as he fills the glass. 'For Christ's sake.'

Who uses an expression like that nowadays? Only his father and mother, who still speak of tins of Coke and packages of crisps, clinging to their antiquated vocabulary like it was something to be proud of.

Henry is conscious of the fact that he is more than a little pissed. The light in the kitchen swims around him, he has to focus several times before locating the glasses. His eyelids have a tendency to droop when he is drunk, giving him a somewhat imbecilic look. His face feels flushed and he opens the button at his collar. He is grateful for the chance to be momentarily alone in the kitchen so that he can splash cold water over his face, rub his eyes vigorously and attempt to bring under control the question that has been racing through his brain: what on earth is his father doing here after ten o'clock at night? Standing over the sink, turning off the tap and passing a tea towel over his face, he cannot find an answer. His head is too fraught with conflicting issues to adapt and make room for another one.

Returning to the sitting room, he finds his father sunk into the sofa, looking uncomfortable and adrift among the sponge and springs and creamy white canvas, his back propped up against two scatter cushions slotted firmly behind him.

'Thanks,' he wheezes, accepting the tumbler and cradling it in his hands. They are big hands, with thick pink fingers like fat sausages, black spindly hairs pushing through the flesh below the knuckles.

Clearing away a clutter of toys, Henry drops his weight into the armchair and leans back expansively, attempting to equal his father's physical presence. Dan has the advantage in terms of weight and height. Despite having shrunk over the past few years, he is still six feet tall, and the girth that has crept over his body, an accumulation of fat cells around a mass of tightly packed muscle, gives him the stature and presence of an ageing work-horse.

The silence that passes between them is uncomfortable, as most of their silences are. Dan clears his throat several times – a sudden hacking exclamation, as if trying to dislodge a stubborn clot of phlegm. Henry masks his revulsion. He is busy trying to appear sober, sitting up straight and concentrating on keeping his eyelids from drooping. His insides have stopped heaving but his brain remains hyperactive, whizzing through a myriad of possibilities, questions whining like sirens, clambering over one another in their efforts to be heard. But it is Dan who asks the first question. 'Elena in bed?' he says, as if just struck by her absence.

'No. No, she's out. At a class reunion,' he answers perfunctorily.

'Oh. School, is it?'

'University.'

Dan nods and sniffs disinterestedly, university being anathema to his conversation. 'Did you not go with her?'

There is a somewhat incredulous look on his face as he asks this. And it is true that Henry cannot imagine an occasion where his mother would venture out without his father.

'No. No, well, I was supposed to, but, em, the babysitter, unfortunately, the babysitter let us down. At the last minute. Otherwise, I'd have gone. I wanted to go, but, as I say, the babysitter...' He is rambling.

His father regards him with solemn eyes and gives the briefest of nods.

'Miserable night for it,' he repeats, and Henry notices again the quiet nervousness in his demeanour. His father seems preoccupied, a tension in the leathery skin of his face, hard, thin concentration lines cutting deep between bushy black eyebrows like caterpillars teetering on a wide expanse of brow.

Dan Butler is not a social caller. Henry can count on one hand the number of unannounced visits his father has paid him in eight years. On any other night, Henry would be quietly bemused by his unexpected and taciturn presence at this late hour. But Henry is not himself, and feels a tickling of fear at the back of his neck. Paranoia nips at his gut, acid spluttering in his bowels. Why is his father here? What does he know? His body is clenching – an involuntary reflex – and he strains to stretch out his legs, a concerted effort to cheat his own body language.

'Kids are in bed, I suppose?'

'Well, it is after ten,' Henry answers tightly, feeling suddenly defensive. To make amends for the shortness of his remark, he adds, 'How's Mum?'

'She's the same as ever. You should ring her.'

Henry feels the twist of this remark and smarts at the implication. He feels raw tonight, overly sensitive. The brash, accusatory tones of his father are not what he needs. He's not sure he can take a lecture about neglecting his family.

'Yes, well…' He trails off, thinking of his mother, the gentle fuzz of hair crowning a permanently flushed face, eyes alert for trouble and an inability to sit still and relax. Although she is not here with them, Henry feels her presence in the careful hemstitching of his father's well-pressed trousers, the bright, clean shirt under the v-neck sweater. There is an ironed and starched hankie in pristine white lurking in one of the pockets, he is sure of it. *Just in case…* his mother's voice echoes in his head. *You never know…*

She is sitting at home now in the big front room, surrounded by her crocheted cushions and china dogs, the television flashing images of fear at her – *Crimeline* or some documentary on Channel Four about drug dealers or kiddie-rapists, real-life accounts of violence to nourish her belief that the world is a dangerous place. She videotapes *Crimeline* and scours it for faces she recognises. On any other night, his father would sit with her, slumped into his green velvet chair, the pile worn at the seat and armrests, barking comments into the space between him and the TV, his mother's nervous contribution – 'Oh

Lord… God help us… What makes them do those things? I just don't know' – filling the gaps.

He closes his eyes to it, immersed in a sudden exhaustion.

'You all right?' Dan regards him with a quizzical eye.

'Yes. I'm fine. A little tired, that's all.'

'Tired?'

'Yes. It's nothing.'

'But you're just back from holidays. You shouldn't be tired.'

'Work's been mental since I got back…'

'Oh, work, is it? I see.'

They drift into silence, the old familiar bugbear already introduced to their conversation. Henry is not sure he has the strength for it tonight.

'Good, was it?'

'What?'

'The holiday.'

'The holiday? Yes, it was fine. Great, I mean.'

And it was great, in some ways. A week in the hills of Andalucia. A rented apartment, a swimming pool, the sun. A temporary reprieve from the concerns regarding his financial affairs. He knew that he was only compounding the problem – buying a holiday with money he didn't have – another bill to add to his spiralling debts. But he forced this to the back of his mind. Concentrating on the children and Elena, he chose to ignore the mounting problems he had left in Ireland. Instead, he threw himself into it with gusto, teaching Emily to dive for coins in the swimming pool, dragging Ben through the water bobbing in his plastic ring. He allowed himself to enjoy the cold beers shared with his wife in the heat of the afternoon sun. And in the evenings, he felt the balmy air rising up from the hot dusty earth as they walked the road to the village, flanked on both sides by groves of lemon trees, stopping at restaurants and bars to peer at menus. Walking back after dark, Ben asleep in the stroller, Emily's body limp in his arms, her head lolling against his shoulder, he would listen to the crickets, his eyes straining through the pitch black, the scent of jasmine filling his senses.

'Of course, this isn't the real Spain,' Elena said on the second or third day.

'Why do you say that?' he asked.

'Well, it's a holiday resort, isn't it? Specially designed. The apartments, the pool, everything.'

'Yes, but it's still in Spain. I mean, there are the hills and the countryside…'

'Then where are all the Spaniards?' she interrupted him. 'The only ones we meet are those serving in the restaurants, and even they speak English. Everybody else is either English or Irish or Dutch.'

She had a point, of course. But when she persisted with this point throughout the holiday, it began to irk him. At the back of each observation was the implication of her knowledge and experience of the 'real' Spain. Henry found there was something boastful about it. And when she began referencing her points to 'the time we were in Barcelona' he thought he would explode. This 'we' did not include Henry. Rather, it referred to *him*, the man without a name, even in his absence invading their holiday, flung at Henry as proof of the existence of a real, authentic Spain lying somewhere outside the resort.

'It would want to be, considering,' Dan says shrewdly, interrupting his thoughts.

'What's that?'

'The holiday. It would want to be good after forking out all that for it.'

Dan Butler is not a well-travelled man. A trip to Lourdes, another to Rome with Henry's mother, Alice, and the occasional jaunt to Cheltenham over the years were as far as he'd ever gone. Religion and horses were the only foreign enticements for him.

'It was worth the money,' Henry counters defensively. 'Elena and the kids had a ball.'

'Good. Things must be going well if you can afford to bring four of you to the continent.'

There is a question in there somewhere, an imperceptible shift in tone. Henry is wary of it. He knows his father – his mild-mannered way of evoking explanations and then pouncing on the information given. He will not be drawn in, not tonight.

Henry remembers their summer holidays as a child. He recalls the rooms above his Aunt Noreen's shop in Waterville, County Kerry, the crash of waves over the pebbled beach. Afternoon tea in the black and white Grand Hotel, the walls lined with framed photos of an old Charlie Chaplin on a visit there, unrecognisable with a shock of white hair and minus his moustache. He remembers sitting in the back of the silver Nissan Bluebird as it roamed the hills and narrow roads of that Kerry peninsula. He loved the balmy exoticism of Valentia Island and that warm breeze from the Gulf Stream wrapping the island in a hazy heat. And the gardens of the great house, alive with species of plants with unpronounceable names, a jungle off the southwest coast of Ireland. In the evenings there would be chips from the Wimpy Bar, served in plastic cartons with little coloured forks, the tang of vinegar on his tongue.

At some stage, his father stopped going. The business couldn't spare him. From then on, it was just Henry and his mum. They would get the train down together and Aunt Noreen would meet them at the station in Killarney and drive them back to the house in her shuddering 2CV. But after a while, the shrill nervy laugh of his mother would grate against the top of Henry's head. Her babbling talk would build to a torrent in the absence of any other stern voice to stem the flow. In his early teens, Henry stopped going altogether.

The wind rushes against the window. Glass rattles in the frame. Henry glances at the clock. It is after eleven. His glass is empty; he shuffles it between his fists, suppressing the longing to refill it, but dreading the effect wearing off. His father's orange squash remains almost untouched. He cannot fix himself another drink and draw attention to the speed at which he is drinking. Already his mind is clouded and feverish. He feels a pressure building in his brain, a need for release, for escape. Suddenly he craves to be anywhere but here – away from this house, the burden of his sleeping children, his creeping doubts about his wife and the stubborn, taciturn presence of his father.

'How's business these days?' Henry croaks, relieved at getting the question out, overcoming the frantic cravings in his mind.

His father's voice fills the room, its sweeping mundanity seeping out to the edges. Henry isn't listening. He doesn't want to know. He is already aware of what kind of a businessman his father is. The kind who is reluctant to plunge his money into things he cannot see or touch. Dan Butler likes to be able to place his hands on his investments. He is suspicious of banks and scours each statement for possible errors, alert for hidden charges and suspect debits. A stranger to the stock market, he is distrustful of PIPs and PEPs and anything with a fluctuating return. 'If it can go up, then it can go down', he is fond of saying. And he would never, in a million years, have been persuaded to part with his money for an investment in a foreign country with the promise of a future up-and-coming area, a potential goldmine. His mind would have jarred on the word 'potential', arousing his suspicion instantly. Whereas Henry only heard 'goldmine'. Perhaps that is the difference between them.

It was Shane Smith who first told him about it – The Hua Hin Development, as it was known. The four of them sitting around the table in Henry and Elena's dining room, the women discussing some French film Kim had seen recently, while Shane extolled the virtues of investing in a developing Asian country that was about to 'take off'. His voice was animated, as were his gestures, outlining the potential return – 'The possibilities are endless,' he said. 'Think of a number and then treble it, quadruple it! I'm telling you Henry, you'll be retiring before you're fifty.' Henry felt himself being swept up in Shane's enthusiasm, feeling that familiar buzz in his brain as it whirred through to the imagined outcome. Gathering up the plates and joining Elena in the kitchen, he turned to her, his eyes lit up with possibility, and whispered his excitement to her. A lucky tip-off, getting in at the ground floor, an incredible opportunity. And, to his complete amazement, she burst out laughing. He stared at her for a few seconds, as she shook her head at the ridiculousness of the suggestion. 'Oh, Henry,' she said, her shoulders still shaking with mirth, 'you must be joking!' But he wasn't joking, he was deadly serious. He felt like someone had just thrown a bucket of cold water over him, dousing the flames of his excitement. 'It's all very well for Shane to plunge his money into some hare-brained scheme. He's got pots of it to waste. But us?' She giggled again. 'Come on!' She continued to shake her head as she prepared the desserts, unaware of the cold blank stare he was directing at her. He felt the put-down keenly. Her remarks diminished him. Ridiculed him. Turned him to stone.

She will be home in an hour or two – flushed with wine and nostalgia. Brimming with forgotten stories, tales of people he doesn't know spilling out, and he will have to smile politely and ask pertinent questions, act like he is interested, when all he will want to ask is, 'Was he there?' Or perhaps she won't say anything at all, remaining tight lipped, keeping that part of her life all locked up and veiled in secrecy.

If his father is still there when she gets back, Henry will have to feign interest and enthusiasm and Elena will be forced to produce details of the evening. But Henry is not convinced that his father will stay around that long. There is something about his awkward stance, his look of discomfort at being here, telling Henry that there is a reason behind this visit.

'Why are you here?' he asks softly.

'What's that you said?'

'I said, "Why are you here?"'

He is somewhat amazed at his own audacity. As is the old man.

'That's what I thought you said.'

Dan's lower lip falls forward, leaving a stupefied look momentarily on his face. He recovers himself quickly, the ire pumping up into his face through veins pulsing in his thick neck. 'Can't a father pay a visit to his son?' he barks. 'Must there be a reason?'

'Does that mean there isn't one? This is purely a social call, is it?'

'What if it is? That's not so surprising.'

'Actually, it is.'

Dan regards his son carefully, through narrowed eyes. 'Are you drunk?'

'What if I am? A man is entitled to get a little pissed in the comfort of his own home.'

He waits for the lecture on responsibility, waits to be reminded that his children are in his care. But it doesn't come. Dan is regarding him with a mixture of disgust and uncertainty, and Henry finds himself relaxing. Somehow his admission of drunkenness has calmed his nerves. His limbs feel warm and heavy, iron hands and fingers hanging over the armrests of his chair. His head feels waterlogged – swimming in brandy – a gloriously muggy velvet crown. Across the room his father is getting to his feet, his lumbering movements hampered by the soft-sinking couch.

'I can't talk to you when you're like this,' Dan mutters gruffly, a look of disgust washing over his hardened features.

'You can't talk to me anyway. Drunk or sober,' Henry shrugs from his armchair, made brave by the alcohol and suddenly sick of all the bullshit. 'So what difference does it make? Just say what it is you came here to say and then you can toddle off home.'

He smiles sweetly as he says this, sliding down and finding the groove in the chair. Aah! Total comfort. He is enjoying this – the tremulous chin and purple complexion of his father's face. Henry feels the power of his position, the warm, balmy sensation of simply not caring. I honestly couldn't care less any more... he thinks, knitting his fingers around the empty glass at rest on his stomach.

Dan is rooted to the spot, quietened by his own lumbering incredulity. He stares at his son with open eyes, dark-brown shadows circling the tea-stained corneas.

'What's got into you tonight?' he asks quietly, trying to control the menace in his voice, the anger rising at the smirk on Henry's face.

Henry shrugs, an exaggerated movement of his shoulders, palms raised and the smirk momentarily disappearing as his face picks up the shrug. But there is something behind his grin, something fragile that's about to break.

'Come on, son. Something's obviously eating you.'

Henry feels a sudden and unexpected surge of warmth towards the old man. Behind the hardened features and the weary disapproval lurks a glimmer of love, a genuine concern. His father has put the question to him, that invitation to speak that he has been waiting for – longing for – but expecting to hear from Elena. And now, from this most unlikely source, he sees a chink of hope, someone to tell, someone to listen. He leans forward, resting his head in his hands. Emotion is welling up inside him. Where to begin? How to word this confession? Tonight, more than anything else, he needs to reach out, to connect, to be understood.

'Well, get on with it, Henry. Spit it out,' his father urges.

And instantly, the moment passes. Pulling back, he feels a mild wave of belligerence pass over him. What does the old man want from him? That he break the habit of a lifetime and pour out the contents of his troubled heart, lay it bare and allow the old man to pick through it? He could throw himself at his father's mercy, confess through a torrent of tears to getting out of his depth, to mismanaging his finances, getting involved in deals where the stakes were higher than he could afford. Between sobs, he could pour out the whole tale of woe, the trail of deceit that has spiralled out of control, forged signatures, delayed payments, lying to his wife. And what then? Would Dan put a strong arm around his shoulders, squeezing tightly and say, *There now, don't worry yourself, we can get this sorted?* Is that what would happen?

Henry sits still, refusing to relinquish his firm occupancy of the chair. The thought of physical contact from his father makes him nauseous. And the prospect of breaking down in front of him – a snivelling, piteous wreck – while his father looks on scornfully, his voice clotting with disgust, is not appealing. Best to maintain the status quo between them.

'It's nothing,' he says tightly.

'Pull the other one.'

'No, really. It's fine.'

He pulls himself into a more upright position in the chair and crosses his legs casually. 'Sit down, Dad. Please. Come on.' The old man is standing in the middle of the room, clenching and unclenching his fists, prevaricating over whether to stay or go.

Henry's eyes fix on the old man's trousers – grey flannels, like a school uniform – well-starched and almost a size too small. There is something indecent about the tightness of them, the starchy fibre clinging to the buttocks and thighs – the unsightly bulge at the front, the straining of fabric and tight puckers and creases of cloth. Where does he buy these trousers, Henry wonders. How many pairs does he possess? Dan reluctantly sits back down and the trouser legs ride up, revealing grey and black diamond-patterned socks.

'So?'

'So.'

The discomfort between them settles under the monosyllables.

'Kids all right?'

'Yep. Fine.'

'Good. And Elena? She in good form?'

'Yeah. She's grand.'

Dan nods his head silently. He is working up to something. Henry can sense it.

'Work going OK?' he asks suddenly, looking away as he says it, avoiding eye contact, trying to dull the sharpness of the question.

'Yes,' Henry answers slowly, his suspicions aroused. 'Look, Dad, what is it?'

'No, I was just asking… just wondering. You know how you hear of people in your line of work, the high levels of burnout.'

'What?'

'And the way the industry looks at the minute, you hear of people looking for a change.'

'What people?'

'I don't know. People. I'm just saying,' he counters with a degree of irritation. 'You never thought about it yourself?'

'A change?'

'Yes, Henry. People do it all the time. They try out one career for a while and then, if they're not happy, they move to something else.'

Henry's eyes narrow. He can see where this is leading. The whiff of old arguments invades his nostrils, their pungent odour filling the room. So that's what this is all about. Butler & Son rearing its ugly head again. He leans forward, shaking his head emphatically.

'No,' he says sternly.

His father looks back blankly. 'What?'

'You know what. My God!' Henry snorts with amusement. 'I thought you'd given up on that notion long ago. I thought I'd made it perfectly clear.'

'Henry, listen…'

'No, Dad, you listen. There is no way I'm joining the business. It's out of the question.'

'But…'

'No, Dad,' he says again, firmer this time, his hand slicing the air with finality.

Something seems to drop about the old man's face, a weariness clouding his features. His physique seems to shrink as he hunches over his empty glass. He attempts to rouse himself, his voice going all roomy and reasonable.

'I know the idea hasn't appealed to you in the past, and I understand that you value your independence…'

'That hasn't changed.'

'Look, Henry, it's not what you think.'

'And what do I think?'

'That I would use you like some kind of skivvy, that you would have no real authority. That I would—'

'Bully me?' Henry's eyes flash dangerously.

'I wouldn't. It wouldn't be like that.'

'The way you've bullied me in the past?'

'Discipline, Henry. That's all it was. You may think it was harsh…'

'The way you bully Mum?'

'Now just you leave your mother out of this,' Dan warns, raising a fat finger threateningly, his elbow coming to rest on a grey-flannelled knee.

Henry smiles solicitously, adopting a more reasoned, quiet tone. But underneath, he feels the angry history between them, stirring and bubbling. This argument is familiar, but the effect it has on him doesn't change.

'I wondered when you'd bring this up again – this father-and-son-working-together dream that you harbour. I just didn't expect it would be this soon.'

He ignores the twitch in his father's face and ploughs ahead. 'Did you really think I'd agree? I mean – building supplies, for Christ's sake!'

'It's good honest work,' Dan counters defensively.

'I don't dispute that, but it's hardly me.'

'Not flash enough, I suppose. Not glamorous.'

'Not stimulating enough,' he corrects between clenched teeth.

'It's a good business,' Dan continues. 'I started that business thirty-five years ago with only a few scraps of old metal and a couple of mounds of bricks and an old van for an office.' He ignores Henry's rolling eyes at hearing these same old lines yet again.

'Here we go. Cry me a river…'

'I've put my back into that business and I am not prepared to just let it slip away.'

'Then sell it!'

'You're my son, Henry. I built that business up and kept it alive for you.'

'I don't want it. I never have.'

'Wait. Just listen…'

'I said I don't want it. Why aren't you listening to me?'

'Don't make a mistake, Henry. Swallow your pride.'

'That's rich coming from you.'

'Don't make a hasty decision that you'll regret later.'

'Oh, I won't regret it.'

'You don't know that.'

'Let's just say I'm prepared to take the risk.'

'Well, if you won't consider it for yourself, then consider it for Ben.'

'Don't you dare bring my kids into this.'

'Businesses pass from father to son...'

'God, you're so antiquated!'

'Or daughters, then – whatever. But you're the only child I have. It's only right that you take it on after me.'

'A dinosaur... do you know that? You're a bloody dinosaur.'

'You could take over the management, modernise it, bring it up to date...'

'Not interested.'

'Run it the way you want to; I wouldn't interfere. I wouldn't stand in your way.'

'Yeah, right!'

'Jesus Christ!' Dan bellows, his face a moving, twisting mass of contorted muscles, his eye twitching crazily, the blood throbbing under his skin. His temper, having been released, is now pulled back, leaving him deflated. His head sinks briefly onto his fleshy hand before he looks back at his son. There is something in his eyes – a hunger, a need. 'I didn't want to ask you,' he says, shaking his head. 'I'm tired of asking. I'm tired of trying to figure out what to do, what is the right thing to do. I wasn't going to come here tonight.'

He breathes deeply. His words seem to demand a lot from him. Henry feels the effort required to get them out.

'I know what you think about the business,' he continues, 'and about me. I wish things could be different between us, especially lately... But I hoped you'd be reasonable. That you'd at least consider it. Just this one last time. I wouldn't have asked if I hadn't...' He trails off, swallowing the words.

'What?'

'Never mind.'

'If you hadn't – what?' Henry sits up, suddenly anxious. The words spoken hang between them. Despite his discomfort and his blanket refusal, something about his father's behaviour sparks concern within him. There is something in his father's demeanour – a fleeting shadow of defeat – that he has not seen before. The tone of his voice, the weariness of it, alarms him.

'Nothing. Don't trouble yourself.'

'Seriously, Dad?'

'I'd better be getting on,' he wheezes, struggling to rise from the soft sofa. 'Or your mother will start phoning the hospitals again.'

Henry senses the deliberate attempt at diffusing the seriousness of their conversation. But something about the previous exchange has chilled him. Perhaps it is the events of the day, the pressure he has been under, that makes him feel unsettled, troubled by something.

In the hall, he finds his father shaking out his still-wet anorak. As he struggles into the jacket, his scalp revealed suddenly through his thinning hair lit by the shine of the hall light, Henry feels a sudden pang of love for this man.

'I'm sorry, you know,' he says awkwardly, wrestling with these foreign emotions, 'for saying no, for not accepting your proposal. I just don't think it would work out, that's all. I just don't think it would be right for me.'

Dan nods his head slowly before reaching out and patting his son's back with his large hand. 'That's all right, son,' he says softly. 'I won't ask again.'

And as he passes out into the night, something flickers across Henry's mind, a shadow of intuition clouding his thoughts.

'You're all right, aren't you, Dad?' he asks nervously. 'I mean, you're not sick or dying or anything?' He laughs as he says this, the notion of illness infiltrating his father's formidable body seeming ridiculous to him.

Dan looks back at him and gives him a smile, a weird grimacing upward twist of his mouth. His face is pale and full of shadows. Something passes between them, something unspoken.

'Goodnight, son,' Dan says quickly. He ducks out under the porch and hurries to his car parked on the other side of the street. He starts the engine and moves away without once turning back to see if his son is still standing there. And even if he had glanced over at the shadow in the doorway, the distance between them meant he couldn't have seen the look on his son's face, or recognised the creeping regret for what has passed between them, and all that remains unspoken.

6

IT IS AFTER six a.m. when he hears the gentle click of a door closing. A brief clatter of shoes dropping is chased by a hush and then the
careful sound of bare feet padding up the stairs. He lies with his back
turned to the door, but he feels the disturbance in the air as it is
pushed slowly open and then closes behind her. Shuffling sounds of
clothes being removed whisper from the corner. He feels the bed
move beneath him, a gentle depression rocking him back as she
climbs in next to him. He holds his body tightly, clinging to the far
corner of the mattress, feigning sleep. *Don't attempt to touch me*, it
says. *Don't even dare*. She doesn't. Whether she can sense his fury or
whether it is owing to her own tiredness, or guilt, she nestles into her
pillow, her back turned to his. He waits.

Light filters through the gap in the curtains. Birdsong is interrupted by the sound of a car starting a few doors down. Soon he can
hear the measured breathing of sleep rising from her. He feels a pang
of envy. How he craves sleep. It will not come to him now. His body
is knotted with tension that has no chance of unravelling while lying
next to her. Too many questions lie between them, poisoning his
chances of rest. Unspoken accusations and fevered demands for
explanations all sweep around him, along with the crushing need to
tell her, to reach out to her, to feel her forgiveness. But that is not
going to happen now. The thought that it would is a product of his
feverish mind. He realises that.

Wearily, he pushes back the duvet and climbs out of bed. His

71

tiredness is chronic, but the need to go is overwhelming. It has been building inside him for hours, steadily rising in pitch, until he feels it screaming inside his skull. Silently, not wanting to disturb her, not able for questions about what he is doing or where he is going, he picks his clothes up from the floor – yesterday's clothes – but he cannot risk the creaking hinges of the wardrobe door. He dresses quickly, slotting limbs into the worn and creased shirt and trousers, before finding his shoes and slipping out into the hallway. Silence fills the house, dust motes tripping through the beams from the skylight, as he creeps past the children's rooms and tiptoes downstairs. His wallet and keys are where he left them. Sweeping them up off the hall table, he fumbles with the locks, bringing the door back and closing it behind him as silently as he can. The air is cold – that bite of early-morning freshness embracing him, pulling him away from the sleeping house and all the trouble that lies within it.

He drives through quiet streets, drives aimlessly. The city is deserted at this early hour and it isn't long before he finds himself leaving the city limits, heading south onto the Wexford road. Buildings fall away from the road, replaced by a wall of hedges and trees flanking the fields and open spaces, the road still slick with rain. Sometime after leaving Dublin, he notices the clouds have moved, clearing away, leaving a cool mist hovering over the fields, hazy in the early-morning sun.

Light breathes through the mist as his head starts to clear. Road passes beneath him, miles and miles of it, his head barely lucid, his body numb. As the rainwater evaporates from the road, the sun licking it dry, details of his surroundings begin to penetrate his senses. Animals lie in lazy clusters in the fields. Cows in mottled, dirty shades of grey and red-brown, and sheep, their coats disfigured by gaudy stains in lurid blue and red. He lowers the window and the car is invaded by the smell of the country – clay-heavy and clotted with animal odours; he breathes it in, battling the staleness of his worn clothes and sleep-filled skin. Passing a lake, its water still and peaceful, he becomes aware of the quietness that surrounds him. The radio is switched off and the road is free of other traffic. Soon, it will burst into life, trucks thundering along to and from the boats at Rosslare. But at this early hour with the morning mist still rising, Henry feels swaddled in the soothing silence that envelops him.

In the end, it was after dawn when he went to bed. His prevaricating, the tug-of-war between his emotions, held him hostage at the kitchen table for several hours. He tried to remain calm, leaned on the methodical side of his brain. 'What are the facts?' he asked himself in a cold lofty voice that didn't sound like his own. And as he listed through the events and options, the calculating, practical voice gave way to a rising pitch of panic. The realisation of what he had done kept slapping him about the head. He had lost the house. Lost it. The admission of this brought no comfort, just a wave of nausea and a tightening in his chest, the blood draining away from his face.

And then his father. The weight of their conversation bore down on him, gripping his temples. That narrow interchange of information, that stilted, awkward request and a vague admission of some unspoken trouble – an illness – all wrapped up in a single night. It pressed upon Henry – the responsibility. Duty. Commitment. It rubbed up against his body, his muscles reflexively tensing to it. It swam around the kitchen, leaving its scent, marking its territory. It mingled with his other duties – those of a father and husband. He felt himself collapsing under the weight of them. It was too much. He couldn't carry it any longer. He could either tell her or else leave. Walk away. The coward's option.

As the night grew, he felt the urge to tell her rising up inside him. He needed to share this with someone, his dirty little secret. He craved redemption, a return to how things used to be – wiping the slate clean. Thoughts came to him of the early days, when they had first met – that easy time punctuated with laughter, joy, embracing the untold possibilities. He fixed himself a cup of coffee, wanting to be sober when she came in. It was important that he explained it clearly, lucidly, with no ambiguities. He twisted the mug in his hands, rehearsing what he might say, how he could open this discussion without alarming her. *Elena, there's something I have to tell you… I've done something, Elena, something I can't keep from you any longer…*

His coffee grew cold and through the black windowpane came grains of light, turning the sky from black to purple to a grey-blue dimness. And as the night died, giving way to the dawn, something stirred in him. Something cold and haunting. His wife had been gone all night. All the doubts and fears he had about her past came creeping back, taking advantage of his weakened state. His tired mind was swamped with thoughts of secret trysts, infidelities. As the kitchen clock measured the passing time, these thoughts incubated inside him, his jealousy taking root, making him cold.

It seems like he has been driving for hours by the time the car swings off the road, tyres crunching over gravel, as he pulls in next to a coffee shop. It sits alone by the side of the road, a long, flat building with neon signs and a thick coating of dust on its walls and windows. An old Pepsi-Cola sign swings from rusty hinges. There is a truck outside and a couple of cars, and Henry finds that it is more than half full when he enters.

He finds a table next to the window and slides along the banquette, feeling the slipperiness of the seat beneath him. The table is coated in linoleum, part of which has peeled away from the metallic rim, revealing chipboard underneath. Henry suppresses the compulsion to slide his finger underneath the linoleum and edge it further away from the chipboard. He folds his hands on the table in front of him, knitting his fingers together, and leans forward, staring at the condiments amassed in front of him. There is a grubbiness about the place that he has noticed. The dust coating the outer walls has transcended to a grimy sheen covering the interior. There are congealed tears of gloop travelling down the necks of the ketchup and mustard bottles in front of him. A history of old spillages marks the table and he feels a stickiness beneath the soles of his shoes. Hygiene is not a priority here, and he tries to draw his mind away from contemplating the cleanliness of the kitchen.

He casts his eyes around at the other diners. For the most part, the café is populated with hairy overweight men who eat voraciously while scanning newspapers, faces hungry for food and information. Working men, refuelling for the day. At a table opposite sits an old couple, side by side. The woman is talking animatedly, making bright sideways remarks in between swift, birdlike mouthfuls. The man's movements are slow and patient. Henry thinks of his mother and father and looks away.

A waitress appears at his side and he gives his order. He feels suddenly famished and remembers that, apart from the apple pie, he has not eaten since lunchtime yesterday. He makes additions to his order – an extra portion of brown bread, two eggs instead of one and extra bacon too. The waitress writes studiously in her notepad.

He looks out the window and waits. The day is brightening, a hazy blue sky appearing through the grey. There is an ache in his body – it travels the length of his legs, which he stretches out beneath the table. The muscles in his back, shoulders and neck are knitted into lozenges of pain. He shifts in his seat, allowing the lozenges to move, willing them to relax and unravel. He has not slept and his eyes feel scratchy behind puffy lids. His hunger is keeping him awake.

The waitress returns with his tea – a stained metallic pot whose lid does not fit properly. He pours the steaming brown liquid into the cup and adds milk and sugar. He raises it to his lips and tastes the metallic taint in it. As he returns the cup to its saucer, feeling the warmth surge down into his stomach, he is violently interrupted by the sudden ringing in his breast pocket. His heart is thumping in his rib cage as he fumbles for the mobile phone, staring at the green letters spelling 'home' on the bleating screen. He is trembling all over, his body spangled with nerves. Conscious of the sideways glances from other diners, he presses the phone into his thigh, muffling the electronic jingle, willing it to end. Which it does. He returns the quietened phone to the table and tries to recover his composure.

He looks at the envelope icon flashing on the screen. A message. She is awake, then. A flash of anger passes over him. Where was she all night? And who was she with? The image from that photograph floats over his brain – those angular features settling on him, the eyes filled with daring, with carelessness – and with it comes a rush of self-pity. He is the victim here. The suffering husband. He winces at all the subtle reminders throughout their marriage of another. One he can't compete with. No. That's not right. Not throughout their marriage, not at the start. But lately he has noticed them. They have crept in while he wasn't looking.

A memory comes to him from a night some years ago, before Ben was born. An old schoolfriend of Elena's had just been dumped by some man whose face and name Henry has since forgotten, and Elena had insisted that she come and stay with them for a few days – 'To get her over the worst of it,' she had explained to him. For a week he crept about his own house, watchful of saying the wrong word, wary of the injured woman's ever-trembling lower lip and the fire in the back of her eyes that seemed to regard him accusatorily. And while he tiptoed and cowered and went about his business, the two women sat in the kitchen drinking endless cups of tea and glasses of wine. They were like two cats licking each other's wounds. The drama and the sheer self-indulgence of it repulsed him. But what he remembers most from that week is the night he stood in the hall with his ear crushed against the kitchen door, listening to his wife tell of a night she had spent with another man in a different country. Filtering through the paint and wood were words he had never heard her use before – at least, not in that context. She spoke of heat, of desire, a longing that drove her crazy. She described body parts as if they were places, geographical landscapes – contours and ridges and silky plains, clefts of flesh and wide expanses of skin. Several minutes were devoted to fingers – travelling, touching, pressing, penetrating. His ear burned as he forced himself to listen to a lover's recounted words. Crude, base, barbaric words – pornographic vocabulary. He was shocked by the words, but even more disturbed by the wistful nostalgia in his wife's voice – her distinct lack of condemnation. Some man had spoken to her – had treated her body – as if she was a whore. And for some mystical, inexplicable and bewildering reason, this had translated itself to her as passion, an all-consuming desire. He remembers the weakness in his limbs as he pushed his body away from the door, guiltily slinking back up the stairs.

When she crept into bed beside him in the small hours and he felt her soft limbs reach for him, her legs tangling in his, he turned away angrily, feigning sleep. He waited, and after a short pause he felt her turn to the edge of the bed, her body flattening into sleep. But he did not sleep. He lay awake, feeling the rage inside him, the pique of betrayal, jealous of this man who had disappeared from her life before he had met her. He remembers the internal battle fought that night, between the wrenching desire to wake her and demand an explanation for her words, crying tears of hurt and indignation, and the pragmatic side, urging him not to be ridiculous, not to stir all that up again.

His breakfast arrives – swimming in a pool of fat on a green plate. The waitress brings the cutlery and offers to refill his tea, which he accepts gratefully. She purses her lips into something close to a smile and takes the teapot from him. His eyes follow her as she moves across the room. She is not much to look at, a small mousy girl with big hips and heavy legs and a nest of non-descript hair. But there is something in her demeanour – an air of passive contentment – that stirs up envy in him. He senses happiness in her, a peace that has been missing from his life for some time.

For a fleeting minute, while he arranges the cutlery and tugs at a napkin from the dispenser, he considers cutting his losses and getting a job in a place like this. The simplicity of it appeals to him. The lack of complications, of guises, speaks to him of ease, a way forward. But by the time he fills his mouth with the first bite – which surprisingly tastes better than it looks – he has already dismissed the notion out of hand.

He recalls boys in his class at school, and later university, friends of his, working in bars and cafés and restaurants as waiters. He remembers their stories about customers and tips and deliveries, and the twinges of envy they evoked in him. Henry, from the age of sixteen, worked every holiday in his father's business. At first he didn't mind, even looked forward to it. It hurts now to think of his enthusiasm, his eager naïveté.

Chewing on his sausage, he pauses to remove some gristle from between his teeth and thinks again of the office he sat in – the small table and grey plastic chair that his father set up for him – that dry colourless room with the window looking out onto the warehouse. That first summer, he shared the office with his father and an equally dour yellow-skinned man from Mullingar named Flynn. Henry never learned his first name. Between them, Dan and Flynn smoked an endless conveyor belt of cigarettes, filling the room with a thick cloud of smoke.

Sitting at his desk, computing endless lists of figures that he had a suspicion didn't relate to anything, Henry fought the boredom with routine trips down to the warehouse. Free from the choking atmosphere of the office, he let his mind wander as he dawdled between wooden pallets stacked high into towers and iron bars roped into place, great mounds of bricks and bags of cement, getting lost among them. The men who worked there ignored him for the most part. There were exceptions, of course, like Stevie Byrne, a small man with a long, thin face that gave him the unfortunate appearance of a weasel. Stevie would stop and chat, passing along tips on the horses, pointing out the favourites in the rolled-up *Racing Post* in his overalls pocket. And it was that first summer, idling in the warehouse, when he first heard his name called out over the tannoy. 'Henry! What are you doing down there? Get back up here now and stop bothering Stevie!' his father's voice belted out across the warehouse.

Henry's face still burns when he thinks of that moment, the pulsing embarrassment of it. He can still hear the great guffaws of the other men echoing in his ears as he climbed the stairs back to the office, the sharp metallic clink of the iron steps underfoot. He remembers the weedy grin on Flynn's face, that asthmatic laugh. But Dan's face was expressionless, apart from the defiance in his eyes – their unspoken taunting fed the bubbling rage inside him.

'It's just his way,' his mother said when he complained of it to her later. 'He's just anxious for you to get on and learn the business. You're there to work, not to dawdle about,' she added, a shrill nervousness in her voice.

That was enough to ensure Henry did not return to her with any more grievances about the business. And so he kept the wincing pain of continued humiliations a secret from her. The following summer, when his father bellowed at him in front of a client, and Henry's lower lip trembled, eyes filling with tears as he stood there bearing the indignity of being labelled an ignorant twit and a stupid little gobshite, he kept the knowledge of the incident to himself. That first summer of university, when he overheard his father saying to one of the foremen that, for all his college education, his son still couldn't complete an order form worth a shit, Henry remained silent. And in the last summer before his final year, when his father lashed out at him, clipping him across the temple so suddenly that he was too shocked to cry out, he still didn't admit it to anyone. He kept his silence. And he never worked there again.

His mobile rings, the shrill bleating wrenching him from his reverie. The waitress shoots him a glance of curiosity as she clears his plate, the phone still bleating on the table. It is Elena again, but this time he is not as shaken. The breakfast has calmed him and he settles comfortably into his seat, sipping his tea. He pictures her, in the house, waiting for the children to wake up and the questions to begin. He wonders what she will tell them. How she will explain his absence on a Saturday morning. And what she will say to the inevitable question, 'When will Daddy be back?' He cannot even answer this himself.

His father never walked out. There were never any unexplained absences during Henry's childhood – none that he can remember, anyhow. His parents' curious relationship – the bullying, the moods, the jittery unease – always maintained a constant knowledge of the other person's whereabouts. Dan would ring from the office if he was going to be late home. And Alice would call Dan before going to the shops in case there was something special he wanted. It used to drive Henry crazy, this system of keeping tabs on each other. But now he realises that there was respect in those gestures, tenderness even.

His father would never have done what Henry has – left his bed, with his wife and children still sleeping, and driven off with no knowledge of where he was going or when he would be back. If he would be back. There are people who do that – who leave their homes in the morning, taking nothing with them except the clothes on their backs and the money in their wallets – and just disappear. Some, of course, turn up dead – their bodies fished out of rivers and canals. In these cases, there is usually drink involved or drugs or depression. They fill his mother's home video collection. But there are others – older men – husbands and fathers, with no obvious reason to walk away from their lives. These are the men he is thinking of. What happens to them? Where is it that they go? And how do they cope with the guilt of all they have left behind?

There is activity at the table opposite him. The old couple have finished their meal and one of them seems to have spilt sugar on the table. Together they attempt to sweep it up, the woman speaking constantly as she sweeps the litter of granules with a cupped hand into the saucer that the man holds to the lip of the table. He reaches out his other hand to assist and his sleeve rides up, revealing a bracelet – green and white, with lettering in blue Biro – a hospital bracelet. Henry is transfixed. He stares at the man, his careful movements, his quiet manners and slow responses. He is a large man, but there is something sedated about him.

Thoughts of his parents creep back into his mind, nudging away the other concerns. It seems unnatural – incredible, even – that illness may have taken root in his father's body. Since before dawn, he has raced through a plethora of questions: What illness does he suffer from? Is it terminal? How aggressive is it? Henry has not contemplated his parents' mortality – it is not something he has had to consider. But his father's visit has brought new concerns, more questions that he does not like to ask. Will illness make his father meek or will it strengthen his aggression? How will his mother cope? Does she even know about it? He imagines not. Dan would want to protect her from it. Her stuttering frailty, that nervous disposition does not inspire confidence.

The ache in his head comes to rest at the nape of his neck. He should go home, hold his children, speak to his wife. She deserves as much – at least a spoken explanation, however mashed and disjointed and senseless it may seem. The weight of his responsibilities bears down upon him. A dutiful son would take over his father's business, look after his mother and come clean to his wife. The thought of doing any of those things fills him with dread. More than anything, he wants to begin again. He wants to disappear. He lets the pain press against his neck and lowers his face into his hands.

'Are you all right?'

He looks up, bleary eyed, into the face of the waitress. It appears ugly, now he looks at it closely – flat and thin lipped, with bulging eyes that suggest a thyroid problem.

'Yes. Yes, I'm fine,' he replies unconvincingly. 'Just a little tired.'

'Were you on the ferry,' she asks, 'from France?'

'I think I've just left my wife and kids.'

These words escape from him without warning, running away from him and falling against the flat face of the waitress. Confusion registers on her features and he instantly regrets it. 'I'm joking,' he lies, forcing a smile to convince her. 'I was on the ferry.'

'Oh,' she says, regarding him warily. 'I thought so. I can always tell.'

He watches her move to the counter and whisper something to the older woman, who turns and looks in his direction before turning back to the girl and making a face. He's not sure what it indicates, something like 'you never can tell' or 'it's always the quiet ones'. Some patronising pat, some hidden warning.

The old couple are getting to their feet, half shuffling, half sliding out of their seat. She pats his hand gently and, when they are both upright, takes his hand in hers and leads him carefully out of the diner. Henry watches them through the window as they make their way to an old Peugeot parked near his own car. She helps the old man into his seat, fastening the belt for him before hurrying around to the driver's side. There is love in her movements – careful and assured. A love that Henry surmises has survived decades and endured sickness. He is amazed by this kind of devotion – this staunch, stalwart affection – and envious too, lustful for such depths of feeling, such boundless commitment.

He finishes his breakfast and looks about him at the other diners. He feels disoriented, shut off from the others, shut out from a world in which the usual standards and words apply. The voices in the room seem overly loud. He doesn't belong in here. He has to get out, but he can't go home either. Not yet.

He pays his bill and steps out into the car park. Traffic is building on the road, with cars careering past, kicking up powder clouds of dust. But the day is fine, and something about the freshness of the morning and his full stomach makes Henry feel expansive and unready to get back into the car again. He needs to be free from enclosed spaces. His mind needs room to breathe.

There was a lake he saw a half-mile or so back, in off the road. With his hands in his pockets, he saunters back, his head held high, breathing in the morning. Some weeks ago he had met with a client in their office. The meeting room was at the top of a twelve-storey building looking out across the growing Dublin skyline. From the window, he could see the striped candy-stick towers at Ringsend, and stretching out in the distance was Bray Head – a lump of land falling forward into the sea. Outside the window was a wide ledge – wide enough for a rooftop garden – and Henry asked the client whether they were able to go outside. 'We're not supposed to' was the answer, as the client reluctantly let him venture out onto the ledge. Years ago, there had been a rooftop garden, Henry was told, with tables and chairs and plants in pots. But then, one Tuesday afternoon, one of the employees had come up for a smoke and promptly thrown himself off the building. 'It was a terrible mess,' the client said, grimacing. And that was the end of the garden. Henry remembers inching to the edge, and peering down. He could feel his stomach clench with fear. The thought of it – the sheer drop. Jesus! Peeping over the edge, he felt a flurry of wind at his back, and his heart bounded in his rib cage. 'Scary, isn't it?' the client grinned. But there was an exhilaration that he felt alongside the fear. Henry imagined that lost soul stubbing out his final cigarette and then taking that great leap out and embracing the sky. Through this act of failure, oddly, there must have also been a kind of relief. There must have been comfort in the fact that this was the end – that whatever particular struggle that nameless person had gone through was going to be over.

Henry is not suicidal, nor was he then. His despair has somehow mutated into this feeling of nothingness – an absence of feeling. And what he wants, more than anything, is to be left alone.

The water ripples with a gentle current, but appears benign and unthreatening. He walks slowly along the bank, feeling the tiredness crawling through his leg muscles. The grass is short and soft underfoot and the noises are pleasing to him – birds in song, the snap of wings and movement of air. A breeze billows through his shirt and ruffles his hair.

He tries to blot out the thoughts of Elena – her worry over his absence. There is no satisfaction in picturing his wife's distress. It takes away from the stillness of the morning, the unspoiled beauty of this lake.

He looks out at the water, sees the sunlight reflected in the silvery surface and feels the breeze scurrying across the lake to him. It fills his senses; he is steeped in the tranquillity of it. The aches in his head, his neck, his back – those lozenges of pain – have dispersed, leaving a sort of levity in his body, a floating sensation, as if he were weightless. He wants to lie down in the grass, to feel the breeze sweeping over his still body as his mind drifts into sleep. He blanks out the memory of the tortured night, and despite the staleness of his clothes and the aches in his body, he feels that he is being cleansed by the stillness of the morning. As he marvels in the redemption that washes through him, his features free from the pinch of worry and distress and guilt, he feels the familiar vibration in his pocket. He reaches inward, retrieving the phone, and checks the identity of the caller. It is Elena, as he knew it would be. He must answer it. He must speak to his wife, assure her of his safety. He will tell her that he loves her and that he needs her to forgive him. He will return to her, to the troubled knot of love that is their marriage.

That is what he should do. But as the mobile bleats its jingle, threatening to break the spell of the morning, he suddenly draws his arm back, pausing to steady his footing, and then, with one sweeping movement, he flings it over his head. It glides through the air, forming an arc. He watches as it hits the water with a satisfying plink – and then it is gone.

ELENA

7

SHE WAKES and he is not there. Looking across, she does not see Henry's head flattened into the other pillow. This morning, she does not want to look into his sleepily staring eyes or see the marks from creased bed linen lining his face. She thinks of his fair hair peppered with grey – the way it stands up as if with surprise, as it always does in the morning – and how it used to prompt a smile on her face. Guiltily, she admits to herself that today it would only have irritated her. That musty early-morning scent from his skin, his stale breath as he leans in to kiss her, the sticky weight of his arm as it circles her waist – these morning habits, the familiarity of them, would only have served as a reminder of all that she risked last night, all that happened between her and Adam. Henry's absence from her bed is a relief. These are terrible thoughts, she admits to herself, treacherous thoughts.

It was reckless, what she did, stupid, she reminds herself sternly as she turns over. But it is not enough to dispel the feeling that has swept around her, gathering her in, pulling her back, making her feel suddenly awake, her senses heightened. It lasted beyond his hotel room. Standing in the lift, watching its progress blinking through the floors, she hugged her arms around herself, feeling wrapped in a warmth of intimacy that raised hairs on the back of her neck. It was quiet in the lobby – almost deserted – the early light from the windows dim against the brightly lit interior. At the reception desk she asked the night porter about taxis and his eyes passed over her briefly while he smiled politely and picked up the phone. 'Fifteen minutes, madam,' he informed her, and after she thanked him and walked away to take a seat, she could feel the question in his gaze, the whirr of his imagination running behind his eyes. He must see women like her all the time – women who drift down into the lobby wearing crumpled clothes and last night's make-up. Women with shamed expressions, anxious for the taxi to come and take them away. But she did not feel shame. Not then.

Sitting in the back seat of the taxi, she looked out at the still-sleeping city as it wheeled past her. The streets were wrapped in a blue-grey blanket of cold. She nestled into the upholstery, imagining Adam, stretched out on his hotel bed, an arm bent at the elbow and tucked behind his head, the other hand idly stroking the hairs on his chest. Is he thinking of me? she wondered. Or is he already pitching through a dream-filled sleep? The street cleaners were out, their tiny stinking vans prowling the curbs, faceless men in heavy clothing sweeping and bending, their breath clouding out, pockets of heat in the sharp air. It was quiet at that time of the morning, the city on the brink of wakefulness, quiet enough to think. A dog was sniffing at some unspeakable mess spilled on the curb and the silence was broken by the raucous din of a woman, still steeped in gin from the night before, tights laddered and clothes askew. She disappeared down an alleyway but her voice lingered. Elena looked out as she passed, observing the ugliness left on the streets from a Friday night in the city. But she didn't feel disgust. Something moved inside her – something old and remembered. 'I need to see you again,' he had whispered to her. An old excitement, stirred up again and coming to life.

She turns over onto her back and stretches out her limbs. A wincing pain hits behind her eyes and she squints through the beam of light falling through the gap in the curtains and stretching across the bed. Her hair smells of smoke and her tongue sticks to the roof of her mouth. Her whole body is wrapped in a brittle shell – every pocket of water sucked dry. From downstairs come noises, the familiar early-morning sounds of the children starting their day. The TV churns out the screeching American voices of cartoons and there is the clatter of hard plastic hitting the floor – Ben is at play. In a few minutes they will come upstairs, hungry, demanding, needing food and attention, pulling at her limbs, dragging her from her bed, and the day will begin. She stretches like a cat, her toes and fingers reaching for the far corners of the bed. Her lips crack as she yawns. Her body craves water. And a shadow of doubt passes over her brain, promising to bloom into a guilty conscience, berating her for what she has done and for what she wanted to do. Enough. She must get up.

Ben sings while he eats. Cereal drops from his mouth as he chants his way through a bowl of Cheerios. It is an unlovely sight. Emily is talking to her Barbie, who is propped against the teapot wearing a lurid pink bikini. She conducts this one-sided conversation with whispered animation and much raising of eyebrows in between mouthfuls. Elena regards them both over the rim of her coffee cup. They always seem so removed from her over breakfast, preoccupied either with their toys or the inner workings of their cluttered minds, or on weekdays still bound up in sleep, silent and puffy eyed.

'Where's Daddy?' Emily asks suddenly.

'Out.'

'Duh! Out where?' she questions, rolling her eyeballs.

'I don't know,' Elena answers truthfully. His sudden disappearance worries her. Getting out of bed that morning, feeling the dull ache swimming around her head, she peered out the bedroom window and noticed the car was gone. When she tried his mobile, it just rang out. She is unsure of how to interpret this. A nagging fear nips at her brain. *He knows,* it whispers to her, *he knows about last night.* And how will she explain it to him? Where will she tell him she was until six in the morning? Future lies gang up on her, grinding at her conscience, crowding out all other thoughts.

'When will he be back?'

Ben is banging the table with his spoon, roaring his own mangled version of 'Bob the Builder'.

'Later.'

'That's very informative.'

Elena regards her daughter carefully. The words coming out of her mouth are not her own. She has picked them up from one of her parents, Elena is not sure which one. Children are like sponges, her mother warned her. They absorb everything. But it troubles Elena that her little girl is picking up their sarcasm, the acerbic comments they use on each other. That cannot be right. 'I'm sure Daddy will be back soon,' Elena says confidently, trying to reassure herself as much as Emily.

She glances at the kitchen clock and feels a twinge of anxiety.

She is a practical person. Grounded. Realistic. 'Elena takes things as they come,' she has heard Henry say. 'She doesn't read too much into things.' And perhaps he is right. But recently she has found that certain things have begun to enrage her. She cannot explain this new anger welling up inside her, these sudden and ferocious eruptions of fury. Why has it suddenly started to annoy her that, first thing each morning, Henry reaches across to the box of tissues on his nightstand to clear his sinuses? He has been doing this ever since they met. But suddenly it bothers her. 'Do that in the bathroom, will you?' she hissed at him, and then lay in bed listening to him padding across the hall and closing the bathroom door behind him, feeling guilty and mean at her bad-tempered little outburst.

There are other vexations. The social column in the Saturday *Times* magazine. Sitting at the kitchen table drinking coffee, Henry scanning the sports pages, the children wreaking havoc in the sitting room, she read the words of some overweight bloated ego spouting on about her night out with some movie star. Elena read some of it out loud for Henry, who gazed at her serenely as she twitched with contempt for this kebab-eating hack and her substandard English. 'Don't take it so seriously,' Henry said, going back to the sports supplement. She flung the magazine at him and stormed out of the kitchen.

When she went to a party not long ago at Shane and Kim Smith's, she was led by Kim into the kitchen, led by the elbow, where the catering staff were pointed out to her. Standing next to the distressed wood island in the cavernous vault of a kitchen, she watched with a growing horror as Kim spoke of the assorted staff in monochrome uniforms as if they weren't even there. 'You simply must get the caterers in for a party,' she said in an urgent voice. 'Why slave away in the kitchen when you can pay someone else to slave for you? There is simply no other option. Trust me, Elena.' It seemed to Elena obscene to speak of slavery in front of these people as they went about their business, earning an honest living. She felt an inexplicable fury growing inside her as she followed Kim's confident strut out of the kitchen, a stream of further instructions issuing forth from her.

Just after Christmas, she had a new haircut – blonde streaks and a sharp fringe, with feathered layers through the sides. 'That's different' was Henry's comment. She liked it at first, liked the newness of it. But the style was hard to maintain, time consuming, requiring a special blow-drying technique that she couldn't quite master. Eventually it grew out and she returned to her straight bob, her hair sleek and shiny and cut along her jawline. 'Ah!' her mother exclaimed when she saw the old haircut's return. 'Now that suits you. That's your style.' But while complimenting her daughter, Rosario was, Elena suspected, stating something else as well: that she had made a mistake with her image before and that she should not do it again. That she should not experiment with her looks, but accept her appearances and not try to deviate. Elena felt the unspoken put-down and it wounded her. She was a grown woman, independent from her parents. Yet still this parental disapproval shadowed her actions, her decisions.

Last week they had Sunday lunch at Henry's parents' house. Lunch was always the same. A roast leg of lamb, mashed potatoes and broccoli – boiled, not steamed; Alice fretting over the children; Dan holding forth on everything from the weather to the state of the government. Elena mentioned that, now Ben was in the crèche, she was looking forward to her morning walks on Dún Laoghaire pier.

'Alone?' Alice asked, looking up, her eyes as round as saucers. 'Oh, no!' she exclaimed, 'Oh, you mustn't, Elena! With all the crime around Dún Laoghaire? The drug addicts? The refugees? Absolutely not! Tell her she can't, Henry. You mustn't let her.'

Elena, with a mouthful of broccoli, felt flustered, and then later furious. 'Does she think that if you order me not to go, I'll just obey?' she stormed to Henry on the way home in the car. 'Does she think we're still living in the Victorian era? Does she even know that women have the vote yet?'

'You're overreacting,' Henry said with a puzzled look.

'Don't tell me how to react!' she countered angrily.

It seems to Elena that she is being instructed from all sources on how to live her life. It isn't done out of malice – more out of habit, but that doesn't make it any less infuriating. And this new-found anger, this explosive rage, seems to bubble close to the surface, threatening to boil over.

She doesn't know where this heightened sensitivity has sprung from. But lately she has felt aware of a growing sense of regret, a new sorrow for all the things she has let slip, let go, abandoned. Her chance meeting with Rachel and then the whole reunion furore have awoken a storm of insecurities, reminders of her unfinished past. And then there is Henry, his growing reticence, the secrecy he seems to wrap himself in, and her sense that beneath his calm exterior is a growing resentment. But there is something else – a quiet voice, a lingering doubt – whispering inside her. The past has caught up with her, its fingers pointing and probing, putting the question to her: has she made a great mistake?

★

Emily has been invited to a birthday party and Elena drops her off on the way to the supermarket with Ben. Pushing the trolley through the aisles, plucking items from the shelves and keeping him amused, she feels a buzz in her head, pain humming alongside the guilt. Leaning over the fruit and veg counter and reaching across for a melon, she catches sight of her reflection in the mirror above the counter. Hair drawn back in an elastic, sweatshirt and cargo pants, she is worse than casual – she is dishevelled. And yet there is something different about her – cheeks that are flushed, eyes that seem brighter than usual. She touches her hand to her face and steps away, the memory of last night pressing against her. She thinks of that kiss – that parting kiss – soft, pressing, a gentleness that belied the urgency it contained. Tantalising and brief, it left her shaking with longing. Her son smiles up at her, a soft pudgy leg dangling from the trolley, and she feels her heart seize with love. This must stop, she thinks as she leans forward and kisses him. I must put this out of my mind.

And then something startling. At the checkout, her Laser card is refused. Insufficient funds. 'Are you sure?' she asks, examining the card that has been passed back to her.

'Do you have another card you'd like me to try, madam?'

'Yes, of course.' Elena fumbles in her wallet, flushed with embarrassment and confusion. 'There must be something wrong with the card; there's money in that account,' she explains as the items are credited to her Visa card successfully.

It itches at her mind as she fills the car with shopping and, after strapping Ben into his seat and taking her position behind the wheel, she tries calling Henry once more. *We're sorry, but the person you are dialling may have their phone switched off or be out of coverage...*

'Damn it!'

She thrusts the key in the ignition, channelling her irritation into the engine.

Later, when Ben is curled up on the couch, lost in his afternoon nap, Elena returns to the bedroom. It feels stale, the mixed odours of last night still lingering. Throwing open the window, she proceeds to strip the bed, feeling the need to purge the events of last night, wanting to cleanse this room of all its treacherous thoughts. She attacks the spillage of discarded clothes on the floor, folding and putting away and filling the laundry basket. After Emily was born, they agreed that this room should be one place that clutter would not enter – no toys, no knick-knacks, nothing to cause distraction. Decorated in restful shades of blue and cream, with light-blond woods and a soft-pile carpet, this room was a sanctuary, a place to escape from the chaos of the children. But its lofty position has recently fallen from grace, and traces of a relaxing in the rules have appeared in the trail of toys that have edged onto the floor, the empty coffee cups left on the nightstands, books and bathroom items lingering on windowsills and chairs.

Fixing the clean sheet around the mattress, Elena thinks of the secrets this bed holds, the acts of love it has borne witness to, the conception of children, the whispered conversations it has overheard, the arguments and hurt-filled silences it has known. She feels flushed with a myriad of memories – of times when she and Henry have lain side by side, staring at each other through the darkness, whispering in the night about the children or how they would cope with growing older or where they wanted their ashes to be scattered or what they would do if they won the lottery. And, more recently, there have been nights when irritation has begun to creep into their bed – a hard, sharp, alien thing, dispelling the warmth and closeness, leaving a lingering presence.

He started working late, very late, the hours growing longer, stretching into the night. She felt him creeping into bed next to her at two in the morning and asked him in a quiet voice where he had been.

'Working,' he replied curtly, his back turned coldly towards her so she couldn't see his face.

'So late?'

'You've no idea, do you?' he hissed in the darkness. 'No idea what kind of pressure I'm under.'

'Well, then, tell me.'

'It's all very well for you, swanning around all day, a lady of leisure—'

'I do not swan around—'

'—while I'm out there working my fingers to the bone. And then, when I come home after a brain-numbing meeting that I thought would never end, I get grief from you…'

'I was worried. Why didn't you call?'

'Why don't you just say it, Elena?'

'What?'

'Go on, just say it.'

'Say what, Henry?'

'That you don't believe me. That you don't trust me.'

'Why are you being so defensive?'

'Jesus. I've had enough of this.'

And with that he got out of bed, snatching a pillow and blanket and making for the door. 'Henry! Don't be like that. Henry, where are you going?'

'Downstairs. I'll sleep on the couch. Maybe then I might get a few hours' peace!'

A week later, when it happened again and she felt his body slipping under the covers next to her and smelled the cigarette smoke on his skin, stale alcohol on his breath, she just lay there, watching the hand of the clock ticking past three, and didn't say a thing.

Filling the pillow cases and throwing the fresh duvet over the bed, she stops for a moment and sits down suddenly, leaning against the bedstead, feeling a rush of blood to her head. The grain of the wood feels smooth and rippling beneath her fingertips. She rubs it slowly, feeling a calmness coming over her again. A memory comes to her suddenly, of a different bed, one with an elaborate wrought-iron frame. She had forgotten that bed, allowing it to become lost over time. But now it is back, she has a hold on it again. She closes her eyes and pictures her hands running along its sleek black frame. Remembering how they marvelled at the iron rising from the four corners of the bed, sweeping up and arching into the centre where the four corners met and formed an iron ring over the heart of the bed. It was such a surprise, that bed, the beauty of it, the romance of its design, in the middle of that puritanical place – a villa in the hills of Catalonia. House-sitting for Adam's boss. A whole week away from the cramped space of their clammy apartment in Barcelona. A real bed instead of a mattress on the floor. The ceiling of the bedroom was lofty, the walls ancient and crumbling, layers of yellow-white paint chipping away. The mattress was wrapped in a harsh ticking fabric that was scratchy against skin and the nights were too hot for blankets. She remembers those nights, the stillness of the air, the citrus smell of oranges they had eaten – peel tossed on the floor – and the sliver of moon seen through the window, a sweaty tangle of limbs, struggling to catch her breath, the cool touch of iron as she reached back and clasped the bed-head, her other hand slipping down into the crevice of his back, sliding down, feeling him rocking over her, believing that it could always be like that.

But a bed can be a dangerous place too – a place where passion gives way to recklessness, an abandonment of reason, a wilful carelessness. That bed in Brussels, that bed she slept in for four months, after Spain, after Adam. She thinks of the risks she took then, leaving herself open, laying herself bare. The nights she spent with men she barely knew, sex temporarily displacing her sadness, making her feel something different, at least for a short time. She cringes from it now, shrinks from the memory, ashamed of the depravity her grief impelled her to. She has lied about this side of her past, preferring to keep it in the shadows, where it belongs.

A history of beds she has slept in lines up in her mind's eye. Her childhood bed – that single bed pushed against the wall of the tiny box-room – that bed she returned to after the loneliness of Belgium, taking refuge, waiting for her wounds to heal, her sorrow to pass. Then there was the bed in the flat in Rathmines – their first bed, Henry's and hers; the hard mattress with the suspicious stains that Elena covered up with plastic mattress covers and refused to think about. The brown spreading stain on the ceiling above them, the musty smell from the carpet below. They were both relieved to leave it behind and move into the house.

She remembers that time with a wistful fondness. How different Henry was then – so upbeat and energetic. His enthusiasm was infectious, she felt buoyed up by his good humour. Before the furniture came, when there was no bed to sleep in, they put a thin mattress on the floor in the living room and surrounded themselves with burning candles to soften the dark corners and distract their attention from the bare floorboards and peeling wallpaper. 'We'll set the bed on fire,' Henry joked, gazing at her across the mattress, shadows flickering over his face.

It was six weeks before the bed arrived, precipitating their move upstairs; when it happened, there was a faint air of disappointment about it. They had been like teenagers, camping out, a blanket tacked up over the window to preserve their modesty. The mattress had been thin and lumpy and they had felt the hardness of the floorboards pushing up through their bodies. They had felt stiff in the mornings, limbs and joints aching, and they had offered up the question 'When will that bed ever arrive?' over and over. And when it did arrive, they welcomed the well-sprung frame, the luxuriant hardness of the mattress, their elevation from the floorboards. They marvelled at the decadence of the size and the regal bedposts. Henry teased her about using her nylon stockings to tie her to the bedposts. But below the high tenor of their excitement and relief, there was a sadness about abandoning their nights on the living room floor. It was like the end of summer – a return to adult sensibilities, no more larking about, no more rolling around unfettered. The move upstairs brought on a new maturity. And it is in this bed that Elena has recently lain awake at night, haunted by the notion that she has made a terrible mistake.

Emily is dropped home, tired and full of sugar. Her crankiness is apparent in the tightness of her face. She refuses to eat dinner and then whines about sharing a bath with Ben. 'Because he's smelly!' she roars, folding her arms resolutely across her small chest. She squeals when put into the bath. 'It's too hot,' she complains, and then when Elena turns the cold tap she mumbles, 'Now it's too cold.' Shampoo suds slide down her face and into her eyes, causing her to scream. Even Ben stops what he is doing and looks up in consternation.

'For God's sake!' Elena hisses, scrubbing the child's head a little roughly, her nerves frayed.

'I want Daddy!' Emily shouts, as she starts to cry.

'Well, he's not here, so you'll just have to make do with me.'

'Where is he?' she wails, tears squeezing from her eyes.

'I don't bloody know.' Elena allows her frustration to come through.

She has given up ringing his mobile and the office. He is not at the squash club either. His mother rang, and made no mention of having seen him, so Elena can only assume he is not there.

Getting the children into their pyjamas, she feels a twinge of fear. What if something has happened to him? She stops what she is doing, a vision of carnage blurring her thoughts – the car in a ditch, Henry bleeding… Don't be ridiculous, she scolds herself. It is quite clear to her what he is doing. She stayed out all night, leaving him alone with the kids. And now it is his turn. Well, if he wants to be petty, then sod him, she thinks savagely.

But later, when the children are finally in bed, after a strenuous protest from Emily, the worry creeps back into her mind. What if something really has happened to him? His behaviour lately has been so erratic, so unpredictable. She doesn't know what is going on in his mind half the time. It is dark outside, a bright moon hangs in the sky. As she stares at it, feeling the worry bubbling in her stomach, something occurs to her. Quietly, so as not to wake the children, she enters the bedroom she shares with Henry, circling their bed before sitting down next to his nightstand. It is in the top drawer. His diary – leather-bound, pocket-sized and emblazoned with the logo of some telecommunications company he was contracted to. She pauses for an instant, some irrational hesitation. *Oh, for God's sake, Elena,* she scolds herself. *It's only a record of his meetings and appointments, not the outpourings of his soul.* Opening it and briskly turning to today's date, she is confronted with a blank page, and while that does not help her ascertain Henry's whereabouts, she feels a wave of relief that there is nothing sinister printed there, no female name to cause anxiety.

Her thumb draws back over the rest of the pages and her eyes travel over a meandering list of places and clients, printed in Henry's scribbled writing. But it is the back pages that catch her eye, the blank lined pages for notes. They hold lists of figures – numbers lined up in neat rows, although growing more erratic in places. She pores over them – a column of numbers, some of which are aligned with dates. Their significance evades her. The letter L appears alongside some of them. They stretch across pages, and one figure, its zeros tripping alarmingly towards the centre of the page, is underlined several times

– the short aggressive expletive 'fuck!!' scribbled hastily alongside it. She stares at the pages, intrigued.

As she ponders the mathematics, the telephone on the nightstand suddenly erupts, making her jump. She grabs the receiver to her ear. 'Henry?'

There is a short pause, an intake of breath. 'No. It's me.'

Her heart leaps wildly in her chest. Her throat closes over.

'I had to call you,' he says softly.

'How did you get my number?' she asks, a nervous quaver in her voice.

'Rachel. I rang Rachel for it.'

'This isn't a good time.'

'Is he there?'

'No. I don't know where he is.'

'Oh.' The silence that follows is filled with his unspoken presumption of a row, some marital discord, and she strives to dispel it.

'But he'll be back soon, so...'

'How can you be sure if you don't know where he is?'

'Adam, this isn't a good idea.'

'I know. But I don't care. I had to call. I'm here at the hospital, bored out of my mind. I needed to talk to someone. I needed to hear your voice.'

'Please. This has to stop.'

'What has to stop? What have we done? Nothing happened last night, nothing for us to be ashamed of.'

'How can you say that?'

'Tell me what it is that we're supposed to have done. It was only a kiss...'

'Now you're being disingenuous.'

She feels the tug of him, drawing her in. But she is sober now, and in control of herself. Her children are asleep in the next rooms. She is leaning back against her husband's pillow. She will not let herself be weak.

'OK. All right,' he surrenders. 'I admit it. I called because I want to see you again.'

'Don't, Adam.'

'Come on, Elena. I know you want it too.'

She bites her lip and stares at the ceiling.

'I'm married, Adam. I'm a mother. What happened… I wish… I shouldn't have gone back to your room. I wish that I hadn't.'

She waits for his response. When it comes it is cool and measured. 'I don't believe you, Elena.'

A surge of indignation, a sudden anger, comes over her. What insolence! Ringing her house, ringing her home! When her husband could have answered the phone, or her daughter! And then the arrogance of bringing up the kiss! What does he expect her to do? Just waltz out and throw herself back into his waiting arms, back to all that she ran from?

'I don't care what you believe,' she says quietly and calmly. 'I don't care what you wish or think or want or desire. I stopped caring about that a long time ago. I'm hanging up the phone now and I don't expect you to call here again.'

And as she delivers the receiver to the cradle of the phone, she hears him, the cool, metallic taint in his voice.

'This isn't the end,' are his words, before the soft click returns her to silence.

8

ONCE, MANY YEARS ago now, a man named Adrian Keneally gave Elena a book entitled *Bornholm Night Ferry*. It was a slender volume of letters – love letters – between a man and a woman over many years, spanning many countries. Elena remembers lying in bed, reading the outpourings of love and grief and anger and longing in the dim light of her bedroom. She remembers the noises of the house surrounding her – the deep, muffled tones of her father's voice travelling up through the walls, the clatter of pans in the kitchen rising to compete with the groaning, angst-ridden melodies emanating from her brother Luis's room across the hall. This soundtrack accompanied the dim weeping of the soul poured out on paper, being sucked up into her consciousness, as she grew increasingly alarmed at the message she perceived to be contained in the book. What was it that Adrian Keneally was trying to tell her? This violent and sexual love portrayed so baldly on paper made her feel uncomfortable. She found her face twisting with distaste as she read explicit descriptions, feeling like a voyeur. She squirmed in her bed, her body clenching in protest at these intimacies she wanted to hear no more about. In the end, she left it unfinished, languishing under her bed until it was swept away with all the other unnecessary clutter in one of her sporadic clean-outs.

When Adrian Keneally asked her a week later how she had liked it, she looked into his face, alarmed by the intensity of his gaze – the warning in his eyes – and promptly lied to him. 'It was great,' she said.

'Very moving.' But the truth was, it left her cold. And his fascination with the book, his eager intensity, frightened her. She could not stir herself to emulate his sentiments. Sitting in the front seat of his car, she felt repelled by the trembling inquisitiveness of his hands, those forceful lips, the flickering greed of his tongue. She broke up with him a week later. The darkness of the look he gave her, the angry embarrassment of his glare, worried her. Two or three times in the weeks afterwards, she could have sworn she saw the black hump of his car crawling by her house. But the weeks and months passed, and then she met Adam. She thinks about Adrian sometimes – not very often – and wonders whether he ever found a willing and grateful recipient for the brooding intensity of his love.

She understands now what it is like to love with that kind of intensity. She has felt the momentum of passion, the heart-stopping, bewildering force of it. And she sees it in others around her. Recently, she was brought upstairs in her friend Ian's house, led proudly into the master bedroom to view a gift from Ian's partner, Graham. Elena remembers staring at it – a gloriously over-the-top French antique bed – and felt something rise inside her, something she couldn't readily identify. A lump appeared in her throat and she felt embarrassed by the sudden tears pricking her eyes. 'It's beautiful,' she managed to say.

'Isn't it?' he responded. 'I mean, some people might think it's a bit, well… rude, I suppose, suggestive, or even just a little naughty. Giving your lover a bed as a gift, I mean!'

She watched him – her friend, with his gentle manners and soft-spoken voice – as he led her on a tour of the well-sprung frame, the well-turned bedposts, the exquisite (if slightly elaborate) carving of the bed-head, the tightly packed mattress. And as they sat together on the edge of the bed, staring out the window at the empty sky lazy with mist, she heard him say solemnly and quietly, 'I just couldn't live without him.'

Later that evening, the TV humming downstairs and the sounds of Henry clearing the dishes, Elena sat in a hot bath, steam rising and misting the mirrors, sweat trickling over her body and angry tears lining her face as she felt a terrible shuddering envy, shameful sobs full of self-pity offered up to the silent, unforgiving bathroom.

Where does love go to, she wonders? What makes it evaporate, misting into a memory, a wistful moment of passing? It leaves a residue behind – a sticky pervasiveness clinging to everyday objects, gathering in the corners of the house, woven and stitched into the customs and fabric of her life. This residue is a smokescreen, a deceitful mundanity. The patterns of love are everywhere, but when did it become just a pattern without the love?

Elena's mother, Rosario, would argue that love could come back again. But it needs coaxing, a careful goading and persuasion to bring it back, to wake it up. Rosario believes that any problem can be solved if you talk around it for long enough. 'Communication' is her thing. Silence is her enemy. And counselling is the cure-all she touts on a regular basis.

'You must talk it out,' she says in her Latin lilt. 'You don't talk about it, it will never be sorted out.'

She discovered counselling while Elena was in her teens. Every Wednesday evening she would wrap her considerable self in a woollen cape-like throw – swaddled in yards of cashmere – to embark on an evening of spiritual and emotional awakening. She would sit on a short-legged chair in the draughty hall of the boys' national school along with twenty or thirty other anxious souls and listen to the stories offered up there, fastening onto the wisdom spoken, seeking a prognosis for all the aggression she was feeling, the terrible sorrow that had come into her home. 'Where has the love gone?' she asked them in anguished hope. 'How has it gone so wrong?'

They would sit on their chairs and stare into their mirrors, pressing themselves to see – to really see – what secrets lay in their own faces. The self-deceptions, the surrendered freedoms, the painful acceptance of all they had allowed to be done to themselves. This self-help group with their hodgepodge amateur psychology and their shared emotional bruises acted as a lifeline for Rosario, a way to cope with the frustrations within her marriage, offering a way forward, suggestions as to how to tackle her husband's drinking problems, his reticence and stony silences. Often there were tears. But there was comfort too. A redemption.

Elena does not know what her mother was told there, or at least very little of it – a mish-mash of information filtered back to her over the years. But she remembers her mother's face those Wednesday nights when she returned home – flushed cheeks, eyes bright with enlightenment; there was excitement in her, a new vigour. She seemed to be charged with an all-consuming energy that swept through the whole house, channelling it into Elena's bewildered father, who looked buffeted about in a storm, lost among this new catechism of psychobabble. And despite his quiet yet persistent protests that he was not and is not an alcoholic – he prefers instead to concede a certain weakness at one point in his life – Rosario would not let it go. She embraced the counselling culture wholeheartedly. She will not be denied her precious support groups. She won't be done out of her weekly meetings. She is a fully paid-up member of Al-Anon; no one can take away from her the wounds the demon drink has inflicted upon her. And if her daughter were to confide in her now, detailing the problems that have taken root within her relationship, Rosario would advise 'a good dollop of counselling' as the way to move forward.

Elena knows that this coldness that has fallen over her marriage has nothing to do with alcohol. The embittered silences and frustrated backbiting cannot be attributed to any addiction that she is aware of. Something is missing, something that she cannot put her finger on. And this newly discovered anger in her, this well of discontent, is threatening to spill over, drowning out any soft sentiment that is left between them. Elena is afraid that soon there will be nothing left to save.

He rang last night. A short, terse conversation imparting the bare minimum of information. The relief that she felt to hear his voice, to know that he was all right, was short lived, chased by a chilly suspicion aroused by his tight-lipped message, the short, cold manner in which he spoke to her. He was staying in a bed & breakfast outside Dublin, he didn't say exactly where. 'But why?' she had asked, feeling the fear creeping into her voice. She is afraid when he becomes like this – secretive, possessive of his private woes. It unnerves her. He was fine, he assured her; he just needed a bit of space, some room to get his thoughts together. They needed to talk, he said, to clear the air. And before they did that, he needed some time alone. She acquiesced, accepting his decision. She could have shouted down the phone, demanded that he return home immediately. She could have railed against the cold manner of his parting, becoming frantic in her expression of worry and disappointment. But inside her was a niggling doubt

– a question regarding her own behaviour. She sensed something in his voice – a warning. And guilt nudged her conscience, reminding her of her own betrayal. So she let it go, accepting his terse explanation, and hung up. And waited.

The night before Elena married Henry, her mother came into her room and sat on the edge of her bed, a sombre expression coming down over her roomy face, and explained to her daughter how she had married a man she had not loved. This may have been said in English or Spanish, Elena cannot remember which. But whatever tongue Rosario spoke in, it was usually in a stream of rapidly ascending syllables, her little pink tongue and tiny square teeth clacking over consonants, vowels treated to her Mediterranean inflections. Her whole body seemed to lift and move through her sentences, her rounded shoulders rising to a shrug, her little hands – those small fat fingers, delicate and feminine – held up, fanning out, forming shapes, descriptive shapes, with a precision that was evocative and elegant.

It was something that Elena had always known – that her mother did not love her father. Not then, anyway. How she came to this suspicion is less clear. Titbits of conversation overheard through the years. Scalding words of anger that her mother had flung at her father, poisoning the air between them, exasperated and desperate. Or perhaps it was just a feeling, one that had seeped through her consciousness as a child, or maybe even earlier. Was it possible that, as she nestled snugly in her mother's womb, the great heaviness of Rosario's disappointment had reached into that safe shadowy place, rubbing a finger of doubt over her even then?

But that night, of all nights, when excitement tinged with apprehension was threatening to keep her from sleep, Elena remembers the change in her mother's voice. Gone was the gusto and exuberance that seemed to inflate Rosario's speech. Her hands were strangely still, the flamboyant gestures put away. Quietness seemed to descend over the room as Rosario spoke. 'I think you should know, Elena, that when I married your father, I did not love him.'

She delivered these words precisely as if she had given them some thought, as if she had mulled over them for some time before arriving at the decision to enunciate them – to deliver them to her daughter, who was sitting upright in her bed, the chenille bedspread pulled up to her armpits, a startled expression spreading across her face.

'I'm not saying that I regret it, I'm not saying that at all. But I've been thinking a lot about it and I've decided that after all that has happened to you – all that nonsense in Spain – it is only right that I share it with you. People get romantic notions about marriage, they think it is all candles and starlight and roses in the garden. But the reality is very different. Now, Elena, I'm not saying that you don't love Henry. That's not what I'm saying at all. But what I'm trying to say is that love is not the be-all and end-all of marriage. Don't look at me like that, Elena. What I mean is that marriage can go through patches where the love slips away, it disappears. But still it can survive. Your father and I, well – how can I put this? – I wanted to get married and we seemed to get along. He had a good job, good prospects, it seemed like a good idea. It was a practical arrangement. I'm not putting this very well, I know. All I'm saying is that while it is exciting and new now, sometimes things can change between a couple. You have to be prepared for certain times when things will seem dull, empty. But this is just a testing time, you can work through it. And I think that, when it happens, it is best not to hark back to earlier times. To previous romances. Making comparisons. All that business before. I know there was something between you and Adam that seemed special, but it's best not to dwell on it. Nothing good came out of it – remember that. And it wouldn't be fair on Henry, it wouldn't give you two a proper chance. Don't look so upset, Elena. I'm just saying that, if you're sure Henry is the one for you, then wipe away everything that went before. Just forget about it. Let it go.'

The memory of that night washes over Elena now as she sits at her own kitchen table, Sunday afternoon settling around her. She feels sidelined, bombarded by her mother's presence in her kitchen, watching Rosario's small hands as they work through a mound of vegetables, chopping and slicing in rapid movements, her sleeves rolled to the elbows, revealing short brown forearms, muscle rolled in fat, and those small hands – their deftness, their strength.

'You see, the trick is to chop everything really small,' she informs Elena, pausing to turn and glance at her daughter, prodding the air with the small kitchen knife.

She is a small woman with a generous frame. Under her clothing are mounds of sweet-smelling flesh pressed in lavender and camomile. She carries her weight with pride, with aplomb, as if each ounce is a trophy – a testament to what she has endured throughout her life. Her face is warm and generous – a dark Spanish complexion, small black eyes that flash and flicker and act as lethal radar for intercepting facial twitches and body-language signals. She is like a terrier, sniffing out unease and tension, worrying away at them until everything comes spilling out. Elena is not sure that she has the energy to resist today.

Elena remains silent, watching her mother's body shuddering and quaking with each truculent chop of the knife. Today Rosario is wearing a long brown hairy cardigan that reaches her knees and stretches tightly over her rounded back and wide bottom. Her bombastic cooking instructions, the endless stream of conversation runs clackety-clack through the kitchen, bouncing off the tiles and the surface of Elena's skull. In the next room, she can hear her father's soft measured tones as he plays with the children.

'Henry is late,' Rosario remarks loudly over the clatter of her industry.

'Yes.' Elena closes her eyes briefly, steadying herself for what is to come. 'Actually, he won't be joining us.'

'Oh?' Rosario stops what she is doing and looks over at her daughter. 'How's that?'

'He has things to do.'

Rosario waits. For her, this is an insufficient explanation. To miss Sunday lunch, especially when there are guests, requires a serious excuse.

'What things?'

'Does it matter?' Elena asks, a rising exasperation sneaking into her tone.

Rosario silently puts the vegetables on to boil before wiping her hands on the chequered tea towel and moving to the table. Her actions are purposeful and direct. The chair screeches on the kitchen floor as it is dragged back before she drops her weight onto it.

'Now. What is the matter?'

'Nothing's the matter, Rosa. I'm just a little tired, that's all.'

'Tired? Tired?'

Rosario is in the habit of taking the pivotal word from people's sentences and repeating it over and over, a habit Elena finds particularly annoying. 'But why tired? You are just back from holiday. You should be rested.'

'It was a long night. I didn't sleep well.'

'You look terrible. This long face, these dark circles around the eyes. What has happened to you?'

'Nothing.'

'Nothing? Nothing? Aah!' She swats the air with her hand – one of her many Mediterranean gestures. 'With you it's always nothing. You are like a clam, closing so tight around your precious pearls of misery.'

Elena resists the temptation to correct the analogy, watching her mother's face as it squeezes into a tight grimace, her whole body crouching in around this illusory clam before she straightens up and holds out her palms in that gesture of supplication, the one that drives Elena crazy.

'And don't raise your eyes to the ceiling!' she admonishes, undeterred by Elena's glare of indignation. 'There are no answers written up there! Now, have you had a fight – you and Henry?'

'No! No, not exactly.'

'What does that mean?'

Elena's mind drifts back to Friday evening – the last time she saw him – and the coldness that was there, the suppressed rage that poisoned the air between them.

'We haven't had a fight. Nothing that open, anyway. It's just that… we don't seem to be getting along so well lately.'

She waits for Rosario to balk at this, to suck the air in through narrowed lips, to shake her head slowly. But to her credit, she says nothing, reaching into the pocket of her cardigan for her cigarettes. Drawing a saucer towards her, she lights up with slow, deliberate movements. Concentration lines appear in her nut-brown face, but the practised routine of lighting the cigarette and drawing deeply on it, puckering her lips, creases appearing around her mouth, then the long, slow exhalation, creates a calmness. Her body seems to relax, to mellow; it welcomes talk, its softness invites confidences. And Elena finds herself opening up.

'There's no reason to it. None that I'm aware of, anyhow. But lately, it's like everything he does is so irritating, it just gets on my nerves, you know?'

Rosario says nothing, reserving judgement.

'And I'm sure he feels it too. It's not one sided. He visibly tenses when I'm near him. He tiptoes around me. It's almost as if he's afraid of me.'

She thinks of the secrecy that veils his actions, his behaviour, keeping his feelings hidden from her.

'He seems so angry with me. So cold. The other night, when I got home from the reunion and got into bed, I knew that he was awake, but he just turned away from me, blanking me, shutting me out.'

'Reunion? What reunion?' Rosario's black eyes narrow and flicker over her daughter's face.

'It was a reunion of my class in college,' she says, swallowing nervously. 'At the Burlington, on Friday night. One of the girls from college that I bumped into recently told me about it. I thought I'd go along, see what everyone looks like after all this time.'

But even as she says this, she sees the change in her mother's posture, the warmth and concern shrinking away, replaced by something hard and worrisome. A new angry disapproval tainted with fear.

'Was he there?' she asks quietly and sternly.

'Who?'

'You know very well who. Don't play games with me.'

Elena breathes deeply. She has been trying not to think of him. Trying not to picture him sitting in a room somewhere across the city, keeping a dying woman company. 'Yes.'

Rosario stubs out her cigarette with finality. Her head of black and grey squashed curls twitches.

'Stupid girl,' she remarks coldly.

'Don't.' Elena raises a hand in warning, but it is not enough.

'What were you thinking?' Rosario charges in with whispered urgency, keeping her voice low so that the children and their grandfather in the next room cannot hear her. 'What did you possibly hope to achieve by going, by seeing him again?'

'Nothing happened, Mother.'

'Hmmph!'

There is irritation and disbelief in that snort. But, more than anything, there is incredulity in her mother's response. She, who never trusted Adam with his easy manners and his casual grin – that he would be casual with her daughter was one thing, but to break her heart was unforgivable. Rosario witnessed the shock of Elena's return, that small tired body, her pallid complexion and the shadows flickering across her face that spoke of untold miseries, a deep private pain. The sound of weeping in the night, a steadfast refusal to speak of it, the sudden anger at the mention of his name, created a hardness in Rosario. And the thought that Elena would see him again, would willingly put herself in his path, after all that he put her through, incenses Rosario.

'You must be out of your mind.'

'Rosa, just leave it, will you? It's none of your business!'

'And what about Henry? I suppose it's none of his business either?'

'Jesus, I wish I'd never mentioned it,' Elena says.

'No wonder he is angry with you. No wonder the poor man turned away from you when you came home.'

'That's enough!' Elena snaps, rising to her feet and turning her attention to preparing lunch, not wanting to be told what she already fears.

Rosario watches her with beady eyes, worry flickering across her features. 'You're playing with fire,' she says softly before getting up and leaving the room.

Something flashes through Elena's head – a memory of Henry shortly after Ben was born. The baby was difficult, crying non-stop, refusing to be placated, denying sleep. The only way to settle him was by driving around, the hum of the engine and the movement of the car lulling him to sleep. After a fractious afternoon, they sat in the car, looking down over Dublin Bay, the sea stretching across the bay to the regal elegance of Sorrento Terrace, watching gentle waves folding back on themselves in endless motion. From the sky high up over Killiney Hill a hang-glider appeared, gently soaring, weaving his way through the air. They watched in silence, Ben finally asleep in the back seat, Emily subdued by the drive.

'I'd love to be him,' she remembers Henry saying, quietly exhaling.

'Really?'

'Way up there, looking down on the rest of us. God, can you imagine the view?'

'It must be pretty scary.'

'Not scary. Exhilarating. Pure adrenalin. Everything else cleared from your mind, except the moment. That one moment floating above the world.'

She can still recall his earnest expression, the wistful glaze over his eyes. 'Seriously, Elena, have you never wanted to do something wild like paragliding or jumping out of an aeroplane or abseiling down a cliff? Something that makes you feel alive?'

'I already feel alive…'

'No, I mean really alive. Not just existing. Not just day-to-day routine existence. I mean something that makes you feel that you are actually living. That you are actually alive in the universe.'

She laughed at this. At that moment he seemed so young to her, bursting with vitality, a new urgency in his voice.

'Well, before you go jumping out of aeroplanes, can you please remember your responsibilities? You have a wife and two children now, not to mention a mortgage to be repaid.'

As soon as these words were uttered, something in his face changed. It seemed to snap shut, the light in his eyes extinguished. A coolness passed over his features and he looked away from her, leaning forward and turning the key in the ignition.

'Henry, I'm sorry. I didn't mean to…'

'No, it's fine,' he said in a low voice. 'We'd best get the kids back.'

He didn't say a word the whole way home.

Where did these silences come from? Why did they let them spring up, creating a wall between them – impenetrable and cold? In the next room, the voices of her children rise. They love their grandparents, their grandfather in particular. Their love towards him is physical. They throw their bodies at him, clinging to his legs, swinging from his arms, climbing into his lap. And then comes Rosario's voice, telling them to calm down, warning Vincent not to get them overexcited. Do they know, Elena wonders? Can they feel the tension that exists between their parents? Emily has become watchful lately, cautious with her in a way that is unnerving in such a young child. She gets the distinct impression that her daughter is handling her. And as she carves the meat and serves up portions onto each plate, she is struck by the unfairness of their behaviour – hers and Henry's – the irresponsibility of it, the futility, the meanness. His secrecy and coldness and her inability to drag herself out of the past and away from all those unanswered questions. What about the children? she hears a voice ask in a stern minor key – her own voice. What about them?

Dinner passes under a cloud of noise, Emily imparting endless information about her forthcoming First Communion, Ben humming continuously, and there are the usual sounds of people eating – the scraping of cutlery against plates, the clink of glasses and the snuffling sounds of masticating food. Rosario says nothing. She is incapable of small talk. If she cannot say what is on her mind, then she will say nothing at all. Although she is silent, her body is brimming with unspoken anger – Elena can feel it reverberating across the table. She chews slowly and steadily, casting hot, dark sideways glances at her daughter. Vincent eats quickly, sweeping the food up into his mouth, making quiet approving noises. He is a man who enjoys his Sunday roast, perhaps more than most, as he was denied them for so long. There was a time when Rosario would have sooner cut off her arm than cook a Sunday roast. Her diet was filled with fish and pasta and rice, much to her husband's dismay. It was one of her ways of punishing him. But now, in latter years, she has allowed a Sunday roast to slip into her culinary repertoire – a small concession that he accepts warmly. And Elena always makes a special point of cooking one for him whenever he comes for lunch.

When Elena was a child, there were always raised voices – Rosario bellowing, Vincent browbeaten and moody. She can remember the crying and wailing, the accusations and the thin line in her father's face, his lips held tightly together as he weathered the storm. Vincent was the type of man that you might call feckless. Now, in later life, he has mellowed into a kind old gentleman whose grandchildren adore him. But Elena can recall the battles that used to rage around their small house in her childhood, Elena and her brother Luis lying in their beds, trying to block out the sounds from downstairs. Vincent enjoys the occasional glass of port now, but in those days he would often return home after closing time, steaming drunk. And that would start Rosario bellowing, her fits of aggression rising to peaks before slipping away into deep troughs of fretfulness and anxiety.

It was her mother's voice Elena listened to – it travelled a greater distance – and her father said little or nothing, which infuriated Rosario further. He would sit in his armchair, his chin tucked into his chest, waiting for her fury to pass over him, like storm clouds releasing their anger and slowly moving on. They fought about drink and about Vincent's absences. And they fought about money. Rosario bullied and coerced him into handing over his wages. She would sit at the kitchen table, a notebook in front of her, scribbling long columns of figures, a frown on her face.

For as long as Elena can remember her mother was in charge of the family finances. She knew the whereabouts of every last penny and channelled all of Vincent's earnings into various outlets – food, clothes, bills, savings – she controlled everything. As a child, Elena would look at her father slumped in his chair, having handed over his earnings, and he seemed diminished, less of a man. At the time, Elena felt that her mother was a bully. After she had barked her orders at him, Rosario would sit with her sleeves rolled up, poring over her books of figures, her little pink tongue flicking to the corners of her mouth as she added and subtracted, oblivious to his slump in the corner. And Elena resented her for it.

But Elena's parents are different now. Small affections have crept back into their relationship. Elena watches her father topping up her mother's glass of wine, his hand resting momentarily on hers, the fleeting tenderness of the gesture. They live in the same house they have lived in for thirty years – a modest semi with small rooms and conservative furniture and the occasional flourish of drama, like the collection of Venetian masks hanging in the hall or the Spanish swords – sharp, glinting ones – crossed over the mantelpiece. They live among this strange mélange of cultures thrown up onto the rooms of their house – plates hang on walls, wall hangings serve as hearth rugs. They sit and eat dinner together every evening in the small dining room, with napkins threaded through silver napkin rings and milk sipped from Waterford Crystal glasses.

The formality of this arrangement does not strike them as being odd. Elena has overheard them reading to each other on occasion – extracts from newspaper articles or long passages from a book recommended by the Book Club. When Vincent retired a few years ago and decided to spend his retirement as a student, returning to UCD and enrolling in an Arts degree course, Rosario backed his decision wholeheartedly. She read his essays, marvelling at his knowledge of Virgil and Homer. She engaged in arguments with him about the existence of the soul and the proof of being. When he graduated a year ago, she went into town and spent more money on an outfit for his graduation ceremony than she had on her clothes for Elena's wedding and sat proudly in the Tony O'Reilly Hall, clapping loudly, her face flushed with happiness, as her husband mounted the steps to collect his degree. She has had it framed since and it sits majestically on the wall in their sitting room. Rosario refers to him proudly as 'an academic'.

Elena regards them from across the table – her father's grave, stoic features, her mother's ponderous form. Her mother did not love her father on the day that she married him, but she loves him now. That much is evident. And as Elena watches them sitting closely together, an easy hum of love weaving in the air between them, she hears the key sliding in the lock of the front door. Her parents look up as the dining-room door opens. Elena doesn't need to turn around. She knows by their expressions and by her own heart – beating high and light near the surface of her chest – that it is Henry.

9

IT IS HER mother's idea to take the children. She reacts quickly, organising overnight bags, getting them into their coats and hats and hurries them out the door. Henry's ghostly demeanour must have frightened her into action, Elena suspects, feeding her worries and hastening her desire to leave them to it. Alone in the house together with no distractions, Rosario would assume they would have no other choice than to talk it out, to get to the nub of the issue. And as the front door closes firmly, leaving them in silence, Elena feels her heart give out a short sideways knock in anticipation of what is coming next. Henry sits in the chair staring straight ahead of him, elbows on the table, his hands clasped together as if in prayer. She wills herself to remain still, to remain calm, as she watches him, the fear creeping around his eyes that refuse to return her gaze.

'Where have you been?' she asks quietly, trying to keep her voice steady.

He breathes deeply, preparing himself, and stares intently at the back of his hands.

'Wexford,' he answers tonelessly. 'I stayed in a B&B last night. On my own,' he adds, as if she might have considered otherwise.

There are so many questions she wants to ask him, all of them flooding her consciousness, tumbling forward, clamouring to be heard. Why did you go? she wants to ask. What made you leave our bed while I was still sleeping and disappear without so much as a note written in explanation? Why have you grown so cold towards me? But the fear of what answers she might hear keeps them down. She waits for him to speak, and when he does, it is in a voice she scarcely recognises – hoarse, choking on his words, a quaver in his voice that speaks of barely suppressed emotion.

'I needed some time away,' he tells her, 'to try and get my head together. To try and sort out my thoughts, to organise how I felt.'

The practicality with which he approaches his feelings makes her balk.

'I've been trying to work out a way of telling you,' he continues, 'but it seems that no matter which way I put it, it sounds equally bad.'

He leans forward, pressing his mouth to his fist, biting it, and Elena feels a new surge of panic rising in her stomach as she realises that, whatever he is about to tell her, it is not something she has anticipated. During his absence, her mind has travelled back over the past few months, tracing the growing prickliness between them, all these thorns that have sprouted. He has grown bored of me, she has thought. We have grown bored of each other. We have nothing left to talk about anymore. We are all talked out. And there were other thoughts – dark thoughts involving third parties. Perhaps he has someone else? It is possible. His work brings him into contact with new people all the time. And he is an attractive man – she is still aware of that – with his blue eyes and solid build, the warmth of his smile. Not that he has been smiling much lately. But while these theories were worrisome in themselves, there was no proof that they were true – no telltale stains or suspicious scents on his clothing, no whispered phone calls in the middle of the night. There remained a kernel of hope. If they have grown bored of each other, then new subjects of interest could be discovered. The spark can be rekindled if it has been extinguished. These are things they can attempt to rectify.

But looking at Henry now, the tired hunch of his shoulders, his face lined with melancholy, he seems so defeated, and she knows that whatever it is that is about to emerge is something they might not be able to resolve.

'You're leaving me,' she says suddenly, surprising them both with the baldness of the statement flung out over the empty plates, the debris of Sunday lunch sitting between them, marshalling this exchange.

He seems shocked, his eyes blinking with disbelief as he brings himself to look at her for the first time since his return. 'No. God, no!' he says emphatically. 'That's the last thing I want. That's not it at all! How could you think that, Elena?'

'Well, what am I supposed to think?' she blurts out. 'You've been tiptoeing around me for months, you avoid being alone with me and when we're together you act like you're afraid of me, shrinking from me like I'm some kind of ogre. I mean, Jesus! I don't know what's going on in your head half the time, Henry. And then… and then… you sneak out of the house before I'm even awake, you don't let anyone know where you're going and then I get this phone call in the middle of the night, telling me you need space to sort your thoughts out? What conclusions am I supposed to draw from that? You tell me! You tell me, Henry!'

She pauses, letting the vitriol of her words hang in the air between them. Her sudden anger leaves her shaking. These words that have been building inside her, suddenly released, leave her feeling empty and colourless. There are more words, more questions lining up to be shot out at him, but she steadies herself, waiting for him to respond.

He nods slowly, bringing his arms down from the table, briefly sweeping at his hair, before resting his hands on his thighs. 'You're right,' he says slowly. 'You're right.'

He pauses, as if reflecting on how quiet and distant he has been, how withdrawn, and she thinks she sees regret in his expression.

'I wish to God I'd talked to you before,' he says, shaking his head, his eyes lowered to the table. 'I've been dreading this – you've no idea…'

Tell me what's wrong, she silently demands of him.

'I just wanted things to be all right between us. I didn't want to worry you…'

'You're worrying me now, Henry.'

'I know. I know. But… God, this is so hard…'

He raises a hand to rub his temple and she notices that it is shaking. His whole body seems sprung with coiled nerves. 'If you only knew,' he says, looking up at her suddenly, the words emerging with an urgency that surprises her, 'how many times I tried to talk to you, tried to tell you about this.'

'When?' she asks, eyebrows knitted with confusion.

'I don't know, loads of times. Like the other night – Friday night –

when I came in and you were in the bathroom with Emily. I wanted to say it to you then.'

'So why didn't you?'

'Because of how you were, so angry, so closed off to me.'

Elena feels that they are straying from the point and opens her mouth to ask him yet again what it is that he can't tell her, but he is there before her, with another accusation. 'So many times I've tried to open up to you.'

'Then why didn't you?' she asks, exasperated.

'I couldn't.'

She is stung by this remark, feeling that he is somehow blaming her – claiming that she has not been receptive to him, that her behaviour has encouraged his silence. She is resentful of the implication. 'I tried calling you,' she says bullishly. 'All day yesterday, I kept trying and trying.'

'I threw my mobile in a lake.'

She stares at him, at the slow smile creeping over his face, the faraway gaze in his eyes as his mind trips back in time.

'What? Why did you do that?'

She starts feeling truly alarmed, watching him shrug off an answer, as if he is past caring.

'Henry? For God's sake! Tell me what is going on!'

And then he looks at her clear in the face and tells her that he loves her. She cannot remember the last time she heard him say those three words to her, and the realisation of this makes her want to cry. But she knows that, while there is truth in his voice, he is saying those words as a preface to what comes next, to soften the blow.

'Tell me,' she whispers, steeling herself for his confession.

But the words that emerge from his mouth are muffled by the hand that covers it, and she has to ask him to repeat them.

'I've lost the house!' she hears him say, and this time the words are blurted out as his voice cracks with emotion, his mouth gasping for breath, tears that come so suddenly that they seem to splutter out, his face becoming a mask of piteous suffering. And while his body shudders in front of her, unburdened of its secret, she stares at him, confused, not understanding what it is he is talking about.

'What?' she asks, shaking her head. 'What are you talking about, Henry? What house?'

He gathers his breath, a hand swipes at his nose and he looks at her, his gaze steadying. 'This house,' he states, as if it were obvious.

'But how can you have lost it? What do you mean? You can't just lose a house.'

She looks at him incredulously, and he holds her gaze and she sees the shadows entering his eyes. 'I haven't made the mortgage repayments. I haven't been able to.'

'How many have you missed?'

'A few.'

Her heart skips a beat.

'But there's money... the money in the savings account... we can dip into that...'

She watches him shake his head slowly, and her chest tightens as she realises that there is no money. That that money is already gone.

A wave of nausea crashes over her and she thinks she is going to be sick.

She listens to him in silence, listens to the cold, harsh tones of his explanation, feeling the angry bitterness of the secrets he has kept from her – the recklessness of his investments, the losses he has suffered, the unpaid mortgage, the mounting debts, his anguish and despair at having to tell her, finally, that they have lost the house.

The first time she saw Henry cry was when Emily was nine months old. An accident – that's all it was; one of those stupid things born out of a temporary lapse in concentration and an active, inquisitive child. It was a misunderstanding, really – each of them thought that the other had strapped her into her high chair. She was a hyperactive baby, always reaching for things out of her grasp, discontent with what was at hand. She was crawling at eight months, eager to find her way around. Elena can still hear that deafening thud as she fell, the cold, hard smack of her head hitting the table. And the roars that followed – pained and piteous. Henry reacted quickly, swooping her up in his arms and hurrying to the sink. The blood came thick and fast – an angry wound gaping through her hairline.

Elena was frozen to the spot, stricken with a sudden terror. It was only later that she remembered Henry's practicality, his cool, swift actions – wrapping a blanket around Emily, pressing a cold towel to the wound and pushing Elena to get into the car quickly. They sat together in the waiting room of Casualty, overwhelmed by anguish;

she held Henry's hand in hers, kneading it, helpless and bereft of comfort. His face was grey, a stricken look taking over his features. As the doctor informed them that Emily was going to be all right, that there were no fractures, nothing that could not be stitched back together, Elena recalls Henry's face dissolving under the weight of relief. His head sank into his hands and he moaned softly, his whole body jerking with emotion, a strangled cry in the back of his throat. 'Thank God,' he said softly, over and over, and when he looked up at her she watched tears rolling down his cheeks, his eyes filming over as he shook his head violently, and she felt her heart seize with love for him.

But this afternoon, as a drizzle of rain patterns the window and she watches Henry's tears falling piteously, she does not feel love or a sudden compassion. She does not feel compelled to move towards him, to take his hands in hers, to smooth his hair with her fingers. Instead, she feels removed, as if it is a stranger sitting there, not the man she has been married to for eight years. *Who are you?* she wants to ask. *Do I even know you at all?*

Elena rises slowly and picks up the stack of plates still covered in congealed gravy and flecks of cold chicken and potatoes and carries them mechanically into the kitchen. As she scrapes the remains of dinner into the bin, she can hear the sound of her husband weeping in the next room. He has been crying for over ten minutes. His face has grown red and damp with tears that he sporadically dashes away with a used napkin from the table – her mother's, she imagines, as she was sitting nearest to him. When she returns to the dining room, she knows she will be confronted with the vision of Henry's body – shuddering and broken – heaving with the weight of his anguish, racked by the revelation of his terrible secret.

But right now, Elena cannot look upon that sight. She cannot cope with her husband's great sadness. Her body is numb, stiffening against the blows it has received, defensively willing itself to remain calm. There are no tears. She cannot feel the full force of her anguish. Not yet. Something is holding it back, so she moves about the kitchen in the manner of a woman anxious to clean up a mess, impatient for order to be returned, stacking the dishwasher, scrubbing out pots and wiping off counters with vigour.

She can feel his presence in the kitchen behind her. The air seems to shrink, like a great heaviness has entered the space, sucking all the air from the room. She looks up at the window above the sink. Grey clouds stretch across the sky, moving swiftly, blown by the wind. He seems to be waiting for something – her reaction, she supposes. For while he explained to her in forthright sentences what has happened – his very pragmatism in the midst of all that emotion baffling in itself – she sat, paralysed by her own bewildered silence.

He clears his throat to announce his presence and she turns slowly to face him. They regard each other cautiously over the space and distance between them.

'Well?' he asks sheepishly. 'Aren't you going to say anything?'

She has been asked that question before – a variant of that question. But it wasn't Henry then. 'For God's sake, say something, will you?' Adam demanded, a desperate plea in his voice. There was rain that day too, cast against the window in long grey threads. But what could she have said then? How could he have expected her to say anything when all the love and hope had been knocked out of her, as surely as if he had punched her?

'I'm not sure what to say,' she says now, finding her voice.

'Please, Elena. Please say something – get angry with me. Get upset. Anything except this awful bloody silence!'

She shakes her head slowly, crossing her arms, hugging herself and staring at her feet. 'It's all such a shock,' she says slowly. 'I haven't really taken it in yet.'

He nods and leans briefly on the back of one of the kitchen chairs. He seems tall and ungainly under the low ceiling. His face is creased with worry and uncertainty. He shrinks from her; his guilt is draped around him, its weight lowering his head. Neither of them is sure of what to do next, and in the absence of anything else, Elena puts the kettle on and makes tea. They sit opposite each other at the kitchen table, two steaming mugs between them, and they begin to talk.

'Is it really that bad?' she asks tentatively, still not wanting to believe, clinging to a glimmer of hope.

He nods slowly, averting his gaze, and there is something defeatist in this gesture that stirs a sudden angry incomprehension in her. 'How long have we got?' she asks in a small voice, shrinking from the answer.

'I'm meeting with the bank on Wednesday. Unless I can come up with something, then…' His voice breaks off. He cannot bring himself to finish the sentence.

'But our savings?'

He shakes his head slowly.

'What have you done with them?' she asks, controlling her voice.

His eyes flicker over her face, and then drop to the table as he starts to tell her.

'It was an investment,' he says quietly. 'One that I'd heard about, I'd been tipped off about. It seemed like a sure thing.'

'Did it?' she says, and the words emerge punched with sarcasm. 'And how much did you invest, Henry? Hmm? How much of our savings went into this tip-off?'

He swallows. 'All of them.'

'All of them,' she repeats. The words catch in her throat.

'And more.'

Her heart feels as if it is travelling up into her throat.

'I borrowed some money – for the investment – I borrowed it against the house.'

She groans softly, the pain of this information seeping through her body. And with it comes the first pang of regret that she allowed this to happen, that she was blind to it, happily relinquishing control of their finances to him. She feels a new anger gathering inside her – anger at her own wilful ignorance, her own pathetic surrender of their assets into his control.

'How could you let this happen?' she asks him, raising her palms, feeling the fury rumbling inside her. 'How did you allow things to get so out of control?'

'I don't know. I just… I kept thinking that it would change, that my luck would change. I kept hoping things would improve, that if I could turn things around…'

'So you ploughed money – our money – into schemes that had no guarantees, that were risky?'

'But they could have worked out,' he argues suddenly. 'How was I to know that they wouldn't? I mean, if they had worked out, you'd be thanking me now. We'd have been laughing all the way to the bank.'

Her stomach twists, a spasm of shocked anger. 'How can you be so naïve?' she demands, enraged by his casual refusal to fully acknowledge the idiocy of what he has done. 'How long has this been going on for?'

He shakes his head. 'Maybe a year. I don't know. I have made some profits,' he says defensively. 'Some of the shares I bought have made money.'

'But you've lost more than we could afford!' Her voice rises shrilly. 'Henry, you've lost our house! Our home! Where are we supposed to live? What's going to happen to us? How can you sit here and argue over piddling shares when we are going to be homeless?'

Her body twitches with rage, a great tide of fury washing over her.

She would like to hit him, to reach out and smack him hard across his face. His irresponsibility, his blind stupidity seems incomprehensible to her.

'I never meant for it to get so out of hand. I wanted so badly to make it work, to please you, to impress you. It was stupid, desperate. But I never meant to hurt you, you or the kids. That was never my intention. You mustn't think that.'

His voice rings with a pained sincerity and she sees the sorrow in his face. His body slumps over his tea and her rage seems to subside momentarily, replaced by a new and sudden longing to reach out and touch the side of his face.

'Why didn't you tell me?' she asks quietly and plaintively. 'Why did you wait until now to let me know? I might have been able to help.'

He bows his head, raises a hand to his hair. 'I couldn't,' he says. 'I thought about it so many times. I tried to, but...'

'But what?'

'I was afraid to. I didn't want to frighten you. I didn't want you to change the way you feel about me, to change the way you look at me – the way you're looking at me now. And I kept thinking that if I could just get myself out of this hole, then things would start to get better between us.' His words wound her, and she stares at the steam wafting lazily from the mug warming her hands. 'And if it hadn't been for that one sour deal – that bloody Hua Hin Development – I might have been able to turn things around.'

She sucks in her breath as it dawns on her what the investment is. 'Oh my God,' she says, her hand raised to her chest. 'It's that Asian deal, isn't it? The one that Shane Smith told you about? That's the one you lost our money on. Isn't it? Isn't it?'

He nods slowly, avoiding the furious disbelief in her eyes.

'How could you be so stupid?' her voice thunders. Her body is engulfed with rage. 'You stupid, stupid fool! After I told you! After I specifically said right here – right here in this kitchen! – I said that it was a ridiculous idea, some feather-brained scheme designed to dupe ignorant twits like you!' She feels convulsed by her gathering fury. It trammels and burns her insides, unleashing a seething stream of vitriol. 'Even I could have told you that it was a scam. But you, with all your qualifications, with all your bloody experience, couldn't see what was right in front of your face. Jesus Christ, Henry! Even Emily could have told you that! But oh, no, you just had to ride in behind Shane, didn't you? Always running to keep up with him. When are you going to realise that he is in a different league to you? When are you going to cop on to the fact that you can't trust him? That you would take his advice over your own wife's...' Her voice softens. 'That you would listen to him instead of me? Henry. That you would open up to him instead of to me?'

His expression has been changing as he has listened to her, and now he glances up at her and she sees the tightness in his skin, a creeping wariness in his eyes.

'Well, you haven't exactly made it easy for me,' he says quietly, his face closing sharply. His tears are all gone now.

'What do you mean by that?'

'Well...' He sits back expansively, thrusting out his chest, squaring up to her, his posture changing to regain some lost pride. 'If I haven't opened up to you, it's probably because of the way you've been. I could just as easily say that you have been cold lately, and secretive.'

His eyes flash dangerously and she fears where he will go with this.

'You know what I'm talking about. You've been wrapped up in yourself ever since you heard about that bloody reunion. Getting lost in the past, shutting me out like you always do. I watch you sometimes, your eyes staring into the distance; you don't see anything. Just that bloody sorrowful look coming over your face. And I know that you're thinking of him.'

'Don't you dare bring him into this.'

'Oh, of course not,' he says viciously, raising his hands in mock surrender. 'We mustn't talk about Adam, must we? That's against the rules. It doesn't matter that you spent all night with him on Friday, so long as I don't mention it!'

'That's not true.'

'Isn't it? So where were you, then? Hmm? Come on, I'm all ears.'

'It wasn't like that.'

'Of course it wasn't. You always have an excuse, don't you, Elena? That's when you deign to offer one. Most of the time I have to content myself with your bloody silence.'

'There is nothing to discuss.'

'And why is that, hmm? Why will you not discuss it? You've never been prepared to talk about him and all that happened in Spain.'

'I told you what happened—'

'Once. And only the briefest version. And I wouldn't even mind if you let go of it, if you could just forget about all that. It wouldn't bother me half so much, believe me. But you can't seem to, Elena. If you could only see yourself. You've been so distracted since you got that invitation – no, worse that that, you've been obsessed! Jesus, the angst over that one bloody night! And don't give me that crap about wanting to meet up with other classmates, relive old times and all that, because I'm not buying it. You went because you wanted to see him.'

His eyes burn with fury, and she realises there's no point in denying it. 'All right,' she says softly. 'I admit it. I wanted to see him. But I wanted you with me.'

'Ha!'

'It's true! I wanted you there to see that what I have with you is far better than what I ever had with him.'

He looks at her intently. 'Is it? Do you really believe that?'

'Of course.' She tries to sound convincing. 'It's different…' She trails off, and his face darkens.

'I don't believe you,' he says softly as he rises from the table and leaves the room.

Evening is growing around her, but it is still bright outside; the rain clouds have passed over and she decides to sit in the garden. When they first bought the house on Windsor Terrace, it was the garden that she marvelled at. The indulgence of space, after the poky stamp of a garden at the back of her parents' semi, was a revelation. When taking a break from the endless cycle of cleaning and painting and varnishing, she would wander around the garden, holding a mug of tea to her chest, peering speculatively at nameless plants and bushes, feeling tired but triumphant. She had plans for this space – something untamed and beautiful. She envisioned grasses, a haze of fuzzy blue lining the walls, flaming blossoms of montbresia nodding their heads, the reckless wildness of Virginia creeper. Peering over the fence at her neighbour's garden, she spied restrained lawns, well-pruned rose bushes, careful rockeries and stately water features – cherubs spouting small bursts of water into mossy ponds. But what she had in mind was something less manicured, a garden that was wilful and unconfined, a space she could breathe in.

'I want it to look like a meadow,' she told Henry one morning.

'I see,' he intoned, not looking up from his paper. 'And will there be a pony grazing in the corner?'

Her enthusiasm for the garden was mildly amusing to him. Her earnest endeavours to create a haven were something he joked about to their friends. 'Elena keeps getting lost in the shrubbery,' he remarked lightly. 'Green fingers? Her arms have turned green up to the elbows.'

But there was pride in her efforts, and the results were rewarding. She had not reckoned with this creative side, this new-found ability to manipulate nature, to encourage growth.

Looking around the garden as it succumbs to the gentle decay of autumn, Elena sees the spot in the middle of the lawn where she used to spread a tartan rug and lay baby Emily down, letting her kick around under the gentle heat of the sun. Those soft summer days, when Henry was at work and it seemed to her that they were the only ones at home on the whole street, she felt a warmth passing through her, a gentle happiness, alone with her baby in the garden, kneeling and bending, tending to its needs. And at that time she had no desire to be anywhere else. Happy in the present, untouched by any alien desires or ancient wants, she pottered around her garden during the day, proudly showing off her handiwork when Henry came home in the evenings.

Lately, she has planted an herb garden in the corner by the kitchen window. Basil, thyme, dill and rosemary all compete for space in the small raised bed, this bricked-in space she has created with cement blocks her father-in-law gave her. His view of her gardening was not altogether favourable. He viewed the wild grasses and the catapulting nasturtia with a disdainful eye. He pointed out shrubs that needed to be cut back. He held forth on the necessity for order in a garden – clean lines and humble plantings. He frowned on the exoticism of the clematis sprawling over the back wall and sniffed at the potted potato plants on the windowsills.

After Emily was born, she planted sweet pea – Emily's birth flower – in the box along the fence. It bloomed in busy tendrils, explosions of pink and purple, delicate and feminine. Daffodil is Ben's birth flower, but at the mention of planting them alongside the opposing fence, Dan openly balked.

'Bit girlie, isn't it?' he remarked astringently, his lip curling.

'He has a point,' Henry chimed in.

And she allowed herself to be swayed.

But lately, she has reversed her decision. Daffodil suits Ben's personality – bright, cheerful and resilient. An everyman flower. A no-nonsense flower.

She looks about the garden for a suitable place and her eyes light on the grass around the cherry blossom. She will wait until the winter is over, after the last frost when the earth begins to soften, and then she will plant them.

And as quickly as her mind wandered into that sleepy dreamy state, it is snapped back again to the cold reality that, when springtime rubs its soft breezes over her garden, it will no longer be hers. All of this – this investment of labour, of love, everything – will be gone. The realisation leaves her gasping.

He is in the kitchen when she comes in from the garden, hunched over a giant sandwich, its contents spilling out onto the plate beneath as he bites into it. He eats hungrily, voraciously, his jaw working furiously. He doesn't notice her for a moment; his concentration keeps him focused on his meal. He appears oblivious to the seething rage she feels pumping in her head. His early sorrow, the tears and lamentations of the afternoon, seems to have given way to this insistent, compelling need to eat. And now, when the true horror of what he has done has finally started to sink in for her, she is to be denied any act of contrition on his part. The flashing anger passing through her, the whittled pain of imminent loss, rises inside her into a ferocious red jet of rage, spurting up through her body, thundering in her skull.

He glances up at her as she stands in the doorway, clenching and unclenching her fists.

'There you are,' he says, swallowing loudly. 'God, I was starving. Can I fix you something to eat?'

She stares at him incredulously. The mundanity of his remarks, the sheer pedestrian practicality enrages her. His soft-cheeked face, that sleepy look of satiated hunger washing over him, vulcanises her fury.

'No!' she shrieks, her body bending forward with the force of this explosive syllable. She rushes at him, wrenching the sandwich from his hand, and it flies across the room, splattering against the wall – a cold splash of coleslaw is momentarily suspended on the cool plaster before it begins to drip to the floor. It is chased by a brown spray of tea as the mug shatters against the wall. She is batting at him with her bare hands and, through the blur of her tears, she sees his hands raised to protect his head from her fury as he pulls himself out of the chair. He is a good six inches taller than her, but powered by her rage she flings herself at him, slapping and kicking, clawing at him, and all the while shouting, screaming, her face a ruddy liquid mass of anguish. 'How could you?' she rages. 'How could you do this?' He grabs hold of her wrists and she feels the strength of his hands as he pins them to her sides, holding her at a distance from his own body.

His expression registers briefly with her. She sees the fear in his eyes, the startled hurt. Her energy is spent and she steps away from him, shaking her head slowly, incomprehensibly, before silently retreating from the room.

After Elena brought Henry home to meet her parents for the first time, she remembers how her mother simply said 'Oh', her voice lilting approvingly up and then down again through the syllable. Rosario liked him from the start. Later, she told Elena that she had been struck by his balance. Yes, he was well mannered and charming, with a certain embarrassed gaucheness about his movements and demeanour, but there was something grounded about him. 'Steady' was the word she used to describe him.

In the early days of their marriage, Elena frequently mentioned his steadiness, his balance – deliberately, proudly, interjecting it in conversation. Even as recently as Friday night, she heard herself referring to him as solid, reliable. 'He's a good man,' she said to Adam, 'solid, dependable.' Now, as she lies curled up on their bed, tears standing in her eyes, she is forced to revise her idea of him.

Her display of temper has exhausted her. She wants to cry ferociously, helplessly, but feels bereft of energy. A small voice inside her whispers that it was unfair – her response to Henry and his sandwich. She realises that he must feel a measure of relief, now that he has told her, now that he has unburdened his dreadful secret. But her anger is too new to let go of – it gushes and sprays and erodes at her insides. Anger at Henry – but also at herself, for being stupid enough to think that surrendering her participation in the financial side of their marriage would make it a better marriage. That it would prevent her from turning into her mother.

Lying in the quiet darkness of their bedroom, she recalls his accusations of coldness, of distraction and obsession with the past. She is not sure she can defend herself against his charges. How did these silences jump up between them, creating this rift, this chasm in communication? Surely there was a moment when she wanted to question him, to point it out to him, to open it up for observation? But the time when she might have begun such a discussion passed. She failed to seize the moment when the question possessed relevance or promise. This one small silence on her part opened to a series of silences, accepted and not challenged by either of them. The poison of inertia seeped into their home.

A grey, comfortless sky presses through the trees outside the window. The house is quiet, stupefyingly quiet. The air feels oppressive. She wants to sleep. But from somewhere deep inside her comes a longing – a physical need to curl up against someone, to feel the warmth of another wrapping around her, to hear a soft voice whispering a litany of comforts into her hair. As she folds into the centre of the bed, the door opens and Henry is standing over her. Looking up, she sees the coolness of his face, his body rigid as he holds the phone out stiffly towards her.

'It's him,' he says shortly, a white rage smothering his features as he drops the phone on the bed beside her and walks from the room.

ADAM

10

IN THE END, she died alone, passing away before he got to the hospital – a matter of minutes, they told him. 'I'm so sorry,' a nurse with a pretty turned-up nose said to him, squeezing his arm. Afterwards, he wondered if her apology had more to do with the fact that he had missed his mother's passing by a few moments than with the fact of her passing itself. It caused a sudden unexpected pain – to know that, while he sat at the traffic lights on the Merrion Road, his mother was slipping away from him. Sometimes, Adam thinks that his whole life has been cursed by poor timing.

They let him sit with her for a while, saying his goodbyes to her cooling body. He looked down at the blue and purple veins threaded through her bony hands and wondered whether he should touch them. She had always been skinny – wiry, he supposes, is the correct term – her body a compacted mass of sinew and nerves and stretched, taut muscle; a strong woman, despite her birdlike appearance. The weakened state he had found her in on his return home from America had shocked him deeply. This was not the woman he remembered. He leaned his elbows on the bed and his eyes passed over the orange powder compressed into the lines and creases of her face – the clumsy eyeliner, like a child had done it, painting black arcs over those aqueous green eyes. Her eyebrows had long departed, succumbing terminally to the tweezers, replaced by kohl marks – hard and cutting through her brow. And those thin lips, sprouting creases on all sides, shaded with a frosty layer of ice-pink lipstick. In death, she looked even less like herself, lost underneath all that make-up, and slightly ridiculous in a blue nightie ruffled with frills, like something a child would wear. His mother, with her abrasive nature, her sharp, quizzical eyes and astringent tongue, would never have picked this for herself. He felt shot through with guilt that it had come to this.

It was not until later, after they had taken her away and he had contacted those few people who needed to be told and had spoken with the funeral directors about the arrangements, that he found himself alone and suddenly overcome with grief. Tears sprang in his eyes, a cry thundering in his chest. He felt an ache in his body, a remorseful pain that circulated through him before settling in a tight band around his head. Up until this moment, he hadn't thought he loved his mother. She had been sharp, cutting and unforgiving. When he was a boy, she had been reluctant to show him physical affection. She spurned his sticky hugs and childish kisses, complaining about getting dirt on her clothes. He came to understand a pat on the head as affection, or a brisk rub on the back or tousle of hair. As a teenager, he had found her meddlesome and demanding. She seemed resentful of his need to get out, to be with other people. She became whiney and clingy, reminding him that he was the only one she had in the world. He endured a litany of abuse against a father he had never known – this faceless, shadowy figure demonised by his mother, this deserter who had abandoned her before their child had even been born. And when Adam went to Spain, he proved to her what she had always suspected – that he was just like his father. He can remember her spitting those words at him – the stinging hurt of betrayal in her voice, a cold fury in those glacial eyes. He had hated her for it.

But some link had remained, a tenuous thread of family strung between them that had not been severed, despite the best efforts of both of them. When he is feeling generous, Adam is willing to offer the age gap between them as an excuse. His mother was in her forties by the time he was born. Too old to care for a new life, he believes. Sitting in the dark, feeling the tug of this thread, he needed suddenly to reach out, to connect with someone. Someone familiar. Someone who had known his mother, who understood the difficult twist of love that had existed between them.

Her husband answered. This was something Adam had not expected. His voice was a shock and left Adam momentarily speechless. The voice was deep and stretched with solemnity, not the clipped, anxious tones he had somehow imagined. Feeling bold and suddenly reckless, Adam announced himself and asked to speak with Elena. There was a wealth of meaning in the pause that followed, a passive aggression in the shallow breathing down the line. He felt the icy shards of the words 'Hold on a moment' echoing through the silence that followed. And then her voice on the line. She sounded dazed, as if woken from sleep. It was only later – after they had spoken, after he had told her of his mother's death, had entreated her to meet with him, even squeezed a few tears to add weight to his plea – that he concluded she was not sleepy but stunned. Incredulous at his audacity to ring again, and this time to speak to her husband. The temerity! The recklessness of it! But that was afterwards, when it occurred to him. And by that stage it didn't matter. She would meet with him. He had made her promise. What happened with her husband was of little consequence to him.

He arranged to meet her in Café en Seine, a large, roomy venue with a dark-wood floor and lofty ceiling. There is noise here, it bustles with shoppers, the clatter of coffee cups, the insistent ring of foreign languages behind the counter. A neutral venue. He is early and finds a seat at a side table with his back to the wall. He orders a cappuccino and fiddles with the packets of sugar in front of him – a nervous need to keep his hands occupied. He used to smoke. That first summer in Spain when everyone around him was smoking, he felt compelled to join in, driven by a need to belong.

He glances at his watch. Eleven forty. Another twenty minutes before she is due to arrive. He will make his cappuccino stretch.

His thoughts return to Friday night and that green dress, the neat haircut, her demure expression; but there was wildness in her eyes – a quiet, simmering rage. Sadness too. He would like to believe that it was a nostalgic kind of grief, like he has felt – grief for all that they have wasted. He recalls how she held her body stiffly – wary of him, and wary of what messages she might be sending him. And how her body relaxed with a few drinks, releasing her anger. He felt the force of her vitriol, understood it. And later, when they were alone and the morning crept up around them, her body seemed to wilt, as if she hadn't the strength to maintain her anger. She lay limply by his side, her defences put away, an honest, clean voice rising from her. Her sadness was palpable – this unhappiness she felt, this unnamed discontent. He wanted her to stay. He wanted to slip his hands under her clothes and feel the smooth warmth of her skin. He wanted to lift her dress up over her head and fold himself around that long-remembered body. But he held back. He knew not to rush her. He knew better than to frighten her.

Perhaps the first phone call from the hospital was a mistake. But he was bored to tears and rigid with impatience, and standing in the echoing corridor, listening to her icy tones, he pictured her sitting clenched over the phone, repelling his unspoken demands, a new frustration in her voice. But he knew it wasn't over between them. He knew that this was not how it would end. Too much had been said that night, secrets whispered in the half light, confidences given, admissions made, a breakdown of emotions, a breakthrough. But more than anything else, he had felt the soft balmy warmth of her forgiveness. She hadn't said it, hadn't uttered those exact words, but it was there, wafting through the room, seeping into the space between them. He had felt it.

The coffee machine is noisy. He listens to the hum and spit of milk frothing, the harsh grating of coffee being ground, its rich aroma rising and sweeping through the length of the building. Looking around him, he takes in the details of his surroundings – the long stretch of the bar, the bronzed statues holding torches, the oversized plants growing out of enormous pots, lush explosions of greenery. The light in here is dim. It casts a faint glow over gilt-edged mirrors, intricate tile mosaics and wrought-iron railings twisting and curling, the whole place awash with art-nouveau chic. It occurs to him why he chose this place to meet her. Because of the similarities. The same dimness around pools of light, the same swirling patterns and casual elegance, the same timelessness, the same noises and smells.

Having made the connection, his mind wanders, drifting through years of events until he is back there. He was waiting for her then, too.

*

It is a sunny afternoon and he feels a flurry of wind rushing up to greet him as he turns from the Avenida Diagonal onto the Paseig de Gracia. The breeze is warm in the September sun, but the city is no longer gripped by the sultry heat that claimed it all summer. Adam feels the air breathing up his T-shirt, his bag feels light on his back. Autumn is in the air today, whispering of an imminent snap in the weather, and he breathes it in, his body welcoming the change, feeling it rinse through him, puffing out his lungs that have felt dry and strangled by the deadly heat of the days and the airless, dusty nights of the last few months.

Today, Barcelona is showing him her good side. Today, she is smiling for him. The Paseig de Gracia hums with life, it buzzes around him as he saunters into the heart of the city. Traffic swarms on either side of him, kamikaze motorcyclists, barelegged girls on scooters, the air punctuated with horns blowing, the impatience of motorists gathering and bursting. A queue has formed outside La Pedrera, tourists craning their necks to look up at Gaudi's work, the bulbous rock swelling into ripples, iron manipulated into tangled shapes like decaying leaves cleaving their way across the façade and dripping over balconies. Adam strolls past, the wind whipping his hair. He walks without purpose, a faint beat of excitement fluttering in his chest. He could have taken the metro or cut down through some of the quieter alleys of Eixample, but he has time to kill and languishes in the luxury of ambling through the busy streets.

Further down, the blues and greens of the broken ceramics covering the Casa Battlo glitter and sparkle in the sun. He eyes it up as he waits at a pedestrian crossing – the tiled roof like the scales on a lizard's back, the bubbles on the walls, an aquatic house, the stone façade hanging in folds like skin. But he does not linger to admire it – he has done that already, months ago, when he wandered wide eyed through the city, marvelling at her beauties and eccentricities. Then he was a stranger, a tourist; pale faced and eager, he stood out among the brown-skinned sons of Catalonia. He didn't fit in. Not like Elena, with her chocolate-brown hair and her skin scorched into darkness by the sun. For once, he was the one who stood out, it was his colouring that marked him out as being different, and he basked in the exoticism that went with it, the interest it provoked. He has enjoyed it, catching people's eyes as they size him up, questioning glances that read his colouring, his height, his northern European looks, and conclude quickly that he isn't one of them. It thrills him. To be apart, to be different. Suddenly aware of his identity, he basks in it, revelling in the wealth of history and culture and language he kept stored within his genes, like a secret he held. But as Barcelona revealed her own secrets to him, he too let go of his, opening up to her, breathing her in.

Today he feels a part of the city, not just a visitor. Today he feels her folding around him, breathing warmly against his neck like a lover. The sun shines on Las Ramblas, illuminating the street performers as they adopt their poses – a gilded Cleopatra, a bronzed Roman centurion on a plinth, a bloody-mouthed Dracula whose eyeballs widen with hunger. The birds trapped in the cages that line the street twitter and squawk, a desperate flap of wings against wire mesh. From La Boqueria comes the animated hum of swift industry as the busy market, with its stalls of neatly displayed fruit and gory animal parts hanging from hooks, conducts its business.

He glances at his watch as he turns away from Las Ramblas and strolls onto Carre de Ferran. It is almost two o'clock. She will be there soon. And then in another couple of hours he will be sitting on a train and heading out of the city. His body experiences a brief thrill of anticipation at the thought. It is almost five months since they arrived in Barcelona on that hot May day, and the memory comes to him of all the promises they made to explore the surrounding countryside, good intentions of using their days off to travel around. They were going to go to the Costa Brava, with its wooded coves and high cliffs and deep-blue water. Cadaques and Figueres were top of the agenda, with their connections to Salvador Dali, and the old town and medieval walls and turrets of Tossa de Mar drew their attention. They talked of going to Madrid and Toledo, and maybe even Seville and Granada when the weather got cooler. But somehow Barcelona crept up around him, drawing him in, swallowing him up in the cramped alleys of the Barri Gotic, luring him with her colours and sounds and smells, her grubby honesty, her relaxed elegance, her sudden and arresting displays of beauty. Her eccentricities rubbed up against him irresistibly and he allowed himself to be seduced.

'Bliss was it in that dawn to be alive, but to be young was very heaven.' The quotation jumps out at him, his mind idling as he ambles through narrow streets. He cannot recall whose words they were. Nor is he sure if he has recalled it correctly; maybe it was 'to be in love was very heaven'? Either one would fit. He thinks of saying it to Elena, to see her reaction. When they first got together, he was always throwing quotations at her, a concerted effort to impress her with his intelligence or his sensitivity, he is not sure which. She used to smile wryly, and he was never certain whether she was quietly impressed or merely bemused at his literary asides.

He is meeting her in Schilling, a favourite haunt, and when he arrives and allows his eyes to adjust to the dimness of the bar after the blinding brightness of the street, he sees that he is there before her. Taking a seat by the window, he gives his order to the waiter, ordering a beer for Elena too. His fingers drum on the marble table, keeping time to the rhythm of funky jazz rumbling from hidden speakers. Schilling has the air of something old and historic, like the city itself. Row upon row of wine bottles line the walls, a gentle film of dust that has gathered on them is lit proudly from above. His eyes travel upwards to the lamps suspended from the ceiling on chains, opaque glass orbs like upside-down spaceships. Great swirls cast out over the walls, the twirls and flourishes of art nouveau creeping like cracks over the plastering. In the centre of the floor, the bar is a bright, shiny island, glittering with hanging glasses, and attended by dour-faced barmen in black shirts and white aprons.

Adam loves this place. He loves the timelessness of it, the classic elegance. Looking around, he sees that the clientèle is mainly Catalan today, the tourists seem to have departed. He sees the dark, slightly pointed features of the locals, engaged in a hum of conversation. At a table opposite, two boys are holding hands and gazing at each other wistfully. He has grown used to seeing this, he has warmed to the tolerance that seems to exist here. The conversation between four girls at the next table rises, voices tripping over each other, lifting to a crescendo before breaking into a smattering of laughter. There are two men at the bar, dressed in black and white, who are casting looks at the girls, admiring glances. The men, oddly, seem to be sharing a suit – one wearing white linen trousers with a black shirt, while the smaller of the two is swamped in a matching white linen jacket. They sip their beer and smile greedily at the girls, who studiously ignore them. Adam's backpack sits on a chair next to him and he stares at it, distractedly peeling the red label from his beer, as he mentally calculates whether he has remembered to bring everything he needs. As he considers this, a new shadow falls across the floor at the entrance, and he looks up and sees her.

Her face is flushed and shiny and he can tell that she ran from the office; her chest is still heaving from the exercise as her eyes travel over the room, searching him out. He sits still, watching her, waiting for her to find him. From the corner of his eye, he spies the men who share the suit casting their gaze in her direction. Adam sees one of them whisper something from the side of his mouth while the other nods in agreement or approval, neither one shifting his gaze during the exchange. He experiences a thrill of pride – this is his girlfriend, his Elena, with her wide expectant eyes and clear face – and, as she spots him, he watches that face break into a broad smile and feels something move within him. She circles the tables and, reaching him, leans forward and kisses him firmly on the mouth. The men in the suit observe this exchange before turning their attention elsewhere.

'Sorry,' she says breathily. 'I couldn't get away any sooner. Work's been mental. Are you waiting long?'

'Nope. Just long enough to get a table and a couple of beers.'

'Hmm.'

She drinks thirstily before returning the bottle to the beer mat, catching her breath and fixing him with the full beam of her gaze. Her body seems to relax, her shoulders dropping, and she grins at him, as if to say, 'You have my full attention, I'm all yours now.'

'What time is the train?'

'Four. I told Carlos I'd meet him at the station.'

'Then you're all mine for the next hour,' she whispers, leaning forward and grasping his forearms. He looks down at the thin white arcs of her pink nails as they stroke back the hairs on his arms.

'So how are the money markets today?' he asks. 'Have you made a decent dent in that first million yet?'

She smiles and rolls her eyes. He frequently teases her about her white-collar job, needling her good naturedly that she should be working behind a bar or waitressing or chambermaiding, like every other self-respecting student, him included. It has taken him by surprise, how much he has grown to enjoy bar work; the physical labour is pleasing to him after a year of studying. The buzz of relaxed conversation embraces him, and he has found his language skills improving as he talks with the customers. But Elena has found something different. Her fluency in both Spanish and English has opened up more opportunities, and he is happy for her, admiring the little outfits she wears, the way she ties her hair up with tendrils working their way free and falling onto her face.

She tells him about her morning, the events at the foreign exchange where she works, and he watches her fiddling with the orange scarf she wears tied over her navy blouse, the uniform she detests but he finds cute in a Miss Moneypenny kind of way. He loves to watch her talk, the animation in her voice, the lilting musical tones and the facial expressions that accompany it, those busy eyebrows and that twitching nose. Her hands rise in gestures that accompany her anecdotes, a part of her Mediterranean inheritance that he notices has become more pronounced in the last few months. She looks so different when she is asleep, the stillness of her features is mesmerising. He thinks of her last night as he crept into bed after returning from his evening shift at the bar. He remembers staring at her as she slept, the narrow light from the hall cast over the mattress, illuminating her dark hair falling over the pillow, an arm curled up under it, the other lying by her side. Over the summer, Adam noticed sharp white lines appearing over his body, the marks from his clothes forming corners and tracts against the blotchy sunburn and sprinklings of freckles that have burnt and singed his pale skin. Lying next to Elena in the half light, he scanned her body for similar markings, but saw only varying shades of milky-brown smoothly running into one another, running over her. As his fingers travelled over her, her body shifted in sleep, a noise like purring turning over in her throat.

'You're so lucky, getting out of the city for the weekend,' she says wistfully, leaning her face on the back of her hand, elbows propped up on the table. 'You know, it's a good thing Carlos isn't a woman, or else I would be getting jealous.'

'What do you mean by that?'

'Nothing. Just that he seems to see more of you lately than I do. I'm beginning to think I've got competition.'

'Why don't you come with us, then?' he asks appeasingly, knowing the answer. 'I've told you, you'd be more than welcome.'

'I know. But I have to work. And besides, it will be good for you boys to get away together.'

Good for Carlos. That is what she means, but neither of them says it. His moods have got worse lately. They have both noticed a change in his behaviour – a new quietness that has crept into him. Elena has concluded that this is because of problems in his relationship with Maria. She has told Adam of conversations she has overheard recently between them, raised voices and the sound of crying behind their closed bedroom door. But Adam suspects it is not as simple as that.

After a few beers one evening, Carlos hinted at a growing pressure from his parents to return to the vineyard near Zaragoza. As the only son, he is expected to take on his father's business, a problem he does not seem ready to face up to yet. For Adam, who has never known a father, this did not seem insurmountable. Surely, if he just explained how he felt... 'It's complicated,' Carlos said curtly, dismissively, his words shutting down fast on the conversation, his eyes misting over with that faraway look that left Adam cold.

He liked Carlos from the start. Since that first day when they met over the bar in La Bodegueta where Adam had been working since his arrival in May, they hit it off instantly. It was hot that day, blisteringly hot, and as he swatted a fly away and prepared another order, Adam felt the ache travelling up his spine and into his neck. 'That fucking tent!' he swore again, and Paul nodded dully, unmoved by Adam's daily bitching about the tent and the commute in the blazing heat between the campsite and the city centre and the flies and the broken sleep and the inadequate washing facilities and the spine-twisting discomfort of sleeping on lumpy, uneven ground. 'Then find a fucking room,' Paul said flatly, sighing with weary indignation.

'I would if I could find one I could afford.'

'I have a room.' This voice came from behind him and, as he twisted around to find the owner, his eyes met a small, dark, square-shaped face. The features were huddled in the centre of that face – a dark-lipped mouth, an inoffensive nose and brown eyes with high eyebrows that gave their owner a permanently startled expression. It was a good face. An open face. A face he warmed to instantly.

Elena was fond of Carlos too. She found his quiet manners charming, his easy, open way with them. The room turned out to be a mattress on the floor of his sitting room, in an apartment that was small and cramped, with no air-conditioning and little privacy. But they were grateful for the convenience of its central location in the business district of Eixample and, as Adam remarked to Carlos, 'Anything would be better than that shagging tent.' But they had not banked on Maria, Carlos's moody, mournful girlfriend with her long, dark looks and large teary eyes. While Adam finds her easy enough to live with, her silences nearly drive Elena berserk; pouting over cups of coffee black as tar, she makes little effort to communicate. Occasionally she chats with Adam in English, a bored expression taking her face hostage, but she seems to openly sneer at Elena, frequently correcting her grammar or her accent.

'Will you miss me?' he asks Elena, grinning at her teasingly.

'No,' she counters, playing the game and smiling coquettishly.

'What will you do without me?'

'Maria and I are planning to put on slutty dresses and high heels and wander down the Ramblas to pick up men.'

He hears the trace of sarcasm in this and looks away. The atmosphere between Elena and Maria has grown worse. It is starting to become a problem.

Lately, nuzzling up to him before getting up for work in the mornings, Elena has murmured suggestions about looking for somewhere new to live, just the two of them. 'Now that we've decided to stay on for the year,' she says. 'Now that we've more money coming in.' He does not want to leave the flat. The thought of traipsing around the city, trawling through piteous accommodation, fills him with inertia. Nor does he want to offend Carlos. But that morning, as they listened for the first signs of movement in the next room and he watched as Elena reached across for his T-shirt to cover her nakedness, he groaned with disappointment as her body was swallowed up in the folds of cotton. She turned to look back at him with an impish smile, saying, 'If we had a place of our own, I wouldn't have to. I could walk around naked all the time', and a new wave of desire broke over him and, with it, he felt his resolve diminish.

Adam knows that Elena does not want to be left alone with Maria for the weekend. He feels vaguely guilty about it. But his desire to get away is greater. If he is honest with himself, it irks him that the two girls do not get on in the same way that he and Carlos do. Secretly, he wonders whether some of the animosity that exists between them owes anything to jealousy on Elena's part. He loves her, but wonders whether she feels occasional pangs of envy. Maria's allure is unmistakable: those giant eyes like pools of ink, the luxury of her long jet-black hair, the sensual movements that accompany her as she wafts into rooms. He has sneaked furtive glances at her emerging from the bathroom, wrapped in a towel. These snatched glances revealed curves and contours that swamped his imagination. And while Elena is pretty – no, she is beautiful – there is something tame about her when compared to Maria's sultry exoticism.

He shakes his head to dispel the image.

'So what are you boys going to get up to?' she asks brightly.

'See the vineyard. Sample the grapes. Ingratiate myself with Carlos's sisters.' He grins at her across the table. 'Drink and carouse with beautiful *señoritas*.'

'Don't you dare,' she says in mock horror.

'Come here.'

He leans across the table towards her and their lips meet over the marble surface. Her face is cool and soft. He will give in to her, he knows this already. They will find a new place, just the two of them. But for now, he remains silent. '*Te quiero*,' she whispers.

'*Me amante*.'

Her nose wrinkles with delight.

*

Memories flood his consciousness. They come to him in waves, his thoughts flickering back through the heady days of those early months in Spain. He stares at the froth hardening against the inside of his empty cup and glances again at his watch. It is twelve ten. She is late. Or maybe she isn't coming at all. It's plausible. He has made it difficult for her with her husband. She will have to make an excuse, invent something; he is forcing her to lie. But all of that is secondary to his need to see her. Friday night has whetted his appetite for her, reminding him of how things were between them, left him craving her even more. The thought that he has frightened her off by his intensity, the realisation that she might not be coming, brings with it a sudden shock. He leans forward and rests his head in cupped hands. His eyes are closed, but the noises and smells remain. Jazzy blues – rich like caramel – seep from the speakers. He wishes he hadn't chosen this place now. It was stupid, sentimental and foolish.

That's it, he says to himself. As he draws his coat to him and rises to go, he sees her. She stands at the entrance, light from the glazed doors behind her, and through the shadows of her face he can see her eyes travelling, searching him out. As he did all those years ago, he waits until she sees him. Their eyes meet and both of them pause as if steadying themselves for what comes next. He feels a tightening in his chest and breathes deeply as he takes his seat and waits for her to join him.

11

SHE WAITS FOR him to speak first. Momentarily distracted by the arrival of their orders, he glances across at her, trying to read her expression, but she keeps her eyes fixed on the table in front of her.

'It's good to see you,' he says eventually. 'I'm glad you came.'

He smiles at her with what he hopes is warmth, tenderness. But his smile is not returned.

'You shouldn't have called my house,' she says coldly. 'You should not have spoken to my husband. What were you thinking of?'

'I was thinking of you.'

'You were thinking of you, Adam. Just like you always have.'

He sits still, considering this for a moment. She is stirring her coffee angrily. Great waves of resentment rise from her – he feels pummelled by them. He will have to go gently with her. 'I'm sorry,' he says quietly. 'I've made things difficult for you with your husband, haven't I?'

A short, mocking burst of laughter greets this statement and she stares at the ceiling, shaking her head, a strange little smile on her lips.

'What?' he asks, suddenly curious.

'Nothing.'

A silence falls between them. Now that she is here, sitting in front of him, he is not sure what he wants to say to her. He hoped to pick up on the intimacy that was between them a few nights ago. But there is something cool about her now, something mocking. He senses a dangerous edge to her today – something strange and brittle that was

141

not there before. She holds her body stiffly apart from him, and he asks himself what it was he hoped to achieve. Why has he brought her here? What are his intentions? At this moment, he is not sure what he wants. As he ponders what to say, it is Elena who breaks the silence.

'I'm sorry about your mother.'

'Oh.' He glances up at her and sees a flicker of concern in her eyes. 'Thanks.'

'Were you there with her, when she…'

'No. No, I was stuck in traffic. One of life's little ironies, eh?' He tries to laugh, but it comes out like a gasp and she looks at him uncertainly.

'Listen, Elena. I'm sorry for dragging you here. I really am. But I just… I suppose I wanted to see a familiar face. No, that's not true. I wanted to see you. And I thought… I thought…' He doesn't know how to say it to her, how to explain that his expectations have been fed by the hours they spent alone together, and how this awkwardness that has come to rest between them is not what he envisaged at all.

'You thought it would be like Friday night,' she says.

He looks up at her.

'That's what I hoped, yes.'

She shakes her head.

'Friday night was a mistake. I wish I'd never gone.'

She sips her coffee and he feels a sudden anger pulsing through him. 'No, you don't.'

She looks up at him, surprised by his reaction.

'Jesus, Elena. This is me you're talking to. Not some bloke you just met—'

'Adam—'

'Can't you at least be honest?' he asks, made bold by his anger. 'You wanted to see me on Friday night – that's why you went. And you've realised since then that you feel the same way about me now as you did all those years ago.'

'You are so arrogant!'

'And you're so deceitful. At least I can be truthful. At least I can admit to wanting something from you. But you, no, you just hide behind this mask, this injured-soul act. It's nice and safe for you like that. That way you don't risk anything, you don't risk admitting how you really feel, what it is you really want!'

He sits back, staring at her. Her features seem to crumple, her expression of dismay falling in on itself. Then from somewhere deep within her comes a small voice. 'What I really want? What I really feel? Since when did you start caring about what mattered to me, Adam? You were always so caught up in your own concerns that what I wanted didn't matter unless it fitted in with your plans!' Her eyes flash dangerously. He knows where she is going with this.

'I wanted us to move away from Carlos and Maria. I wanted you to stay in Barcelona and not go to Muel with Carlos for those few days. I wanted you to come to Zaragoza with me, to go to the funeral of your friend. But that didn't matter to you then, did it? What I wanted had no bearing on you back then, so why should it matter to you now?'

He is tired suddenly. He feels the weight of his limbs, the sudden airlessness of the café. Regret creeps up around him, fastening itself to his thoughts. He sighs deeply. His weariness washes over him.

He looks at her, his eyes shadowy and tired. 'If it's any consolation,' he offers, 'I wish I hadn't gone to Muel too.'

*

In hindsight, it must have been Adam himself who suggested the trip, although at the time he managed to convince himself that Carlos had issued the invitation willingly. A weekend in the country, an opportunity to see the real Spain, away from the crowded streets of Barcelona, away from the tourists and the shoppers and the day-trippers, a chance to visit a vineyard and sample some of Aragon's finest wine, to meet with Carlos's family, and – although neither of them said it – a welcome break from the tense atmosphere that was building up in the apartment, threatening to reach crisis point.

Carlos slept throughout the journey, his shaven head pressed against the train window, while Adam stared out, hungry for the view, his eyes eating up the flat, dry plains, the short, squat olive trees that huddled in rows over stony soil. Long, flat hills rose suddenly out of the plains, and yellow grass grew in scrubs at the base, the soil becoming darker as they pressed deeper into Aragon.

The train dropped them in Zaragoza's hangar-like station and they got a taxi away from the city, south to the village of Muel. Adam sat in the back seat, silently observing a village that had seen better days – run-down shops, graffiti on the walls, the vacant gaze of an ageing population propped up on stools outside their houses, dogs sniffing at street corners, ripped and filthy awnings stretching out over dusty windows. The taxi dropped them at the foot of a dry, stony road that stretched up a gentle hill. 'We walk from here,' said Carlos, and Adam threw his bag over his shoulder and followed his friend, past the fields of vines to their right – long furrows cutting through the turned black soil. Walking up the hill, he glanced across at Carlos, taking in the short stature, the blocky limbs of his friend, hair cropped close to his skull like black stubble. His eyes were creased as though smiling but his mouth was set firmly, until he became aware of Adam's glance and his face broke up in smiles, lines stretching from the corners of his eyes across his temples into his hairline.

The setting sun cast its red glow on a small clutch of flat-roofed buildings at the top of the hill and, as they drew nearer, he spied a small, squat woman with a brown raisin-like face hurrying out of the main building, her hand shielding her eyes from the last rays of the disappearing sun. She saw them and hurried towards them, her hands flapping in the air. She moved quickly, as though powered by worry, and as she came upon them Adam could see the neat print of her dress, the black stockings under blue carpet slippers and those hands – large hands for a woman – fluttering in the air, the flutters accompanying the changing expressions of her face, from anxiety to bashful joy to embarrassed laughter and back again. 'Mama,' Carlos said softly as she took his face in her hands, examined it carefully, worry lines etched into her forehead, before leaning forward and kissing him on the lips.

The wine is strong and throaty. He swirls it in his glass, the lamplight reflected in its dark surface, and he raises it to his lips, tasting the black earth, the hint of flowers, and something else, something warm and dry tipping down into the pit of his stomach. Leaning back in his chair, he lets out a long, satisfied sigh into the night air. Crickets click in the darkness, a hum coming up through the fields, and Adam feels the warmth of the day dying in the breeze, his stomach replete, his head heavy with wine. It seems to him that his whole body is untangling, slowed by the quiet ease of this place.

'God, you're a lucky bastard,' he breathes, shaking his head slowly with envy, with incredulity that anyone could come from such a place.

Looking across the table, he can only see one half of Carlos's face; the other half is in shadow as he gazes into the darkness, cradling his glass in his hands. His eyelids have grown heavy, and his silences have also grown since their arrival earlier that evening, becoming more morose as the evening faded into dusk. At first, Adam didn't notice it, too busy with the introductions, the shaking of hands, the exchanging of brief pleasantries in his pidgin Spanish. The roughened brown faces of the parents; the hardened skin of Señor Quintenal's strong hands, his thick neck, those fierce little eyes, an unspeaking mouth hidden under a heavy moustache, his rubbery face deeply lined as though a fork had been scraped through it; Señora Quintenal's searching eyes, a thin-lipped mouth that quivered nervously through smiles and frowns, worry pinching at the skin between her eyebrows; and two of the sisters – one plump and bashful like the mother; the younger one, with eyes that were alert and bold, holding his gaze and later becoming talkative, eager to practise her English, peppering him with questions, giving lengthy answers to his, until Carlos told her to give it a rest and leave them be.

Their home is simple; the lack of luxuries is apparent. But what appeals to Adam is the humility of the place, the lack of artifice. It is what he expected – what he hoped for. But while he feels his mind and body relax into the surroundings, he senses a different change in his friend. The introductions were brisk; Carlos seemed unusually curt, as if unwilling to linger there too long. The thought momentarily flashed across Adam's mind that Carlos is embarrassed by these relatives, hanging back, examining the floor in front of his feet, while his friend shook hands with each one of them. That thought wasn't allowed time to grow, chased away by the food and drink that followed.

But now as he slides lower into his seat, the scent of jasmine from the garden filling his senses, the notion returns to him as he regards his quiet, contemplative companion. The others have departed for their beds, leaving the two of them alone to finish another bottle of the family label.

'A lucky, lucky bastard,' he repeats, and this time Carlos turns his face to respond.

'Why do you say that?'

'This place. I mean, look at it.' His arm sweeps in a wide arc, taking in the surroundings, before falling back in his lap. 'This place is amazing! It's like something out of a movie. Fields full of vines, an olive grove, a kitchen garden? Is that… are they lemon trees over there?' He stares blearily at the misshapen yellow fruit nestling into the branches. 'Not to mention your own wine cellar, for Chrissakes!'

Carlos says nothing, regarding him strangely, his eyebrows perched in their lofty position high above his eyes. But the eyes are unsmiling, his mouth a flat line in his face.

'It must have been great growing up here. All that space to roam around in. And then your family…'

'My family?' Carlos's voice rises with a snap out of the darkness.

'Yeah – your mother and father, all of your sisters; it must have been fantastic when you were all kids, growing up together. To have so many people around you, so much company.'

Adam, who grew up in a small house with an embittered middle-aged woman for company, has always craved the comfort and closeness of siblings. Carlos's four sisters are something of a revelation, and it seems to Adam that, while it is not the same as having a brother, it must surely be better than growing up alone.

In the wait for an answer, something about the coldness of the silence holds Adam back from questioning him further. Across the dimly lit terraza a candle flickers beneath a whisper of a breeze while Carlos continues to stare at him, and there is something dark and unknowable in his expression that causes a shiver to pass across the back of Adam's neck. He holds his gaze a moment longer before draining his glass and looking away. The bottle is empty and he feels sleep creeping up on him, and after a few minutes he declares his fatigue and says goodnight to his friend, retiring into the dark, quiet house.

Adam wakes late, his bedroom darkened by shutters still closed to the late-morning sun. Stumbling from his room, bleary eyed with sleep, his brain rocking in his skull from the wine of the previous evening, he wanders through the quiet house. His footsteps echo over the stone floor as he moves through silent rooms in the long villa. As he nears the kitchen, he hears signs of life.

'*Buenos dias*,' he says sheepishly, standing awkwardly under the doorframe as Carlos's mother and sister look up simultaneously.

'Good morning, sleepy-head,' smiles Pilar. 'We were beginning to wonder about you.'

'I'm really sorry. I didn't realise the time.'

Carlos's mother steps towards him, ushering him to the table with those flapping hands.

'Please, please,' she says insistently, as he reluctantly takes his seat, embarrassed to see that he has interrupted the two women in their preparation of lunch. He looks at the food spread across the table – the plates of plump tomatoes doused in olive oil and garlic, a dish of broad beans glistening with vinaigrette, baskets of crusty bread, platters of cold meats and cheese and a bowl of exotic fruit salad – mango, papaya, kiwi and pineapple.

Pilar watches with smiling eyes, rinsing asparagus in a plastic bowl, as her mother bustles around the kitchen pouring steaming coffee, her short, squat body quivering as she slices bread and places it in front of him. 'Please,' she repeats, raising fingers to her mouth, miming eating the bread.

'*Muchas gracias*,' he replies, and tucks in hungrily. The bitter tannin residue from the wine has coated his palate, and his mouth feels stale; it craves a new taste.

'Carlos is very rude to leave without waking you,' Pilar states as she empties the asparagus into a bowl.

'Where's he gone?' asks Adam, savouring the hot coffee, feeling it revive his limp stomach.

'Who knows?' she shrugs. 'Down to the village, probably.'

'Oh.'

'He is avoiding Papa.'

Pilar is the youngest of the sisters, barely a year older than Carlos. Adam regards her from over his coffee cup, taking in her sharp black eyes framed by thick dark brows, a startlingly sensitive mouth in her strong, almost mannish face. Her intelligence flickers behind her eyes as she continues her work, waiting for him to speak.

'Why would he avoid your father?' he asks tentatively.

'He always avoids Papa!' she exclaims with a sudden burst of laughter. 'Carlos hates to row, don't you know? And he has fought with Mama already this morning. Didn't you hear them?'

'No.' He watches the dark, rounded figure of Señora Quintenal retreating from the room.

'Mama was shrieking. I'm surprised it didn't wake you.'

'What were they fighting about?'

'Oh, the usual. Mama doesn't approve of Carlos living with Maria when they are not married.'

'Oh?'

'She wants him to marry a nice girl, a good Catholic girl from the right background.'

'What's wrong with him marrying Maria? Is she not Catholic?'

Pilar shakes her head. 'It's not that. But any girl who will live with a man who is not married to her is a *marrana*.' She looks up and sees the surprise on his face and quickly adds, 'That's what Mama thinks, anyway.'

'I see.' An image of Maria strays into his head, walking from the kitchen in her underwear – those long stalking legs, that shapely flesh.

'Well, you live with them. Can you see Carlos and Maria getting married?'

Adam shrugs noncommittally. He thinks of the arguments that have raged lately and Carlos's moody withdrawal into silence. But it is not his business. And he is wary of Pilar's persistence.

When she has finished with the asparagus she takes a seat opposite him, pushing the salad bowl away from her, her chin leaning earnestly in the cup of her hand.

'So you are living with your girlfriend too?'

'That's right.'

'And she is Spanish?'

'Half Spanish. Her mother is from Andalucia.'

'Ah. And tell me, you are in love with this girl?'

Coal-black eyes glitter at him, and he notices her finger twisting a tendril of hair around it. She flirts playfully, but he feels the danger of her attentions. There is fire beneath that innocent exterior. He imagines there are vengeful facets to her personality. He smiles at her innocuously and avoids answering the question.

But later, as he walks alone through the dusty field, his eyes staring out at the neat rows of vines stretching over the natural idiosyncrasies of the land, his mind wanders back to Pilar's question. Why didn't he answer it? He loves Elena, he's sure of that. And yet... He thinks back to all the hopes and expectations that clamoured within him before leaving for Spain. He was aching to get away, needing to be alone with her, somewhere he could feel free of his mother's abiding disapproval and Elena's mother's constant interference. Those Sunday afternoon lunches with Rosario and Vincent depressed the hell out of him. Vincent hardly uttered a word, frightened into silence, while Rosario's persistent questioning left Adam feeling battered and raw. 'Don't take it so seriously,' Elena said when he complained of it to her. But it seemed to Adam that, no matter what answer he offered, Rosario's lip seemed to rise into a sneer, projecting her unspoken view that he was not good enough for her daughter.

Adam, on the other hand, was reluctant to bring Elena anywhere near his mother. On the one occasion that he did, his mother was steeped in gin, her make-up scarily garish, and she scowled at Elena, openly referring to her as 'that girl'.

A summer away, with no exams to study for – and the promise of sun, cheap wine and fiestas – seemed like a blessing. And it has been wonderful. Exhilarating. So much so that he hardly had to think about it when Elena first raised the possibility of extending their stay in Barcelona, deferring their studies for another year. It came about so unexpectedly, that night in the stifling heat of August, when they strolled down to the harbour, needing to feel the coolness that skimmed across the sea. The lights were coming on along the marina, night closing in swiftly. They sat together on the harbour wall, shoulders touching, Elena with her knees clasped into her chest, her hair drawn back off her face, Adam with his legs dangling over the ten-foot drop. They watched the sun disappear, the light on the boats fading into shadow as a deep navy swept down over the sky – a last glow shimmering on the horizon before the sky met the sea and colour blended into darkness. The boats rocked in the harbour, a forest of masts clinking together, and the hum from the bars and restaurants grew loud, stretching out into the night.

'I don't want to go home,' Elena said, breaking the silence between them.

She stared wistfully into the darkness, her small body rocking back and forth.

'To the apartment or to Ireland?'

She shrugged and thought for a minute. 'To Ireland,' she said at last.

'Then let's not.'

These words escaped from him without thought. But announcing them into the darkness, he heard the honest ring of truth in them. He felt her hand reach for his in the darkness, and possibility flowed through him like the gentle breeze, and the rightness of the words announced filled him with a sudden excitement.

But now, in the vineyard, kicking clumps of dry soil, he is visited by a new doubt. He thinks of Elena, their meeting in Schilling. Did he hear a whine in her voice at the prospect of being without him for the weekend? Are they becoming too dependent on each other, living in each other's pocket? He thinks again of Pilar's questioning eyes, that finger twirling her hair, and wonders for the first time what this year away might mean to Elena. A cementing of their relationship? A deeper commitment? He begins to understand that something might be expected of him at the end of it. Some kind of grand gesture, an expression of his intentions. Despite the heat, a shadow passes through him. But this is quickly chased by a sharp pang of guilt. An image of Elena comes to him, throwing her arms about his neck as she said goodbye to him outside Schilling; drawing her head back, she kissed him – a loud, warm, smacking kiss – and he felt the love in that kiss. These guilty, disloyal thoughts in the vineyard cannot dispel that. No matter how much they trouble him.

Lunch is a family affair and Pilar and her mother spread a richly embroidered tablecloth across the long deal table on the terraze outside the kitchen. An old yew tree provides a natural shade. The wind is gathering, rustling under the branches and lifting the edges of the cloth that is weighed down with bowls and dishes laden with food. The eldest sister, Silvia, and her husband, Domingo, arrive with their two small children and more introductions are made. They find their places around the table, a noisy, moving body of people. Adam feels bashful in their company – and embarrassed too, like a debutant whose date has abandoned him. Señor Quintenal says nothing about his son's disappearance, but his eyes reflect a troubled mind. A few terse instructions issue from under his moustache, his gaze flickering at the faces gathered around the table. His wife wrings her hands with exasperation, trying to organise her unruly family. Pilar sits next to Adam. The warmth of her thigh presses against his, and he feels something stirring within him.

There is a brief silence, with heads bowed during grace, before the table erupts again into a cacophony of sounds, hands reaching, bowls and dishes being passed around, the clink of cutlery against crockery, voices raised, talking together, talking over each other. They ignore him for the most part, their conversation racing past him, a few words comprehensible, but most of them lost to him, beyond his grasp. Only Pilar has time for him with her whispered asides, her sharply acidic commentary on her siblings and their spouses. 'See how he snorts his food?' she hisses. 'What a pig! He drives Mama crazy. And you see Elise, the way she scowls? She cannot stand Silvia. Never could.'

What Adam notices first is a tightening about the features in the old man's face. His moustache seems to draw in and the lines on his face grow taut, air sucked into his cheeks. Following his gaze down into the fields, he sees Carlos moving through the vines, slowly and deliberately, his body bent forward as though walking into the wind. From that distance, even before he staggers and clutches at a vine to regain his balance, Adam can see that his friend is drunk. That faraway gaze, that patient smile, and as he approaches the diners he gives a brief salute. Picking his way around the table he finds a seat, and taking hold of the back of it he seems surprised by how solid it is, and then tries to mask his surprise. He falls into the chair and immediately reaches for the wine bottle. Oblivious to the uneasy silence that greets his arrival, he pours liberally, filling his glass and drinking deeply. Adam watches silently, feeling the cold breath of trouble stirring around him, at his friend's slow movements, the deliberate way in which he reaches for the bread, his eyes focusing carefully before selecting a slice. Carlos picks at his food, a thoughtful smile on his face, lowering his gaze and not speaking to any of them. A hush has fallen over the table, conversation has died away, as have appetites; food is left on plates uneaten, cutlery has been laid aside along with half-eaten crusts of bread. It is as if everyone is waiting for something to happen.

And then something happens.

The old man's moustache twitches and he clears his throat, his muscular forearms leaning on the table in front of him. From deep in his throat comes a rumble of words that Adam does not understand – a rattled question thrown out across the food. The table seems to heave around it. Adam sneaks a glance at the other faces and reads apprehension there, and a weary jaded recognition. Only Carlos remains grinning. He looks up and smiles sweetly at his father, holding his palms up in mock surrender.

'*Si*,' he answers softly. '*En el taberna.*'

Adam feels Pilar stiffening next to him. 'Here we go,' she breathes out of the side of her mouth.

Señor Quintenal's face seems to swell, turning red, then purple, lines and folds and creases in his skin becoming stretched. Adam can see a vein throbbing in his temple – it ripples under his skin like a tributary flowing down from his skull. When he speaks it is in a low voice, a hoarse whisper, but his moustache moves angrily over the words, which Adam doesn't understand. It quivers and fumes as the voice builds, a river of bitter words rising to a crescendo, and all the while Carlos smiles implacably, absently chewing on his bread. Señor Quintenal's coal-black eyes narrow with fury, and suddenly incensed, he is moved to bring his fists down with a slam against the table. As his rage consumes him and he casts it out, sweeping over the whole table to reach the intended recipient, his wife trembles, her hands rising to her face, hiding this scene from her eyes. No one says a word, frozen by fear, as the full force of Señor Quintenal's fury pitches forward and rises to a peak – a pivotal question, asked threateningly. Although Adam is lost amid this incomprehensible argument, he understands from the tone and the direction of all eyes on Carlos that the argument is teetering on the brink of a fall. An ultimatum has been served.

The air seems to still in that moment. There are no breezes now billowing the tablecloth. All sounds are suspended. The tree above them stands silent, as though listening. Even the children are motionless, cowed by the ferocity of their grandfather's wrath. Adam feels himself holding his breath.

Carlos reaches forward with measured deliberateness, his fingers selecting a plump green olive from the bowl. He examines it – the slick smooth skin, the fleshy wall – then, glancing briefly at his father, he enunciates the clear, flat syllable – 'No' – before popping the olive cleanly into his mouth.

The table seems to deflate. An exhalation of hot air. Adam can feel Pilar wilting next to him. Around the table, bodies seem to imperceptibly slump, a release of tension, a reprise. Señor Quintenal, his question answered, is silent. He rises slowly out of his chair and moves with weariness around the table, as if holding his body together with sheer will. Arriving at his son's chair, he gently lays his hands on Carlos's shoulders. They rest there – strong brown hands, a tight weave of toughened muscle and sinew – as if channelling warmth into the son's body. Adam, misunderstanding the outcome, perceives this to be an act of forgiveness. His eyes open wide when, next, the small, short man with his thickly packed muscle draws his arm back before bringing a fist down sharply against the side of Carlos's head. A collective cry rises up from the table; chairs scrape back in fright as the family gets to its feet. Señora Quintenal rises wailing, her hands fluttering around her face. Carlos slumps forward, his eyes wide and unblinking, stunned by the blow, a dark trickle of blood emerging from his ear. His father is gone, his exit brief, and when Adam looks for him he sees a figure down in the fields, holding himself upright with forced pride, but his movements are stumbling and rushed as he hurries through his beloved vines, away, away from the debacle he has left behind. The table seems to break up amidst a rising pitch of anguished female voices. Hands flap around Carlos's head, torn between concern for him and berating him. He swats them away, irritated, hurt and recovering from his daze; he gets to his feet clumsily, swaying from the drink and the sudden blow.

Ignoring the pleas of his mother and his sisters, he staggers from the table, across the terraza towards the car parked in the shade of the grove. His intentions cause more wails of anguish and Adam finds himself lurching forward.

'Wait!' he calls out urgently.

Getting to his feet, he shrugs off Pilar's restraining arm and tears past the others. Carlos is already behind the wheel, turning the key in the ignition, when Adam reaches the passenger door, flinging it wide.

'What are you doing?' he asks, breathless and hoarse.

But Carlos is oblivious to him and the car jerks suddenly as he starts to reverse, the open door flapping as the vehicle lurches and skids.

'Wait!' he cries and the car shudders to a halt, and leaning in he sees Carlos looking up at him, a weird grin on his face.

'Are you getting in?'

'You're crazy,' Adam says, shaking his head in disbelief. 'You can't drive, you're in no condition…'

'Either get in or fuck off,' Carlos cuts him off, his voice chill and cutting in the hot, stale air of the car. Despite his better judgement, Adam finds himself sitting in the front seat, his knuckles whitening as he grips the dashboard with one hand, the door with the other.

'This is fucking madness,' he says breathlessly as the car swings around. Carlos whoops wildly, crying out, 'Hold on to your pants!' before screeching out onto the narrow stone road, a cloud of dust kicked up behind them, his foot flooring the accelerator and a gleam in his eyes as they speed away from the house, the nose of the car pointing towards the city.

Zaragoza is teeming with activity. The city is crammed with traffic, and Adam is grateful for it, the car forced to come to an unwilling halt. He feels Carlos's body grow quiet and tense as he sounds the horn and growls with impatience. Glancing across, Adam recognises the same alarming gleam of brightness in his eyes. But the high, shrill laugh that has accompanied their race from Muel, and the forced high spirit, seem to have dissipated. Adam's fingers are sore from clutching his seat and his limbs feel weak. His attempts at placating Carlos have failed, and now he watches as his friend pulls the car up onto the curb and switches off the engine. 'Let's go,' he says quickly, abandoning the car.

The streets are busy, a moving mass of people gathering and following the streets down to the Plaza del Pilar. Adam looks about, confused at the growing crowd; there is a festive atmosphere in the air, a purpose to the congregation. He sees brightly coloured masks, costumes adorned with streaming ribbons, faces painted in gaudy hues that fluctuate from the menacing to the ridiculous.

'What's going on?' he asks, hurrying to catch up, afraid of losing Carlos in the swelling crowd.

'It's party time!' his voice sings out shrilly. 'The fiesta of Nuestra Señora del Pilar! Look! I'll show you.'

He plunges into the crowd and Adam has to charge in after him, feeling elbows digging into his ribs as he pushes past, eyes flashing in irritation at him. The crowd swarms around the Plaza del Pilar, and Adam pauses for a moment to take in the huge stone square packed with life, the noise and clamour that rises from it with the pigeons that flock and rise up over imperious buildings, bricks reddened by the sun. In the distance, he can see a statue of the Virgin Mary, teetering precariously as she is stretchered through the crowds, traversing the square on the shoulders of four burly men.

'You see?' Carlos calls to him. 'Over there is the Basilica de Nuestra Señora del Pilar. That is where they are going. Don't you know? The Virgin appeared at the top of a pillar, right here in Zaragoza – if you can believe that! The pillar is still there – right in the middle of the church. You can go in and kiss it if you like.'

His laughter soars – thin and mocking – his arm waving crazily in the direction of the Basilica, and his elbow cracks against the head of another man, causing angry words to rise up. But Carlos is oblivious to the annoyance he is causing, that high, shrill laugh sending a shiver through Adam.

'Carlos!' he calls out. 'Why don't we go somewhere a bit quieter, huh? Let's find somewhere quiet to sit down.'

The crowd pulses around him and the noise of the throng echoes in his ears, competing with the crashing sound of panic within him. He is out of his depth. Today, Carlos is a loose cannon. The light in his eyes is worrying; the tenor of his voice has changed. He is distracted, self-destructive. Adam feels how dangerous he is.

'Good idea,' Carlos replies with a grin. 'Let's go and get a drink.'

The narrow streets that swarm around the plaza are filled with bodegas, bars and cafés. They hurry past them, Carlos leading the way, driven by a new sense of purpose. Avoiding the bars along Carre de Don Jaime with their slot machines and supermarket lighting, they duck down a side street and into La Republicana. The bar is full, and they squeeze past the counter and into the back, where they find a table decked out in cheerful red gingham. It is noisy, crammed with families and couples and groups of revellers here for the fiesta. Adam looks about him at the yellow walls, the antique advertisements, the faded sepia portraits, while Carlos calls to the waitress. An enormous old oak dresser stands against the back wall, cluttered with bits and pieces gathering dust – a collection of thimbles, old sweet jars still holding their saccharine treasure, a set of weighing scales, rusting jelly moulds. From the ceiling, bundles of dried flowers hang from hooks driven into the beams – lavender and roses, parched and dusty. At the other tables, people are tucking into tapas served in tin plates with spoons, without fuss, without ceremony. Adam eyes up the plump tomatoes glistening with olive oil, he smells the fish stewed in aubergines and courgettes. He thinks of the lunch he left behind. It seems like hours ago. His stomach growls, registering its complaint.

A bottle arrives and is left on the table between them. Carlos tips the neck and the glasses fill with a liquid the colour of dirty water. Leaning forward, Adam sniffs at his and draws back with distaste. 'What the hell is it?'

'Orujo,' Carlos answers tersely. 'Taste it. It's better than you think.'

With that he tips back his own glass, emptying the contents down his open throat with a flourish. Adam watches as he refills it quickly, barely pausing to belch.

'Easy there, Carlos.'

'Drink!' His eyes flare open and he growls with impatience.

It smells of old socks, but as he draws the syrupy liquid into the back of his throat, feeling it slide down into his belly, the sweet, unexpected flavours of dates and almonds ripple over his tongue.

'Good?' Carlos is smiling at him now, looking pleased with himself as Adam nods. 'Come along, have another.'

They knock back three or four shots, and Adam feels the warmth of liquid surging down into his stomach. His body begins to loosen, a needling sensation runs through his legs, his face relaxing into a sloppy grin.

The bar drums with activity as evening draws in, chasing away the daylight. Adam no longer knows what time it is. He has lost count of how many glasses of Orujo he has swallowed. Carlos's cheeks are shiny, his lips peeled back revealing rows of white teeth. His eyebrows strain to reach his hairline, a comic expression to mask the day's events.

'Carlos?'

'Hmm.'

'What happened back there? Earlier. That row with your father…'

Carlos swats at the air dismissively, his head tilting back violently as he downs another shot.

'Was it about the vineyard?' Adam persists.

'It is always about the vineyard,' Carlos says, leaning forward over the table for effect.

'So what? He wants you to come home and take it over and you don't want to?'

'Something like that.'

Adam pauses to digest the dilemma. He thinks of the long, simple house, the rolling fields, vines running in strips across the land. He remembers the sun setting red against the house, the smell of jasmine, the rich, fruity taste of the wine, the plump lemons. Shaking his head from side to side as if trying to dislodge something caught between his ears, he looks into his friend's eyes and professes his inability to see what the problem is.

'Oh, come on, Adam ...'

'No, really, I don't. It's such a beautiful place. Can't you see that?'

'Muel? Are you crazy? There is nothing there! Old women and dogs – that's all there is to Muel. Just a group of run-down buildings that should be demolished. Even the taberna is dead, visited only by old men still arguing over the civil war.'

'But the vineyard, your home...'

'Yes, yes, I know what it is you see. You see the old farmhouse, the simple life, the fresh air, no? One big happy family living together?'

Adam shrugs in agreement.

'But it's not like that. It's not like that at all.' His lips narrow and his face seems to close in around this one thought, his eyes looking inward at memories and images that Adam cannot see. 'He's a bully. He always has been. Maybe you don't see it, because he's on his best behaviour in front of visitors, but when you're not around...' He breaks off and shakes his head. And then, as if struck with a thought, he sits up in his seat and, rolling up his T-shirt, twists to show Adam a small scar, like a half-moon, nestling into his shoulder blade. 'Do you see that? He did that with a shoe-iron when I was thirteen because I forgot to close the gate of the hen-house. And this...' Adam watches uncomfortably, a growing sense of disgust rumbling inside him as another scar is brought out on display, this time a white notch in Carlos's shin. 'This was when he kicked me once for telling Mama to shut up.'

'Jesus.'

'And he thinks that I'm going to go back to that? Settle down in that dead-end hole with that bully watching over me every minute of the day and night?'

'I had no idea,' Adam whispers, stirred by what he has seen.

'No way.' He shakes his head with determination. '"It's time to come home now, and if you don't, then you can forget about coming back here again." That's what he said to me. Well, if that's the way he wants it, that's the way he shall have it.'

'Wait. I'm sure once he calms down, once he realises what he said… I'm sure he didn't mean it.'

'I mean it,' Carlos retorts quickly. Looking up suddenly, his eyes burn with conviction.

And in this dim corner of La Republicana, in that one fiery gaze, Adam sees a lifetime of acrimony hardening into an unbreakable resolve. Carlos won't ever go back. He can see that now.

*

Night draws in around them. A second bottle of Orujo appears. Adam can feel it thundering in his ears. The bar is hot; clammy bodies brush past the back of his chair, and sweat forms under his clothes, a damp layer over his skin. But the anxiety over the day's events has ebbed away. Carlos's irrational behaviour seems to have dissipated, and in the closeness brought about by alcohol and the warmth generated by the convivial surroundings, he finds himself leaning towards Carlos over the table in a circle of intimacy, moved to express feelings of friendship that feel deeper – more weighty with importance – tonight than on any previous occasion.

'You're like a brother to me,' he admits solemnly, feeling his tongue thick in his mouth, clotting his speech. Carlos nods steadily in agreement as he listens. 'I never had a brother. Or a sister. And I know that, although you have four sisters…'

'Sisters aren't the same,' Carlos interjects, his eyelids lowering as if weighted down.

'That's right. That's right. Sisters aren't the same. We're like brothers, you and me. You're like the brother I never had.'

'Yes. And for me… and for me…'

'And for you the same.'

'I always wanted a brother,' Carlos admits wistfully.

'Me too!' These words emerge like a point of wonder, as if a great discovery has been made. 'And you're more than just a brother. You're my best friend too!'

'Yes. And you are to me, Adam.' Carlos stretches across the table and grips Adam's forearm to drive home his point.

'You're my best friend, Carlos,' he admits, alcohol swarming through his bloodstream, filtering through his brain. He feels light headed suddenly, giddy with drink. 'I fucking love you, you know.'

'Yes,' Carlos nods, kneading Adam's arm with the hand that still rests there. 'I love you too.'

The room sways around him, light skimming at the corners of his vision; the table seems to sway underneath the weight of his arms, furniture taking on new dimensions. His thoughts are thick and heavy and he struggles to focus his vision. Through the blur of images that clog his addled mind, there is a face coming towards him, hands are on his cheeks, cupping his face with a strange tenderness, and in that moment he feels lips pressing into his, his mouth meeting with another. Confusion clogs his mind and he struggles to clear it, aching for illumination. A pressure is building inside him, a negative force, bubbling up, threatening to burst through the surface. With a sudden crack of clarity, he breaks away, fuelled by a wave of revulsion. His hands press against Carlos's chest and with a tremor of disgust he shoves him violently, sending him flying backwards onto the ground.

Adam's legs tremble beneath him as he pulls himself upright, horror flooding his senses. His head is still muggy with drink, but a new sensation has taken root there, one of angry indignation, revulsion at what has happened. He is mortified by the misunderstanding, but most of all, he feels betrayed – that his friend could think such a thing, that he could pervert their friendship like that, read something alien into it. And as he watches Carlos curling up on the floor, his body closing in on itself, he knows that the damage is irreparable. There can be no excuses, no hiding behind a curtain of alcohol, no pleas to forget it ever happened. Neither of them will be able to do that.

As he continues to stare in horror, he watches Carlos's features crumpling – his face falling in on itself. Getting to his feet, he takes one last look at Adam, and in that look there is shame, and regret, and pain. A look that takes root. An indelible look that Adam will not forget. And, as quickly as he realises this, Carlos is gone.

*

'That was the last time I saw him alive,' Adam says.

Elena listens but says nothing. She appears to be struggling with all that he has told her – this secret he has kept from her all these years. She drops her head into her hands, hiding her face from him. He sees the narrow shake of her head that registers her disbelief.

'I did try to find him, you know. After a time. I needed to get my head together first. I traipsed around all those bars, went back to the Plaza del Pilar, around to the Roman Wall...' His eyes stare blankly, as if retracing his movements all over again in his mind. 'He didn't go home that night. And the next morning... well, I was just too embarrassed – humiliated – to wait around for him.'

He shakes his head, rocked by the memory.

'God, I was so angry,' he says wistfully. 'Everything we had, spoiled. Although I didn't know then that he would spoil things irrevocably.'

'Why are you telling me this?' she asks him, emerging from the shelter of her cupped hands, and he reads her shock and wariness in those glassy brown eyes.

'So that you know,' he shrugs. 'So that maybe you'll understand.'

'It's too late for that, Adam.'

His chest feels tight. The air around him seems to contract, sucking at his lungs. 'I need air,' he says quickly. 'Let's get out of here.'

He rises from his seat and goes to the counter to pay for their coffee. She walks ahead of him, out into the daylight, the sun breaking through the clouds.

12

THEY SIT SIDE by side on the bench, looking out across the stagnant water of the pond in St Stephen's Green. Ducks huddle on the edge as if revolted by the filth that mars the water. Together they watch a woman strolling past pushing a buggy, a small leg kicking out from under a pink blanket. Elena stares straight ahead, her hands driven deep into her pockets, a scarf covering her jaw. She appears pale in the clear light of day, her face taut and stretched.

'I knew something had happened,' she is telling him, shaking her head, her eyes narrowing with righteousness. 'How you were that evening when you arrived back. There was something shifty about you. You were so jumpy.'

He remembers the nervousness of his behaviour, his eyes darting, forced giddiness consuming him. And the way she looked at him quizzically, wary of him.

'I can't believe you didn't tell me then,' she says, still balking at the enormity of all he hid from her. 'My God. If you had... It would have explained why you refused to go back to Zaragoza with me.'

He nods his head slowly. But how could he explain to her the confusion he found himself in that night, the trembling shock of it, the burning humiliation? He wanted to tell her, but not there in that crowded bar. And then later that night, after they had found Carlos – well, he couldn't tell her then. It was wrong to speak ill of the dead.

He hasn't spoken of that night in many years. He has tried not to think of it. His mind treats that memory like a dangerous package kept in a dark corner, to be approached with extreme caution.

Now, looking out across the park, wind skipping in over the water, he watches the birds swoop overhead and hears himself begin, 'It was so hot that night. Do you remember?'

*

She is tired, weary from work, restless with boredom. The weekend was a washout, she says. Maria ignored her and, tired of the pervading animosity, she wandered along to the Picasso Museum, getting lost among the white walls and vivid paintings, that jumble of angular mismatched limbs, those distorted features.

'I couldn't wait for you to get back,' she says.

He tries to ignore the whine in her voice, the pique of irritation it causes in his brain. He smiles at her briskly and races on.

'Let's go out,' he suggests. 'Let's go to a bar and get really pissed. Absolutely off our faces drunk. C'mon. What do you say?'

'OK!' she laughs. 'But I would have thought you had enough to drink last night.'

'Yeah, well…'

His hangover rages over his whole body. The journey on the train was excruciating – the rattle and clatter of the carriage over the tracks, the endless rocking motion, his stomach fitful, and the few snatched moments of sleep invaded by dreams of entwining arms wrapping around him, suffocating him, strangling him. He woke, his neck stiff and his heart racing.

His body aches for sleep. He would love to go back to the flat, close the shutters and lie in the darkness, his body drifting into unconsciousness. But Carlos may be there, and he is not ready for that. He dreads the awkwardness that is inevitable, regardless of explanations or apologies. He shuts his mind to it and orders the first round.

It is a long time since they have done this, sat through an endless stream of beer, their talk becoming livelier and more animated with each drink. At least Elena's does. But tonight his mind seems deadened to the effects of alcohol, desensitised from the night before, heavy with the weight of what has happened – this new knowledge spreading like a poison through his brain. He shakes it off – laughs loudly and shrilly at her jokes, recounts anecdotes that tonight sound tired and threadbare. He tells her that she is beautiful. He tells her that he loves her. But he hears his own voice and recognises a desperate urgency in it. He is not sure who he is trying to convince – her or himself? And convince of what?

She gives him a watery smile, her features made soft and pliable with beer. She grins inanely and laughs too long and he feels himself grow impatient with her.

He wants something, but he is not sure what. He feels a vacuum between them. It sucks his mind to places he does not want it to go. Their conversation dies away, Elena overcome with hiccups that rack her body and make her giggle. He is depressingly sober, his mind frantically awake. He needs more stimulation.

'Let's go dancing!' he suggests, and she brightens at the prospect.

But when they get outside, she staggers in the street and he realises that she can hardly walk. He has to half carry her to the bus shelter, where her nodding head and the weight of her dragging limbs cause him to snap at her with sudden anger. 'For fuck's sake, Elena!'

'What?' she drawls, her tone registering a surprised, bewildered hurt that makes him instantly remorseful.

'Nothing,' he murmurs, his arm around her waist, holding her against his hip as she sways in the darkness.

It is after one a.m. when they arrive at their building. The lift is broken and Adam curses it and kicks the doors, venting his frustration. Someone shouts out from an apartment and he yells back, 'Ah, fuck off, will ye!'

Elena is quiet as she half stumbles, is half dragged, up the stairs. It takes them ten minutes and all of Adam's patience to reach the third floor. Sweat runs down his back, rivulets drenching his shirt. He feels sticky and tired, and wary of the emotion nipping at his heart. This rawness is new to him, like his shell has been stripped away, peeling some of his skin away with it – a quick, harsh tear, like a plaster being removed. It stings. His head hurts. His body aches.

He turns the key and the flat is in darkness. Elena stumbles through the door and makes her way blindly to the mattress under the window. He hears the soft thud of her body falling onto it as he closes the door behind him.

He doesn't turn on the light. The flat is still. All he can hear is the measured breathing from the mattress. His eyes are scratchy and he wants to sleep. He pulls his shirt over his head. It lands in a ball in the corner. He takes small steps across the floor, his eyes growing accustomed to the dark. Shadows announce themselves to him as a table, a chair, a wardrobe, a door. A chink of light falls through the gap beneath the bathroom door and he hesitates before knocking gently. Only silence answers him. His bladder presses against the belt of his jeans, demanding with a renewed urgency that he enter, so his hand finds the handle and he pushes the door, blinking in the light, and rushes to the toilet.

Relief comes to him as he stands and listens to the loud hiss of his own piss hitting the enamel. He closes his eyes and waits to finish, drops the lid and pulls the chain before zipping his fly and turning away, and then he stops. His breathing stops. His heart stops. All movement is suspended. The room seems to change dimension. It becomes brighter, whiter, light bouncing off the surfaces of tiles, off white walls, off the murky surface of bath water, off the stained enamel bath. He hears a gasp and realises it is his own chest heaving, air wrenched into his lungs – air from this poisoned room.

Carlos lies in the water, his eyelids drawn down but not fully closed, so that he appears to be staring drowsily down at the space below the taps where his toes break free of the surface of the water. Adam stares at the toes and then the feet, and then through the darkness of the water he sees the dark gashes where the ankles have also been cut, the veins opened, revealing a blackly dark blood that has dyed the bath water. A brownish stain runs down the outside of the bath where a hand rests on the ledge, the fingers dangling – that small brown hand that held his face. He is naked and, through the murky water, Adam sees the tangled darkness of hair and hooded flesh – his penis, small and shrivelled, pointing upwards.

He must have made a noise. He must have screamed, although afterwards when he replays it over and over in his mind, he cannot recall it. But it must have happened. For Elena is by his side, swaying, staring bleary eyed; her limbs weakening, she sinks to the floor. He hears her low moan, she whispers his name over and over, but Carlos will not answer now. Her arms are delving into the water, clutching at the lifeless body, shaking it, imploring it. The water, disturbed, laps angrily against the enamel, spreading its dark tide, smearing the surface with brown droplets.

Standing in that bathroom under the harsh fluorescent light, listening to Elena's hysterical pleas, he feels his anger rise sharply, flowering within him, a more vivid angry red than the blood emptied from Carlos's body. This anger, now uncovered, engulfs him – shivering and fluid, propelling him into a set of actions – calming Elena, phoning an ambulance, and coolly waiting for them to come for the body of his friend.

*

'I felt dizzy,' she tells him, her hair whipped back by a sudden wind, and she raises her hand to draw a strand away from her face. 'The whole room seemed to swirl around me. I felt drunk and weirdly sober all at once.'

He shifts, changing his position on the bench so that his body turns to look at her, so he can watch her face. She stares earnestly into the middle distance, her eyes clouding with memory.

'I suppose I just couldn't believe it. I remember shaking him and shouting at him, convinced he would snap out of it. Like it was all just some sick joke.'

She shakes her head at her own foolishness. And then, turning to look at him, she continues, 'And I remember how calm you were. So in control. You went and did everything – the ambulance, and then later contacting his family, Maria…' Her voice trails off. 'You were so practical. While I just sat there uselessly.'

'You stayed with him,' he says softly, as if to comfort her, to provide some evidence of her contribution that night. 'You never left his side. That was something.'

'I had never seen a dead body before him. He seemed so… I don't know… waxen or something. Not like Carlos. Not like him at all.'

Adam looks away. The image floats into his mind, that unsmiling face, those heavy-lidded, lifeless eyes. The silence of it, the indignity. He closes his eyes to it.

'Poor Carlos,' he hears her say softly.

*

Poor Carlos. That is not what Adam thought as he looked at the body in the bath. And later, after they had fished him out and taken him away and left them with that bloodied bathroom, that is still not what he thought. And when he rang the Quintenals and explained what their son had done to himself, listening to the pitched anguish of their wails – that haunting sound that still comes to him sometimes in the night – 'poor Carlos' is not what occurred to him. Nor was it what he thought when Maria arrived home in the height of her grief, arms flailing, lashing out at him, beating at his head and his chest in disbelief, in a piteous denial as he tried to overpower her, clasping her arms and pulling her to him, rocking her back and forth, feeling her moans humming into his chest. Poor Carlos. No. That was not how he saw it.

For Adam could only see the selfishness of the act. Everything had been spoiled. Everything had been ruined. They had been happy before that. Well, he had been, anyway. He thought back to Carlos and those dark looks that would come over his face sometimes, his eyes lost in a different world, those long, brooding silences. What had been going through his mind then, Adam wonders? What secret desires had haunted him? What hidden fears played on his conscience? But the foolishness of his admission to Adam – the recklessness of that kiss – the memory of it drew blood to his face, a sweeping embarrassment came over him. He cringed from it – shrinking from those words still ringing in his ears.

In the hours that followed, as night gave way to day, as Maria finally slept and Elena gave in to exhaustion, Adam sat on the floor staring at the bathroom door, feeling his anger incubate inside. Anger at Carlos for what he had done – for the sheer thoughtlessness of his act, uncaring of its consequences. Staring at the body in the bath; those gashes across his wrists and ankles were like giving the finger to the rest of them. *Fuck you,* they said to Adam. *Fuck the lot of you.* A loud, emphatic, 'Ha!' This anger blossomed inside him in the darkness, and over the following days, he felt it grow, stretching out to fill every part of him, consuming him.

It is Maria who says it first.

'I'm not going,' she announces, standing in the doorway of the kitchen, wearing one of Carlos's shirts.

They stop what they are doing, Elena switching off the cooker, removing the pan from the hob, Adam looking up from the toast he is buttering.

'What do you mean?' Elena asks in that gentle voice she has been using with Maria since that night, treating her carefully, like she might break.

'Just that. I've decided not to go.'

Adam watches her, saying nothing. Her face is drawn, her skin stretched tight across it. She seems to have aged overnight. And yet there is something in her eyes – a defiance – that seems to balance out the defeated slump of her shoulders.

'But you must go.'

'Why must I?' she flashes suddenly. 'It's not as if his family even want me there. And, of course, his mother will blame me. I won't suffer her black looks, her accusations.'

'But, Maria, it's his funeral…'

'I know that! And it would make me sick to stand in a church, to hear people talk about what a great young man Carlos was, with so much potential, his whole future ahead of him, and how it is such a tragedy, his life cut short, how he will be missed, and so on and so on.' Her eyes flash brightly, charged with a vibrant jet of anger. 'This was his choice! He did this. He caused this tragedy. Don't you see, Elena? He didn't give a damn about me. He didn't care how this would hurt me. He gave no consideration to breaking my heart. So why should I go to his funeral?'

Tears spill from her eyes as she turns back into her bedroom, closing the door behind her.

'One of us should go in there.'

'What for?' he murmurs, returning to his toast.

'To talk to her, persuade her to go.'

'We can't make her go, Elena.'

'She was Carlos's girlfriend. She knew him better than anyone. Of course she must go.'

She turns away, busying herself at the cooker, clattering pans, her frustration showing. He listens to her sighing, watches the irritation etching itself into her face. It has been three days since they found him. And for three days, Elena has been asking why. Why would he do this? She has plagued him with questions about what happened in Zaragoza, pestering him for clues, worrying away at his flimsy excuses, trying to find a reason for Carlos's desperate actions. But Adam held back. His fury paralysed him, preventing him from telling her. He listens to her, the worry in her voice, the drive for practicality, for level-headedness.

'Oh, Christ, I've nothing to wear,' she moans, raising her hand to her mouth. 'I'll have to go into town today, see what I can find. Anything black I suppose. How about you? Should I pick up a black tie for you while I'm there?'

He swallows his toast and takes a sip from his coffee, knowing what will come next.

'I'm not going to go either,' he says flatly. He doesn't look at her, but he can feel her body tense, the muscles stiffening, a bewildered, questioning look spreading across her face.

'Why not?' she asks lightly, still holding the pan in one hand.

'Maria is right,' he shrugs. 'This was Carlos's decision. I don't have to agree with it. And I choose not to support it.'

'I see,' she says coldly. 'And what about me?'

He shakes his head. 'You do what you want.'

She brings the pan down on the counter with a slam and, without speaking, grabs her bag and within seconds is gone.

★

'You still should have gone,' she says to him.

He shakes his head.

'You shouldn't have let me go alone.'

There is a quiver in her voice. Of anger? he wonders. Bitterness? Regret?

'Have you any idea what it was like for me, going there, meeting his family, seeing their terrible grief? And having to explain why neither his best friend nor his girlfriend would attend the funeral, when I didn't even understand it myself?'

He bows his head, his chin resting into his collar. Her hands are folded in her lap in front of her. They look cold, the knuckles white. He feels an urge to reach out and take her hand, to knit his fingers through hers. But he doesn't. His hands ball into fists in his coat pockets.

'I'm sorry,' he says into the wind.

'For not going? Or for what you did after I left?'

Her voice slices through the air between them and he looks away.

★

Neither of them goes to work. He lies on the mattress rereading a book, the sentences passing under his eyes like clouds of words, a misty strand of letters not penetrating his brain. Maria slinks around like a cat, not speaking, insistent on wearing Carlos's T-shirts over her underwear. He watches those long legs stalk past him and tries with renewed vigour to concentrate on his book.

When the phone rings after ten that night, he realises that he has hardly moved all day, lying slumped on the mattress, drifting between sleep and a kind of sedated wakefulness.

It is Elena. Her voice sounds distant to him, like she is in a different country.

'How was it?' he asks her, not wanting to know, but feeling that he should ask anyway.

'It was… difficult.' The pause that follows is strained with the burden she has been carrying all day. He feels a crack in the silence, a shuddering, noiseless crying at the end of the phone. His heart is snatched with remorse – a pained sympathy for her, a flash of guilt.

'Ellie…'

He hears her draw breath and her words come out in a tear-filled stream of emotion.

'Oh, God. It was horrible, Adam. I… I just wish… Jesus, if you'd only seen them. They were distraught. His mother…'

She stops, her tears taking over her words. He clutches the receiver, his knuckles white, and bends over the kitchen counter, his head hurting with anguish, a confusion of emotions tumbling over each other.

'I wish…' he begins, faltering. What does he wish? That he had gone with her? That she hadn't gone at all? That none of this had ever happened? 'I… I…'

'It's all right,' he hears her say briskly. He has a picture of her wiping her tears quickly with the back of her hand, her chin jutting forward, that look of determination coming over her.

'Elena.'

'I'm fine, Adam. Really.'

He hears the sudden irritation in her voice, a warning, and he backs away from it. He is too raw for an argument. 'Where are you staying?'

'In Zaragoza. I got a room in a hotel near the station. It's OK. It will do, I suppose.'

'What train are you getting tomorrow?' he asks. 'I could come and meet you at the station. We could go somewhere to talk, just the two of us, maybe get something to eat…'

'Look, Adam, I thought that I might stay on here a bit longer.'

'What do you mean?'

'I thought I might as well. To see a little bit of the city.'

He pauses, thinking about this.

'Is this because I wouldn't go with you? Is that it?'

'No! No, I just feel that I need to be on my own for a while. That maybe we both do.'

'I see,' he says coldly, feeling petulant and snubbed. 'How long do you think you'll stay there?'

'I'm not sure. Six, seven days maybe.'

Neither of them says anything, each waiting for the other to speak.

'I'll call you again in a couple of days,' she says finally, a weary resignation in her voice.

'Fine,' he answers tightly, and hangs up the phone.

He can feel his temples pounding, hot blood pulsing around his brain. What does she mean by this? Why does he feel she has abandoned him? That he is being punished? She cannot know what happened, can she?

'So, she is not coming home?'

He turns suddenly, startled by the voice behind him. Maria stands in the doorway, her shadow cast by the light behind her – a long, dark shape across the kitchen floor. Darkness has crept up in the room as the evening falls outside. She pads softly across the floor in her bare feet; her long, blue-black hair hangs loose down the length of her back.

'I wish you wouldn't do that,' he says irritably, pushing the phone back against the wall. 'It's rude to listen to other people's conversations.'

'Oh, please,' she laughs, emerging from behind the fridge door with a beer in hand. 'You want one?'

'No.'

He returns to the mattress on the floor, throwing his body on it and picking up the book he has been trying to read. He avoids her gaze, staring sulkily at his book.

'Well, did she say how it was?'

He ignores her, sensing the danger in her voice. High and shrill, it is barely controlled.

'No matter,' she shrugs. 'I can imagine what it was like. I can see them all now, his mother and all those sisters, lined up in their black clothes, their mantillas, like beetles, all of them crying and wailing. And the father, that short, fat, mean little man, looking stern, but no tears from him. Lord, no!' She laughs suddenly and Adam shifts uncomfortably.

'And afterwards,' she continues, 'when they all go back to the house – all those people, all that food… Why do people eat so much at funerals?' She pauses to consider. 'And they will all talk in loud voices about the tragedy of it, the terrible loss, the bravery of the family, the way they are holding up. But to each other they will whisper, "Why? What made him do it?" And what do you suppose they will answer to that?'

Adam shoots a glance across at her. She sits on the counter, her long legs crossed at the ankles, swigging from her bottle of beer.

'I don't care,' he says coldly.

'If you didn't care, you would have gone to the funeral.'

'That's why you think I didn't go? Because I feel in some way responsible?'

'Well, don't you?'

'No!' he yells at her, infuriated by the questioning eyebrows, the smirk on her face. 'I'm not responsible! I didn't do this! If anyone is to blame it's you!'

Her eyes widen, their dark orbs burn, scalding him.

'Me?'

'I've heard you, don't think I haven't!' he hisses. 'And Elena too. We've had to listen to you going on and on at him, that endless whining, always at him. Nagging him. Plaguing him. Where have you been, Carlos? Who were you with? Why didn't you come home, Carlos? Do you love me, Carlos? Do you need me, Carlos? How much? Nag, nag, nag.'

He stops, breathless, shocked by his own outburst. He reads her bewilderment in her shocked expression. He thinks she is about to cry, and instantly regrets his outburst.

'Oh, Maria… Jesus, look, I didn't mean that. I'm sorry, OK? I'm just upset. Hey, the only person to blame here is Carlos.' He shakes his head and sighs in defeat. 'And we'll never know why it was he did it.'

'I know,' she says quietly.

He looks at her across the room. Her face is in shadow but he can see the glint in her eyes.

'What?'

'I know why he did it.'

'But… how could you possibly…'

'He left a note.'

Her words, flung at him in the darkness, wound and sting. Their sharpness, and the prospect of what words the note might hold, leave him gasping.

'Why didn't you say so before now?' he asks, confused. 'Where is it?'

'I burned it.'

'What? But why? What did it say?'

'I think you can guess.' Her voice is cold, strangled with emotion. He feels the spite of them. His mouth is dry. Something cold plunges through his body and he shakes his head, but his denial comes too late for her.

'I should have let you read it, I suppose. You'd have found it funny, really.' Her voice lilts, she is almost hysterical. 'He was never a very good writer, Carlos, and believe me, this was not his best work.'

'What did it say?' he asks quietly, his anger simmering close to the surface.

'In fact, I should have kept it. Just for the entertainment value alone…'

'What did it say?' He jumps up from the mattress, rushing at her from across the room. His eyes are wild with fury, lit with an insane desire to know. Her sarcasm, this mark of nonchalance she wears, infuriates him.

'What it said,' she counters angrily, 'what it said was pathetic. Unrequited love – tragic, really. That sorry little show of affection during your weekend in Zaragoza. Now really, Adam, that wasn't nice. The way you looked at him, your scorn, your horror. How he couldn't forget it. How he would never be able to forget it.'

Adam feels his heart tipping in his chest. It feels cold, like a stone.

'Oh, there was all the usual stuff as well – how his father hates him, how no one understands him – and that includes me, by the way.' She laughs mockingly. 'Just your average – how do you say it? – garden-variety depression. But you? You were the last straw.'

Her words slice the air. They cut through him.

'Jesus Christ,' he whispers, shaking his head.

'I know!' she laughs. 'Ridiculous, isn't it? I mean, who the hell kills themselves because of embarrassment!'

'Shut up,' he whispers.

'Oh, Adam. You're not going to cry, are you? A big man like you? Carlos would be touched, I'm sure. To finally see your feminine side. It might have given him some hope…'

He reaches across and slaps her, hard across the mouth.

Her hand goes to her mouth instinctively and her eyes fill with tears. She stares at him, silenced, incredulous.

'Jesus, Maria. I didn't mean to do that.'

Her eyes continue to stare at him, tears spilling noiselessly down her cheeks.

'Are you hurt?' He moves to examine her cheek, but she turns her head away.

'Maria.'

He touches a finger to her cheek, feels the dampness there, a pearl of salt water dissolving at his touch. The room is quiet. Her hand moves away from her mouth, revealing a new redness that will become a bruise over the next few hours. He touches it gently, his fingers linger. He looks in her eyes – pools of blackness – and as he gazes down at her, she folds his fingers in hers and moves them slowly, guiding them into her mouth. He feels the warm wetness of her tongue, the inside of her lip. Her eyes do not break his gaze as she sucks them further into her mouth. He feels her tongue flickering and something jolts inside him. The night feels warm and still around them.

'This is wrong,' he murmurs, his mind misting with desire; his body craves her.

She releases his finger from her mouth and regards him plaintively with those deep, soulful eyes. But he doesn't remove his hand from her clasp and she moves forward, slipping from the counter, pushing her body against him, and lifts her face up to his; he feels the heat from her breath before her lips brush his, and his hand twists around to the small of her back and he feels her crushing into him. Her lips crushing his, her breasts pressed against his chest, those long bare legs rubbing against his thighs. The voice inside him, telling him this is wrong – that whining, narrow voice – is drowned out by the clamour of desire, the overwhelming rush of blood that sweeps through his body, making him weak. It is pointless to fight it. He wants to be defeated. He wants it to win. Their bodies tangle on the mattress and he marvels at the length of her, the softness, softer than he had imagined. She feels cool, like a drink of water, and he drinks greedily, needing to quench his terrible thirst.

ELENA

13

HER FACE STINGS as the wind whips hair across her cheek. She gathers the strands with her fingers and releases them back into the breeze. His words whip around her too. They cut and sting as sharply as the wind. These painful memories, brought out into the daylight. Reliving them through his perspective causes an ache in her chest. She doesn't like to think of that time. Her mind was tortured by it for long enough – those persistent wonderings about how he filled those seven days and nights while she was in Zaragoza. In her mind's eye, she has watched him with her, the heat of the night, their passions inflamed, a thrusting, achingly physical togetherness, blue-black hair on the pillow, long legs clasped around his hips. Her imagination has allowed them a steamy, erotic affair, a callous disregard for anyone or anything else apart from their own lustful carnal pleasures.

'Was it just that one night?' she asks tentatively. She is not sure why she wants to know this. Clarity, she expects, a need to tie up loose ends. This spirit of confession, coming clean, demands a cold, hard look at the facts.

The pause before he answers is an answer in itself. It confirms what she had feared.

'That night. And then one other,' he says feebly. And then he charges on, as if needing to explain, to justify, 'I was angry with you, you see? I couldn't understand why you were staying away for so long. It felt as though you were punishing me, cutting yourself off from me. You can be so cold sometimes, Elena. Isolating yourself.'

She listens to the chilliness of his accusations. It could be Henry sitting next to her, making the same remarks, pointing out the same character flaws, using them as justification for his own shameful deeds. Weariness descends on her. She is too tired to fight any more. The patterns of her life cast out around her and she is struck by the repetition of them – this endless cycle, the persistent recurrence of the same arguments, the same accusations, the grooves and patterns of the same dreary mistakes.

She closes her eyes and hears his voice asking softly if she is all right. Thinking about this, considering her state of mind, the present lying in tatters around her, pitching forward uncertainly into the future – the past still clawing at her, pulling her back – she answers feebly, a noncommittal response, shrugging off the probing nature of the question. She lifts her face to the breeze.

'I've often wondered,' he says to her, 'why you stayed in Zaragoza for that week. I mean, I understand why you would want to go to the funeral, but… well, it was never clear to me why you had to stay away so long.' He pauses, waiting for a response that doesn't come, and then adds tentatively, 'I thought, perhaps, you were trying to punish me.'

He is needling her, she knows this – pushing her into giving an answer – and while part of her resists this subtle bullying tactic, another part of her is travelling back to Zaragoza.

'Maybe I was punishing you,' she says softly. 'I felt let down, confused. You were hiding something from me, I knew that much. And the funeral, it was so shocking, so violent – the grief that I witnessed there, like Carlos had cut a giant gash through that whole family, as easily as he had taken a razor to his wrists and ankles. It left me feeling raw and emotional. And I knew that if I went back home, back to that apartment with Maria hovering blackly around us, I knew if I did that, then things could explode between us – that I would say things to you that I could never take back. I wasn't prepared for that anger, for that confrontation. I needed to be alone for a while. Can you understand that?'

He is leaning forward, his forearms resting on his knees, but his head is turned back to look at her. His eyes have been fixed on her for the duration of her explanation. She looks into them and thinks she sees a glimmering of understanding. They travel over her face, a settled frown softening somewhat. He gives the faintest of nods before turning away to give his attention to a duck launching itself into the pond, ripples trailing out behind as it glides through the water.

*

On the first day, she wandered down to the Plaza del Pilar and, like a pilgrim, stepped through the tall, heavy doors and into the lofty palatial expanse of the Basilica. She drifted through the long marbled corridors, her deadened gaze travelling over the blue walls and creamy columns, up, up to the lofty ceiling. It wasn't like the other churches – not grey and dark and brooding – not like the church she had stood in the day before, with her head bowed, so she wouldn't have to look on those faces stretched and dampened with a disbelieving grief. It was enough, having to stand there listening to that pitiful wail like an animal suffering beyond endurance. But the Basilica was quiet, wrapped in the hushed awe of visitors witnessing its dignified magnificence for the first time. Light streamed through the windows, filling the immense airy spaces. She walked through rays of sunshine, dust motes eternally descending through them. Her feet moved mechanically over the cold marble floor and she leaned her head back to look up at the frescoes by Goya, dark colours, brooding images, saints and men in voluminous robes with troubled faces, fingers pointed in accusation or instruction, hands clutched in prayer or covering hearts. At the capella, she lit a candle for Carlos – a long pillar of wax – a candle that must burn for weeks, she thought. Planting it firmly in place, she watched the flame flicker before steadying itself, burning strongly. The musty smell of incense filled her senses, and as she stared at the flame licking upwards into a thread of thin black smoke, she tried to harness some emotion, tried to access her grief or anger or sadness. But inside was full of smoke too – black, ethereal, intangible, masking whatever secrets lay within her soul.

Perhaps I should go back, she thought. Standing in line, waiting to come forward and kiss the pillar, she turned this idea over in her head. Her decision to stay in Zaragoza seemed like an act of defiance. But what exactly was she rebelling against? Adam's silence that had greeted the announcement of her decision was still ringing in her head as she inched towards the pillar. That silence was weighty with his indignation and annoyance and her own unspoken protest, and she felt the cold wedge of distance it placed between them. Feet shuffled forward and she glanced sideways at the open confessional, the bored stare of an elderly priest who sat and listened to a continuous litany of misdeeds as the sinners queued up to unburden themselves. Adam should have come with her. She felt the harsh sting of his failure. He had let her down. She reached the pillar and was confronted by an oval of eroded stone locked in a marble surround, the groove created by countless believers who had stroked and kissed this piece of rock, strengthened by the belief that the Virgin Mary had appeared on this pillar, hundreds of years ago. As she bent down to apply her lips to the holy stone, she felt the coolness of the kiss, and something whispered to her that it would not be the last betrayal, that he would let her down again.

*

'Churches,' she says to him. 'Zaragoza has a lot of churches.'

'Well, it's a religious country,' he adds, with a brief, hoarse laugh. 'Did you experience a religious conversion while you were there?'

She smiles and doesn't answer.

It felt as if she visited them all during that long, lonely week. All those dark, hushed temples, the masses and masses of sculptures and paintings, scenes from Armageddon flooding her senses, crowding out any peace that was there. She went to the churches to sit in the quiet cavernous spaces and listen carefully to the echoes of her soul. But the clamour of religious fervour in the throngs of holy images that assaulted her proved too much, drowning out the whisperings of her conscience.

*

On the fourth day, needful of some secular images to occupy her imagination, she found herself alone in the Museum of Zaragoza, her shoes squeaking over the stone floors, their solitary echo a testament to the emptiness of the building. But the paintings that crowded the walls were despairingly religious too. Her heart sank, and she felt a new impatience as her eyes cast about her from one dark image to the next, medieval impressions of biblical scenes, drawn faces – pale and green at the edges – stared back at her, eyes filled with melancholy or dread or lit with the light of religious zeal. One painting out of all tugged at her consciousness, drawing her to it – *The Interrogation of Saint Apollonia*. She bent forward to get a better view and her eyes widened with horror as they travelled over the scenes depicting the pale-skinned woman, her long hair like ropes of gold and russet, her green robes, as she was systematically tortured. Something moved inside Elena as she silently observed the indignity of Apollonia's clothes being stripped from her body, revealing pale breasts, the next scene showing the rips and lacerations cutting through that alabaster skin. As her eyes travelled to the penultimate image of Apollonia's head being held and one of her torturers brandishing pliers clasping a tooth, she saw other teeth lying on the ground, blood streaming from the woman's mouth. Elena felt her stomach lurch, a heaving nausea washing down over her. She had to get out, where she could breathe, away from these images of pain and death.

The courtyard was quiet and airy and she sat with her back to the egg-yolk-yellow walls, closing her eyes to the fragments of Roman sculpture that surrounded her, and felt her tears coming quickly, hot licks of breath searing her chest. Images of death and birth and sacrifice and pain clamoured behind her, pictures she had seen and would in time forget. But one image had left its bloody stain on her mind indelibly. She saw his body again, those staring eyes, that filthy bath water and the violence of those cuts in his skin, those veins ripped open. She had tried to forget, but the memory of it rose up and lapped at her. Sitting with her head in her hands in that quiet courtyard, she felt the events of the previous week closing in around her, rubbing against her, leaving her raw and alone.

It was the evenings that she found difficult. Sitting in a bar, nursing a glass of wine, she avoided eye contact with other people, not wanting to be disturbed, not wanting to make small talk or explain her presence there or ward off any unwanted attention. Or else, lying in her hotel room, staring at the ceiling, she willed herself not to pick up the phone and call him, steadfastly maintaining her distance, remaining aloof. It was stubbornness, sheer bloody-mindedness, and she knew it. But something was making her do this, forcing her to remain apart from him, like a test, to see if she could do it. A test for him, too – so that he would be aware of how he had hurt her, how disappointed she was by his actions, or rather his omissions. And while she craved his company and the sound of his voice, there was another voice, deep inside her, needling her, cajoling her into doing this, into keeping herself apart from him, just for that week, to gain some perspective and allow the wounds to heal.

After her experience in the museum, she shunned her hotel room and the perils of her minibar and instead strolled through the narrow streets down to the river. The Plaza del Pilar was still busy with people as she sat down on the steps, facing the Basilica. The sun was setting, casting an orange glow over the buildings. The plaza was wide and open, feeling more Italian than Spanish with its Florentine-style exchange building, those arched cloisters. And as she sat on the steps, the Basilica appeared to Elena to be incredibly, impossibly big. The sunlight was on her back, but soon she would be in shadow. It was growing late, the evening creeping up around her, another night alone. She pulled her cardigan about her and watched as the pigeons and the people congregated in groups across the plaza. Some nuns emerged from the Basilica, wearing black habits and white starched wimples – they scurried along like a group of puffins, their crucifixes dangling from long beaded chains. A breeze rippled in the air and Elena breathed it in and thought of Carlos. Her friend had been dead for nearly two weeks. As she sat on the steps on that beautiful evening, listening to the noises of the day relax into night, she wondered how it could have been possible that he had not had enough hope that he would live to see an evening like this. That it had not been enough for him to experience the comfort of the fading light of day, the hazy sky shot through with the flaming orange of a dying sun, the air filled with the music of bells chiming through their pattern of notes high up above the domed roofs. That his pain was great enough to dull his senses to such beauty.

Choirboys emerged from behind the Basilica, summoned by the bells, and marched in pairs around to the entrance, their red and white vestments blowing in the breeze. They laughed and joked and talked loudly to one another. A gypsy woman approached her, offering birdseed for sale, but Elena shook her head and smiled and the woman moved on. A short, fat, tough-looking woman wandered around the square selling lottery tickets. Her voice – hardened into a squawk – called out her wares, competing with the hypnotic chant echoing inside the church. Water slipped from the fountain near the Roman wall, sliding over the smooth surface of rock before plunging from the jagged precipice to the pool beneath. She sat, her arms clasped around her knees drawn up to her chin, and watched the Spaniards indulging their small children, who in turn indulged the pigeons, scattering seed. Elena felt her body relax, each muscle folding out and expanding, each tendon and sinew relaxing and loosening. And for the first time that week, she felt joy in her solitary view of all around her. Something inside her heart began to melt, anger dissipating into acceptance; the blood released through pumping valves flowed warmly into her veins, carrying the first drops of something generous and forgiving.

As she sat there, a small child – no more than three years old – was chasing a pigeon in front of her, his face set with determination. Elena watched as he crept up behind it stealthily, his feet hastening into a run as the pigeon hurried away. Yet still he persisted, until his impatient dash spurred the pigeon to use its wings and it was gone. It soared above the plaza, up to the heights of the dome, while the boy's face collapsed into tears, his mouth a down-turned U of despair. As his father swept the boy up in his arms, asking him with amusement why he was crying over that one pigeon when there were so many more left to feed, Elena heard the boy say clearly, 'But I wanted that one.' Something inside her recognised the senseless truth in that quest – the fathomless need to pursue that one elusive being. And she felt, in that moment, ready to go back to him.

By the time the train pulled into the station, the heat and fumes rose up to greet them. People pushed through the doors out onto the platform, another hot, damp blanket of heat greeting them. Grit rose up in the smoke, caking their lips with a dry dust. Elena felt herself carried along by a wave of people – a surge of humanity pushing towards the gates. Her heart beat loudly in her rib cage, a rising excitement pulsing through her, bringing a sudden smile to her face. Her eyes scanned the crowd, eager and hungry for him. And there he was. Taller than the others, his head rising above the crowd, that shock of hair falling forward onto his face, those sharp angular features – the humour of them, the openness. For a moment he looked without seeing her, not noticing her approach; and as she came towards him, waiting to be found, waiting to be gathered up in his arms, she saw something in his face – a wariness, an anxiety – that she had not read there before. His hand rose to his head, rubbed down over his features, leaving them briefly drawn, stretched with a nervous anticipation. The smile fell from her face, something cold settling on the floor of her stomach, and at that moment he saw her, almost jumping with fright. A smile sprang onto his face. But there was something hard and tight about that smile, his eyes remaining watchful, as he pushed through the crowds and found her, taking her with uncertain arms and a hard, urgent kiss.

★

'I knew then that there was something wrong,' she tells him. 'I could feel it. I could sense it.'

He looked guilty, that was it. His eyes tried to hide his thoughts while at the same time searching her expression for some sign of recognition, a hint that she knew what he had done, that she could see it in him.

She cannot see his eyes now as they stare ahead of him. She hears his release of breath as he shakes his head slowly.

'I know,' he concedes. 'It was so stupid. When I think about it now…' His head sinks momentarily, and he repeats that same gesture of anguish – passing his long, narrow hand over his face. 'I dreaded meeting you off the train. Did you know that? I was sure you would be able to tell. One look at my face, and I was sure you would guess what had happened.'

But she didn't want to see it. She wilfully ignored it. She accepted his forced cheerfulness, allowed herself to believe that it was genuine. She let herself be deceived, ignoring the nagging tone of doubt at the back of her mind, choosing not to hear the desperation at the edges of his voice. Instead, she went along with it, allowing herself to be duped, willingly surrendering herself to the deception.

'Perhaps I should have told you there and then,' he says, his hands spreading wide as if balancing the arguments for and against. 'I did think about it, you know. In fact, I was still debating in my mind what I should do when I saw you coming towards me on the platform. But as soon as I looked into your face, I knew I couldn't do it. And at that point, I couldn't think of any reason why you should have to know about it. I thought, so long as you didn't find out, the whole thing could be forgotten about, that it would fade into oblivion.'

She sucks air into her lungs, suddenly breathless, his regret leaving her cold.

'What a secret to carry inside you,' she says to him and, despite her best efforts, she cannot avoid a hint of disapproval in her voice.

'I should have told you then,' he says quickly, shaking his head in disbelief at his youthful stupidity. 'To think that I could hide that from you, that we could just move forward as if nothing had happened…'

'Maybe we could have,' she volunteers, 'if it hadn't been for…'

The words hang between them, unspoken and swelling in the space. *If it hadn't been for the baby.* The baby that never was. And with this realisation, Elena is hit by a renewed wave of anger – anger at the futility of all that happened, the tragedy of the errors that were made between them.

'If only we had talked,' he says solemnly. 'If only we had been able to talk things through then… All of the things we've missed, the sheer waste of it all. Sometimes I think about everything we threw away, what we could have had, the life we could have lived, the children we might have had. It's not something I like to think too much about; it might drive me crazy.'

Her eyes bear down on him, her fury and indignation rising with each word that he utters.

'We?' she says, struggling to contain her temper. 'It was you, Adam. You did this. You threw it all away.'

He glances back at her, his eyes implacable.

'Yes. I suppose it was me, in the end.'

Evening is closing in over the city, darkness streaking across the sky. Elena thinks of the night that lies ahead, the routine pedestrian activities that must be gone through – dinners to be made, children to be washed and put to bed, and then the terrible stand-off with Henry, the avoidance of that aching wound that has opened between them, not wanting to touch the scar, to pick away at the scab. She hasn't the will or the energy tonight. Any argument will raise questions that she does not want to consider the answers to – notably, where do they go from here? And will they move on together or embark on separate lives? The pain that that will entail, the long wait for her heart to mend, seems inevitable to her at this stage. But it is something that for now she wants to put off, although she cannot put it off indefinitely.

'It's getting late,' she says with finality, bringing their conversation to a close. 'I have to go; the children will be waiting for me, and Henry...'

He glances up quickly at the mention of her husband.

'Of course.'

They rise and turn into the wind, striding purposefully back along the path, past the flowerbeds, neither of them speaking, an awkward silence accompanying them. They stop at the Arch, preparing to go their separate ways, and she turns to him. His face arranges itself into an expression of earnest seriousness.

'My mother's funeral,' he begins. 'I'd really like it... I'd very much appreciate it if you could attend.'

The formality of his address strikes her as awkward. She feels the difficulty of his request.

'Of course,' she answers generously, suddenly feeling a surge of pity towards him rising out of the hollows of her tired body.

He nods and gives her the details, avoiding her eyes.

'Well, until tomorrow, then.'

He holds himself stiffly away from her, and the sorrow of his loneliness moves her to step towards him and wrap her arms around him. The sudden warmth of this gesture, the spontaneity, takes both of them by surprise and for a moment they stand there, clinging to each other. And in that moment, she feels the warmth of him, the sinewy tautness of his long body, the sudden surprise of the softness of his cheek against hers. With the autumn wind whipping around them, they stand holding on to each other as the traffic builds and the day slips away into night.

HENRY

14

HE WAKES TO a beam of light entering the bedroom through a break in the curtains. Something is wrong, he thinks, it should not be this bright. He must have slept in. Heaving himself up onto his elbows, he squints across at the radio alarm. Only it isn't there. As his eyes adjust to the new day, the room settles into his vision. Ben's room. The quiet neatness of it, the cheerful primary colours, the room ablaze; from the small bed Henry surveys the empty cot in the corner, the mobile hanging still, stuffed toys lined up in a row on the shelf along with Ben's books, the stencils of Winnie-the-Pooh and Eeyore – stencils that he did himself, and not very well.

He pulls himself up into a slumped seated position. Observing the blocky brightness of the room, he remembers how he came to spend the night here, his sleep broken by the sporadic and insistent kicking of his little boy, thrashing through his sleep. Elena said little all evening, looking grey and washed out, preoccupied with her own thoughts. He sensed a calming in her, the anger of the previous day simmered down into a dull, hard disappointment. But the cold shell of her exterior, the frosty sadness, seemed to warn him off wordlessly. 'I'll sleep in Ben's room,' he said to her, offering it up as a gesture, a show of sensitivity, an unspoken understanding that he knew she didn't want him near her, that she would flinch were he to touch her. He knew that she could not relax into sleep were his body lying next to hers and risk an unintentional brushing of limbs, their unconscious bodies gravitating towards each other, betraying her waking thoughts, her conscious desires. But after he offered up this gesture of goodwill, she barely looked up at him in acknowledgement.

Henry lay awake in the tiny room that night, in that cramped bed, staring up at the ceiling, listening to the sounds of the house around him: the creaking floorboards, the cistern bubbling, taps spilling water into the basin in the bathroom – and the sigh of their bed when Elena climbed in. He watched the light seeping under Ben's bedroom door changing as doors opened and closed, and he could read from it too when Elena switched her light off, the last light in the house. He lay in the darkness, listening to the gentle sounds of his son's breathing, feeling drained and weak and a little hammered.

The day had been a washout. He had gone into the office, driven by a sense of duty, a weird need to clear up around him, to create some semblance of order before everything went asunder. He had sat at his desk, peering at his inbox, all those unanswered e-mails, and briefly considered composing something explanatory, something final, that he could send to everyone in his address book. It would have to be short and snappy, something with a bit of zing to it. *Sorry, folks, you're out of luck and we're out of business! Cheerio, everyone, the fat lady has gone to get her coat. So long, my friends, it's been a privilege sailing with you. Roger, over and out.* The screen had blinked at him, offering no answers, so he had shut it down. The phone had rung a few times, until he disconnected it. In the cupboard behind his desk, he had found a bottle of Beaujolais – a gift from a client – that he had forgotten to bring home. Taking a plastic cup from the water-cooler stand, he had sat in his chair, surrounded by unopened letters and stacks of files, with all means of communication switched off. Leaning back in his chair, he had peered across his desk and raised a cup of wine to his crumbling empire. 'So long,' he had announced to the empty room, 'and happy hunting.'

He can't face another day like that. He sits up in bed, blinking away the sleep, his eyes scanning the ceiling. The thought of going back to the office, another restless, fruitless grey day, just depresses him. He needs to shower – needs to feel the force of hot water between his shoulder blades, galvanising him, clearing his head.

He creeps across the landing in bare feet; the house feels empty around him. The bedrooms are empty. He has no idea what time it is.

Padding downstairs, he feels the stillness rubbing up against him. His house. Their house. All these rooms, these familiar smells, how his house sounds when it is empty. But it is not empty. He finds her seated at the kitchen table. Elena glances up briefly as he enters but then looks away again, her brow furrowed with concentration. He stands at the threshold of the kitchen, watching her, the way her head bends over her work, her hair falling forward, the way she sucks in her lower lip, her eyes lost from him, only heavy lashes sweeping her cheeks. She is writing something, the page in front of her filling up with her neat square writing.

'What are you doing?' he asks hesitantly, leaning against the doorframe.

She sighs heavily, and he feels the weight of her disappointment in him. 'Making a list.'

'I see.'

He comes forward gingerly, feeling unsure of himself, hesitating before taking a seat. She does not want him here, he can feel it. But something is compelling him, some last need to salvage something.

'A list of what?'

She looks up at him and her eyes travel over his face quickly, a flickering movement, but there is something searching in that look, as if seeking something hidden there.

'A "to do" list,' she says solemnly. 'So far I have cancel squash club membership, collect dry cleaning, contact employment agencies and find new place to live.'

Her words crush him. There is no sarcasm in her voice, just a melancholy strain, as if she is deflated yet still slightly disbelieving that this is happening to her.

'I know it's ridiculous,' she continues, 'but I felt that if I made a list then at least I would be doing something, making a stab at sorting things out. But I don't know where to begin. Everything seems so huge. So desperate.'

Her hands lie on the table, palms up – *What am I to do?* she seems to be saying. And he, in return, has no answers to give her. A sudden perception of his weakness comes to him.

'I'm sorry.' The words sound flat as they escape his mouth. He looks away from her as he says them.

'Please stop saying that.' She caps her pen quickly, snapping it shut, and he feels the contained ferocity of her actions. Her chair is pushed back suddenly and she picks up her mug and moves to the sink.

'Where are the kids?' he asks after her.

'I've dropped them to school and the crèche. Your mother is going to collect them.'

'My mother?'

'Yes. I have things to do, things to sort out. And so do you.'

He nods his head slowly, feeling the ache of what is to come. This conversation. This sorting through the mess. And the questions that will fall out of it, the reasons sought and his baffling lack of explanations. But, more than that, he fears the decisions that will have to be made – the momentous, life-altering choices that will be played out in this kitchen.

'Are you going into the office?'

He shakes his head. 'I can't face it. Not today. Later in the week, once the meeting is over and all of this is…' He can't bring himself to say it. His unfinished sentence hangs in the air between them. *Once all of this is over.* The finality of it – the imminent closure – cuts through the air with a truculent chop.

'I see.'

She dries her hands briskly on the tea towel before flinging it on the counter – a display of irritation. He notices her clothes – the starched elegance of them. She is wearing a black wool dress and tiny kitten heels. Black glass beads swarm at her throat, her hemline skims her knees.

'You look nice,' he says softly, inquisitively. 'Are you going somewhere?'

'To a funeral.'

'Who died?'

She pauses, considering what to say, before shaking her head. 'No one you know. It doesn't matter.'

'Shall I come with you?'

She shakes her head vigorously, her eyes squeezed tight, and he nods gently, an acknowledgement of her understandable need to be alone. He looks down at his hands, the large knuckles, the spindly hairs pushing through the skin, and notices for the first time how like his father's hands they have become.

'What are we going to do?' he asks quietly. He doesn't look up, feeling her body held tightly, pressed against the kitchen cupboards, as if leaning away from a precipice. She says nothing. He can feel her holding back, silenced by her indecision, bewildered by the decisions she has been confronted with.

'Those things I said,' he tries uncertainly, 'those things I said on Sunday, about you and him. About the way you've been lately. I didn't mean them. I was just – I don't know... I suppose I wanted to blame you for something. I wanted you to feel bad too. But it's only because I feel so guilty myself.'

His voice cracks suddenly, emotion swelling in his chest. These words that are being spoken sound small and paltry, echoing around this cold kitchen. He feels their inadequacy. They are not enough to breach the gap between them, not enough to make up for everything that has happened. They both know that.

'Are you going to leave me?' he asks, not daring to look her in the face, not wanting to see the truth in her eyes. 'I'd understand if you wanted to. I couldn't blame you, after all this...'

She raises her hands to her face – he sees this action from the corner of his eye – her fingers laced together, hiding her face. From within that shelter, behind that woven mask of flesh, comes a small, uncertain voice. 'I don't know,' she says honestly. 'I don't know what I want, what I'm going to do.'

Something cracks in his chest, he feels like he has been punched in the gut, and a loud gasp escapes him; he bends forward with the blow.

'Oh, God,' he moans. Until this moment, he had not conceived it possible. And now he is confronted with the blinding reality that she might leave him. It makes him weak. He feels hollowed out. There is a push of pressure in his chest.

She moves away from the sink and takes the seat next to him. Her movements are awkward; her hands flutter, looking for a place to rest. Her arms reach out to him and then snap back, as if reminded of what he has done and how it would betray her principle of hurt to touch him, to comfort him. He swipes away a single tear with the back of his hand, willing himself not to break down, not yet, not in front of her. He is not yet dressed and feels hideously dishevelled in his pyjamas, sitting next to Elena and her elegant dress.

'It's just that you're a different person to me now,' she tries to explain. 'I always thought of you as someone I could rely on, someone I could trust. That's what made me love you – well, part of it, anyway. But a big part. I never thought you would do anything to hurt me.'

'I didn't mean to…'

'But you did. It happened, Henry, and it has shocked me. Tomorrow, my home will become the possession of an institution. Our children will have no place to live. And I have no idea what we will do for money. I can't even begin to think about what other debts have built up that you haven't told me about. These are things that I thought would never happen. I would never have dreamed that you would allow this to happen, that you would be so careless, take such risks. I don't know what to think about you any more. Don't you understand that? You're changed to me. I don't know who you are any more. I don't know if I can still be with you. If I can still love you.'

He wants to say yes, that he understands, but he fears the entrapment of words, fears that she would mistake this for acceptance on his part, a letting go. Instead he covers her hand with his. She lets it rest there, unmoving. Through the mist of his gathering tears, he sees marks on the kitchen wall – pencil markings stepping up through the wall, dates alongside each notch. Elena's careful handwriting. *Emily aged three and a half. Emily aged five and three quarters. Ben at fifteen months.* These tender recordings of their children's progress make his heart heavy. This woman whose hand lies under his, this woman he has loved for a decade, who has carried, given birth to and nursed his children; her gentle, pragmatic responses to the world, her studious endeavours to build a home, a family, her staunch heart, the bravery of her efforts – all of these things are slipping from his grasp. His fingers close around her hand, feeling the pulse running through her flesh, and he has a sudden glimpse of the futility of his efforts, the greed of his endeavours, the uselessness of it, the waste.

'Oh, Lord,' she breathes, her hand slipping out from under the weight of his, and she reaches across the table for a napkin to dry her face. 'I have to get going.'

She gets up and straightens her dress.

But before she can move away, he grabs her by the wrist, overcome by his sudden impulse to keep her there, to hang on to her, to them, for just a little longer. 'Elena,' he says, looking up into her wide eyes, teary and alarmed. 'What's happened to us? How did we get to be like this?'

She shakes her head, unsure of what to say.

'When did we grow so distant from each other?' he asks plaintively. 'We used to talk. We used to be able to tell each other anything.'

'I remember.'

'We swore that we would never lose that. Do you remember? We promised each other that we would always be open and honest. Where did all these secrets come from? How did we let them creep in?'

She is struggling with her emotions; her eyebrows peak into the centre of her brow, her eyes fill with pain. 'Henry, don't…'

'And we used to have fun,' he charges on, 'don't you remember? When we first moved in here. We used to take baths together. I used to wash your hair for you. And afterwards, you would sit on the sofa wearing only my shirt, and I would rub your feet, which were always cold, while you ate ice-cream from a tub.' He smiles, a wistful smile, the glow of memory warming him.

'I remember.'

Her hand rests on his shoulder and he looks up into her eyes and for a moment he feels a glimmer of the closeness that used to exist between them. But then something flickers across her face, a sudden realisation, grabbing her back from the past and into the cold, harsh present. She breaks away from him, composing herself.

'You'll collect the children from your mother's later?' she asks quickly, restoring the distance between them with her tone.

He nods, his body leaning forward, defeated, and listens to her moving about the house, gathering her things. A few minutes later the front door bangs shut.

He sits still at the table, watching the markings on the wall, his shadow pitched against them. He feels panic, a shortness of breath. A sharp pain lodges in his chest. From within him comes a new longing – a longing to hold on to Elena for just a little longer. Surely there must be a way, if only he had the wit to find it.

And then comes a brainwave. As he stands at the kitchen sink, drinking a glass of water, it occurs to him. Shane. His friend. The one who gave him the idea in the first place. The realisation comes to him quickly – more a remembrance, the return of the knowledge that should he need help, Shane can supply it. Shane would stand by him, help him out of this rut.

The phone call is brief, the meeting arranged. Henry finds himself taken by a surge of energy. He bounds up the stairs, showers vigorously, whips clothes out of the wardrobe and hops about on one foot as he shoves the other into the leg of his trousers. During the drive into town, he finds himself tapping the steering wheel, humming to the radio, his eyes darting from traffic to rear-view mirror, darting all around him. Having parked the car – scraping the door handle against a pillar in his haste, leaving a smear of yellow paint etched into the black plastic – he hurries across the bridge, watching impatiently for a break in the traffic before racing across the road and into Pravda.

It takes him a few minutes to adjust his eyes to the dimly lit interior, the floorboards creaking as he steps past the bar down into the cavernous interior. He finds Shane on the mezzanine, waving to him to come up and join them. Them. As Henry comes closer, he notices the other suit at the table and is introduced to Gerald, one of Shane's colleagues from the office. Both men are sipping white wine while perusing the menus, and Henry eyes the bottle of Chardonnay cooling in a bucket at the side of the table.

'Sit yourself down there,' Shane says voluminously. 'You'll have some wine, won't you?'

Henry quietly acquiesces, feeling his early enthusiasm draining away as Gerald enquires loudly of them whether the chicken wings here are very salty.

'I'm sorry, I didn't know you had lunch plans,' Henry says nervously to Shane. 'I didn't mean to intrude on you.'

'Nonsense! Gerald's just started with us at the firm, thought I'd bring him out for lunch. Didn't I mention it on the phone?'

'No, you didn't.'

'You don't mind, do you?' He looks at Henry's face, his anxious features, and Henry shakes his head quickly, shrugging and holding up his palms.

'No. No, of course not.'

But he does mind. He hoped for a quiet lunch, a quiet word with Shane, with his friend. It is his own fault, of course; he should have said as much on the phone earlier, he should have clarified his intent. And now there is this third party with his narrow aquiline face and busy tie, whose sudden smile displayed too many teeth and whose obvious need to impress, to fit in, threatens to spoil Henry's lunch.

'I was just telling Gerald here that he really ought to join a club – squash or tennis or golf, whichever he prefers. Henry and I are in the same squash club. That's how we know each other, isn't that right, Henry?'

Henry smiles and nods, his order arriving – a cheeseburger crammed full with salad and skinny chips piled high in a separate bowl. For eight years now he has been a member of the squash club. Eight years pounding a black rubber ball against the wall. Eight years and countless pints in the bar afterwards with Shane, leaning over the tall round tables, discussing their game, the stock market, the state of the economy, whether to buy a holiday home abroad or in Ireland, the benefits of private education over public at primary level. Their conversations roll back over him, the clamouring good humour of them, the warmth and sense of purpose, the information passing back and forth, the in-jokes that crept into their conversations, the whispered gossip about other club members, the invitations to each other's house, dinner parties and Sunday afternoon barbecues; lately they spoke of maybe a foreign holiday together, although Henry doubted it would ever come to pass. He couldn't see Elena being too thrilled at the prospect of a week in Kim's company, and then there were the problems that accompanied Alex, Shane's difficult son.

'It's not as if we're that close to them,' Elena remarked to him once, a remark that stung him. He considers this friendship with Shane to be the closest he has. 'What does he ever talk to you about, except his portfolio and the quality of his serve?' she asked him. To Elena, a close friendship takes the form of something secretive – confidences offered and invited, souls bared. He thinks of all the hours she spends on the phone in their bedroom, perched on the side of the bed, her low voice travelling into the receiver, occasional gasps and whispers of 'No way', 'He didn't' and 'I don't believe it' travelling the phone line to Clodagh or Sinéad or Ian – these people with their difficult love lives, their awkward, stilted dilemmas that he sometimes listens to, but more often than not avoids. He is unwilling to consider what stories they might have been told about him. These are Elena's close friends. It is hard for her to grasp that something else is involved in his friendship with Shane.

And there have been occasional confidences over the years. Shane has opened up to him on more than one occasion about the difficulties involved in rearing a boy like Alex, the emotional strain, the additional pressures it puts on a marriage. Henry tried to arrange his features into a serious, understanding pose, nodding his head, making sympathetic noises and offering words of encouragement. And over a few pints one evening, after a particularly crushing defeat of opponents in a tournament, Henry felt open and magnanimous enough to confide in Shane the troubled history of his relationship with his father. For this, he was rewarded with the knowledge that Shane's dad used to slap his mother around until Shane became big enough to threaten the old man himself. This exchange of confidences, this rare moment of openness, left him feeling profoundly happy. A connection had been made between them that would transcend the hours and hours of straight above-counter conversations that they would have in the future. And it was this connection that led him here today to ask for help.

His opportunity arrives when Gerald's mobile rings and he excuses himself to go and take the call. Henry, sensing that there will not be much time, takes a deep breath and delves right in.

'Shane, I need to talk to you about something.'

'Oh? Something up?'

'Yeah, I'm… well, I've got myself into a bit of trouble.' He laughs hastily, watching Shane sawing at his steak, a chunk of meat disappearing into his mouth, his eyes resting momentarily on Henry's face before looking back at his plate.

'What sort of trouble?'

'The Hua Hin project. I invested a little heavily in it. A little too heavily.'

'Uh-huh.' Shane puts down his cutlery and picks his napkin from his lap, wiping his mouth quickly. 'I lost a lot on that one myself. Fucking SARS virus. Completely screwed us. Otherwise, it would have been a sweet deal. Terrible shame.'

'Right, but you see, the thing is, it's left me in a bit of a state. Financially.'

'Golden rule of investments, Henry. Never invest what you can't afford to lose. You know that one as well as I do.'

'I know, I know,' he says, trying to hide his rising irritation at the teacherly tone he is being subjected to. He glances down from the mezzanine and sees Gerald pacing back and forth, his head thrown back, his mouth wide open with laughter. 'And it's not just the Hua Hin deal – there were others. I just seem to be going through a streak of bad luck at the moment.'

'Why? How much have you lost?'

Henry watches the alteration in his friend's face as he tells him the sum. Shane's eyes widen, bald staring orbs naked with incredulity; his mouth drops slightly open and he blinks rapidly, drawing his face back with a deep intake of breath so that his chin seems to double.

'Jesus fucking Christ,' he breathes. 'Whoa. That is some loss. Does Elena know about this?'

'She does now.'

'And what does she think?'

Henry covers his face with his hands, not wanting to answer, not wanting to think about it. He draws his hands down from his face. He can imagine what he looks like. The blood is draining from his cheeks, he feels light headed. 'We're going to lose the house.'

'Fuck. Are you sure?'

'Unless I can find some money from somewhere within the next twenty-four hours.'

He looks at Shane, whose face at that moment seems to register what this lunch meeting is really about. His eyes narrow and flicker over Henry's face and something seems to close down in his features, like a guard dropping over them.

'Right,' he says softly, sitting back in his chair, removing himself from the cloud of confidence over the table. 'I see.'

'Shit, I hate asking you this, Shane, but I don't have anywhere else to turn.' He hears the pleading whine in his voice and despises himself for it. Below them, he can see Gerald pocketing his phone and turning towards the stairs. Panic surges up through him, making him desperate. 'I really need the money, Shane. If there was any way… I'd pay you back, of course. With interest. What do you say?'

Shane seems to be examining the leftover steak on his plate. A look of consternation, which could be mistaken for indigestion, crosses his face. Henry wants to shake him; the urgency of the situation presses upon him, needing an answer. But before there is time for Shane to give one, Gerald is back.

'Sorry about that, guys. Bloody workmen. I swear to God, they wait until they know I've sat down to lunch before they ring. They are the biggest curse on God's earth. If I had known they would be half this much trouble, I would never have bought the place. Old houses may have character, but dealing with the fucking builders renovating it certainly builds character, that's for sure! Next time, I'm buying a new build. No question about it!'

'Henry has an old house,' Shane interjects suddenly. 'Beautiful late-Victorian. Very classy. It was a mess when they bought it. But they've turned it into something really special now.'

'Is that so?' Gerald raises his eyebrows appreciatively. 'And tell me, did you spend a lot on the renovations?'

Henry can't answer, paralysed by his nerves.

'It was a good investment,' Shane continues. 'A wise investment. In this day and age, you have to be careful with your money. Put it into bricks and mortar, that's what I say.'

'Absolutely,' from Gerald, between mouthfuls. 'Couldn't agree more.'

'Because you can't expect anyone to help you out if your investments fail, can you? It's not as if any of us has extra to spare.'

He directs these comments at Gerald, but Henry feels the dead weight of them. His eyes are smouldering. They bore holes into Shane's heavy jowled face, the cruelty of his mouth – those carved lips, the arrogance of a tyrant's mouth. Look at me, he demands silently. At least have the decency to look me in the eye. But the voice that escapes from him is gravely whispered, and lit with barely contained rage.

'You sanctimonious bastard.'

Shane is looking down at his plate, concentrating on his lunch, but Gerald, who has stopped eating, looks up, a nervous stare coming over his face.

'You and your big mouth, your big ideas. It was you who got me involved in this Hua Hin mess, and now you haven't even got the decency to look me in the eye and tell me you won't help me out.'

'I never forced you to get into it.' Shane looks at him coldly, putting distance between them. 'I let you in on an investment opportunity that could have made us both very rich men. But you knew the risks, and you took them. Don't blame me for your losses, Henry. You made your bed.'

His words are delivered with precision and hardness, and in that instant Henry can hear their friendship twisting apart. He looks at Shane and sees in him a vanity he was faintly aware of and a condescension that he always attributed to self-confidence, but now sees as cold arrogance. This man he considered his friend is now looking at him as if he is someone he has tolerated, some poor fool who hardly registered as consequential, someone he is seeking to distance himself from.

'I did get myself into this. And I don't blame anyone else but myself for that. But I was wrong to think I could rely on you, to think you were my friend.'

He rises from his chair, trying to salvage some of his dignity. As he reaches into his wallet for his last remaining note, Shane touches him lightly on his sleeve.

'Self-reliance, Henry, is the most important thing. I would have thought your father would have instilled that in you.'

Disgust boils over and he drops the note on the table, all of his energy focused on not leaning across and smacking the supercilious prick in the jaw.

'Go to hell,' he says quietly, before turning and walking out of the restaurant.

ELENA

15

SHE DRIVES LIKE an automaton, her eyes fixed on the road, her deadened gaze passing over the city as she weaves through the traffic. Overhead, the sky is darkening, rain clouds threatening to relieve their contents all over the grey city. She turns the volume of the radio up in an effort to stifle her worries, an effort to blot out Henry's voice and the whisper of inquisitiveness it feeds.

She slept fitfully and had nightmares that she couldn't remember when she woke up. As she woke alone in their bed, the weariness of the previous days came flooding back, uprooting the repose of sleep, restoring its place inside her addled brain. With the children gone and the house echoing around her, she dressed carefully, conscious of the sleeping presence in Ben's room, not wanting to disturb him, not wanting to wake all that up again. 'What would be the point?' she asked herself. There were no conclusions to be drawn, no solutions offered.

Her brain hurts from pondering the myriad questions that have arisen in the past few days. She is conscious that, tomorrow morning, her husband will meet with the bank and end his struggle to save the house. There will be a period of sixty days or so, and then they will be forced to vacate. They have yet to discuss what happens then – where will they go? What will they tell the children? How will she explain it to their relatives and friends? She feels the pressure of the imminent shame bearing down on her. The need to escape, to run free of all these woes, grows inside her as she drives towards the west of the city.

The landscape changes, becoming industrial. Tall chimneys rise up against a grey sky, the sloping hills far off in the distance. Hot clouds rise up into the sky. Spiked fences in grey metal surround factories and warehouses. Poppies grow at the side of the road among gorse and weed. A voice crackles from the radio and she flicks channels. But the tinny clanging of music and the dull, thudding beats only compound her headache, so she switches it off, allowing her thoughts to stretch out and fill the car. They sweep around her, rubbing against her, needling her for conclusions to be drawn, inferences to be made, analysis and suggestion.

Her anger of the past few days seems to have dissipated, leaving in its wake this awful flat feeling of nothingness. She feels deadened, desensitised, and when Henry entered the kitchen that morning, a cold, hard flatness seemed to fall between them. She recalls how he hovered by the door, shrunken and dishevelled in his pyjamas. Unshaven, he peered at her through dull eyes, the lines on his face and the brittle way he held his body speaking of a restless night. He too had slept fitfully, troubled by his dreams. Most of all, she remembers the way he looked at her, whey faced and anxious – the face of a small boy, a pleading look, fearful of her response.

'How did this happen?' he asked her. 'How did we drift apart, each of us caught up in our own catalogue of woes?' Feeling his hand clutching her wrist, the tenacity of his grip, she read desperation in his eyes, and something else. Something forgotten. There had been a time when that look came to her regularly. His eyes had shone with it once. Warmth had flowed from him. He had seemed lighter then, less weighed down. But these last days have become an ordeal. He seems to drag his weight around with him. And as she watched his tears flow, instinct told her to reach out to him, to fold him in her arms, to shelter him from this blackness that could wither the last fragments of love between them. But she held back, anxious and uncertain – caught up in a destructive stream of memories, her mind trapped in another time, another place, another man. She stepped away from Henry. That was her choice.

Now, as she drives through the industrial heartland and out towards the Dublin mountains, pangs of guilt rip through her. She should have stayed with him. She should have talked it out. Why is she so reluctant to salvage her marriage? As the car winds its way slowly up a hill, the wasteland giving way to hedgerows and fields, the suburban landscape petering out, the answer to that question whispers to her. The spectre of that time – that old love – hangs over her, taunting her, beckoning her. Everything inside tells her it is a mistake to be drawn in again, but the lure of him is beguiling. If she is honest with herself, she can acknowledge that she wants to be drawn in, to be seduced. It complicates matters, she knows this, but it is difficult for her to turn away from the wrenching draw. As the car reaches the little church of Bothar na Bríne, tucked away at the side of a curling road, she feels her heart leap at the prospect of seeing him again. The first drops of rain splatter on the windscreen as she pulls into the nearly empty car park. She sees the hearse parked by the entrance and draws in her breath deeply. Locking her car door behind her, she hurries into the church, the patter of rain thickening as she ducks for cover.

The church echoes as she enters and some heads turn to see who the latecomer is. It echoes with emptiness – there cannot be more than twenty people here – as she slips into one of the pews near the back and kneels down, lowering her head in prayer. The droning voice of the priest rises above her and she lifts her eyes, scanning the congregation for Adam. His head rises above the others, distinguished by the presence of hair, as well as his height; he stares ahead of him, holding his body stiffly. She watches him, noticing him turn slightly, sneaking glances at the coffin parked in the centre aisle, adorned by a sheaf of lilies.

Elena remembers that one occasion when she met Adam's mother. She was not sure what she had expected, but the apparition that greeted her came as a shock. Crimped grey hair, black kohl-pencil lines instead of eyebrows, and those wide, watery green eyes, the way they stared while hardly blinking. Sitting on the hard sofa in that stuffy sitting room, Elena got the distinct impression that this was not a house you could easily relax in. Nothing was out of place. The cold austerity of the furniture matched the glacial gaze of Adam's mother. She sat opposite Elena, her posture stiff and strenuously elegant, with her knees to one side, her back ramrod-straight and those knurled bony hands folded neatly in her lap. Her smile was brittle and never reached her eyes, powder tunnelling into the lines of her face. They sat regarding each other over the distance of the hearthrug, while

Adam flapped around them, his movements made enormous by his nerves. He had not wanted to bring her there, Elena knew that, but had felt compelled by the regular welcome her parents extended to him. 'That girl will want something to drink,' his mother said pointedly, her voice clearly enunciating each syllable, her eyes widening, nostrils flaring as she inhaled deeply. It was then that Elena realised that she was drunk. Steeped in gin at two thirty in the afternoon. Elena looked at that cold, inebriated woman in those clinical surroundings and felt a hollow emptiness surround her. Poor Adam – to grow up in this loveless environment, a small boy with this withered old woman and her immaculate living room... It made her heart seize for him, wanting to reach out and hold him, to allow warmth and love to seep into him through her embrace. For all of her own mother's bellowing and her father's stubborn reluctance to give in, she could not compare them to the bloodless, antiseptic environment Adam had been subjected to.

What is he feeling now? she wonders as he sits in the front pew, so alone amongst the small gathering there. Sadness hits her at the thought of his lonely position – no wife or partner sitting next to him, holding his hand, no close friend or relative to comfort him. The back of his head betrays no trace of feeling. Perhaps he is relieved at his mother's passing – no longer burdened with the worry of how to care for her. She thinks again of the pinprick pupils in those icy green eyes, the way they fixed on him accusatorily as he hovered around trying to make his girlfriend welcome. And she remembers, too, the words said in cold anger when he departed for Spain, words that were stinging and razor sharp and could never be taken back.

The mass ends, and the skeletal congregation files out behind the coffin as it makes its journey towards the entrance. Outside, the rain is falling in straight sheets, bouncing off the concrete, pooling thick and fast in dips and hollows. The coffin is bundled quickly into the hearse and umbrellas are snapped open, hair and clothes flapping viciously in the wind.

She sees him through the small mass of people that crowd around him, solemnly shaking his hand and offering their condolences. His face is drawn and gaunt looking, pale from lack of sleep, and his eyes seek her out, beckoning her to him.

'You came,' he states clearly as they huddle under her inadequate umbrella, rain slapping against one of his cheeks. 'I wasn't sure if you would.'

'How are you holding up?' she asks.

'Oh, OK. A little worn out, I guess.'

She nods, her eyes passing over his face, concern mixed with a shrinking pain from the bitter elements clouding her features.

'Thank you for coming,' he says, looking clear into her face. 'It means a lot to me.'

'It's nothing.'

'No, really. I was worried there'd only be a couple of us here.' He looks about at the sparse group that is whittling away as the weather sends people scattering to the comfort and warmth of their cars. 'And I know how much you disliked her...'

'Adam.'

'No, it's all right. I disliked her myself a fair bit.'

'Still.'

'Yes. I know.'

He nods his head gravely and a brief silence falls between them. She is aware of the pointed sideways glances they are receiving from some of the other mourners, wondering who she might be and what her relationship to Adam is. Beady eyes needle her and she feels naked in front of them.

'Adam, I'd better go.'

'Wait,' he says, urgency swelling in his voice as he grabs her arm. 'Will you come to the grave with me?'

'Oh, Adam, I...'

'I know I've no right to ask you. Especially on this miserable day.' He glances out from under the umbrella before fixing her with the full force of his gaze. 'Please, Elena. It would really mean a lot to me.'

That wistful tone of voice, those eyes, the steadiness of their gaze – she feels something buckle within her. She nods quickly, forcing a weak smile, and feels his hand release her arm as he turns away from her and prepares to take his mother to her final resting place.

When they bought their house, Henry and Elena made wills, marking out their intentions in the events of their deaths. Later that night, in their bed in the rented flat in Rathmines, they lay side by side, staring at each other in the shadowy dimness of the room, and discussed what would happen if one of them died.

'Do you think you would remarry?' she asked him playfully, propping herself up on her elbow to look down on his face.

'No,' he said quickly, emphatically.

'Really?'

'Of course,' he answered earnestly. 'There could never be anyone else to take your place. I wouldn't want anyone else.'

'Aww!' She leaned forward, planting a full-lipped kiss in his hairline.

'How about you?' he asked.

'Nope,' she answered reciprocally.

'Not at all? Not even after seven years of mourning?'

She laughed then, and pulled his head into her chest, arms worming around his neck, pulling him to her.

'Not even then,' she said happily.

And she meant it. She was swollen with love, feeling warm and happy and buoyed up by this immense feeling of security, of certainty; it seemed probable to her that she could never love anyone like that again.

Standing in the graveyard, gusts of wind whinnying through the pocket of mourners gathered around a hole in the ground, she thinks about that promise again. Next to her, a man she once loved is staring at a coffin entering the ground. Rivulets of mud run past them, her heels sink into the soft earth, and she listens to the words of the priest competing with the howling weather around them. Then, suddenly, as the prayers rise into the screeching wind and mourners battle with their umbrellas, he reaches for her hand, and she lets him take it. The suddenness of this gesture, and the persistent kneading of his fingers, leave her gasping for breath. She does not look at him; she stares solemnly ahead, feeling something inside her crumpling – her last resolve, fading without a whimper.

*

'Why does it always rain at funerals?' her friend Clodagh once asked.

And it is true; at every funeral Elena has ever been to, the weather seemed to harmonise with the sad occasion, weeping in tune with the loved ones left behind. Every funeral, except for one. It is eleven years now since they buried Carlos. Eleven years since that October afternoon, when the first cool breezes of autumn, softening the heat, licked gently at the crowd gathered outside the small church high up in the hills of Aragon.

The ground was dusty, it turned her black shoes orange, great clouds were kicked up by cars driving up the hill and pulling in under the shade of a grove of yew trees. The church – austere and puritanical on the outside – was filled with ornate and elaborate pieces, candlesticks and sceptres in spiked bronze, intricate cornicing painted with gold leaf, and the pained, martyred faces of saints locked within stained-glass windows. They frowned down on the moving congregation as prayers and cries rose up to greet them. Pitched wails emerged from the crowd, rising to a crescendo and falling away again, the piteous sounds of people being pushed beyond endurance. The noisy responses were drowned out by the persistent weeping. For the duration of the ceremony, tears rolling down her cheeks, dampening her collar, she stared at that wooden casket, trying to fathom what it contained. Their friend, with his dark smiling eyes, his flippant, casual turn of phrase, all that time masking this inner sadness. It didn't make sense to her. She could not understand his reasons for doing it. Looking into the bewildered faces of his family, damp with tears, she could read their own questioning predicament. A lifetime of questions stretched out ahead of them, questions that would never be answered.

Later, back at the Quintenals' house, she felt awkward, standing about clutching a plate of food she had no desire to eat, uncertain of what she was doing there, longing to get away. It seemed insensitive, somehow, to witness the raw anguish of the family. Señor Quintenal, stoic and unspeaking, his chin tucked deep into his chest, avoiding eye contact; Señora Quintenal, sleepy as if drugged by her grief, eyes half closed and unfocused, sitting in a chair, surrounded by women patting her hands and rubbing her shoulders, a moving group of attendants buzzing around her and her grief. One of Carlos's sisters, the youngest, with the darting eyes and thick black hair, asked her about Adam and why he had not come to the funeral. Elena shrugged, at a loss to explain and too weary and heartsore to make excuses for him. The girl's eyes narrowed and she muttered something about Maria – her inability to see past her own selfish hurt, not bothering to attend the funeral. Elena smarted at the remarks, twisting with discomfort at words that were not aimed directly at her, but she was the only one there to absorb their acidity.

Later that day, as she sat on a bus bringing her back into Zaragoza, she thought of Pilar's words, the sharpness of them, the way they cut through her, nicking at her conscience, and she felt a wave of anger take her. Anger at Adam – and Maria – for letting her go alone, to face the grief and bewilderment, armed with no answers and no excuses. It wasn't fair. It was cruel. She felt the injustice and callousness of it. As the bus lurched and rocked forward into the city, she looked out of the dust-smeared window, her bag clutched to her knees, her dress sticking to her body, and quietly observed the passing streets. As they entered the central square the Basilica towered above them, faintly threatening in its size and magnificence. She thought of the train journey back to Barcelona. She thought of returning to that small stuffy apartment. A string of bitter arguments stretched out in her mind's eye. And as she stepped off the bus out into the square, among a scattering of strangers going about their daily business, the thought came to her, sudden and welcoming, of staying in Zaragoza. Just for a week. Some time to herself. Time to get her head together. And time for the others to let the dust settle in her absence, and perhaps resolve whatever issues they had.

*

She shakes her head at the memory, her foolishness, her naïveté. How could she have been so stupid, so trustworthy? She feels his hand in hers, twisting, the fingers knitting with hers, a sudden squeeze bringing her back into the reality of the present. The other mourners have moved away, scurrying back across the graves to their cars. He turns to look at her.

'What now?' she asks quietly.

'Come on,' he replies quickly, turning to follow the departing few, hurrying through the rain, still holding her hand as he leads her towards his car.

HENRY

16

THE RAIN SLAPS hard against the windscreen, and Henry watches the wipers flick it away steadily, whipping back and forth to clear the view. Cars charge past him, their headlights distorted through the wet glass – smudges of yellow and white flashing past, his eyes blinking against them. He feels tired, exhausted. His head is heavy with sleep, threatening to bring his eyelids down, the slow whirr of his brain coming to a halt, slumped in the seat of his car. He lowers the window and feels the rain falling in on his face, cold, wet needles nudging him, keeping him awake. The car feels stale; he needs to stop, to get out and walk, but already the sky is darkening, clouds travelling to meet one another in thick grey formations. And the children are waiting for him to collect them and bring them home. He presses the accelerator and listens to the hum of the engine. He feels depressed, all hollowed out of emotion.

A car brakes suddenly in front of him, jerking his concentration back as he slams on the pedals, a sharp intake of breath. The red tail-lights rear up in front of him and his heart beats madly, a narrow escape. The rain is getting heavier, the road is slippery. He must get home.

*

'Mum?'

'Henry! My God, you scared me! I didn't hear you come in.'

'The back door was open. Sorry, I didn't mean to startle you.'

'Goodness.'

She leans against the counter, her hand resting over her left breast, protecting the wildly beating heart underneath her floral apron and neat blue jumper.

'Sorry, Mum. You OK?'

'Oh, fine, fine.' Her hand flutters away from her chest and she releases a sharp breath of relief before turning back to the counter, where a pile of vegetable peelings is poised to be swept away by her cupped hand into a small plastic bag, which is duly knotted and then deposited on the floor by the back door. 'For the compost,' his mother explains breathily.

'Are the kids inside?'

'Yes, yes. They're in watching TV.'

'Have they been behaving themselves?'

'Oh, yes. You know. Ben does like to make noise, doesn't he?'

Her cheeks are flushed, and her small eyes remain trained on the countertop that she is scrubbing. Lines shoot out across the sides of her face, and the skin around her jaw is slack and loose; it quivers with her efforts. He notes the vigour with which she attacks the worktop and sees her stress in the tight clench of her shoulders.

'And Emily?'

'Fine, fine. A little quiet. I think she might be coming down with a cold.'

'Oh?'

'So I've wrapped her up a bit. Given her a hot drink.'

The musical tone of her voice pleases him for some reason. Even the way her hands move busily across the counter, her matter-of-factness, speak to him of something safe and enduring.

'Grand. I'll just pop in and say hello.'

'Okey dokey. Dinner will be ready soon.'

The living room is in darkness, lit only by the flickering blue light from the television. 'Daddy!' Ben hurls himself at his father's legs, and Henry feels the small sticky hands gripping the backs of his knees.

'Whoa there.'

'Daddy, Daddy, Daddy!' He jumps up and down, his open face looking up, soft crushed curls bobbing, and a grin full of tiny white teeth smiling up.

'Hey, Emily.'

'Hi, Daddy.'

She stays on the sofa, her dark head peering out from under a heavy duvet, a watery smile momentarily illuminated by the changing light from the TV. Crossing the room, with Ben clamped to his leg, Henry switches on a lamp and, turning back, observes her face, pale and shadowy, eyes filling up with a cold.

'Poor old you,' he says softly, peeling the boy from his leg as he sits next to her. 'Not feeling the best?'

She shakes her head and he reaches out and presses the back of his hand to her forehead, feeling the pressure of heat seeping into his skin.

'Poor baby,' he murmurs. 'Did Granny give you a hot drink?'

'Yes. It tasted horrible, but I drank it anyway.'

'Good girl.'

She turns her attention back to the cartoon and he feels a twinge of love for his little girl, her obedience, her quiet acceptance. He watches the stillness of her head, eyes trained on the coloured images, her expression grave and subdued, unchanging as the cartoon rumbles and screeches to its conclusion. Her little body is lost under the voluminous quilt and her eyelids are heavy.

'Are you up to eating dinner, pumpkin?' he asks gently, and she shakes her head in response, her eyes unmoving.

'All right, so.'

'When's Mummy coming?' she asks.

'We'll see Mummy at home later,' he answers in a voice that is meant to be soothing, but sounds croaky and thin.

She glances at him briefly, a look that raises questions within him over how much his little girl knows. What she has witnessed recently. Something cold trips down the length of his spine.

Ben's attention has shifted to a toy ship that he is hammering away at with a hole punch, intent on destruction. Emily sighs and slumps further down into the quilt. Henry rises from the couch, feeling the room resume the pace and tone it held before he disturbed it. He closes the door softly behind him.

His mother is peering anxiously out of the kitchen window. The sky is black now and full of wind. The snapping sound of trees being pummelled by the storm seeps through into the house.

'It's turning nasty,' his mother says, shaking her head.

She pulls the curtains over – thick red curtains with a ladybird print; they have been hanging there for as long as Henry can remember.

With the dark, threatening sky shut out, the kitchen becomes a cube of comfort. It feels dry and warm and snug – the redness of the curtains, the heat from the oven, the industry of his mother. She is lifting the receiver on the wall phone and punching in the numbers for his father's office, her face knit with silent worry. Henry slides onto the bench and leans back against the radiator, feeling the heat travelling through his clothes. Cooking smells fill his nostrils – something warm and nourishing heating in the oven. Looking about him, he sees a kitchen unchanged since his childhood. The orange plastic façade of the cupboard doors, the old white tiles, cracked in places and punctuated with the occasional bronze tile embossed with an image of rosemary or thyme or basil – these printed herbs, a hallmark of his youth.

'Why don't they ever change that kitchen?' Elena asked him once. 'It's not as if they don't have the money.' Henry shrugged; the reason was inexplicable to him. Or rather, it was impossible to formulate into words – this need of his parents to hold on to existing structures, the value placed on the original pieces that had come with the house, the beauty boards in the hall, the stone cladding on the fireplace, the swirling patterns in busy colours of the hall carpets. All of these things are woven into the fabric of this house in which he was brought up.

His mother puts down the phone, her call unanswered. 'It's engaged,' she mutters distractedly, and he can almost see the whirr of anxiety in the pinched expression on her face. She checks on the casserole in the oven and then begins filling the sink to start on the dishes.

His mother is meticulous. She takes pride in the cleanliness with which her house is enveloped. Her cushions plump up proudly on the blue velvet sofa and the white covers on the armrests are a pristine snowy white. The linoleum floor in the kitchen is mopped down every evening, a cloth is passed over each cupboard door; she uses a harsh chemical-smelling polish on their silvery edges. She vacuums like a woman possessed. Henry remembers calling to see her once and being amazed at her strength and agility as she swept through the sitting room with her Nilfisk 90, tipping up a heavy armchair with one hand, poking the nozzle under it with the other. He wonders if his mother sees the shabbiness of the furniture that she has lived with for over thirty years. Is she aware how dated it has become, how tired the prints and patterns appear? But as he watches his mother now, elbow-deep in suds, humming to herself, the strings of her apron tied in a neat bow at the back of her waist, she seems to belong here. Despite her nervous disposition, she seems relaxed in this dated seventies kitchen.

Henry remembers his mother's face when they were renovating their own house, as Elena led her through the new kitchen with its distressed wood finish, its Belfast sink and copper taps, the Smeg fridge and gas-fired stove. His mother smiled politely and made approving noises, admiring the chrome accessories and the chequered tiles. But Henry saw a flicker of consternation cross her face. He saw alarm in her eyes as she examined the elaborate juicer with its levers and chrome surfaces. She looked bewildered when the carousel cupboard was displayed for her. She papered over these feelings with her quivering, uncertain smile, but seemed relieved once the tour was over.

Elena thinks that it is meanness on his father's part – that that is the reason why his mother has to put up with this tired décor. But Henry knows that it is something different. His mother feels at home here. She feels secure, safe in her refuge.

'What a miserable evening,' she says. 'I hope Dad will be all right.'

His parents call each other Dad and Mum. They have adopted his names for them and continue to use them on each other. Henry has found that irritating in the past. But not tonight.

'Real funeral weather,' she continues. 'Elena will be soaked. I hope she dressed up warm and had a decent pair of boots on. And a good umbrella. The last thing you want is to be standing in a windy graveyard with no proper protection.'

He watches his mother, the grey frizz of her hair crowning her perplexed face. He sees her cheeks pink from her kitchen exertions, powder pressed into the lines and cracks of her face and neck, a faint shadow above her lip. She will be seventy in February. Seventy! It is hard for Henry to accept that his mother has reached that age. She was thirty when she married his father, who is four years her junior; thirty had been considered old at that time. There was another man before that – his mother spoke of him once, and once only, and that was just to say that he had 'let her down'. Henry is not sure what kind of disappointment or betrayal those words embody. But he knows there was a gap of some years while she waited for her broken heart to mend. He feels a surge of warmth for his mother in her careful blue jumper and gabardine skirt, the pleats ironed into crisp creases, and her ever-present worry for her family, that small inadequate group of people who have assembled around her and who occasionally mock her, albeit in a good-natured way.

'You didn't go to the funeral?'

Henry hears the lightness of her tone, a paltry attempt to veil the worry she tries to conceal.

'No. No, I didn't.'

'I expect you didn't know the person – the deceased.'

He doesn't respond, doesn't tell her of his complete ignorance of whose death Elena is mourning.

'And you had to work today, anyway, I'm sure?'

The kitchen feels warm around him. He feels snug, cosseted. He is aware of the onset of a feeling of relief – relief that things cannot get any worse. That he can sink no further. There is a certain comfort to be drawn from that. Tomorrow he will have the meeting with the bank and that will be that. Somewhere outside in the city, Elena is sitting among people he doesn't know, her presence there a message of her sympathy while masking her own private pain. He remembers the look on her face that morning, the hurt, compromised expression. Already, she feels lost to him.

'I didn't go into the office today.'

'I see,' she says in a slow, contemplative way.

His mother is fishing in a drawer for cutlery, preparing the table for their meal. But something in the way she holds herself changes. A stiffening, imperceptible to most, apart from her son and her husband, who can read these subtle changes. For a moment, he considers telling her about the imminent demise of his business, the loss of his house and very probably his wife too. He seldom confides in his mother – or in his father, for that matter, but for different reasons. She carries horrors around inside her, perceived dangers lurking outside, threatening the people she holds dear; the battery of thugs and rapists and murderers, the new wave of refugees, the increasing traffic deaths and the surge in road rage, even the weather. She is twitching at the curtains, eyeing up the gathering storm, her alarm pitching through her clenched muscles. Her only child has inherited some of these fears, not all of them irrational. Sometimes, Henry feels that his whole life has been lived out in the shadow of those fears. But his mother is possessed of courage too. Courage to recover from the disappointment of an earlier shadowy romance, her staunch heart mending itself enough to be entrusted to another. And perhaps it is for this reason that he has sought to protect her, sheltering her from his own problems; hiding his troubled thoughts, not wanting to alarm her needlessly. In fact, he has made it a point never to alarm her. And yet, tonight, he is reluctant to become embroiled in another catalogue of lies. He is weary at the thought of inventing excuses, however implausible, to placate his mother, to keep her from worrying. He needs to make a clean breast of it, to offload the burden of pretence.

'Actually,' he begins, 'actually, I'm not going to go back to the office. I've decided… I've decided to let it go.'

'Let it go?' She eyes him cautiously, her voice crotchety with worry.

Before he can explain himself, a loud crack from outside causes her to wheel around and fling the curtains wide open.

'Lord, what was that?' Her eyelids shoot back in alarm, eyes wide with sudden fear.

A branch of the tree at the back of the garden – an apple tree – has splintered and is hanging loosely like a broken arm, dangling and redundant.

'Mercy!' she declares. 'Oh, it's getting bad out there.'

He joins her at the window, observing the wounded tree. Rain is streaming down the glass pane, forming rivulets that course and flow.

'I hope Dad will be all right driving home,' she says anxiously, hurrying to the phone and punching in the numbers with a new urgency.

His eyes strain to make out the tree in the darkness. He used to climb it as a boy, sitting between knots and knurled branches.

'Still engaged,' she says breathily, exasperated. 'And what about Elena? Will she be all right? Maybe you should phone her.'

He remains unmoving.

'She might be at home. What do you think? Will she come here?'

'I don't know where she is,' he answers tonelessly. 'And I don't know whether she is coming home or not.'

His mother turns to look at him. She hangs the receiver back on the hook and wipes her hands on her apron. He doesn't turn to look at her, but hears the slow pad of her slippers crossing the linoleum floor. He senses the heaviness of her breathing next to him, the beating of that staunch heart under her apron. He feels her arm circling his waist, the warmth of her body through her machine-knit sweater, tough little fingers kneading his side. She says nothing as the storm rages outside. Something rattles high up on the roof as the house is pelted with relentless rain. They stand together by the kitchen sink and, in the window, Henry watches their reflections framed by the red curtains – a plump little woman, her features a blur in the darkened pane of glass, one hand clutched to her waist, the other tight around him; a tall, thin shadow of a man, locked in the uncontested forgiveness of her embrace.

He eats voraciously, the hunger that has built inside him silenced by the comfort of his mother's cooking. The plate steams and the food burns his tongue and he hunches over it, not pausing while he works his way through meat and vegetables. His mother watches him eat from across the kitchen as she listens again to the engaged tone humming through the receiver. She has surprised him tonight with her calmness, her controlled reaction to his distress. She listened to what he had to say without needling him for further information or for explanations or reasons, doing her best to mask her anxiety in front of him. In the sitting room, Emily lounges under the duvet, a hot lemon drink in her hand. Ben has fallen asleep on the rug and is covered over with the blanket from the back of the sofa.

'The children should stay here tonight,' she informs him in a softly instructional tone. 'It's getting late, and it's too wild out there to be dragging them across the city.'

'What about Elena?'

'I'll ring and let her know. Maybe she'll come over here and stay the night too?' she says with a brightness that is unconvincing, and he bows his head and finishes his meal.

Her eyes move to the clock on the wall and he sees the flicker of worry crossing her face.

'Dad is late,' he remarks casually, but watchful for her reaction.

'Yes. And that line is still engaged.' She stands with one hand raised to her face, fingers rubbing her jaw distractedly.

'Perhaps the line is down?' Henry suggests.

'Perhaps.'

But she does not seem reassured and wanders across to the window again for another peep at the foul weather.

He crosses his cutlery on the empty plate and pushes it aside. He feels fortified, re-energised by the meal, and conscious of his mother's unspoken concern.

'I'm sure he's fine,' he says reassuringly.

'Yes, yes. It's just... he hasn't been himself lately... he's been...'

'What?'

'It's nothing,' she answers with a dismissive shake of her head, tugging the curtains shut again and hurrying to the table to clear away his plate. 'It's just that, on a night like this, I worry about him being alone in the warehouse, or driving home in that rain.'

As he watches her, Henry considers his father's demeanour a few nights ago, the unspoken worry, the distracted consternation, and a shadow of doubt passes over him.

'Why don't I drive over there and see where he is?' he suggests.

'Oh, no, Henry. You can't go out there in this weather.'

'I'll be fine, Mum, really. I won't be gone long.'

'Only if you're sure?'

'I'm sure.'

She seems somewhat comforted by this and fusses around him, fetching his coat and scarf, while he looks in on the children, both asleep on the couch.

'Drive carefully,' she warns him, her face wreathed in worry, as he opens the door and steps out into the night.

ELENA

17

THEY SIT IN the car, staring out past the pine trees across the stretch of the city. The car seems overwhelmingly quiet now that the insistent buzz of the engine has been cut off. Neither of them spoke as the car wound its way about curling roads stretching up into the Dublin Mountains. She didn't ask where they were going, didn't comment on the speed he was doing, but leaned her elbow against the window, chewing the corner of her nail. And now, as they sit in silence, she can see the lights of the city coming on as the darkness grows around them.

The car is warmed by the radiator, hot air blowing into her face. It feels stuffy, muggy and humid from the damp weather. It is late, and the rain is coming in over the mountains, gusts of wind assaulting the car, rattling the doors and windows. Her children will be at their grandparents' house. Maybe Henry is there too. Guiltily, she acknowledges to herself a reluctance to join them.

'You probably think it's strange,' he says, breaking the silence, 'that there's no reception after the funeral.'

She says nothing.

'It is strange,' he answers for her. 'Bizarre. Anti-social. But that's how she wanted it. Imagine that' – he gives a short gasp of a laugh – 'imagine declaring specifically your desire is not to have a funeral party.' He shakes his head, the acts of his mother, even after death, still baffling him. 'And it wasn't a question of money. I'd have paid for the damn send-off myself. But she actually stipulated that not one person was to raise a glass to her over a couple of sandwiches. She was adamant.'

'Maybe she didn't like the idea of having a party without her.'

He grins suddenly, pleased with the notion, and nods his head vigorously.

'I think you may have hit on it,' he says.

Silence falls between them, a silence that prickles with unspoken goodbyes. His business here is done. His mother has been buried. What now? Elena wants to ask. What happens now?

'Would you want a big party after your funeral?' he asks her, twisting in his seat to look at her.

'That's a bit morbid,' she smiles, trying to lighten the mood, trying to diffuse the closeness that seems to be growing around them.

'Haven't you ever thought about it? Haven't you and Henry discussed what you want to happen if one of you dies?'

Her husband's name coming from Adam's mouth seems wrong to her. She flinches inadvertently and he mistakes this for discomfort at the thought of death.

'Sorry, it's the day that's in it,' he says quickly, shaking his head.

'No, no, it's not that, it's…'

'What?'

'Nothing.'

It occurs to her that they cannot talk to each other the way they used to. There was a time when she could have told him anything.

'They used to have wakes for people when they emigrated,' he says brightly, struck by the thought. 'Remember that?'

'Did you have one?' she asks, and he shakes his head.

'I didn't think I was going for good, to be honest. I always thought I'd come back.'

'And now?'

He turns to look at her.

'Now?' He seems briefly confused before the question dies on his face, realisation creeping over it. 'I see what you mean. Now that my mother is dead, there's no reason for me to come back here again.'

She shrugs, feeling suddenly afraid of his answer.

'No. No wake for me. It's too late for that. Or too early, depending on your point of view.'

So that's it. He's not coming back. She feels a shortness of breath in her lungs. The car is too warm, the air too oppressive. She lowers the window a fraction and feels the flick of rain dash against her cheek.

'When?' she asks quietly.

'The day after tomorrow.'

She nods but doesn't look at him. She cannot risk the betrayal of her own face.

'You could come with me.'

He says these words pensively. It is a question, an open one. As if he thinks it is actually something she could possibly agree to. The navïeté of it makes her smile, despite the turmoil of her emotions. For a fleeting moment, she imagines saying yes to him. Turning away from all the problems with Henry, with the debts and the bank and the house that tomorrow will not be theirs any more. But the children. That she could contemplate leaving them, even for a second, or that he could think that she would, causes a stabbing pain in her heart.

Today is a day for goodbyes. She thinks of all that he has said, all that he has told her of what happened in Spain. But this new know-ledge doesn't change the fact that they are not together. Nor can they be. That day in Barcelona – that wet, wet day – they never got to say goodbye. Then there was only the coldness of her anger and the bit-terness of unspoken recriminations. But today is a gift, she thinks to herself, a reprise. Her eyes roam out over the city landscape. She leaves his question hanging there, unanswered, and watches the drops splattering against the windshield as she casts her mind back.

*

It was a Tuesday when the rains came. They arrived from the Pyrenees and spread outwards across Catalonia, hovering over Barcelona in damp, grey, voluminous clouds like great brooding monsters. Sheets of white rain hit the streets, bubbling up in drains, making the pavements slick and treacherous. Tables and chairs along the Ramblas and Paseig de Gracia were hastily withdrawn, the greased awnings snapped back, leaving the streets looking suddenly bare and naked. On the metro, Elena held herself stiffly, trying to avoid brushing against the other drenched bodies, a stale, damp odour assaulting her nostrils. In the evenings, she stretched out on the mattress reading her book, fighting the boredom, while listening to the relentless drum of rain splatter and break against the windows.

'When will it stop?' she moaned.

She was answered by Adam's grim monotone, 'Soon.'

He had been quiet lately, moody and withdrawn, since her return from Zaragoza. He seemed to move from high-pitched excitement to a sudden irascibility to long brooding silences where his eyebrows veered towards each other over eyes that stared vacantly ahead, fixed on something that she couldn't see. He appeared troubled, but when she tentatively tried to draw him out, he snapped out a smile and an empty laugh, holding his secrets close to himself.

The rain persisted and by Friday Maria declared that she had had enough and boarded a train for Seville, where her parents lived. The apartment seemed to breathe a sigh of relief after she'd left. It was as if the walls themselves had been holding their breath, anxious not to upset her, wary of the brittle shell she had wrapped herself in. Yet still a tension persisted. It was there when Elena woke on Saturday, her eyelids leaden and her head sore. The air hung heavily around her. She was growing used to the same bleak greyness of the sky, the constant stream of water. It hissed around them, temporarily giving way to brief spells of noiseless drizzle before flurrying up into a storm again.

The flat felt cold. The floor crawled with books and clothes strewn about. A stack of dirty dishes was growing in the sink. All the old habits and rituals of cleaning and tidying and maintaining order had been abandoned. They felt empty now – there was a hollow ring to them. The place was in need of a good clean. But, more than that, it needed new tenants. Too many ghosts lingered there, fingering the walls, rubbing their odourless scent against the furniture. The bathroom was treated with a cursory disdain, each person using it as if holding their breath, anxious to get out of there as quickly as possible.

Silence had fallen over them. Conversation seemed hollow. Their voices were too loud in the small space, casting echoes around the rooms, and so they found themselves communicating in whispers, skirting around the unspoken thought, suppressing what it was they wanted to say. But Elena could feel the words building inside her. They jostled for position, each climbing over the others, climbing up her throat, filling her mouth, threatening to be released in a torrent.

Let's leave here, they said. Let's get out of here, find somewhere new. Just the two of us. But they were never spoken aloud. She couldn't allow them to be.

In the end, it was Adam who spoke first.

She was standing at the window, staring out at the buildings surrounding theirs, when he told her. She was thinking how even the rain could not wash away the ugliness of the grey walls, the stained stone and wires and air-conditioning boxes that sat on iron arms. Washing lines stretched from window to window, but there were no clothes hanging in the rain. Shallow balconies held an assortment of items – small clues to the identities of the tenants, baskets of clothes pegs, potted plants, satellite dishes, a rusting exercise bike, a cylinder of gas, a cat litter-box. The rain had washed away the dust and stains like rust bled from windowsills.

'We need to talk,' he said behind her.

'Mmm,' she hummed absently, her eyes travelling over the windows of the building opposite, looking for signs of life.

'Why don't you sit down?' he suggested.

'I'm fine standing.'

'Please, Elena. Please sit down.'

She turned to look at him. It was his voice that made her do it – the slight quaver of indecision in it, as if he was not convinced he wanted to have this conversation, as if he had not thought it through properly.

'I'm fine,' she repeated, holding her position, watching his face, which appeared pale and drawn in the shadowy room.

He took a breath and held it before letting it out slowly, staring down at his hands; in that second, she read the sum of his feelings. He was afraid – afraid of her. This new knowledge pulled tightly across her chest and she felt the words inside her clambering upwards in a panic, fuelled by an alarm that she could not yet account for.

'I've been thinking,' she said quickly. 'We've stayed here too long. This apartment – we need to get out of here, find somewhere new.'

'Elena.'

'Maybe even move on from Barcelona. Now that the weather has turned, it'll soon be winter. We might as well be in Ireland, with this rain.' She laughed suddenly and felt how forced it was. 'We could go south, to Andalucia. We could find work there, I'm sure of it. And if nothing else, it will be easier…'

231

He stared at her, bewildered, as she rambled on. His face settled into a patient arrangement of features. He was waiting for her to finish, waiting to tell her what she didn't want to hear.

The words ran out and she came to a halt, and he said into the vacuum – 'I have something to tell you.'

She turned away from the gravity of his voice and resumed her window gazing. Her heart was beating high and loud in her chest. She counted the windows in the opposite building. Most of the shutters were pulled down against the rain. Some were green, some were brown, others again had once been white. All were filthy.

'It's Maria,' she heard him say.

Her eyes travelled to the older, more well-to-do buildings on the far side of the square. Most days, they reminded Elena of colonial dwellings, with their striped awnings and fluttering trims, their elegantly curling wrought-iron balconies, terracotta pots spilling leafy verdant foliage. Most days. But not that day.

'She's pregnant.'

This came out as a half whisper and he swallowed loudly, as if the words had dried his mouth out.

Something jolted within her, a sudden charge of electricity running through, prickling the back of her neck, causing the hairs on her forearms to stand erect.

'Pregnant?' She turned to stare at his bowed head.

The enormity of it struck her forcefully and she leaned back against the windowsill, shaking her head slowly, trying to fathom the consequences.

'Poor Maria.'

He ran his hand through his hair and continued to stare at the floor in front of him.

Questions swarmed through her brain and some of them leaked out. 'What is she going to do?' she asked. 'She'll keep the baby, of course? Oh my God, what about Carlos's parents – do they know yet?' And then she paused, struck by a new and shocking thought. 'Carlos didn't know about the baby, did he?'

Her heart was still as he looked up wearily and shook his head. Exhaustion was etched into his face. He looked haggard and spent.

'No,' he said at last, his voice rasping in his throat. 'Elena, it's not as simple as that.'

'How come?'

She watched as he shifted the weight of his head from one hand to the other, fingers travelling across that drawn face; through them, an open mouth drew thick, deep breaths. He could not bring himself to look her in the eye. The pounding in her chest had spread through her body. Blood thundered in her ears. A lump rose in her throat as she watched him struggling to express himself.

'Adam?' she asked quietly.

'Oh, God,' he moaned, and something icy slipped through to her insides.

'You're scaring me,' she admitted in a tiny voice.

'You're going to hate me…' he began.

And with the rain sliding down the windowpane, he started to tell her. 'It happened the week you were in Zaragoza…'

She leaned against the window, suddenly in need of support. Her legs felt weak, her stomach lurched. His words echoed around the room, swarming about her, pressing up against her threateningly. She felt her body tighten. It closed in around her protectively, shielding her from the slice of his words. She could not bring herself to look at him. There were tears in his voice, but she didn't want to see them. He offered up excuses, but she didn't want to hear them.

Instead, she was bombarded by a rush of images, a torrent of memories that rose up from deep within her, bursting like a fountain, rising up and slipping down over her edges and surfaces, drenching her. She allowed her mind to slip back there, absenting itself from the dreary room and the misery it contained. Instead she saw green eyes smiling at her over a row of heads, a knowing grin catching her daydreaming during a lecture. And there was more: cherry blossoms shedding petals like confetti, holding hands at the lake, breath clouding out in hazy puffs, the coarse weave of his jacket rough against her cheek; stolen kisses among a warren of lockers, misting over with a rising wave of desire; that first time in a borrowed room under a blanket that kept slipping off them, her legs clasped around him, drawing him in, her eyes fluttering open suddenly and seeing Che Guevara peering down at them from a poster on the wall; a lurching, nauseous feeling – her stomach full of hormones – not eating for a week; lunch in the canteen, the way his hands curled around his tray protectively; in the library, the struggle to concentrate on tortious liability and the defence of insanity and the laws governing marriage, while resisting the draw of his bent head, the way his eyes narrowed with concentration, the way he tapped his pen against his teeth; the taut range of his body, gripped with excitement, his long legs crossing and recrossing, too long for the narrow seats of the plane; the deep honey sound of his laugh in the dying light of day as they struggled to pitch their tent; his arms circling her waist as she stared up at La Sagrada Familia; his breath on her neck, mingling with the hot breaths of the night; the warmth and familiarity of his body held against hers in the darkness; and talking, talking deep into the night, holding his head against her chest, her leg slung over his hip, feeling his words murmured against her breast, his words pouring into her, spoken to her heart, the peace that came to her in those moments, locked in a tender, shadowy embrace.

His words dried up. He had told his story. In the silence that followed, Elena felt those memories slipping over her, filling with cracks, as they slipped perilously before shattering on the floor about her. He looked at her expectantly, waiting for her reaction. His shoulders curved, his whole body seemed to slump forward in defeat, tension hovering over his face, watchful of her, wary of her, fearful of her reaction.

But she didn't react. She did not know how to. Her body was paralysed, frozen by its utter powerlessness to alter the situation. She was aware of the space in between them. The distance seemed to grow in the silence that followed. Her heart rocked in her chest and she felt a terrible aching need to reach out to him, to hold him in her arms, to feel the muffled warmth of his breath in her chest and the cool softness of his hair against her cheek. But that was impossible. His betrayal had opened a wound between them – a giant chasm – and all of her compassion and love for him would fall into that chasm, tumbling into that great hole, devoured by it, chewed up and discarded. She could feel it beginning already. She was starting to unravel.

He grew impatient. Her silence baffled him. He needed a reaction; he needed to see the colour of her anger – the vibrant red of her rage, the ice-white of her chilly withdrawal. But instead she remained colourless. Her feelings were translucent. Some part of her was conscious of future pain. But she did not know yet the searing depth of it.

'Elena?' he prompted her, anxiously drawing her eyes back to his, and then waiting.

She looked into his face, that face she had loved for so long. She knew the freckle above his lip, the tiny white scar nicked into his forehead, the coarse reddish hairs of his sideburns. If she closed her eyes, she could trace those features, the hard ridge of bone at the bridge of his nose, the length and straightness of it, the cool sweep of his eyebrows, the feathery lightness of his eyelashes, the smooth straightness of his lips, the sudden dimple in his left cheek – still a surprise to her, even now. But, of all these features, it was his eyes that had changed. It was in the way they were looking at her. Love had fled from them, replaced by fear. It flickered behind them, stalking her.

'Aren't you going to say something?'

He looked at her expectantly, irritation hovering over his face, jostling for position amongst the fear and anxiety that huddled there.

What was there to say? She turned her back to him and stared out the window. Behind her, she felt his anger inflate in the short gasp of air that escaped his lips. 'For God's sake, Elena, say something!'

The first drops of anger began to colour her emotion, like spots of ink striking water, dropping deeply and clouding out, passing particles, filling out and expanding.

But she did not give vent to it. That didn't happen yet. And later, when it exploded inside her, he would no longer be there to witness it.

She stared out through the window at the water gathering in dips and crevices on the balcony. She could not remember the last time she had sat out there and felt the sun warming her limbs, a lightness in her chest, the sound of laughter in her ears.

He was badgering her now, pushing her to say something. But what could she tell him? Her body had taken a blow, all the love had been punched out of her. What could she say to that?

She stared at the balcony, at the green plastic chairs, at the rusting ring-pulls littering the ground. She would not sit there again. In that one moment, she understood that it would be impossible for her to stay. And before night had fallen, she was gone.

In the days and nights that followed, after she had hastily packed the bits and pieces of her life with her broken heart and fled north across Europe, needing to get away – far, far away – those unspoken words incubated inside her. The words grew teeth and began to gnaw at her insides. She was tortured by what she might have said, reliving the scene a hundred different ways. She felt the shuddering force of her anger, crying hot tears of murderous rage. The wounds fixed to her body like welts and she carried herself carefully.

She found somewhere new to live – Brussels, where it rained every day. She found a job and went to work, and in the evenings went out and met new people. At weekends, she walked through the narrow cobbled streets and forced her gaze over the medieval beauty of the Grand Place, the quirkiness of Mannekin Pis, the majesty of the Palais de Justice. She sat in dark pubs sampling Belgian beer and ate *Speculoos* bought at St Katherine's market. She took trains to Antwerp and Bruges and wore down the soles of her shoes, feet pounding over foreign pavements, all the time waiting for the novelty and beauty of these places to seep into her soul, to awaken it again. But it had become a stone. And while her dry eyes passed over art and sculpture, palace and museum, inside she wept. There were men, too, nights of sweaty limbs, soulless exchanges, and while her body tried to lose itself in oblivion, her grief raged and moaned, maintaining its red-hot grip.

And still the questions came. The eternal *Why?* The wrenching plea of *How could you?* The torturous *What if?* But these questions were offered into the darkness and no answers returned.

*

Outside, the pine trees grow dark. Their black silhouettes push threateningly against the night sky. She thinks of those questions, hears the whisper of them that still lingers. It accompanies the shadow of pain that has remained long since the wound was first made. She could ask him now. She could line her questions up along the dashboard in a neat row and pass each one by him, noting the answers and boxing them off neatly in her mind. Would that help? Would that satisfy the longing within her? Would the restlessness diminish, or the new discontent she has known lately – would they dissipate and fade into nothing once she had the answers?

She looks at him, taking in the side of his face that she can view, trying to read him, trying to find him. His head tilts sideways towards the window, his gaze passing over the lights of the city, their glow strengthening as the light dims. There is a strange smile lingering on his lips.

'You know, when I was in college, it used to kill me that I didn't have a car,' he says. 'I used to fantasise about coming up here to watch the lights coming on, a beautiful girl in the car with me.'

'And then a drink in Johnny Fox's?'

'Oh, please – the Blue Light!' he corrects her playfully. 'And then, on the way home across the mountains, stop somewhere quiet, secluded…'

'And steam up the windows?'

He laughs, a loud burst of laughter that seems too big for the car. He draws a finger to his teeth, the laugh softening into a pensive smile as he stares at her intently.

'Would you have liked that?' he asks her, his eyes darting over her face, searching it, guarded but needful.

'Yes,' she replies, holding his gaze.

'And here we are now, alone in this car, the city lights stretched out ahead of us, a whole warren of quiet mountain roads behind us, and yet…' His voice breaks off as he shakes his head, struck by the irony. 'Poor timing, huh?'

She stares out at the city. Her head feels hot and full of blood. The clouds are scudding across the sky, racing towards nightfall. The storm is gathering around them, she can hear the low rumble of thunder in the distance. The car rocks with a sudden gust of wind and she watches as a flock of birds wheels across the sky. Leaves are tearing away from branches, crowds of them scurrying across the breezes. The air seems to be filling up with goodbyes.

She watches as he sucks in his lower lip, squeezing it with his teeth, so that the lip turns white and bloodless. His eyes are lost to her, staring into the distance, and he sucks in his breath, his cheeks filling, before the air escapes through pursed lips, whistling between his teeth; and what she feels suddenly is a longing and a regret, so achingly deep it seems to cut into her flesh, and there is only one thing left she can do.

'It's getting dark,' he says. 'You must want to be getting back?'

'Soon,' she answers quietly. 'But not yet.'

HENRY

18

THE CAR COMES shuddering to a halt. Henry sits stunned for a moment, watching the rain leaping off the bonnet in wet splashy strides. Oh, no, he thinks to himself, a long sigh of a thought. It is at least another mile to the warehouse, if not more. He does not like the way the wind is howling around the car. Leaves scutter along the road, flurrying up with the litter, lifted and tossed about on the wind. There are few cars on the road; the storm has driven people indoors. A bin is blown over and swept across the road in front of him, a black barrel like an animal fleeing pursuit. He turns the key in the ignition and hears a horrible choking noise. The engine heaves asthmatically, then falls silent. 'Damn, damn, damn,' he swears under his breath, trying the ignition once more. He will flood the engine at this rate, he knows. 'Fuck it!' His head leans forward and rests momentarily on the steering wheel. The night feels large and threatening around him. 'Oh, to hell with it,' he says quickly, taken by a surge of impatience, unclipping his seatbelt and opening the car door. The wind takes it, whipping the door back. Henry scrambles for the handle and just makes it as the hinges are pressured, the door flung wide. 'Christ!'

He is outside, ankle deep in water as the rain laps at his feet, seeping into his shoes and socks, making them suddenly cold, then warm and muggy. Slamming the car door, he locks it, pulling his anorak tightly around him. He struggles with the zipper holding his hood captive, managing to unravel it, but not before his hair and ears and face become soaked. The hood turns out to be hopelessly inadequate, barely covering his ears and not reaching his forehead, making his neck feel hot and clammy.

He walks with his head bent, leaning into the wind. It is a struggle moving against this force of nature that beats at his muscles, sapping his strength. By the time he reaches the warehouse, he is exhausted and soaked to the skin. He finds the place in darkness. Banging on the door, he peers in through the slatted windows, looking for a sign of life inside. There is no reply. His father's car sits in the car park – a solitary vehicle. Hammering on the doorway, he calls out – 'Hello!' – but only the echo of his own voice greets him.

The rain beats into his back, punishing and relentless, as he fishes in his pocket for his spare set of keys. He tries a few before finding the right one and hurriedly pulls the door open, letting it slam shut behind him. Pressing his back against the door, he allows himself a minute or two to catch his breath, waiting for the heaving in his chest to stop. His clothes are plastered to his body, his limbs feel heavy, wrung clean of energy. He pulls down his hood and runs his hands through his hair, then down over his face, which feels hot and damp. Blinking in the darkness, he pushes himself away from the doors, stumbling out onto the workroom floor. Great towers of wooden pallets rise up in front of him, dark and intimidating. His feet make angry slapping sounds on the stone floor as he moves into the heart of the building, feeling the dampness of his socks rubbing against raw, chafed feet. His voice echoes as he calls 'Hello' to the silent walls.

A dim grainy light floats down through the darkness, and he raises his head to the window of his father's office. A bare seam of light seeps out into the grey space beyond. As he climbs the metal stairs, Henry's muscles groan and kick, sore and angry at the night's exertions. He knocks gently on the door before pushing it open.

The room is in near darkness. A dim lamp casts a faint shadowy glow from the corner. And next to it is his father, slumped in a chair, staring into space.

'Dad?' Henry asks, feeling something leap in his chest. Dan's eyes are glazed. He is lost in a different world of thought, oblivious to his son's presence. Alarm nips at Henry's heart as he observes the emptiness of his father's gaze. Slumped in the chair, he seems smaller, strangely diminished, the harsh clipped tones notably absent, the steely glare replaced by a bewildered stare. He seems lost, abandoned.

'Dad?' Henry says again, awkwardly reaching out to touch his father's shoulder.

Dan looks up briefly, still dazed, but his eyes clearing, returning to the present, and he makes an effort at pulling himself up in his chair.

'Henry,' he says sleepily, a confusion settling on his features. 'What are you doing here? I didn't hear you come in.'

'I banged on the doors for ages. I called out to you. You didn't hear me?'

Dan shakes his head, and Henry reads the fear in his eyes.

'Are you OK, Dad?'

'Yes, yes, I'm fine,' he answers, scratching his bristly head.

'Mum was worried. She tried calling you several times, but there was no answer.'

'Yes, well, I've been busy.'

Henry glances across at the desk and sees that the phone has been taken off the hook, the receiver lost amid a ream of paperwork. For as long as Henry can remember, his father has been meticulous about tidiness, fastidiously maintaining an ordered desk, reluctant to leave paperwork lying about undone. Henry's eyes absorb the papers that are now strewn across the desk, a paper trail that has stretched, tipping over the edge and snaking along the floor, making its way across to form a pool around Dan's feet. Alarm bells ring in Henry's head. What has happened to his stoic father, his stern, unyielding, orderly ways?

'I'm just going to ring Mum, let her know you're all right,' he says, but Dan barely looks up in acknowledgement. As Henry speaks to his mother in a low voice, telling her not to worry, he casts his eyes briefly over his father's shadowy face and feels a sudden flurry of feeling race up his spine. It tingles all over, the rawness of it, this new sensitivity.

Putting the phone down, he looks about uncertainly. The papers stare up at him, forlornly scattered, and he bends down to reach for them.

'Leave them be,' Dan intones solemnly, and Henry straightens up reluctantly.

'What's going on, Dad?' he asks quietly, slipping his hands into his pockets, feeling like a teenager again, skulking and wary and needful.

He watches his dad's hand rise slowly before falling limply back by his side – a gesture of weary defeat. His brow wrinkles with dismay, a forlorn look washing down over his features, tiredness swamping his bulky frame slumped in the chair.

'This. All this,' he says, his eyes sweeping casually in the direction of the paper trail, 'this must all be sorted out. For the solicitor. Tomorrow. I've been going through it, going through everything. Trying to get things ready, trying to take care of things.'

Henry is mystified. He shakes his head, shifting his weight from one foot to the other. His shoes are sodden, and the musty smell from his clothes rises up and invades his nostrils.

'What do you mean?'

'Tomorrow. I have to see the solicitor tomorrow.'

'What for?'

'To make arrangements.'

Henry looks from his father to the pile of papers in his lap, weighted down with his left hand.

'What arrangements?'

'The business. Everything.' Dan glances over his shoulder, his small eyes creeping towards the factory floor. 'I'm getting rid of it. I have to. You don't want it. You've made that clear. And I accept that. I want you to know, Henry, that I accept your decision.' He nods earnestly in his son's direction, his eyes intent and narrowed with seriousness. 'This place isn't for you. I know that. I've always known it. And I'm not going to be able to... I... I just can't do it any more. So I'm going to get rid of it. To sell it off.'

Henry feels the air escaping his lungs. He sinks into the chair opposite his father. The wind screeches outside and he feels the echo of it in his head. It is something he cannot fathom – his father without the business. To Henry, they are one and the same. And, in spite of his resentment of this marriage between his father and his work, and regardless of Henry's stubborn refusal to take on the business, this news leaves him gasping. He feels winded by it.

'But you love this business. It's been your life...'

His words hang in the air between them. They have been uttered before, but then they were flung accusatorily, something blameworthy and shameful. This time they ring out plaintively, gently, in the dark office.

'I know.' Dan's chin sinks into his chest, his voice disappearing in his rib cage. 'But I can't carry it any longer. It's... it's too much.'

The table lamp shines on his face and he seems smaller than he really is, diminished by the cold hospital sterility of the pale walls around him. It occurs to Henry that something has physically altered about his father in the last few days – his body has been invaded by a new frailness, a sharp, hard, alien fragility. It alarms him.

'What's wrong, Dad?' Henry asks, a tremble in his voice. His father's frailty claws at his heart.

And then Dan raises his hands to his face, pressing the balls of his fists into his closed eyes, squeezing them tight, his large body clenched in protest, his face turning red, then purple, with the exertion of fighting this emotion. He seems to gasp for breath before pulling his hands away with a violent shake of his head. Tears stream over his rounded cheeks and he gasps again, a great sob emerging from his chest. The papers slide off his lap and he lets them fall without making any effort to save them. And in that gesture, that sudden sob, Henry sees the depth of his despair.

'I... I...' His voice quavers as he sucks in his lower lip, his eyes trained on the wall ahead of him as if scouring it for a reason, an explanation for his turmoil.

Henry leans towards him, wanting to reach out, to place his hand on his father's shoulder, to steady him. But he feels suddenly faint with tiredness, a dizzying fatigue filling out his body, the drench of emotions dulling his reflexes. In that moment, he realises his own hopeless inadequacy in the face of crisis. Elena would know what to do here. Elena, who has always given herself with warmth and understanding, would be out of her chair like a shot, folding Dan in the generosity of her embrace. Elena, who has always been willing to make excuses for the old man's shortcomings. 'He loves you really, you know,' she has assured him on occasions when he felt bruised by his father's formidable temper. 'He's a sweetheart, underneath it all, deep down,' she told him.

'Very deep down,' he grumbled, full of misgivings and reluctant to allow his father the warmth she seemed so willing to bestow on him. Elena, were she here instead of him, would find words to utter to fill this quiet room, to make it safe again. But he is left stumbling over his own inadequacy, bereft of words, hopelessly clenching and unclenching his fists.

It takes Dan a minute to compose himself. His eyes reflect an internal struggle, and when he speaks, the words come out broken and uneven.

'My heart,' he begins, 'it's been playing up. I… I have to…'

'What?' Henry asks quietly, feeling his own heart beating loud and slow in his chest.

'I… God, I didn't want to tell you this.'

'Tell me.'

'I have to have surgery.'

'When?'

'Next week. Thursday.'

'What sort of surgery?'

'A triple bypass.' His mouth falls open as if stunned again at the prospect, overwhelmed by the heft of his announcement.

Henry feels a long, weak breath rising up from his chest.

'Jesus. Have you had a heart attack?' The words feel cold and round in his mouth, like pebbles.

'No. Not yet. A few months ago there were some chest pains. Nothing dramatic, just the odd shooting pain. I didn't think much of it at the time. Put it down to stress, and just got on with things.'

Henry thinks of his father, his stalwart approach to work, his silent refusal to be deterred by the cries of his own body.

'But then, a couple of weeks ago I had a bad one. Not a heart attack. Not that. But it frightened me. That's when I got it checked out.'

Henry sees the fear flickering in his father's eyes; he seems dazed by the workings of his own body. He looks like a man who has been betrayed, his eyes grown opaque with hurt. Henry wants to say something comforting, something reassuring. He reaches out a hand involuntarily, and for a second it hangs there between them, before he snatches it back, rescuing himself from a sentimentality that his father would despise. He feels a rackety pity for the old man but, unable to express it, he floats away on a wave of uncertainty.

For a minute they sit in silence. Henry can hear the wind whining outside the window, a sudden crackle of rain on the corrugated roof. He wonders how his father has been able to sit here in this room, listening to the pounding elements – and not just on this night, but on all those other ones that have lined up in his history, that endless series of days and nights knitting together to form the tapestry of his life.

'At least you caught it in time,' he says gently, optimistically. 'I mean, this way, the surgery might pre-empt any heart problems that might have developed later, might stop you from having a heart attack. Right?'

He watches his father, this elderly gentleman, slightly stooped, in a green button-down cardigan and grey flannel trousers. His small dark eyes are regarding his son forlornly. They flicker with a question, as if to say, Don't you understand? Isn't it clear enough? His eyebrows float upwards in dismay, his lungs releasing air in a bewildered sigh.

'My father died when he was sixty-four,' he says softly. 'He worked hard all his life. And it was difficult work. Hard slog. Then, two days after retiring, he dropped dead of a heart attack. Just like that. I can still remember it. That awful thud, his body stretched out on the kitchen floor.'

His face pales to grey as he recounts the memory.

'And his father before him. Another heart attack, at fifty-eight.' His voice rises as he makes his point. 'And now there's me. I'm sixty-six. Now it's my heart that's failing. Don't you see, Henry? It's in the genes. It's in our blood. There is absolutely nothing I can do about it. And now that it's my turn, I'm… I'm just not ready.'

The room feels unbearably hot. Henry begins to understand. His clothes feel musty and clammy, sticking to his limbs, making him sweat. What he wants more than anything is to bridge the gap that exists between them. He feels pained and shocked by his father's raw emotion. His admission of fear, of frailty, has left Henry grasping for some way of reaching him.

'But that might not happen,' he says, trying to sound encouraging, but his voice coming out reedy and inadequate. 'You've caught it in time.'

'No.' Dan shakes his head firmly, his anxiety leaking into his voice. 'You don't understand. Everything is in such a mess! This place, this place that I have devoted my whole life to, and now I have to give it up, just like that? I'm expected to just hand it over to some stranger, who doesn't know what it's meant to me? I've been sitting here these past few hours, looking through all of this, and it keeps coming back to me – what has it all been for? What has it all meant?' His voice, forlorn and aching, rings out cleanly in the small room as his eyes travel upwards to the ceiling, sweeping out over the walls and furniture.

'When I think of the time I've spent in this room, all those hours, all those years...'

The weight of it labours his breathing. His voice drifts into silence, an aching regret released into the air between them.

Henry looks at his feet, unable to look his father in the eye, racking his brain for some paltry words of comfort. But Henry has long resented his father's devotion to the business. He has felt the loss of it throughout his life. And for that reason, he feels illqualified to console him, to say that it was worth it, when he doesn't believe it himself.

'Does Mum know?' he asks instead, and watches in amazement as Dan shakes his head. 'She's worried about you. She suspects something.'

'I know. I'll tell her later.' His chin sinks into his chest again, his eyes clouding over at the prospect of that conversation.

Henry, struggling with the burden of his own dark secret, feels suddenly protective of Dan. An unexpected, inexplicable urge to please his father takes him, and he finds himself on the brink of giving in to everything, submitting to his father's wishes, taking on the business despite his stubborn resistance over all these years – all of this he is willing to offer up as a poultice to press on his father's wounded spirit; an offer of help, to shoulder some of Dan's cares.

Outside, the storm is shrieking, the rattle of rain echoing loudly through the building, clamouring over the workroom floor. As Henry grapples with his courage, the words tumbling up inside him, he is interrupted by a sudden crack of lightning overhead. A change comes over the room. The dark rumble of thunder seems to jolt Dan from his faraway thoughts. He shakes himself to attention, shoulders back, head up; drawing a hankie from his pocket, he blows his nose loudly. He stands abruptly, running his hands quickly down the sides of his cardigan. Looking about him, he straightens his tie, composing himself.

Glancing over at his son, he seems to notice Henry's sodden appearance for the first time.

'What happened to you? You're soaked!' The sudden bark of his voice and the iron in his stare stun Henry into silence.

'You'd better get out of those wet clothes before you catch your death.' He steps in behind his desk and rummages in a drawer, fishing out a small key. 'Here. Get yourself downstairs; there's a change of clothes in my locker – number thirteen – by the far door. Put those on you.'

These orders are delivered briskly and Henry feels the dismissiveness of them. And in that moment, something is dispelled between them; that rare moment of intimacy is snuffed out. As he steps out of the office, closing the door softly behind him, Henry feels the coldness of the rejection, and of his own failure – his failure as a son, as well as a husband – the pitiful wreckage of it.

Save me, he wants to cry out. Save me from all of this.

ELENA

19

THIS TIME, THEY do not linger in the lobby or at the bar. Adam crosses the well-lit lobby with its bank of bright receptionists and its ceiling speckled with light bulbs. He walks purposefully ahead of her, and she watches those long legs, a loping walk that gives him a casual air despite his brisk movements. His walk has not changed. As they approach the lift, her eyes pass over the length of his body, the long, narrow back, those square shoulders hunched awkwardly within his suit jacket, rolling and shrugging as if anxious to escape their confinement. The hair at the back of his head is peppered with grey, and it occurs to her as the lift arrives that soon she will encounter other changes in his body, more markings of age that she might not have anticipated – a thickening about the waist, the hint of slackness about his torso? These are small things, minor details that she will not linger over. She can only hope that he will afford her the same dignity.

'Here we are again,' he says quietly as the lift opens onto the fourth floor. He smiles at her, creases travelling up the sides of his face into his eyes, and she sees something there – a wild kind of hope. As if her being there, as if what they both know will come next, this unspoken agreement, as if he believes this to be the start of something. Or worse, more dangerously, the continuation of what existed a long time ago. She feels a needle of fear and wants to stop him, to say something to curb his expectation, a gentle warning that this is not a new episode or the unfolding of something long lasting. She wants to place a steadying hand on his arm and speak softly in his ear this is goodbye. But she does not feel composed. Be careful, she whispers to herself.

There is a moment of awkwardness after they enter the room, both staring about them, and she is conscious of her body, knowing that any movement could betray what she feels inside. She is also conscious of the furniture, the positioning of the beds. Unsure of where to sit, not knowing how this should begin, how they should approach each other, which one of them should reach out, she looks about her, seeking a distraction.

Feeling her awkwardness, Adam begins to move about the room, attending to a series of tasks. She doesn't stir from her standing position by the bed, but watches him, his brisk, hurried movements becoming less hurried as the room starts to breathe around them. Sounds seem elevated to a clarity she was not aware of on her previous visit to this room. She hears clearly the spatter of raindrops against the window. She feels the rush of wind as it flings itself against the walls, rattling the doors and windows that push back the threat robustly. A thrill goes through her as he draws the curtains and she hears the rush of hooks along the rail and the swish of fabric swinging to a halt in folds. The sound of his jacket slipping off his shoulders and down his arms causes a bead of sweat to run slowly between her breasts. The room is warm. It relaxes around them. It feels bigger than she remembered it. Or maybe it is her memory of his place in it that has changed. He no longer seems ungainly, or crowding to the room. He drops his jacket over the back of the chair. 'Elena,' he says quietly and steps towards her. They stand facing each other for an instant, and then she reaches out and finds him as the wind gathers and pummels the window, banging in protest.

His arms are around her, folding her into him, and at that moment she realises that she has been thinking about this for days. She is trembling. He looks at her face and kisses her tenderly. Her mouth opens and she feels as if he is pouring himself into her. It wakens something inside her, stirring up a slumbering desire that is whipped alive and comes tumbling up in waves. His touch is familiar – the dry softness of the palms of his hands – but there is a tentativeness about his fingertips that is new to her. As he unzips her dress and nudges the fabric away from her shoulders, allowing it to slip and fall in a pool about her feet, she realises that what is there now is a sort of

deference that wasn't there before. A new respect, a lingering knowledge, and the tingling excitement of a new lover. Her arms slip
around his waist and her hands travel to the deep crevice in his back.
Tracing the groove of his spine, she closes her eyes and, like a blind
woman, feels the contours and ridges of his back and shoulders. They
unveil themselves to her like a memory swimming up from the murky
waters of the past.

They draw apart briefly to take their places side by side under the
covers – a solemn arrangement. As he reaches for her under the
sheets, she remembers again how, before, all their beds were borrowed or rented. There was never any ownership to the place of their
lovemaking. This transience settles around her in the darkness of the
hotel room, the storm gathering and raging outside.

Guilt slips under the covers alongside them and she pushes it aside,
pushes it away, out to the far reaches of the bed, the far corners of her
mind. She aches with wanting him and her body tightens. This is
goodbye, she reminds herself. Goodbye, her body sings as it cleaves to
his kisses. She is willing herself to remember this, to absorb every
detail, each caress, the soft pluck of his lips against her collarbone, the
brush of his fingers against her thigh. She stores them up, these sen-
sory delights, welding them into a memory that will have to last a lifetime.

He smooths the hair back from her forehead, leaning on his elbows
and gazing down at her. They are bound to each other, moving in a
deep, slow rhythm. In a few hours they will leave each other, sucked
back into their separate lives. She senses the press of time against
them, of minutes passing already, before she has to leave him. And as
if suddenly realising it too, that their minutes together are short and
numbered, that gestures and words cannot be wasted, he is taken with
a new urgency. As she feels her body rise, moving towards a shuddering moment of departure, her mind opens up a seam of memory
that was lost to her, small moments obliterated by all that came after.
She smells a dark salt-scented harbour, the bobbing forest of masts
clinking together. She sees ribbons of light trailing away into darkness, the dying embers of a setting sun. She feels her chin balancing
on her bare knees, watching the day dying in a foreign country. She
sees a boy with tousled hair, his skin scorched by the sun, his long legs
dangling over a sheer ten-foot drop to the harbour below. She hears

his voice ringing out into the night, the clear pitch of it, the honeyed undertones. She sees glints upon the water as they sit together overlooking the Mediterranean, the bright lights behind them casting their bodies in silhouettes. She feels the swell of anticipation in her stomach, a fizzing excitement masking something deeper, something rooted and lasting. And then she feels his hand travelling around her body, drawing her to him, his breath on her neck, and a loosening in her body as it breathed in the warm night air.

Goodbye, her body sings out as she lets them go. Goodbye, as they fade away into darkness.

They lie together in the quiet stillness that has returned to the room. After a while he releases her head from the crook of his arm and turns over in sleep. Outside, the storm is inflicting its rage on the city, but Elena feels strangely at peace. The violence outside does not touch her. For something has returned to her, something that had been lost over time and forgotten under a mound of details that had become her life. The person she was, that soft, open girl so full of hope and possibility – something of her has been resurrected. She feels a faint thrill of excitement, a whisper of hope, at her return.

Adam moans in his sleep, a long sigh released into the night. She feels as if she too has exhaled her relief into this room. She watches the shadow of his body next to hers; there is so much to recognise, and yet it was different between them. There was an urgency that had not existed before, because then, they had all the time in the world, and neither of them had seen how it could change or end abruptly. There had been no dissipation in sentiment, no slow descent into feelings of ambivalence or a nagging dissatisfaction. What had existed between them – all that love and hope and possibility – had come crashing to an end, wiped out in a few moments of madness. The grief of this stayed with her over years, how she had been cheated out of her goodbye, and it silently ate away at her until she learned to forget it and found solace in her husband, her children, her home. These people, these places served as a consolation for her loss. Now, lying in the stillness of this strange room, she is wrapped in a peace that she understands to be forgiveness, a healing of wounds. The bitterness that she has tasted seems to have fermented into something sweeter. She knows that this is the end for them. And her knowledge of that passing does not bring with it a renewed grief, but rather a peaceful acceptance, a new opening, a way to move on.

He lies on his side, with one arm tucked up under the pillow and the other arm raised above his head, touching the headboard. She remembers how he used to lie like that, and stops to consider the vulnerability of this sleeping posture. She considers what has passed between them – what she has allowed him to believe. She knows that he can sense her marriage is foundering. She has dropped hints, small clues that alluded to an emptiness in the relationship, a lack of fulfilment, and in this respect she feels guilty. He has seized upon these clues and possibly made more of them, hoping that... what? That she will run away with him? That she will leave her husband and children and go back with him?

What he wants of her, she cannot give him. The impossibility of it is overwhelming. To be together would require sacrifices too great for her to consider. But, more than that, he wants a return to something that belongs in the past, as though by returning to each other they might recapture something of that lost youth, that fallen hope, that dying possibility. She too has been a victim of the same fantasy. But as she lies there watching him sleep, the futility of this fantasy strikes her forcefully. She is a different person now; they both are. Life has chipped away at them, teaching them harsh lessons, shaping them into older, flawed people.

But something else occurs to her as she listens to the steady rhythm of his breathing. She has been deceitful, to him and to herself. The emptiness in her marriage, the lack of fulfilment – she attributed these deficits in her life to marrying the wrong man. Somehow, she has allowed her broken heart to blind her to her own complicity. Thinking of the person she was in Spain, she looks back on that girl and sees a strength about her, a confidence, an independence, that has been stripped away, a sacrifice to assuage her torn love.

She remembers, too, her mother, the way she used to sit at the kitchen table working through her lists of figures, tut-tutting loudly, her eyebrows knit into an angry concentration, while Elena's father sat in his chair, his body slumped in defeat, diminished by the bullying and the surrendered dignity. Elena remembers how she felt shame for him, how she resented her mother and the way she dominated them all.

Later, after Adam had left her tired and spent and heartsore, she felt like all the life had been ripped out of her. In that weakened state, she just wanted someone who would take care of her, who would shoulder the responsibilities, protecting her from life's chips and stings, shielding her from all the pain she had known. Her willingness to surrender that independence, the ease with which she allowed her grip on responsibilities to be loosened, letting Henry take control of their finances – she thought all along that this was his decision. But in the dying moments of the day, she realises that she is the guilty one, that it was her doing. She wanted to be taken care of. She absented herself from her responsibilities, seeking shelter in the cosy patriarchal marriage that she nurtured. Her collusion in this brings a fresh shame. But, more than that, it brings a new resolve.

She slips out from underneath the covers and finds her clothes in the dark. She dresses quietly, and as she presses her feet into her shoes, a voice comes out of the darkness.

'You're leaving?'

She turns to look at him. In the shadowy half light, he has raised himself up onto his elbows and is staring at her. She tries to read the expression on his face, tries to find what expectations lie there.

'I have to go home,' she says. 'I need to go home.'

A silence falls between them, a silence that reverberates with the need she has expressed, her decision implicit in its declarative intent, and he sucks in his breath and drops his chin onto his chest.

'So this is it,' he states.

A lump rises suddenly in her throat and she doesn't trust herself to speak.

'I suppose there's no point in giving you my address, just in case you ever decide to...'

His voice trails away as she shakes her head.

He sits up and runs a hand through his hair and in the shadowy darkness he floats a lazy smile across to her.

'You're sure this is what you want?'

'Yes.' Her voice rings out strongly, not betrayed by any hint of tears.

She wants to tell him that it is too late for them. That he is not what she needs, and neither is she the answer to his questions. She wants to tell him to look within himself, to find the person he used to be.

She wants to urge him to be closer to his son, to find some happiness there. She wants to persuade him to let go of the bitterness of the past, to find hope in his future. But she doesn't say any of this. A part of her senses that he knows this already. And another part of her realises that these are lessons he must learn himself.

She gathers her coat and bag and moves towards the door. She is struggling to find something to say. As she opens the door and light falls across the room, he speaks softly. 'Be happy, Elena.'

His words shoot through her, expanding and filling out all her hollow spaces, warming the coldest parts of her. She glances back at him from the doorway, his tousled hair, the paleness of his skin, light in those green eyes.

'Goodbye, Adam,' she whispers before stepping away, closing the door softly behind her.

HENRY

20

THE LOCKER ROOM is in darkness and echoes as Henry enters. There is a blinking spasm from the fluorescent light when he flicks the switch before the whole room is illuminated – silent and comfortless, the tiled floor and dour walls reflecting the chill from outside. There is an unplaceable odour, a whiff of old socks doing battle with the smell of bleach. The patter of rain on the roof seems amplified in this narrow space.

Upstairs, his father is in the office, clearing away his papers, wallowing in the futility of all that he has built up around him. But down here, among the stout grey lockers, Henry feels the daily rituals that have made up the fabric of his father's life impressing themselves upon him. They nudge up against him like the lurking shadows of ghosts – the old man's actions over the years, his deliberate and steadfast efforts to remain part of the workforce, part of the team, not removed from them, determined not to become some shark in a suit. Henry thinks of his father enjoying the idle gossip in the mornings with the other men as they change at their lockers or sharing a joke in the kitchen as he makes his tea, waiting in turn for the kettle to boil. Every week he chips in his two euro for the Lotto syndicate, sharing the hope that this week will be their turn and cursing with the rest of them when it isn't.

It occurs to Henry as he fiddles with the lock that his father's success as a businessman has not sat comfortably with him. He thinks of his parents' house, unchanged in so many years, the lack of holidays they have allowed themselves, their failure to indulge in certain luxuries, and it comes to him now that these sacrifices have something to do with his father's reluctance to accept his success and the financial rewards that have come with it. The tragedy of this bears down upon him heavily, compounding his own sense of loss.

He turns the key and the lock springs back, the locker opening and revealing itself to him. Henry stops. He draws in his breath and holds it, his throat suddenly plugged with emotion. Stuck to the inside of the locker door is a solitary photograph. Henry finds his eyes blurring as his gaze passes over it, his mind fumbling back through a field of memories, trying to locate the time, the occasion of its taking. His fingers reach for it and he touches the white edging of the old photograph – thirty years old – the face trapped within those neat borders. Henry looks at the boy in the photograph, perched on the bonnet of the old Nissan Bluebird, a carton of chips in his lap, the tuft of hair whipped back by the sea breeze and a wide grin exposing a gap in his teeth where new white frills were breaking through the gums. There is something delicate about the boy's mouth, an uncertain smile. His eyes are round with anticipation, his face – freckled and open – staring straight into the camera.

Henry feels a twinge at his heart. This old holiday photograph, this forgotten memory. How long has it been stuck to this door? He thinks of his father and his perceived lack of sentiment. And yet here – this one photograph that has greeted him every morning and every evening for the last thirty years – here is evidence of a feeling that he thought his father incapable of possessing. Henry, wet and dishevelled under the bright lights, begins to feel the warmth seeping back into his body, rinsing through his bones again, as he stares at the image of a younger, untainted Henry, when his life was still bursting with possibilities, his father behind the camera, that ever-present protective force, capturing his innocence on that breezy summer's day.

Tears stand in his eyes, emotion bubbling up around his heart, and he stumbles backwards; finding a low narrow bench, he drops his weight onto it and sinks his head into his hands. The life that is his, ruptured and sorrowful in recent days, crowds around him. His body feels stretched, weary, ready to snap. His brain is crowded, needful of sleep. His thoughts turn to his own children, their rapturous clamouring love for him – How long before his shortcomings as a father impinge on that unquestioning love? he wonders. How long before they start to realise his failings? And Elena, his only love, where is she? She is somewhere in the city and yet she feels a million miles away, lost to him now, her faith in him shattered. But despite these thoughts, these quavering doubts, he is visited by the realisation that through all his recent pain, his seeming despair – throughout all of this – his father's stern, unyielding and difficult love for him has endured, quiet and undemanding of reciprocation, and the knowledge of this seems to drill straight through him, right to the core of his being.

*

When Henry was eight, around the time the photograph was taken, he started going to piano lessons. He can still remember sitting at his mother's piano, looking up at her collection of china dogs and Belleek vases, and amongst the clutter the metronome struck its steady beat. Henry remembers watching the thin stick moving back and forth, calmly hitting each beat as his fingers stumbled over the keys trying to keep time. He was not a musical child. His fingers seemed awkward and stubby as they stretched to reach notes and slipped over keys, ugly mishits punctuating melodies. A scattering of quavers and crotchets and minims swam in front of his eyes, black spots with their flicking tails dancing over bars and spaces, confusing and headache inducing.

The lessons continued for two and a half years before ending abruptly. Henry can recall clearly the last time he played the piano. The occasion has lingered long in his memory. He can still remember that draughty competition hall and the icy chill of his own fear as he looked down at the sheet music, those dog-eared, tea-stained pages, fluttering in his shaking hands. His father sat in the audience, still and composed, saying little as he observed the other competitors through narrowed eyes, arms folded over his broad chest. He was oblivious to the growing terror flooding his son's body, numbing his extremities, causing waves of nausea to tip up from his stomach into the back of his throat.

There were others there Henry recognised, other pupils of his own music teacher, Ms Cavendish. 'Now, Henry,' she said, her voice a low hiss, giving him a last pep talk as he stood in the wings, his body spangled with nerves, 'just relax, you'll be fine.' He nodded gravely, something fluttering in his bowel. Then she did something to send his heart freewheeling down through his small body. 'It would be better,' she said quietly, spittle gathering in the corners of her mouth, 'more professional, to play without the sheet music.' She smiled intently, fixing him with stone-grey eyes. 'It's not as if you need it any more. You know that piece backwards.'

'But, but...' Henry croaked, his voice caught somewhere back in his throat.

'That's a good boy. You'll be just fine.' And in that instant, as she snatched the sheet music from his grasp, he felt something slipping away from him, his lifejacket whipped off him by his swimming instructor.

As he crossed the stage, the piano loomed up in front of him like an albatross. Underneath carefully pressed trousers, his legs quivered and shook, feeling weak at the knees as he reached the stool and sat down. The adjudicator sat at a small table, illuminated by a desk lamp that reflected glaringly through the large square lenses of her glasses. Her blonde hair lay neat as a wig, unmoving as she looked up, gave him the briefest of smiles and nodded at him to begin.

In his mind's eye, the opening notes of Bach's 'Adagio' floated in front of him. His thumbs reached for the white keys and his fingers aligned themselves for the opening chords. It was a shaky start, nerves channelling through his arms down to his fingertips as he struck notes gingerly, lurching from bar to bar. The room seemed to swell around him. The stage dipped, the piano and stool that carried him threatened to pitch down into the orchestra pit. The light from the adjudicator's desk sent sparks flying from the darkened auditorium. Heat from the lights above the stage brought beads of sweat to his forehead and his jumper pulled tightly across his rounded back, bent over the keys. Notes danced in his head as his fingers stumbled and mashed through the first page and, as the notes dipped and then rose to a crescendo, he could see the end of the page in his mind, the dog-eared corner, stained with his grimy fingerprints; he imagined touching it, taking it between finger and thumb, flipping over the page, and then, and then... And then nothing. A blank. White, blinding, nothing. An awkward silence fell over the auditorium. He could hear someone near the back clearing his throat. Sudden tears pricked his eyes, a dull thud emanating from his chest. With his head bent in concentration, he replayed the final bars of the first page, praying for inspiration, but his fingers came stumbling to a stop, the notes trailing away into an echoing silence.

'Perhaps you'd like to start from the beginning again?' the adjudicator suggested. But that was of no use. He could feel his thighs sticky with sweat. He was taken with a deep longing to flee the building, his tears very close now.

Then, from across the stage, a figure emerged from the wings – a bulky frame, short gunmetal-grey hair cut in a military style. Henry sat, paralysed, as his father crossed the stage, slowly, purposefully, his face expressionless. When he reached the piano, he leaned forward and propped the sheet music up in front of Henry.

'There now,' he said tonelessly. 'Start again from the top, that's a good lad.'

He stepped away silently, striding back across the stage and down the steps into the auditorium. Henry played badly, abysmally, racing through the piece, desperate to reach the end. When he did, it was to a small scattering of sympathetic applause, which hardly registered amid his shame as he raced offstage, scurrying down into the hall, finding his seat. Dan sat motionless, staring gravely ahead, not saying a word. When all the pieces had been played, the winner announced, the medals distributed and the comments sheets pored over, Henry felt the weight of his father's hand on his shoulder. He looked up into those small dark eyes, feeling the shame of his pitiful grade slicing through him.

'Never mind, son,' Dan intoned quietly, his hand warm and heavy, the sudden squeeze. 'You're a good lad. You did well.'

On the way home they stopped at McDonald's for a chocolate milkshake and a bag of chips ('Don't tell your mother,' Dan said gruffly). Sitting in the car, digging into the bag for the last dry salty chip, Henry said in a quiet voice, 'I don't want to play the piano any more.'

He remembers his father staring straight ahead – 'Not to worry, son,' he said loudly, 'it's not the end of the world. The earth will keep turning even if you're not playing the piano.'

Later, when they saw his mother and were greeted by her shrill questioning about the competition, and Henry felt his heart sink at the naked anticipation in her voice, his father answered with finality, 'The boy did great.' And no more was said on the matter.

Why this memory returns to him now, Henry is not sure. The day his father rescued him. That small kindness, that gesture of compassion, spoke to Henry of a love his father has seemed unable to utter or express since. Were he to mention it now, he is sure his father would fix him with that quizzical eye and claim to have no recollection of it.

*

Dan stands in front of the window, his back to Henry as he re-enters. He is looking out at the storm that continues to rage.

'It's a bad one,' he says over his shoulder. 'We might be here a while yet.'

On his desk, the neat mound of paper sits primly, recovered from the temporary lapse into disorder.

Henry watches his father, his large frame, the strong, proud set of his shoulders, his hair – spiky and severe – framed by the moonlight. He has railed against him for so many years, has loathed and despised him, mocked and derided him. This man with his bullish temper, his mean, scrimping frugality, his quick temper and caustic tongue, has been capable of shattering his son's faith with the easiest of kicks. But this is a man who has also harboured hidden fears, private yearnings. This man rescued him once before. And he has kept a photograph of his six-year-old son pinned to his locker door throughout the next thirty years of that son's life. As he stands in this small grey room, with the weather screaming outside and his life in pieces, it seems to Henry that, for the first time, he is beginning to understand his father.

Henry stands there waiting, a man with nothing left to lose, a man who needs to be rescued and who is prepared to wait for the blessing of recovery, hopeful that it will come.

'Dad?' he starts slowly, watching the old man turning around, his bushy eyebrows raised into a question. 'There's something I have to tell you.'

He takes a deep breath and begins.

ELENA

21

'I'M THINKING,' ELENA says to her mother-in-law Alice, 'I'm thinking about going back to college.'

She watches as Alice pauses in her slicing of bread to consider this before resuming the carving of thick slices and silently lifting them onto a china plate that she carries to the table. Alice's eyes are on her, she can feel them – watchful and pensive. Her mother-in-law is different tonight. The usual jittery motions that accompany her conversation seem to have smoothed out into a gentle stillness. And the anxious quaver in her voice has mellowed away.

'What brought this on?' she asks, not unkindly, drawing back a chair and dropping into it with a sigh.

'I don't know.' Elena shrugs. 'Something and nothing. I never finished my degree and lately it's been bothering me. I just thought it might be a good thing to do. If they'll still let me.'

They sit opposite each other in the warm kitchen, staring at the puritan spread of bread and cheese and a pot of tea between them. Night lingers outside the window, but the storm has abated, the full extent of the damage yet to be exposed by the dawn. They are alone, and there is a certain awkwardness between them. Alice has not asked her where she has been until now, and Elena has not offered an excuse. She has not the heart to lie. Upstairs her children are sleeping in the big double bed of the spare room. Soon she will join them. Her mind is foggy with tiredness, weary from the events of the day. And yet there is a sharpness to it, a clarity that seems fresh as the new day, a clarity that has been evasive for so long that she is not quite sure what to do with it.

'Have you spoken to Henry about this?'

'No. No, not yet. I haven't really thought it out fully myself yet. I wanted to think it out properly first before talking to him about it.'

When did we get like this? she wonders. How long has it been since ideas started having to be thought out properly, the pros and cons weighed up, before being discussed openly between them? When did this sense of formality slip into their relationship?

'Well, it sounds like a good idea.'

'Do you think so?' she blurts out, eager for affirmation. 'I hadn't considered it before now, but I think it might be a good thing to finish it. A good thing for me to do.'

'Well, do you think it will make you happy?'

This question slips into the air between them, hovering over the table as Elena considers it. When she arrived at the house an hour ago, Alice folded her in a warm embrace before holding Elena away from her at arm's length and, looking carefully into her face, she asked her, 'How are you doing, Elena?' There was a probing sincerity in that question. Elena felt the warmth of it. Something lay beneath the thin veil of that seemingly innocent enquiry – an inkling of her discontent, the stalking presence of this unnameable unhappiness that has shadowed her in recent days, and Alice's unspoken perception of this. That her mother-in-law should be aware of it, that she should have recognised it and held off speaking about it, strikes Elena as a gentle compassion that is strangely moving.

'I don't know,' she admits quietly. 'I don't know if it's what I really want. All I know is that I feel unfinished. I feel incomplete.' This admission stirs up emotion and she endeavours to contain it. 'And it has nothing to do with anyone else; it's me. Who I have allowed myself to become. What I have allowed to be taken from me. I need to get something back. I need to reclaim something that is just my own – not Henry's, not anyone else's, just mine.'

Alice pours a thin stream of brown tea into mugs, her blue eyes bright between the creases and lines that spread out to her snowy white hairline. She is dressed in a pink crinoline dressing gown and there are three blue curlers lined up above her forehead. Under the bright fluorescent kitchen light, amid the orange cupboard doors and the red ladybird curtains, she appears old – older than Elena has pre- viously considered. And yet the set of her face, that quiet demeanour, speaks of a contentment that Elena can only strive for. The solid com- fort of Alice's presence in this warm room, the steam from the mugs of tea, the artless domesticity of her fur-lined slippers, all wrap around Elena's senses, swaddling her in a feeling of safety, cushioned by that unquantifiable sentiment – the protectiveness of home, of family. Alice nods her head, and Elena sees the gathers and folds of flesh beneath her chin wrinkling above her nightgown.

'Henry told me about the house,' Alice says.

'Oh.' Something drops within her – this new sorrow, still raw and fresh, dousing her like cold water.

She waits to hear Alice's response, anticipating a fretful admonish- ment, an anxious quizzing over what is to be done. But what Alice gives instead is a tentative response, reserving judgement, filled with a gentle compassion, warm and reassuring.

'It's just a house,' she says quietly. 'I know how much effort you've put into it, and how much you both adore it. But in the end, it's just bricks and mortar; it's not flesh and blood. That would be much harder to let go of.'

Elena bites her lip, her forehead knitting into a frown and says quietly under her breath, 'But it's the betrayal.' Emotion rises suddenly in a wave, threatening to drench her. Speaking of it here in the kitchen to Henry's mother makes her feel disloyal somehow. And yet, there is a compulsion to give utterance to it, to allow her grievances to come spilling out – what the house means to her, the work she put into it, how she cannot fathom that he could put it at risk, their children's home, the utter carelessness of it, and for what? What was it all for? But then she remembers her own betrayal. In an instant, it comes back, rushing through her – an image of Adam leaning over her, shadows filling his face and the warm heaviness of his body. She closes her eyes to it, but it remains, that gentle rocking, the heat of his breath on her face, her legs locked around him, her body rising to meet his. Her cheeks redden at the memory and she looks down at her placemat, hiding her face. She locks away her secret, keeping it from Alice's steady gaze. He is gone from her now. She will not go back there. Her decision has been made.

'He thinks he's lost you.'

This statement, flung baldly across the table, causes Elena to catch her breath suddenly, emotion snagging in her throat.

'Has he?' Alice presses gently.

'I... I don't know,' she responds, shaking her head.

Alice puts down her tea and, leaning forward across the table, places her hand on top of Elena's. She feels the warmth and the softness of the fleshy palm and the short fingers with their bare nails and simple wedding band.

'I remember the first time you came to this house,' Alice tells her. 'You sat inside on the couch, in that big duffel coat you used to wear, do you remember? And I said to myself, "How young she is." Those enormous brown eyes peering out of that tiny face. You didn't seem to know where to look.'

Elena smiles sheepishly.

'I think you were a little frightened,' Alice says teasingly.

'I think I was,' Elena nods.

'We offered you tea and coffee and you wouldn't have anything – all politeness, not wanting to be any trouble. This strange, shy little girl, and how she had bewitched our son. You hardly said two sentences the whole time you were here.'

She draws her hand away from Elena's and gazes wistfully into the middle distance, a new remembrance occurring to her.

'And after the two of you left, Dan turned to me and said, "He's going to marry that girl."' She shakes her head, her eyes clouding as she bites on her lip. 'And I was so surprised at that, shocked. I had been so busy taking you in, I hadn't stopped to notice Henry. But Dan noticed him. "Didn't you see the way he was looking at her?" he asked me. "Couldn't take his eyes off her," he said. And this made me suddenly afraid.'

'Afraid?'

'Yes. You were both so young, and Henry was such an innocent – I don't think he had any girlfriends before you, certainly none that we were ever introduced to. But it was something more than that, something about you that made me worry.'

'What?'

'Your sadness.' The word emerges like a stone, and Elena feels her eyes grow hot with tears. 'There was such sadness in your eyes. I could feel the weight of it in you. And I couldn't help but think of what a burden it would be for Henry, how hard he would have to strive to make those eyes happy.'

Tears leak from the corners of Elena's eyes and she dashes them away with the backs of her hands.

'You didn't want him to marry me?' she asks in disbelief.

'Oh, my dear,' Alice says hurriedly, moving to rectify the damage, 'it's not that I didn't want him to... I just didn't want to see him hurt.'

'I can't believe you're telling me this.'

'Oh, Elena, wait—'

'I can't believe you waited till now to say something. I mean, if you really felt strongly about it, you should have said something then.'

'No, Elena—'

'I bet you wish you had, now, considering the mess we've made of everything—'

'No!' Alice barks out this word sharply and Elena looks up, surprised at this new firmness, this new authority in her gentle, reticent mother-in-law. 'Don't you see? I'm glad I didn't say anything. I'm glad I kept my worries and fears to myself. Because it's Henry's life, and your life. And you have made him so happy, so proud – I've seen that.'

'Really?' Elena needs to hear this, needs to know that it hasn't all been a mistake. Her desire for affirmation surprises her, almost as much as Alice's perception.

'And I think you were happy too, Elena.' She nods her head sagely as she says this. 'I've seen you with him, the way you two were together – that natural weave of love between you. When Emily was born, and the two of you were struggling with sleepless nights and all the stress that a new baby brings, I remember looking at you and thinking how I had never seen anyone look as tired and as happy at the same time. Despite those dark shadows around your eyes, you simply glowed. And Henry, as proud as punch, so in love with his new daughter. And so in love with you.'

Elena cannot help but smile at the memory.

'Don't forget it,' Alice says to her. 'Don't forget how things were once. People do that too easily. They allow the dark days to cloud a whole marriage, instead of waiting a while for the clouds to pass.'

Elena feels tired suddenly, exhausted by the battles of recent days – too tired to refute the points made.

'Who knows?' she says with a shrug, a piece of her already opening to the possibility.

'This is just part of it,' Alice says with a smile.

'Part of what?'

'The pleasures and the pains of life. Of love.'

Elena's elbow is on the edge of the table and she leans her chin onto the palm of her hand, fingers curling and covering her mouth. She is struck by the beautiful simplicity of her mother-in-law's philosophy. Alice, with her fretful nature, her timid anxiety, the way she fusses over them all – that she should have felt heartache and loss, as well as ecstasy and joy, opens Elena's eyes to her, causing her to regard her anew from a different perspective. This mother, this grandmother, has also been a lover. She had forgotten that.

But Alice is already glancing up at the kitchen clock.

'Lord,' she says with a sigh, her voice elevating suddenly, breaking the veil of intimacy that has fallen over them, 'it's almost morning.'

Elena follows her gaze, and a cloud of concern passes over her mind. 'They've been gone a long time,' she says. 'Maybe we should call…?'

Alice is on her feet and clearing the table, taken with a new and different urgency.

'They have things to discuss,' she says briskly. 'Best leave them to it.'

Elena watches the bulk of her frame wrapped up cosily in her pink dressing gown, the belt tied in a neat bow at her side. Alice turns from the sink and comes towards her with arms outstretched, and Elena allows herself to be gathered up and drawn into the warmth and strength of her embrace. She feels the pucker of soft, dry lips pressing against her cheek and hears her mother-in-law speak quietly. 'You take care of yourself,' she says slowly and deliberately, 'and everything else will follow.'

Elena opens her mouth to speak, but Alice has already released her and is moving away, back to the business at hand, and Elena understands that their conversation is over. Alice has said all that she is going to on the matter. Instead, she turns her back to her daughter-in-law and begins rinsing cutlery under the running tap, a hum of industry rising up from the vigorous quivering of her body. Elena stands for a moment, immersed in the realisation that she has lost something tonight, but it is something she lost a long time ago, and now she is reconciled to it. Her eyes are red and scratchy. She needs to sleep. 'Be happy,' he said to her. The words expand and fill her, they echo around her as she makes her way up the stairs, tiredness drawing her towards bed. Behind her, she can still hear Alice in the kitchen, busying herself with the return of order before the day begins to break.

HENRY

22

THE SUN HAS yet to appear, but already the first rays of light are creeping through the morning sky, warming it into a grainy blue, free of the grey clouds that have been swarming over the city for days. The silence swells around them and seems enormous. Now that the howls and screams of the storm have fallen away, there is not even a whisper of wind left as a reminder. It feels as if, on this morning, winter has stepped into the city, snatching the last warm breath of autumn.

Henry sits wordlessly in the passenger seat as his father drives through deserted streets. Silently, they witness the devastation the storm has left in its wake. Trees that stood like flares of gold, laden with autumn colours, have been brutally stripped overnight. The leaves clog together in gutters, rolled over and drenched with rain, forming a thick mulch that coats the paths and makes the road slippery. The ferocity of the previous night's weather is evident in the split branches that have come away from their parents, dangling perilously, a mass of jagged splinters, or lying as though wounded across the road or fallen into the gutter, their twigs like fingers reaching up in appeal. Bins have been overturned, spilling their filthy contents. Milk cartons, orange peels, used nappies – the litter of domesticity lies strewn across the road like the fallen casualties of a disaster.

Henry sees the slight shake of his father's head. The litter is displeasing to the old man's fastidious nature. He drives slowly, choosing his route carefully to avoid the pooling of water on narrow roads. Twice, he has to make a U-turn to escape the flooding. His headlights swing around corners, illuminating quiet buildings that seem to be holding their breath, as though shocked in the wake of the storm. Other cars travel equally cautiously, creeping through the streets, anxious not to create a new disturbance. All the traffic lights appear to be broken; flashing amber greets them at every junction. Street lamps shine like orange lozenges, casting a warm, hazy glow from their high perches.

They pass Henry's car, abandoned at the side of the road. It is disappearing under a weight of debris, and there are leaves shored up against the wheels, rotting into puddles, disappearing into the gutter. His head turns as they pass, his eyes fixed on the vehicle.

'We'll come back for it later,' his father says tonelessly.

Henry finds something comforting in his father's voice, the words emanating from the depths of that cavernous chest, an unspoken reassurance in that guileless statement. The car is warm around him. His joints ache, the muscles in his body pinch around his bones. His spine, curving into the groove of the car seat, demands to be stretched out flat, each vertebrae baying for its own space. But while his body screams around him, his mind feels strangely at peace. The steaming cauldron of worry and anxiety that has been bubbling and spitting and threatening to boil over in a scalding flood of anguish seems to have simmered down. A great weight has been lifted from him. The knowledge that he can sink no lower seems to shore him up. And for the first time in the slow descent into nightmare, he sees a glimmer of hope. The shame of his admission still clings to him; he tries to shake away the memory of it, the stammer of words spoken under an averted gaze, the pain he saw in his father's face, and the disappointment – he hadn't imagined that. Henry glimpses a future endeavouring to atone for his mistake, trying to shake off that clinging shame, striving to regain that trust – in his father's eyes as well as Elena's. But, in spite of his weariness, he feels eager to start, anxious to prove himself. This burst of adrenalin is new to him; he cannot remember the last time he has felt it – the warm spark of possibility.

Looking out the window, he sees the sky is lightening. A clear bright blue pushes through the spines and spindles of the naked trees. Winter stretches across the city, bringing with it a new withering, a new frugality. This day has arrived, the day he has been dreading. In a few hours he will meet with the bank and the future will be decided.

But, now that it is upon him, he doesn't feel the usual instinctive flavour of acid in his throat or the agitated pulse at his neck. For he knows now that he will not be alone. Of course, it may be too late to put forward their proposal; he is aware of this. But a glimmer of possibility sparks in his chest. A stay of execution. Perhaps, it whispers. Perhaps.

The car is parked safely in the drive, and Henry raises a mild protest as he looks ahead at his parents' house.

'I should go home,' he says weakly. 'Elena... the children...'

'You'll stay here,' Dan answers with firmness, bringing the car door shut behind him and moving towards the house. Henry, too tired to protest, follows him.

Once inside, they stand in the hallway of the still house and Henry feels a certain awkwardness returning as they regard each other.

'Look, Dad, I want you to know – I just want to say that I really appreciate what you've done... what I mean is that I'm grateful for...'

'Best get to bed,' Dan says briskly, cutting through his apologetic appreciation and pushing it aside with a clean sweep. 'We still have two or three hours.'

He nods his head dismissively and Henry understands that the exchange is over. He also understands that there will be no thanks given, no apologies offered or accepted, no grateful speeches or heartfelt thanks. That is not his father's way. Nor will there be any reference made to his father's lapse into dismay, his temporary loss of hope. Dan will not speak of that night again, but will address the future in his usual brisk manner, his no-nonsense approach, stern and determined; for once, Henry can feel only gratitude for these characteristics he has railed against for so long.

Light falls through a gap in the curtains and the shape of the bed lies beneath its grainy beam. The bed is speckled with flowers, a tight weave of lilac, an old duvet cover, one that Henry remembers from childhood. An ironing board is folded and leaning against one wall, a basket full of crumpled washing waits at its side. He squeezes past it, and past the old wardrobe with the rusting hinges and the missing handles, packed with his old toys and games, clothes long outgrown that his mother has never been able to throw away, labouring under the belief that they will be worn by his offspring in time.

His son's small body floats up from the top of the duvet. Ben sleeps

283

with his hands thrown up over his head, hair matted to his forehead with sweat. He lies between his mother and sister, their hair on the pillows framing his small pale face, the duvet pulled up to their chins.

Henry undresses silently, anxious not to disturb them, and hangs his trousers and shirt over the back of a chair. He regards the sleeping bodies. There is barely enough room for him. Lifting the covers, he slips across the edge of the bed, feeling the coldness of the sheet against his skin. But Emily's body is warm. She moans slightly as he nudges her, gently manoeuvring her sleeping body towards the centre of the bed. His bones seem to creak as he lies back into the pillow, each muscle straining as he resists collapsing into the mattress. He does not want to disturb them, but lets them sleep. Across his children's heads, he sees Elena curled into the far corner of the bed. He cannot see her face, just the shadow of her hair on the pillow, the brush of eyelashes on her cheek. Turning onto his side, he suppresses the desire to reach across to her, to trace her smooth eyebrow with his finger, to run his hand along the slope of her cheek. He doesn't want to wake her, doesn't want to see her eyes opening, that flicker of confusion before remembering where she is. Most of all, he doesn't want to risk seeing that steel entering her gaze, that needle of disappointment. For now, he is content to listen to the ebb and flow of their breathing. He closes his eyes and hears his own breath joining their chorus.

ZARAGOZA

23

ELENA SITS WITH her hands folded neatly in her lap, staring ahead at the domed altar. Light streams through the windows, but it does not reach her, cloistered here at the back of the Basilica. So much is familiar to her – the marble floor and the sound her feet make echoing through the long corridors, the darkness of the capellas, the splendour and apocalyptic doom of the frescoes, the thickness and the height of the oversized candles, the dry musk of incense filling her nostrils – all of these things surround her, swamping her senses, stirring up old memories, the soft hammer of recognition in the back of her mind. And yet there are things that weren't here before, or rather she didn't notice them. Like the framed painting on the west wall, depicting the Miracle of Zaragoza – the tale of an amputee who dreamed he was in the Basilica de Nuestra Señora del Pilar, and awoke with his limb returned to him. Or the bombs hanging from a pillar near the altar – two unexploded missiles that were dropped on the Basilica during the Civil War but failed to detonate – another miracle. Elena would like to believe in these miracles, she would like to accept faith as the only reasoning behind them. But a cynical voice inside whispers that these are untruths, that there is a scientific or mechanical reason why the bombs did not go off, and that the miracle of Zaragoza was some sort of elaborate hoax, merely an illusion.

Two cleaners dressed in blue overalls are sweeping the marble floor. Elena listens to the gentle whoosh of the brooms. A speaker buzzes at the altar. She hears the solid click of a woman's sturdy platform shoe striking the marble. Henry stands close to the altar, his gaze drawn skyward to the sculptures and paintings that adorn it – the billowing robes, the looks of wonder and awe, poses from Armageddon or the occurrence of something momentous. Elena watches him, the relaxed set of his shoulders, folded arms, the gentle lick of honey-brown hair at the back of his head. He doesn't like these zealous depictions of the might of God, he has told her. He finds them vaguely offensive. This old-world wrath and fury is at odds with his vision of a gentle, compassionate God. He prefers the more modern, angular sculptures adorning the entrance to La Sagrada Familia in Barcelona. These speak to him of compassion, a gentle understanding, forgiveness.

A group of tourists has entered the inner dome, all short, stout elderly people with brown faces and grey hair. They wear identical vests over their clothes with a pattern on the back, identifying their group. One of them gets close to Elena and she reads the words printed between the shoulder blades – 'San Daniel Comboni, Peru'. A religious tour group. Nearly every one of them holds a camcorder, and they wander around, absorbing the details of the church through camera lenses, accompanied by a loud chatter, which strikes Elena as curiously disrespectful. Henry has noticed them too. He doesn't turn around but she can tell by the tensing of his shoulders, the stiffening of his stance, that their noisy intrusion has disturbed him. She watches with a growing amusement as one of the Peruvians clears his throat noisily behind Henry, who is blocking the view of the camcorder. These guttural eruptions grow into a hacking cough as Henry stands his ground, doggedly refusing to be moved. Elena observes his stubbornness from her seat near the back and feels a tickle of hilarity rising up inside her, a giggle filling her chest and throat.

It is a gift from her parents, this time away together. Rosario, sensing the coldness that was slow in thawing between them, suggested a few days away. 'It will do you the world of good,' she said to Elena, 'to be away from the children and the house and the business, just for a few days. You need time alone together, time to sort things out, time to talk things through.'

It seemed to Elena that time was being prescribed to her from every angle. 'Just give it time,' Alice counselled her, 'and things will soon be back on track.'

'You hang in there,' Ian said to her, 'just sit tight, and the worst of it will soon be over.'

But how much time would they need, Elena wanted to know, before they could put all those recriminations behind them, along with the nights of screaming rows, the tearful accusations and the long solitary silences where she couldn't bear to look at him or even hear his voice? Is one week away enough? It seemed like a plaster being applied to a great gaping wound. The prospect of sharing a bed for the first time in months sent a shiver of nerves through her; she was haunted by the thought of clinging to the edge of a foreign mattress, holding her body stiffly apart from his.

Time is a great healer. That is what they all told her. But alongside her nerves sat a cold rod of fear. What if? she asked herself, over and over. What if they can't work it out? What if they spend the time together and she still can't avoid returning to those doubts that have dogged her in recent months? What then?

She looks up and sees him striding towards her. Now that the Peruvians have moved on, he can step away from his position in silent victory. His mouth twitches, the edges curving upwards into a hint of a smile as he approaches her. 'Well?' he asks her. 'It's something else, isn't it?'

'It certainly is.'

He stands with his hands on his hips, looking all around him, his eyes busy, distracted. She waits patiently. She is content to wait.

'I thought I'd slip around and kiss the pillar,' he says with a bashful shrug of his shoulders. 'Sure, I may as well, hmm?'

She is moved to smile at his embarrassed admission.

'How about you?'

'I've kissed it already,' she says quietly. 'Once was enough.'

'Fair enough. I'll be back in a mo.'

He walks away, slipping his hands into his pockets, affecting a casual air to mask his sense of purpose.

They are here at Henry's suggestion. 'How about Barcelona and Zaragoza?' he said when Rosario first made her offer. Elena looked up quickly, searching his face for some trace of malice, some hint of provocation, a cheap attempt at stirring up another row. But there was nothing sinister hidden there, no secret plan of entrapment, and she let it go. Lately, she has grown weary of being defensive. She is tired of circling over the same old questions, the same jaded demands. Her coldness is wearing thin. She cannot keep it up much longer.

These spasms of anger have taken their toll on both of them. Elena's need to punish and Henry's weary regret weigh heavily on their home. She has to keep reminding herself that the house is safe, for the time being at least. The bank accepted the last-minute pitch to save it, a plan to pay off the loans, with Dan acting as guarantor. The relief was overwhelming, like something exploding inside her, a burst of emotion – joy and anger in equal measure; it rocked her whole body, leaving it heaving and spent. But Henry could not be let off the hook; she could not allow him to forget. And so she pursued her campaign of chilly disappointment punctuated by wild bursts of rage, allowing it to take over their home. The children looked on, bewildered, unsure of whose side to take, and that they should be expected to take sides at all brought Elena a fresh wave of sadness.

Henry is being careful with her lately, respectful, kind. Not that he wasn't those things before. But it feels forced to her, after all that has happened. She cannot help but think that he is trying to ingratiate himself with her, worming his way back into her affections. When she first voiced her plan to go back to university, and he received it so readily, with an enthusiasm that seemed overblown, she had to suppress the irritation that swelled up inside her at his response. 'Absolutely!' he said. 'Definitely, you should do it. Go back and finish what you started. It will do you a power of good.' This new tone of trying to please grates on her. She feels that no matter what she suggested he would agree to it, so desperate is his need to return to how things were.

It hasn't been mentioned much of late – the university idea. She has allowed it to die away. It is tempting to blame Henry for that, but if she is honest with herself, she realises that the real reason has more to do with her own indecision, her wavering insecurity. 'You don't know what you want!' Henry bawled at her during one argument before she slammed the door and stormed up the stairs, the whisper of truth tunnelling into her brain. She threw words and phrases about, talking of regaining her independence and finding herself. But what did these words mean? And would a degree achieve that sense of arrival that she yearned for?

Her determination to re-establish some control remains. In fact, it has galvanised into something steely and aggressive, powered by an energy she wasn't aware she possessed. Six weeks ago, after dropping Emily at school and Ben at the crèche, she drove to Butler & Sons Building Supplies, walked across the factory floor, climbed the metal staircase – high heels clanging, announcing her arrival – and, entering the office, presented herself for work, to the startled faces of her husband and father-in-law.

'I want to know everything,' she said on the first day, her words like hot needles pricking at Henry. Nothing was to be hidden from her – that was the implication. She wanted no more surprises, no more shocks or revelations.

It took time, grappling with a business she knew nothing about, learning slowly and steadily how the orders worked, who the clients were, the black art of ordering the right amount of stock, the antiquated accounts systems they operated. She took the work home with her and pored over lists of figures at her kitchen table, filling up pages and pages with scribbled calculations, trying to fathom how it all worked. At other times she sat at her small desk in the office, going through the accounts with knitted eyebrows and an assortment of heavy sighs, this performance for Henry's benefit. But she has to remind herself to keep it up. Her mask has been slipping lately. It is becoming increasingly difficult to keep up a façade of annoyance. For secretly, she enjoys her work, silently revelling in the new-found status it gives her. Learning something new, taking control of something meaningful, she finds herself experiencing a rush as she mounts the metal staircase in the mornings.

Still, there are worries. Their money problems have not gone away. If anything they have been compounded by this new debt they owe Henry's father, whose slow recuperation from surgery has necessitated a redoubling of effort on their parts. But at least she is aware of the financial situation. She scrupulously keeps an account of it, planning repayments, revising those plans, in a continuous circling of figures, round and round they go, making her dizzy.

She leaves her seat and wanders around the altar in search of Henry. She finds him near the far end of the Basilica, his gaze passing over the alabaster engravings of the second altar. For a moment he doesn't see her, and she stops to consider him from her hiding place in the shadows. In recent days, it feels as if she is getting to know him anew, trying to find the person he is, the person who has eluded her for some time now. He appears older to her. The events of the past few months have taken their toll, adding density to the grey in his hair, multiplying the new lines that have begun to appear on his face. The shame of losing his business and the pride-swallowing feat of returning to his father's company have given him a new humility, a new vulnerability. There are days when she looks at him bent over his work, chewing his lip with concentration, and wonders if he is happy here. Or is happiness the price he has paid for his misdemeanours?

And what of her own acts of betrayal? The memory of that stormy night comes back to her, flushing through her like blood rinsed out of her heart. How many times has she replayed it in her mind, over and over? She hasn't told Henry, not wishing to stir all that up again. It is unfair on him, she is aware. It creates an imbalance. He is shouldering the guilt of his admission, facing up to the blame, weathering her fury and her disappointment, and all the while she has her own guilty secret, a secret he could use as ammunition against her. And it is the knowledge of this that makes her feel guilty. She has almost told him on several occasions, particularly in the last few days. But what would be the point? It would only set them back again, returning them to square one and the whole bitter circle of arguments whirling into life again. Better to let it lie.

In Barcelona it was difficult. She felt the memories raw against her skin. Everywhere they went, she pictured Adam, his tousled hair, his laughing green eyes. She shook her head, trying to dislodge the image, trying to lose it among a jumble of thoughts. It made her irritable. She snapped at Henry for no reason. Her temper got hold of her and made her jumpy and eager to get away from him. Frosty silences took hold of her.

But here in Zaragoza, the atmosphere has begun to thaw. She finds herself loosening, letting go of her angst, opening up again. In the restaurant on the first night, Henry made a joke, some throwaway remark that she cannot remember now, but at the time it struck her as hilarious. She laughed out loud, a sudden burst of unconscious mirth, and once she felt the laugh passing through her, she realised it had been building inside for months. Released into the restaurant, it was followed by a string of giggles that tickled her, sending her into a fit of hilarity. Tears filled up her eyes, and she bent over double, clutching her belly. It was contagious. Henry was laughing too – a deep baritone laugh – his whole body shaking. The relief of letting it out, letting it into the open, was overwhelming. Her body felt light, her head still giddy. Henry looked at her across the table and said suddenly, 'It's good to see you laughing again.' The truth in this statement, the genuine tone in his voice, touched her, and this time she felt no compulsion to shut it down with an acerbic comment or sarcastic quip.

That night, he reached across the expanse of mattress to her, a tentative gesture, and she responded willingly. They made love like strangers, with an awkward timidity that belied the hundreds of times they had slept together. His hands passed over her body as if touching it for the first time, as if the knowledge of all her curves and hollows had departed from him. Their coupling was stilted – his movements trying to impart respect and a sense of apology, hers trying to force an affection that was bigger than her disappointment, that embodied her forgiveness. They could not avoid the underlying air of panic. But afterwards, as they lay together in the darkness, she felt his body curling around hers, felt his warmth pressing into her back. In her sleep, she didn't move away from him and she felt the fresh rush of surprise when she awoke the next morning locked in the embrace of his arm thrown over her waist, resting warmly and heavily on her body.

He sees her and starts coming towards her, his features warming up into a smile.

'Did you kiss it?' she asks, adopting a playful, mocking tone.

'I did.'

'And how was it?'

'Cold,' he replies with a grin.

'No flash of inspiration? You weren't struck with sudden illumination?'

'Come on.' He shrugs off her teasing good naturedly and ushers her away, his hand in the small of her back. 'Let's get the lift up to the roof. See what the view is like from the celestial heights.'

The lift is ancient – a creaking grey metal casket, manned by a toughened old man who sits on a stool, listening to an old transistor radio humming the sports results. They pay for their tickets and squeeze into the back, forced into the corner by the collective bulk of eight Peruvians, all clutching their cameras. The lift ascends slowly, accompanied by a series of creaking, groaning noises. Elena looks up at Henry and he pulls a face of mock anxiety. She slaps him playfully in the stomach. The lift comes to a screeching halt and the doors open and they file out, finding themselves on a wooden platform, facing a stairway that rises around and up into the tower. The lift attendant points a tobacco-stained finger and offers terse instructions and they begin the climb, Henry leading the way, followed by Elena and the string of pilgrims.

The stairway twists and winds. The steps change from wood to metal as they climb higher. Peeping over the banisters, Elena sees the lift descending, caught inside its cage, suspended on wires and metal. She sees the sheer drop and feels a sudden fear surging within her. The air is hot and tight in here as they near the top. The inside of the roof is lined with metal and heat seeps through it like an oven. Her head feels light, sweat forming above her lip, and she reaches for Henry's hand to lead her up. She sees his fingers curling around her hand and feels the cool grasp of them leading her on, up into the light, a cool breeze coming for her as they reach the top.

The viewing deck is a narrow, cloistered space, and they shuffle around, making room for the Peruvians, who hoist their cameras onto the ledge to film the streets of Zaragoza far below them. Elena peers over the edge, looking past the green of the dome and the terracotta roofs, down to the plaza below, lit up by the early-evening sun. From her perch high up above the square, she can see the pigeons scattering out, scavenging for seed. The tables outside bars and restaurants are filling up, and the hard squawk of the lottery-ticket seller echoes up to greet her.

It has been eleven years since she sat on the steps of the Plaza del Pilar, watching the last rays of the setting sun warming the Basilica and thinking of her friend Carlos and the terrible thing he had done. So much time has passed since then. So many lives set on different courses. And yet, something of the peace she felt on that evening returns to her now as she rises up on the tips of her toes, craning her neck to see the choirboys as they emerge, chattering, their red skirts billowing under white soutaines. How tiny they appear from this height. Henry leans forward too, and she can feel his hand still holding hers, their fingers laced together.

The Peruvians begin to file back down the steps, having captured as much footage as they need. But Henry and Elena linger, feeling the heat from the red sun warming their faces. She wants to say something to him, but is afraid to break the silence and splinter the peace between them. I've missed you, she wants to say. It seems to Elena that they are learning a new language, a new way of communicating with each other – a slow and cautious stumbling of words, a tentative movement towards each other. As the bells peal out over the city and the pigeons wheel past them, she feels his hand move in hers, a slight push of pressure, a gentle kneading; and, in that moment, something echoes within her – a new calmness, a quiet gratitude – emerging out of her dark hollows and slowly rising to the surface.

Acknowledgements

A number of people have read the manuscript for this book and offered suggestions and encouragement. I thank Dominic Bennett, Steven E Byrne, Lynn Caldwell, Catherine Dunne, Bridget Maher and Brendan O'Mahony.

For their enthusiasm and support, I am indebted to Breda Purdue, Ciara Considine, Claire Rourke and Hodder Headline Ireland.

I am particularly grateful to my agent, Faith O'Grady, for her advice and commitment.

Thanks to all my friends for their enormous morale-boosting skills.

Most of all, deepest thanks to my family for their constant support during the ups and downs of writing this book.